spin

K.J. Farnham

more books by k.j.

Don't Call Me Kit Kat

Click Date Repeat
Click Date Repeat Again

A Case of Serendipity

Visit kjfarnham.com for more information.

For my Grandma Esther

prologue

Bonnie Kemp
Friday, May 11, 2018
Six and a Half Months After Jenna's Disappearance

I take a deep, cleansing breath as I grip the knob of Jenna's bedroom door. It's been thirteen days since I was last in there—a record since bringing her home from the hospital and laying her in her bassinet sixteen years ago.

"Quick in and out, Lulu. Okay?" I look down at Jenna's dog. Every few days, the black lab incessantly whines and scratches where the door meets the floor, eager to enter her beloved owner's room. Today happens to be one of those days.

As soon as I open the door a crack, Lulu bolts inside, causing me to lose my grip on the knob and forcing the door to fly wide open. The energetic dog quickly gets to work sniffing every square inch of Jenna's room as if searching for clues that might reveal her whereabouts.

I smile somberly and shake my head before stepping inside and glancing around the room. The sting in my heart isn't nearly as sharp as I anticipated it would be, but it's there, nonetheless.

My gaze falls to Jenna's desk, which has been left untouched since the police came through to look for items of interest. Surrounding Jenna's Chromebook are a holder for pens and Post-it notes, a tube of lip balm, a basket with random keepsakes, and a few notebooks and textbooks—all items that the police had left behind.

To me, Jenna is missing, not gone for good. Missing, not dead, despite what the Briarwood Police Department may think. I'm furious that they've given up the search. It's like a slap in the face, thinking about all the stones that have probably been left unturned.

I scan the room one last time.

"Come on, Lulu," I say as I head for the hallway. I begin to pull Jenna's door closed, expecting Lulu to make her exit any moment, but she remains seated next to Jenna's nightstand.

"Lulu," I press, "let's go, girl."

The dog still doesn't budge. Instead, she whines, her tail sweeping the floor maniacally. Then she sniffs Jenna's nightstand.

"Ohhh," I say, joining Lulu next to Jenna's bed. "I know what you want." I place my phone on the nightstand and reach for the handle of the second drawer. I close my eyes for a moment, and images of the night I invaded Jenna's privacy by reading her diary play behind my eyelids. It wasn't long after that Jenna started changing, and then she went missing. I'll always wonder if my betrayal was partly to blame.

The guilt in my heart causes me to bring my hands to my face. I press my fingers against my eyelids as if they're buttons intended to deactivate the troubling thoughts that are always lingering in the back of my mind. The sensation of Lulu's cold, wet nose against my elbow snaps me out of the trance I've fallen under, and before I have a chance to change my mind, I pull open the drawer.

My gaze immediately falls on Jenna's new diary. It's a replica of the same diary I so callously peeked at last summer, the one Jenna had tossed in the kitchen trash can after we had a blowout over my betrayal. I'd been shocked to see this new, nearly identical diary (save for the Briarwood High Cross Country sticker on the back) when we did a frantic sweep of Jenna's room after two full days with no contact from her.

Lulu whines, once again pulling me from my thoughts and prompting me to pick up the quart-sized Ziploc bag full of dog bones next to the diary. Lulu's tail thumps wildly, zigzagging from the floor to the nightstand as I pull open the bag and remove a bone. The dog happily accepts a treat, and immediately begs for another, so I give the command Jenna used to give as I toss a second bone a couple feet into the air. "Leap, Lulu!"

Lulu isn't quite ready, so the treat bounces off the tip of her nose and falls to the floor, sliding under the two-inch gap beneath the nightstand.

"A little rusty, huh, Lulu?" I ask with an amused grin as I get down on my knees and slide a hand under the nightstand to search for the fallen goodie.

Lulu whines and pokes her nose under too, but neither of us can seem to find the treat. "I guess I'll have to get it with the vacuum later today. Or whenever I feel like vacuuming . . ." I say, leaving the treat for now. But Lulu continues whining and scratching at the base of the nightstand, so I sigh, grab my phone from the nightstand, and give it a shake to activate the flashlight.

I get back down on my knees, press my cheek to the floor, and with the help of the light, I spot the treat right away. As I reach my hand all the way into the back-left corner, my knuckles brush against a smooth surface on the underside of the nightstand. The texture strikes me as odd, so as soon as I hand the rescued treat over to Lulu, I return my cheek to the floor and shine the light under the nightstand again, this time tilting my gaze upward toward the underside where I see something that causes my breath to halt. I collapse onto my stomach, momentarily paralyzed.

Could it really be?

A gentle tug results in the sound Velcro makes when its hook and loop fasteners separate. Sitting cross-legged with my mouth ajar, I examine my discovery: a diary identical to the one in Jenna's drawer.

It can't be.

I run the fingers of my right hand across the cover and flip it over to reveal something that makes me shudder uncontrollably. Smack-dab in the center of the back cover is a worn Briarwood High School Cross Country team sticker. It's the diary Jenna had thrown away on the night of our big blowout. She must have fished it out of the garbage after everyone had gone to bed.

Realizing what my find could reveal, I frantically open the tattered notebook and flip to the last entry dated *Thursday, October 26, 2017.*

I exhale a hard, swift breath when recognition sets in. The final entry was written the day before Jenna went missing.

As I read the entry, I have to remind myself to breathe, and I pause several times to ensure I don't pass out. I can't process everything and have to reread the most alarming parts . . . *I can't talk to him anymore . . . he was upset . . . starting to creep me out . . . planned to meet him tomorrow night . . .*

I know the howl that echoed through my brain must have escaped me when Joseph rushes into the room. In a daze, I look up at him. His lips are moving, but I can't hear what he's saying. I look over at Lulu who's cowering in the corner and wonder if she knew all along that Jenna's diary was under the nightstand. If so, why didn't she let us know? We would have known about his lies much sooner.

I glance around the spinning room and realize my thoughts are irrational and my anger toward Lulu is misplaced.

I look back at Joseph and can finally hear him.

"Bonnie? What's wrong?" He's crouched at my side, his hands cradling my face. "What is it?"

I stare at him, still speechless.

He maintains eye contact for a moment but then follows my gaze as I glance down at the long-lost diary in my lap. "What's . . . Is that . . ." His eyes widen and remain focused on the object in my lap as he settles onto the floor next to me.

I burst into tears and jump to my feet, clutching the open diary to my chest. "It was him . . . it had to be him . . ."

"Bonnie, wait . . ." Joseph scrambles to his feet and reaches for me, but all he gets is a strand of hair because I'm moving too fast.

"He lied. Dear Lord, Joseph, he lied! And he got away with it!"

Joseph enters the hallway behind me just as Shaina jumps out of my way. I glance back to see her with her back pinned to the wall. Joseph gives her a comforting squeeze on the upper arm as he rushes past. I turn and continue down the stairs and into the kitchen. Joseph rounds the corner as I frantically grab my oversized purse from the coat hook next to the garage door and shove Jenna's recovered diary inside.

"Who? Who lied? And where are you going?!" Joseph asks as he grasps my shoulder. He spins me around with one hand and reaches over my head with the other to hold the door to the garage closed.

"Move your hand, Joseph! I need to get to the police station!" I can barely see through the tears that are flooding my eyes and streaming down my cheeks so fast that the top half of my T-shirt is speckled with drops.

"Okay . . . it's okay," he says, slowly removing his hand from the door and raising both into the air in submission. "Just tell me what's going on. Please. Then I'll drive you wherever you need to go."

I squeeze my eyes closed, acutely aware of each painful breath I'm taking. When I open them, Joseph is looking at Shaina, who's made her way into the kitchen but remains next to the refrigerator. Just like Joseph, Shaina has become accustomed to tiptoeing around the house, especially when I'm having a rough time. A single tear trails down her left cheek in response to my outburst. I want to rush to her, to comfort her, but I can't right now. Not when the key to Jenna's whereabouts could now be in my possession.

"No," I say, calling Joseph's attention back to me. I reach into my bag to retrieve the diary and hold it out to him. "I'll drive. You read." After he takes it, I sniffle and straighten my posture, my expression once again strong, determined, and resolute. "It's the last entry. The one from October twenty-sixth. We're going to find her, Joseph."

chapter one

KEELEY SIMON
SATURDAY, OCTOBER 28, 2017
ONE DAY AFTER JENNA'S DISAPPEARANCE

"Hello?" My mom tilts her head slightly, pinning the phone between her shoulder and the dangly silver earring hanging from her right earlobe. She pours a dash of half and half into her coffee. "Uh, nope. Sorry, Bonnie, we haven't seen her."

Bonnie? Jenna's mom? I look up from my scrambled eggs.

My mom stops stirring, her thumb and forefinger gently gripping the spoon handle sticking out from the oversized coffee mug she always uses. A look of concern spreads across her face, and her eyes meet mine for a split second before she steps away from the kitchen table and turns toward the island. I lower my eyes to her mug, and my thoughts begin to race. It sounds like Mrs. Kemp is talking faster than normal, but I can't make out anything she's saying.

"No, I don't think . . . Okay, hold on. I'll ask her." My mom holds the phone to her chest as she turns to face me. Her voice quickly shifts from casual to a concerned whisper. "Bonnie says the car Jenna uses is parked in the driveway, but she doesn't think she slept at home. And her phone has been going straight to voicemail all morning. Do you have any idea where she might be? Did you and Delaney see her while you were out last night?"

She knows we haven't been hanging out with Jenna lately, but her eyes are wide, hopeful that I'll say yes. I shake my head, doing my best to mask the panic bubbling up inside me and deciding not to mention the texts

Jenna sent me last night. My mom inches the phone back to her ear, maintaining eye contact as she relays my response to Mrs. Kemp.

"I'm so sorry, Bonnie, but . . ." There's some rapid mumbling, and my mom's chest deflates. "Well, are you sure she didn't sneak in without your knowledge? Maybe she's gone for a run? Or maybe she spent the night at . . ."

Spent the night where, Mom? You have no idea who Jenna has been hanging out with lately. If you did, you probably wouldn't continue asking why we haven't been spending time together. Because you'd be relieved.

Then again, if my mom knew, she probably would have called Jenna's mom weeks ago, and maybe Mrs. Kemp wouldn't be looking for Jenna now.

Does me not wanting to be a nark make me a shitty friend?

"Hmm . . . okay. Can you please hold for a second, Bonnie?" This time my mom looks at me suspiciously. "Keeley, Bonnie says Jenna has been spending a lot of time with a girl named Leighton, and she seems to think you and Delaney have been too. I'm confused . . . why haven't I heard of this girl before?"

I clench my jaw and take a quick sip of orange juice to buy some think time. "I don't know," I say with a shrug as I place my glass back on the table. "Leighton is new, and Jenna has some classes with her, so they study together sometimes. But Delaney and I haven't really hung out with them." I look down at my plate and wonder if Mrs. Kemp is really this clueless about what Jenna has been up to lately? Does she even know anything at all about Leighton?

"So that's it? They just study together, and Jenna never invited this new girl to hang out with you or any of your other friends?" I can hear the confusion in her voice.

"Yeah, that's it," I say, rising to join my mom at the island. "None of us really know much about Leighton. But *Jenna* seems to really like her." *Oops.* The hint of jealousy in my voice was unintentional.

"Wait. Is that why you and Jenna haven't been spending time together lately? Because of this girl? Why haven't you mentioned her before? Do you *not* like her?"

Wonderful. Rapid-fire questioning. "I guess that's part of it. But friendships change too, right? I mean, you've told me that a bunch of times. So, it's not really that big a deal." *Or is it?* "And I didn't mention Leighton because she's just . . ." I break eye contact. I've never been good at lying to someone's face.

"She's what?" my mom whispers as she presses the phone tighter to her chest.

I prop my elbows on the counter and twist my palms into my eyes.

"Keeley, she's *what?*"

"She just doesn't seem like the kind of person I'd want to be friends with," I say, standing upright and folding my arms.

My mom flexes what she refers to as her "eleven lines"—aka the vertical creases in the middle of her forehead. "Well, if you think *that* then why has Jenna been hanging out with her instead of you and Delaney and all your other friends?"

"Because. I've already told you. Jenna's been acting different lately. She's trying to . . ." I pause, frustration welling up inside me. ". . . find herself or something. Did Mrs. Kemp try to call Leighton? Maybe Jenna's over there."

My mom sighs and returns to Mrs. Kemp, and I return to my seat. I can barely contain my racing thoughts as I cut through the slice of avocado next to my eggs with the edge of my fork. *Jenna's fine. She's probably just sleeping off a hangover at Leighton's house. She was probably drunk when she texted me. But what if something happened to her? What if I'm the shittiest friend ever for not returning her text and for not telling my parents or Jenna's parents how weird she's been acting?*

"Okay, Bonnie. That's a good idea. Please keep us posted." My mom ends the call with Mrs. Kemp then turns to me. "She tried to call Leighton earlier, but there was no answer. She's trying again right now . . . Keeley? You okay?" She sets her phone on the table and pulls out the chair next to mine. She sits then laces her fingers around her coffee mug.

I want to tell her how much Jenna has changed, and that she's probably just passed out with a hangover at Leighton's. But I don't. After all, Jenna's not the only one who's no longer the goodie-goodie her parents think she is. We've all done things that our parents would be upset about. Besides, Jenna will probably show up at home any minute, and I don't want to be known as the girl who ratted out her best friend for no good reason. Or maybe I should say *former* best friend. I really don't know anymore. "Yeah, I'm fine. Just thinking she'll probably show up any minute."

My mom studies my face as she takes her first sip of coffee. She's about to say something else when her phone vibrates. We both glance at the screen. It's Mrs. Kemp again.

"See, I bet she found her."

"Let's hope so," my mom says, bringing the phone to her ear. "Hey, Bonnie. Is she home?"

I scoop up my dishes as I stand but freeze mid-step when I hear my mom say, "Oh no . . ." I return to the table, still standing, still holding my plate and glass. "Okay . . . Yes, I'll talk to Keeley again. And please let us know if you hear from her . . . Okay. Talk to you soon."

"Talk to me again about what? What did she say?" I ask.

"Leighton says she hasn't seen Jenna since around nine last night. Bonnie is going to try calling Delaney and Dustin next. If neither of them can help, the Kemps will be calling the police."

"Seriously?" I pick up my phone and scroll through the call log to verify I didn't miss a call from Mrs. Kemp this morning. She probably called my mom instead since they've spoken with each other hundreds of times over the years. "Delaney and Dustin aren't going to know where she is either. They were in the same place as I was last night. But even if the three of us don't know—"

"Four. Don't forget about Leighton," my mom interjects. But Leighton could be lying about not knowing where Jenna is. Maybe she's just trying to buy her time while she recovers from drinking too much or from whatever else they may have taken last night.

"Right. Just because the four of us don't know where she is doesn't mean they need to call the police just yet."

"Keeley," she turns in her seat to face me, "why do you seem to think this is no big deal? If it was you who was missing, and your phone was going straight to voicemail, I would have already called the police. What's going on with Jenna anyway?" She stands, takes the dishes out of my hands, and storms to the sink. "The Jenna I've known all these years has always been such a rule follower. She would never leave without a word to her parents. When did Bonnie and Joseph start letting her do that?" She places my dishes in the sink and turns to me for an answer. Her arms are now folded, and she's leaning against the counter.

"I don't think they *let* her, Mom. I'm pretty sure she just does it."

"Since when?"

"Since about . . . I don't know, end of September?" I shrug and grab my phone off the table again to see if Delaney or Dustin have messaged me yet. No one has.

"That was around the time you girls began spending less time with each other." It wasn't a question, but the deepening of her eleven lines indicates she suspects I'm withholding information. "Keeley, Bonnie and Joseph are worried out of their minds, so if you have any idea where Jenna could be or if there's *anything* you'd like to share, now's the time."

I look up from my phone, suddenly wondering if Jenna may have texted Dustin last night too. Maybe he decided to meet up with her. He did ditch out on Delaney after the movie, saying he didn't feel well. No, that couldn't have had anything to do with Jenna. He would have said something to Delaney, and she would have called me already to complain about it. I wonder if *she'll* tell Mrs. Kemp that Jenna texted me last night. "Nothing I haven't already told you."

"All right then." She turns to open the dishwasher and begins loading it. "Maybe you can call other mutual friends to find out if anyone knows where Jenna is? What about her cousin Eli? I wonder if Bonnie has spoken with him yet." She turns to face me, a few dirty utensils in hand. "He hangs out with some of your friends too, doesn't he?"

Eli. A subtle knot forms in my chest. "Yeah, a few, I guess," I say, shaking my head. "But he was working the concession stand at the movie theater last night, so I doubt he'd have seen her either."

"Oh, okay. You'll call some other friends, though?"

I nod, more out of habit than agreement, and she turns to put the silverware she's holding into the dishwasher.

As I exit the kitchen, my mom starts up again, "Keeley, this girl, Leighton, who else does she hang out with?"

I peek my head back into the room and shrug. "She's new, so no one really. Not that I know of, anyway. Just Jenna, I guess."

"Well, when Jenna gets home, I think it would be a good idea for you to invite her over. Yes, people grow and change, but you two have been friends for a long time, so there's no reason for you to stop talking to each other altogether." She glances back and forth from me to the dishes as she talks. "I'm not saying you have to go back to spending all your free time with each other but getting together every now and then would be nice. Even just to go for a run. You two have always been running buddies . . ." She pauses with a sigh. "Maybe you could even invite Leighton. You know, so you can get to know her a little too?"

Having Leighton over is a terrible idea but telling my mom that will only prolong this conversation. "Yeah, maybe. Good idea."

She smiles, but I can tell by the way she's gripping the edge of the counter that she's struggling to let this go. Even though she's been working on not being so nosey when it comes to my social life, sometimes she just doesn't know when to quit. It's something Jenna, Delaney, and I have all struggled with to varying degrees since around seventh grade—nosey parents, mine and Jenna's moms especially. The funny thing is, Jenna's parents have always been the worst—not just nosey but strict and way overprotective. So it's hard to believe Jenna's the one who's gone wild. If someone would have asked me before we started high school three years ago which one of us would end up being the biggest rebel, I would have guessed Delaney. But Jenna? She's always been the rule follower and most levelheaded out of the three of us. For her to spin out of control the way she has must be a fluke. Maybe scaring the crap out of her parents like she has today will put an end to it all.

I look up and see my mom watching me. She sighs and says, "All right then. I know you're dying to call Delaney, so we'll talk later."

Without another word, I duck out of the kitchen and head down the hall and upstairs to my room. As I close my door, I hear my dad return from his Saturday morning trip to the gym. Perfect timing. After my mom fills him in on our conversation about Jenna, he'll most likely remind her to give me space and trust that I'll confide in her about my problems with Jenna when I'm ready. Gotta love having a therapist for a dad.

Taking a seat on my bed, I pull up Jenna's number on my phone. I don't expect her to answer, but I call her anyway. It goes straight to voicemail, and I hang up without leaving a message. Then I stare at my phone and wonder if there's a chance Jenna could really be missing. I start typing a text but erase it after a few words. A text won't do any good. What's the point if her phone isn't even on?

Sighing heavily, I stand and plug my nearly dead phone in before setting it on my desk. Then my gaze wanders out the window into our wooded backyard, coming to rest on the worn, weathered, and abandoned playset Jenna, Delaney, and I used to play on. My mom has been asking my dad to take it down for years, ever since we grew out of it and started going to Jolliet Park instead, but his response is always the same. *Leslie, one day we're going to have grandkids, and they'll need a place to play.* Then my mom always laughs and warns him how dangerous the old "deathtrap" is. Does he really want their grandkids at risk for contracting tetanus from a rusty old nail?

He always promises to inspect the play structure's integrity come spring. Every year, I secretly hope it passes inspection, because there's something comforting about seeing it when I look out my bedroom window.

Of course, I see more than just the slide, the three swings, the teeter-totter, and the fort at the top of the slide; I also see my best childhood friends and I having contests to see who could swing the highest or who could walk across the teeter-totter the fastest. I see us in the fort with an arsenal of snowballs meant for my unsuspecting big brother and his dorky friends.

And I see us sliding down the slide into one of those hard, plastic swimming pools on humid summer days.

The memories prompt me to walk over to the pin board hanging above my desk. I poke around a bit before I find what I'm looking for tacked underneath a strip of three photo booth pictures from this year's homecoming dance, taken the last time Delaney and I hung out with Jenna. Even though it was only five weeks ago, it feels like months have passed. I run my thumb across Jenna's face in one of the three photos, trying to decipher her odd expression. Guilt swells within me, prompting me to slide the strip into a wicker keepsake box on top of my desk instead of tacking it back up. Then I return my attention to the old, forgotten picture that was tacked underneath the homecoming photo. It's of Delaney, Jenna, and me lying on the old merry-go-round at Jolliet Park the summer before we started seventh grade. I scan the ancient photo and then zero in on Jenna's face, which has the same faraway expression she always used to have in impromptu snapshots. It suddenly occurs to me the expression isn't all that different from the one she has in the homecoming photo. I guess it's just been a long time since I've seen her look like that. Sighing, I tack the old photo back in place then take a step back and wonder if there will ever be another photo taken of the three of us again.

A vibration brings me back to the here and now. I lunge for my phone, unplugging and answering it without looking to see who it is. "Hello?" I say before it's even to my ear.

"Did you talk to Mrs. Kemp?" Delaney asks without returning my harried greeting.

"No, my mom did. Why? Did you?"

"Yeah. She called my mom, but my mom can't talk because she's at the salon. So she texted me and said Mrs. Kemp left a weird voicemail about

Jenna and that I should call her back. What the hell? Where do you think she is?"

"I don't know. Leighton's is my best guess."

"Uh-uh. Leighton told Mrs. Kemp she hasn't seen Jenna since last night."

"Right, but maybe Jenna's hungover and Leighton is covering for her." I glance at the old photo and wish I could ask the tan-skinned girl with the brown side ponytail if she knows what's wrong with her sixteen-year-old self.

"You really think Leighton cares enough about Jenna to lie for her like that?" She huffs. "I doubt she could care less if Jenna gets in trouble."

"I don't know, Delaney. I'm just throwing stuff out there. Where else would she be if she really didn't go home last night?" As an afterthought, I mumble, "And how did she get there without her car?" Delaney's silence is enough to elevate my worries over Jenna's recent actions, but we've already decided half a dozen times to give Jenna a little more time before we say something. Then again, we've never discussed who we'd say something to or if our concerns would be voiced anonymously. I guess we're close to being forced to make those decisions, though, now that she's decided it's okay to stay out all night without a word to her parents about where she'll be. This isn't the same Jenna we grew up with. "Anyway . . . now what? Have you talked to Dustin? I guess Mrs. Kemp was going to call him too."

"No," she says with an edge to her voice. "I tried to call him a few times this morning, but he isn't answering . . . And he never responded when I texted him goodnight last night . . . Whatever."

"You don't think Jenna texted Dustin last night too, do you?" I ask, my gaze falling back on the old photo.

"Well, if she did, he didn't tell me about it," she snips.

Whoops. What started out as a '*We both miss the old Jenna so why don't we lean on each other?*' sort of thing between Dustin and Delaney has evolved into more than anyone thought it would.

"Anyway," she continues, her tone back to normal, "should we try to hunt her down or something? You know, for her mom and dad? I already tried to call her, but it went straight to voicemail."

"Same here. And yeah, I mean . . . I promised my mom I would ask around, so . . . When we find her, we can give her a heads up that her mom has been calling around looking for her. Do you want to meet at Jolliet?" I ask.

"Jolliet? Why don't you just come over here?"

"Nah, I feel like getting outside. Going for a run."

"All right, I guess." She sighs heavily. "How long? Ten? Fifteen minutes?"

"I'll leave right away, so yeah, about ten." Our house is a little farther away from Jolliet Park than Delaney's, but since I'm running, we'll probably get there about the same time if we both leave now.

"Okay. See you there."

chapter two

Friday, July 21, 2017
Three Months Before Jenna's Disappearance

Jenna Kemp's first instinct when Dustin's hand found its way under her shirt was to flinch.

"Sorry," Dustin said, quickly moving to withdraw the advance. For months, he'd been dreaming of doing more than just kissing Jenna, and for years before that, he'd dreamt of doing more than talking on the phone with her, holding her hand, or putting his arm around her while they watched a movie. He knew he had to take things slow with her. Not because he had much experience in the sex department (for a seventeen-year-old, he had *way* less than many of his friends), but because he never wanted to do anything to jeopardize their nearly decade of friendship if dating didn't work out for them. But his friends had been giving him a hard time lately about being stuck on first base with her, so he couldn't deny his growing frustration and paranoia that maybe Jenna didn't feel the same way about him as he felt about her. He worried she was too nice to outright reject him.

Jenna grabbed his hand, pinning his palm against her hip and his fingertips to the flesh of her lower abdomen. "It's okay," she whispered. It really wasn't, but Jenna wanted so badly to forget the past. Her head and heart wanted him to touch her, but the memories wouldn't stop appearing out of nowhere, stifling her desire to be physical with him.

As Jenna's grip loosened around his hand, Dustin's fingers moved cautiously, slowly tracing a path along the lower portion of her stomach, then a little faster upward and across her ribs. Her breath hitched when the edge of his palm touched her bra, but the doom she felt was accompanied by desire, so she thought maybe she was okay.

Until suddenly she wasn't.

"STOP," she said as the panic overtook her, hurriedly elbowing her way into an upright position in the back seat of Mr. and Mrs. Bock's black Chevy Malibu.

She shrank back against the door and brought her hands to her face as Dustin watched from a slumped position against the opposite door.

He sighed more gruffly than intended, once again not understanding what he'd done wrong.

"I'm sorry. I don't know why I keep doing this," Jenna whispered. She could never seem to bring herself to tell Dustin the truth.

Doing what? Dustin wondered. *Trying to convince yourself we should be more than just friends?* He couldn't say it out loud because he was too afraid it was the truth, and he wasn't ready to give up on her just yet.

"Hey," he said, sliding closer to her, "it's okay."

Jenna met him halfway, allowing him to put his arm around her. She rested her head against his chest and closed her eyes, thinking about how badly she wanted to take their relationship to the next level and how badly she wanted to be a willing participant, even if it was only to bury the memories of all the times she wasn't.

"I can't believe summer is already half over," Dustin said, changing the subject. He ran a hand through his hair. "We haven't even been to the beach or gone to the drive-in yet."

Jenna peeked up at him, a grateful smile forming on her lips. "Well, maybe if *someone* hadn't decided to take a full-time summer job . . ."

"I know, I know. But *someone* doesn't get straight A's like his girlfriend, so he really needs to save up for college even if it means tuning up bikes and test riding them around a parking lot every day."

Jenna laughed and kissed Dustin's neck. It was a quick, innocent peck, but it made Dustin wish he could be on top of her again. He cupped her chin and turned her face toward his. When he found her lips, his pulse quickened, and he fantasized about undressing her. Instead of acting on this fantasy, he somehow mustered the willpower to stop kissing her and wrapped his arms around her as they stretched out across the back seat.

The last thing Jenna remembered before dozing off was Dustin kissing her hair and telling her it smelled good.

"Oh my God!" Jenna jumped up, waking Dustin. "What time is it?"

Dustin sat up slowly and rubbed his eyes, Jenna's words not quite registering. His heart skipped a beat as a car headed toward the undeveloped cul-de-sac. He thought it might be a police car at first, but from what he could tell, it was just another couple looking for a private place to park.

"Dustin! We have to go! My mom is going to kill me!" Jenna scaled the middle console and was already buckling her seatbelt before Dustin fully understood the situation.

"Okay. It's okay. Calm down," he said, as he climbed awkwardly over the console and into the driver's seat. He glanced at Jenna as he started the car and put it into gear. Her eyes were wide, and her chest was heaving. "Jenna, it's not like we're out partying. We fell asleep."

"Right, but my mom would probably be less upset if she knew we were at a party instead of alone . . . in the back seat of your parents' car," Jenna said.

Dustin kept his gaze on the road, but he could feel Jenna's eyes on him. "Then we'll tell them we were at a party and lost track of time instead," he offered.

With a heavy sigh, Jenna slumped back into her seat and focused on the road ahead, keeping her thoughts to herself. This had been the third time in a month she'd been with Dustin and missed curfew, so she knew an interrogation awaited her at home.

Less than ten minutes later, they pulled under the streetlamp in front of the Kemps' modest Lannon stone Tudor on Berkeley Street. Dustin put the car in park and reached for the keys in the ignition, but Jenna stopped him.

"It'll be better if you don't walk me to the door." She removed her hand from his and unbuckled her seatbelt.

"Why? I can back your story about us being at a party."

"Dustin, I'm not going to lie. So trust me, it's better if you just go." Jenna leaned over to kiss his cheek. Before he had a chance to object, she already had one foot out the door.

"Text me to let me know how it goes!" he rushed to say before Jenna closed the door, but most of his words had been trapped inside the car. He watched as she jogged up the sidewalk to the house then held the front storm door open with her back and fumbled with her keys. She didn't find them fast enough, though, because the inner door flew wide open within seconds. After Jenna disappeared inside, he got a glimpse of Mrs. Kemp saying something to her before peering out into the darkness at Dustin's car. He waved, but her only response was to shake her head as she closed the door.

With an exasperated sigh, Dustin drove off. He wondered the whole way home why Mrs. Kemp no longer seemed to condone his relationship with Jenna after all the years they'd been friends. He'd talked to his mom about it a few weeks ago, and she tried to explain it from a mom's point of view, but he still didn't get it. Would Mrs. Kemp rather Jenna date some dude who only wanted to get into her pants? His mom said to give Jenna's parents some time to get used to the idea that Jenna (and pretty much all their classmates) were at the age when hormones started raging. Dustin did his best to hide his amusement over this advice because most of his friends, himself included, had hit that age years ago. But his amusement was short-lived because Jenna didn't seem anywhere near as interested in sex as he was.

Some of his friends called Jenna a prude and joked about her uncle being a pastor. *Dude, you're never going to get into the pants of a pastor's niece.* His rebuttal was always some sort of jab, such as calling them assholes or saying they couldn't get a girl like Jenna even if it was in their dreams. The passive-aggressive smile Dustin always had plastered on his face at times like these was only there to hide how pissed off it made him when they talked about Jenna that way. It also hid his hypocrisy because Dustin wasn't innocent of dating girls whose pants were known to offer easy access. But that was never the reason why he wanted to date Jenna.

chapter three

KEELEY
SATURDAY, OCTOBER 28, 2017
ONE DAY AFTER JENNA'S DISAPPEARANCE

"I'm leaving . . . Bye!" I call out as I'm about to walk out the door, but I pause when I hear quick footsteps moving down the hall.

"Hey, Keeley?" my dad says as he enters the mudroom. "Make sure you let us know if you get in touch with Jenna. And if not, please check in soon. Your mom is a bit shaken up about this whole situation."

"I don't understand why. I told her there's probably nothing to worry about. I'm sure Jenna's fine."

"Yeah, well, you know your mom. Hey . . ." he fingers the thick scruff along his cheeks and chin. ". . . if you ever want to talk about anything—you know, friends, boys, school—my door is always open. Like, literally, just pop in anytime." He chuckles as he gestures in the direction of the hallway, which leads to his home office.

"Yeah, I know, Dad. Thanks." I return his warm smile as I step outside.

As soon as I close the door, I take off running. The weather has been mild for October in Wisconsin, so I instantly feel warm and wish I hadn't thrown on a third layer. But my mom was insistent. *Better to be warm than cold, Keeley, and you can always remove a layer.*

Delaney lives about six blocks from the north side of Jolliet Park, and Jenna and I are on the south side. Whenever Jenna and I run to the park, we meet on the corner of her street, right next to the streetlight and the KEEP OFF sign Mr. Fitzgibbon's has had on his lawn for as long as I can remember. Out of habit, I stop when I reach the streetlight and look down the block at Jenna's house. I'm tempted to make a pitstop, just in case. Is it possible Jenna went home already and her parents are too busy interrogating her to let my mom know she's okay?

No, I can't. If she isn't there, Mrs. Kemp will ask me questions that I don't have the answers to. Questions I don't want to answer. I'm afraid I won't be able to look Jenna's mom in the eyes and not tell her the truth.

The faint sound of a dog barking reminds me that I'm no longer moving. I glance up from the spot where Jenna and I always used to meet and see Mr. Fitzgibbons peeking through his curtains at me, his rusty-colored poodle beside him pawing at the window. I wave at my retired high school math teacher. He returns the gesture and promptly turns away from the window, letting the curtains fall closed. I guess that's my cue to be on my way.

As I run the final few blocks to Jolliet, memories of my childhood come flooding back. Jenna, Delaney, and I have been meeting at this park ever since sixth grade when our parents agreed that, as long as we stuck together, we were old enough to hang out here without adult supervision. It was about the same time the playset in my backyard began to feel babyish, but we still used the playground equipment at Jolliet when no one else was there. When we entered middle school, our main priority became talking about boys and pretending we were too old for things like swings and monkey bars. But there is one piece of equipment we never stopped using.

The Jolliet merry-go-round holds a special place in my heart—and probably in Jenna and Delaney's hearts too. I'd bet money on it. When we became teenagers, instead of running until we couldn't pick up any more speed and hopping on, we would just sit—none of us wanting to admit that spinning was way more fun. After all, we had to act cool. If there were little kids on it, we'd sit on a bench and wait for them to leave. Sometimes we'd offer to give them a spin, laughing at their dizzy smiles and occasional screams. Then when we became freshmen, for some reason, it was cool again to get the merry-go-round going as fast as we could before hopping on. But instead of laughing hysterically like when we were kids, we would lay still and enjoy the dizzying effect it had on us, wondering if that was what it would feel like to be drunk. Of course, we all know now that it isn't quite the same.

But the merry-go-round has never been just a place for us to play or try to act cool. It's also a place we would go when life sucked. Like when we were ten and Jenna's first dog got hit by a car and had to be put down. Or when we were thirteen and Delaney's dad moved out. Or in eighth grade when Haley Tompkins started spreading rumors about us, which was ridiculous and probably a result of Haley's crush on Dustin, who was always hanging around Delaney, Jenna, and me at lunch and during school dances. According to Haley, Jenna was flirting with Delaney's crush and I was seen coming out of the bathroom stall where it said "Jenna Kemp is a lesbo" on the wall. There was also something about Delaney's dad having an affair with my mom. That one really made us laugh. All of Haley's efforts might have turned us against each other if she hadn't started mixing our names with the alleged offenses. After a horrific week of classmates whispering behind our backs and us hearing bits and pieces of the lies, we ended up at Jolliet. Instead of discussing any of the crap Haley was saying about us, we sat on our merry-go-round and made a Haley Tompkins voodoo doll out of sticks and leaves and dandelion stems. We burned that ugly thing to a crisp, and none of us have spoken to the real Haley by choice since.

It's been nearly two years since we last spun on the merry-go-round, probably because we've been too busy hanging out in the woods instead, where kids our age sometimes smoke or drink if it isn't too cold outside. Delaney and I have steered clear of most of that. Jenna's another story, of course.

When I see the Jolliet Park sign, I reduce my pace to a slow jog. Delaney catches sight of me but doesn't wave like she normally would. Instead, she continues sitting cross-legged, hands gripping the edge of the merry-go-round, and looks back down at the ground. As I move along the tree-lined path Jenna and I have jogged along together so many times, a knot forms in my stomach. I can't decide if it's because of all the childhood memories we've shared here or because the last time I was here, Jenna was too.

"Hey," I say as I bend and place my hands on my knees to catch my breath. I crane my neck to glance up at Delaney.

"Hey," she responds, uncrossing her legs and dropping them over the edge.

"So, how did Mrs. Kemp sound? What else did she say?" I ask, standing upright and taking a seat next to her. I grip the bar next to me and lean my head against it, my chest still heaving.

Delaney sighs and remains silent for a few seconds as she checks her phone. "She was calm at first . . . sniffled a few times while we caught up.

She asked how I am, how's school, how's my mom . . . said she's due for a haircut so she'll probably pay my mom's salon a visit soon." She glances over at me. "You know Mrs. Kemp . . . always really nice." I nod, and she continues. "Anyway, then she asked if I saw Jenna last night, and when I told her I've hardly spoken to Jenna for two months, she started bawling. Said she had no idea we haven't hung out for that long. Then she started rambling and saying things like she was just trying to be understanding, thought Jenna breaking curfew so often lately was just typical teenager rebellion—nothing to worry about. She didn't want to make things worse by butting in, and that she was trying to make amends with Jenna over the whole diary situation. Then she asked—"

"Wait . . . what diary situation?"

"No idea," Delaney says. "I thought maybe you knew." I shake my head as she continues. "So then she asked about Leighton. I mean, Keeley," we lock eyes, "she thought we'd been hanging out with Leighton too. They have zero idea what's going on with Jenna. How is that even possible?"

I shrug and shake my head. "All I know is Mrs. Kemp has been busy taking on more roles at church since Pastor Steele took over, and of course, Jenna's dad is always super busy until it gets too cold to work outside, but I still don't get it either. You didn't . . . tell her anything, did you?"

"No. I didn't know what you might have said, so I didn't say anything. This is it, though, right? I mean, now they're probably going to interrogate her big time and find out about everything. Don't you think?"

"For sure. And there's no way she's not getting grounded for, like, the rest of high school." We both laugh, but the lighthearted moment is fleeting because the things Jenna has been doing aren't anything to laugh about. "Anyway," I clear my throat, "where should we start? Do you want to try calling Dustin again?"

Delaney pulls her phone out of her pocket and looks at the screen. "No. I already have . . . a few times. And I texted once." She sighs. "You'd think after talking to Mrs. Kemp he'd call right away."

"Maybe he didn't talk to her yet. Maybe he's still sleeping," I offer.

"Yeah, maybe. Or maybe he's already trying to find Jenna on his own." She rolls her eyes. "It wouldn't surprise me."

"Maybe we shouldn't assume anything until you hear from him . . ." *I'm staying out of this love triangle.* "Should we talk to Leighton?"

"How? Neither of us has her number? And I certainly don't feel like calling Mrs. Kemp to get it."

"Me either . . . She doesn't live far from here. Should we just go to her house?"

Delaney looks at me as if I've suggested we walk across hot coals. "Are you serious? Leighton hates us."

She hates you, Delaney. I have no idea how she feels about me.

"And what if Jenna *is* there? How do you think she'll react to us showing up? I'd rather call. I bet Lou Tang knows Leighton's number. We can easily get his number, or we can DM him on Insta."

"We're not calling the resident drug dealer, Delaney. Besides, who cares if Jenna gets mad at us for showing up at Leighton's? Her mom and dad think she's missing, and they're going to call the cops if she doesn't get her butt home. Whether she likes it or not, we'd be doing her a favor."

I get why Delaney is nervous about showing up at Leighton's house, and it has nothing to do with the rumors about Leighton being expelled from her last school for fighting. (Word has it she ripped out a chunk of another girl's hair, big enough that it left a huge bloody bald spot.) I'd be uneasy around Leighton too if she'd called me out on being a shitty friend to Jenna. Not so much because of the shitty friend part, really, but more because of the reason.

Most people were shocked when Delaney and Dustin started spending time together, even me. But after his split from Jenna, and the way she pulled away from us, who's to tell them who they can and can't date? Besides, Jenna's the one who broke up with Dustin. Leighton's the only one who ever said anything. And she didn't do it discreetly, nor did she sugarcoat her opinion about their "betrayal."

But I'm not going to Leighton's by myself, so Delaney needs to forget about the scene Leighton caused, even if it's only for the next hour or so.

Delaney and I walk the first half of the ten-block trip to Leighton's neighborhood mostly in silence. But as we pass the Mobil gas station on the corner of Hampton and Santa Monica, a guy pumping gas into a white Chevy yells, "Hey, you ladies cold? We got plenty a room if you want a ride." He taps the top of the car a few times, and the rear driver's side window opens, releasing a cloud of smoke and my grandpa's idea of noise pollution at its worst: gangster rap.

"Well, isn't that impressive?" Delaney whispers under her breath. She gives my elbow a tug, encouraging me to keep up with her quickening pace, but I fall behind a few steps as I sneak a peek inside the car, which is filled with guys about our age. I don't recognize any of them, though, so I lose interest and pick up my pace to catch up with Delaney.

"Oh, okay, I see how it is!" the guy at the pump yells. Then he adds, "Typical white girls," just loud enough for us to hear.

Delaney stops dead in her tracks, but before she can turn around, I link my elbow with hers to keep her moving. "Don't even bother. It's no big deal." If Jenna was with us, she'd have gone back to confront the guy before I had a chance to stop her. She's always been the outspoken one, but only when it's on behalf of someone else, never herself.

"Fine," she says with a sigh. "But it pisses me off. You know?" She presses the pedestrian crosswalk button, and we wait for the light to change.

"I know. But why bother? Clearly, he's an idiot," I say, wondering if I should have just let Delaney tell him off. It might have been fun to see his face when he got a better look at me and realized the white girl label doesn't quite fit. That's life when you're a mixed kid.

Three blocks later, we turn into the Juniper Court cul-de-sac.

"I think it's that one," I say pointing at the fourth townhouse in on the left side of the circle. "I remember those tiered planters from that time we picked up Jenna."

"Me too," Delaney says.

We're about to cross the circle when she stops and turns to face me.

"What?" I ask, looking around to see if there are any cars backing out or turning into the cul-de-sac.

"Are you sure you want to do this? Maybe we should just get Leighton's number instead. Or . . ." She pulls her phone out of her pocket and pokes at the screen. "Maybe Jenna turned her phone back on." She puts the phone to her ear, and even if I couldn't hear Jenna's voicemail greeting, I'd know she didn't answer based on the frustrated expression on Delaney's face.

"Come on, Delaney. Yes, Leighton totally embarrassed you, and she was wrong to stick her nose in where it doesn't belong. But can you just let it go? At least until we find out if Jenna is here? You can't make me go to the door by myself." *Because Leighton scares the shit out of me.*

"Yeah, sure. Fine." She looks over at Leighton's house. "You lead the way."

Delaney walks beside me as we cross the center of the cul-de-sac. When we reach the stairs, she falls back and stays on the top step as I ring the doorbell then fold my arms across my chest like I mean business. Seconds tick by without a peep from inside, so I ring it again.

Still nothing.

"Okay . . . no one's home," Delaney says.

I glance back at her and knock, unwilling to believe Leighton and Jenna aren't inside. Or maybe even Leighton's mom or dad or someone else who might live here. Surely, they could tell us if Jenna spent the night.

"Keeley, they're either not home or they know it's us and they aren't going to answer, so let's just—"

"Shh. Did you hear that? That ding? It sounded like a phone." I glance back at Delaney and lean my ear toward the door. After a few seconds of silence, I back away with a sigh. I raise my hand to ring the doorbell one final time but lower it when I hear the door being unlocked. As the door slowly opens, I quickly refold my arms and contemplate whether I'm going to play good cop or bad cop. The next thing I know, I'm face to face with Leighton, her multi-colored hair, and a blank stare.

chapter four

"Hey, Mom. Sorry I'm late," Jenna said, trying to maintain a steady, lighthearted tone as she breezed past her mother into the house. "Dustin and I fell asleep listening to music." It wasn't a lie, she'd told herself. There *was* music playing in the car. Following the greeting, Jenna said a nervous, silent prayer promising to never break curfew again if her mom would just let this one slide without a huge argument. She headed straight for the stairs, Lulu's tail wagging happily by her side. "Hey, girl," Jenna whispered, patting Lulu's head as they climbed the first few steps together.

"Whoa, whoa, whoa. Get back here, young lady." Nothing short-circuited Bonnie's usual soft-spoken nature like the fear that her teenage daughter would follow in her naive footsteps and have sex before she was ready. She knew from experience what the consequences could be.

Jenna froze on the third step, closing her eyes and taking a deep breath before heading back downstairs where her furious mother was waiting. When she and Lulu returned to the entryway next to the open concept living room, her dad was there now too. He was in his usual evening attire—flannel pajama bottoms and a ratty old classic rock band T-shirt (tonight it was AC/DC)—and he was holding a mug with a Tazo tea label hanging over the side.

"Oh, good. You're home," Joseph said to Jenna as he handed the mug to his wife. He then leaned over and gave his daughter a peck on her forehead. "I assume there's a good reason for you being late again?"

Grateful for her dad's presence, Jenna's posture relaxed a little. Even when he'd first entered their lives, back when Jenna was three and her mom was struggling to make ends meet as a single parent, he'd always seemed to buffer any turbulence between them.

"Yeah, of course. Dustin and I were listening to music, and we fell asleep." Jenna shrugged. "It's not a big deal. Besides, I'm only—"

"Not a big deal?" Mrs. Kemp's voice boomed. She handed the hot mug of tea back to her sighing husband. "You're almost an hour late! Where were the two of you? It must have been someplace pretty darn cozy if you fell asleep."

"God, Mom!" Jenna threw her hands up only for them to come crashing down to her thighs. "It's not like we were out partying or robbing gas stations. We were just hanging out, talking, listening to music. Why are you the only parent I know who overreacts like this?" Lulu nudged Jenna's hand with her nose, but Jenna ignored her, causing the dog to wander off to her bed in the corner.

"Jenna, how many times do we have to—"

"Okay, okay," Joseph said moving a few feet into the living room and setting the mug of tea down on a coaster. "How about we all just sit down and *talk* this out?" He gave Bonnie a pointed look as he finished his sentence. Then he took a seat on the sofa.

"Fine," Bonnie said before following in Joseph's footsteps and taking a seat next to him.

Jenna followed too, but she chose to sit in the lounge chair clear across the room from her parents. She dropped her bag to the floor as she swiveled the chair to face them. Lulu reappeared at her side, and this time, Jenna indulged her canine bestie with a few scratches behind her ear.

"You know, Jenna, we've been understanding in the past when you've broken curfew but only because you were never habitual about it. But this is the *third* time this month, and you've been with Dustin every time. So, what's going on?"

"*Nothing* is going on. I told you we fell asleep. That's the truth."

"Right. You fell asleep this time. Last time you lost track of time. And the time before that, traffic was terrible on the freeway on your way home from the concert." Bonnie waved her hand in the air dramatically, dismissing all of Jenna's excuses. "Your dad and I weren't born yesterday, and we were both teenagers once, you know? And *you* should know better than any of your friends how important it is to abstain from sex at your age. I need you to learn from my mistakes, Jenna."

Jenna rolled her eyes and huffed, feeling defiant. She was tired of being reminded that she was the result of an unplanned pregnancy when her mom and biological father were in high school, and it was moments like this that made her think about telling her mom exactly why she didn't have to worry about her losing her virginity to Dustin. "I said I was sorry. I don't know what else you want me to say."

"I want you to tell me the truth . . . are you and Dustin having sex?"

Jenna catapulted to her feet, bent down to grab her bag, and said, "Just because you and your friends were all having sex when you were my age doesn't mean I am." Then she headed for the stairs.

"Jenna," Bonnie gasped. Joseph put a firm hand on her knee, but it didn't have the effect he was hoping for. Instead, his wife rose to her feet and followed their daughter. "Where do you think you're going?" she demanded.

Jenna paused at the base of the stairs. "Do you really think I'm that stupid? After all the times you've lectured me about how hard it was to have me when you were still in high school? About how hard it was when the sperm donor dumped you and left you to raise me on your own? Well, I'm not an idiot! And Dustin is a good guy, but you've been horrible to him ever since we started dating."

"Oh, Jenna . . . that's not true."

"Yes, it is! You barely acknowledge him anymore when he comes over. Why do you have to be like that?"

Bonnie was worried that Dustin Bock only wanted one thing from her daughter, but she couldn't admit it out loud. Not when she also knew deep down it was an unfair assumption. "Sweetie, he didn't even walk you to the door. What kind of boy—"

"Seriously?" Jenna's frustration had almost reached a boiling point.

"Bonnie, just let her go. She said she was sorry." Joseph looked at Jenna. "Go to bed, Jenna."

Without a word, Jenna turned to escape upstairs but paused when she heard her mother's agitated voice again.

"Wait. Don't you think she should have some sort of consequence for breaking curfew again?"

"Bonnie, she's a good kid . . . can we just figure it out in the morning? After you've had a chance to cool down?"

Only when she heard her mother's sigh of resignation did Jenna stomp herself the rest of the way upstairs. She was about to enter the bathroom when she heard her little sister's voice.

"Jenna?" Shaina whispered, poking her head out of her bedroom directly across from the bathroom.

"Oh, hey. It's late. You should go back to bed."

Ignoring her big sister, Shaina stepped into the hallway, yawning and rubbing her eyes. "I have to pee."

Jenna sighed and crossed her arms as Shaina groggily stumbled past her into the bathroom, closing the door behind her.

As she stood there waiting to get in the bathroom, Jenna tried to eavesdrop on her parents' continued arguing, but all she could make out was her dad pleading with her mom. *You need to loosen the leash a little, Bonnie!* That was when Shaina exited the bathroom.

"Are they talking about you or Lulu?" Shaina asked as she disappeared into her bedroom.

"Smart aleck," Jenna mumbled with a grin before entering the bathroom.

While Jenna got ready for bed, she and Dustin exchanged a few texts.

DUSTIN: EVERYTHING OKAY?

JENNA: NOT REALLY. SHE'S RIDICULOUS.

DUSTIN: ARE YOU GROUNDED?

JENNA: NOT SURE YET. THE SENTENCING IS TOMORROW.

DUSTIN: HAHA. IF NOT, WANT TO HANG OUT AGAIN?

Once in her bedroom, Jenna placed her phone on her nightstand instead of answering Dustin's last text right away. She retrieved her diary and a pen from the second drawer as a hopeful Lulu looked on, tail wagging.

"It's too late for treats, Lulu. You know that. Come on," Jenna said, motioning for Lulu to hop on the bed before climbing under the covers.

With Lulu curled up next to her, she opened her diary, which was a simple hard cover magenta notebook with an elastic strap for securing it closed when not in use. For her seventh birthday, her Aunt Lenore had given her a real diary, with a lock and two miniature gold keys. From that point forward, Jenna started chronicling her life, writing about everything and anything. Back then, it was mostly stuff about what she did in school or during recess, her likes and dislikes, and her general state of mind. When that first diary wore out, she asked for a new one for Christmas, and so the trend began. When she started sixth grade, she decided locked diaries were too babyish, so she'd asked her mom for something more grown up. Then for her eleventh birthday, she received a bundle of twelve hardcover notebooks in various colors. Of the twelve, only two remained.

July 21, 2017

Dear Diary,

I don't understand my mom. Sure, I was late again, but it was an accident, and it's not like Dustin and I were doing anything wrong. Or maybe that's why she's been acting so strict with me this summer. Because of Dustin. How could she even think I'd make the same mistake she did when she was my age? I'm not an idiot. I know how babies are made. (Although she did too, but whatever.) And there's also all the other stuff holding me back, the stuff no one knows about. Part of me thinks I should just go through with it with Dustin, that maybe it would help me forget, but the other part of me worries it'll only make my memories more vivid. I know he's frustrated, and I'm scared he might dump me if I keep acting so weird every time we make out. So what do I do? Sometimes I think telling him might help, but it could also scare him off. How would he feel if he knew I'm not as innocent as he thinks? He might not want anything to do with me, as my boyfriend or even as just friends.

Sometimes I wish Dustin and I, and all our other friends, could just go back to playing kickball, riding our bikes together, and hanging out at the pool or park. It was much easier back then.

On a brighter note, I ran well this morning. Keeley did too. We ran farther than usual—about six miles straight through Jolliet and then all the way to the end of the Parkway. Then we stopped at Jolliet on the way back (so I guess it was more like five and a half miles because we walked home from

Jolliet). It was getting hot out, so we didn't stay long, but we did take a spin on the old merry-go-round. Did we spin that fast when we were kids? I wish Delaney had been with us, but she doesn't run because she prefers a matte finish to sweat. Funny how the three of us are so different, yet still such close friends.

Well, gotta go. Keeley and I are supposed to meet for another run in the morning. It's going to be really hot again, so I need to wake up early. Hopefully, this heat lets up by the time cross country practice starts in a few weeks.

~Jenna

Jenna closed her diary, pulled the strap around it, and clipped the purple pen she'd used that night to the strap. Then she opened the second drawer of her nightstand and dropped the diary inside. She began sliding the drawer closed but hesitated with about two inches to go. She wondered if maybe it was time to start hiding her diary again. When she was younger, she hid it under her mattress, but it got to be a pain digging it out whenever she wrote in it, so she started hiding it among her stack of teen magazines. Then come freshman year, she stopped hiding it, figuring if the elastic band wasn't enough to let someone know the notebook was off limits, so be it. But unlike some of her friends' moms, Jenna's mom wasn't the type who snooped, at least she didn't used to be. Now, with her mom's suspicions about Jenna and Dustin, Jenna began to wonder if she could still trust her mom not to invade her privacy. In the end, she shrugged off her leeriness and closed the drawer.

Before she went to sleep, she grabbed her phone and responded to Dustin.

Jenna: Yes. xx

chapter five

LEIGHTON PIERCE
SATURDAY, OCTOBER 28, 2017
ONE DAY AFTER JENNA'S DISAPPEARANCE

I've just started the dryer and put in a second load of laundry when another text from my mom comes through.

MOM: AFTER YOU FINISH YOUR CHORES, WHY DON'T YOU GO TO THE STORE AND PICK UP SOMETHING FOR DINNER TONIGHT? MILK AND EGGS TOO IF YOU CAN.

The last time I took care of dinner, which was two nights ago, she didn't even bother to come home after her shift at the hospital. Instead, she went to her boyfriend's house over in Glendale, but at least she was here when I woke up the next morning. That's starting to happen less and less, though. Only one year to go. Then she can be rid of me, free to start over. Hell, she might still even be young enough to have another kid, one that won't ruin her life by "chasing off" her man. My father is no man, though. He's a selfish asshole who only cares about himself.

ME: MONEY?

MOM: SHOULD BE A TWENTY IN THE BOWL ON MY DRESSER. AND USE CHANGE FROM LAST TIME.

Not wanting to walk a mile home from the grocery store with milk and eggs, I text my friend Sticks to see if he's around to give me a ride.

ME: HEY, ANY CHANCE YOU'LL BE OVER BY ME TODAY?

The doorbell rings when I step out into the hallway. Not interested in telling another Boy Scout selling wreaths or popcorn to get lost, I ignore it and retrieve the money from my mom's dresser. Then I shove the twenty in my pocket and head toward the bathroom, but the doorbell rings again, so I change course and run downstairs, realizing it might be Jenna. I peek through the living room blinds and see two people I never expected standing on my porch.

What the hell? Why are Keeley Simon and Delaney Burns here?

I move to the door and place my hand on the deadbolt, contemplating whether or not to talk to them. A definitive *don't answer* echoes through my brain, but then my phone pings with a response from Sticks asking what I need, and I hear Keeley. *Shh. Did you hear that?* As if she isn't perfect enough, she also has supersonic hearing.

Whatever. Might as well see what they want. Who knows? Maybe after the epiphany Jenna had last night, she told them everything, and they're just here to thank me for being there for her when they weren't. Or maybe instead of thanking me, they're here to tell me to stay away from Jenna now that she's decided to come clean about all the shit she's been through. I wouldn't be surprised. I'll never be a candidate for best influence.

I unlock and open the door, then wait a few seconds for one of them to say something. But these Ugg-wearing princesses just stare at me, Keeley with her arms folded across her chest like she's a prosecutor on some court drama and Delaney shifting from one foot to the other.

I sigh and ask, "What do you want?"

"Hey, Leighton," Keeley says, unfolding her arms. She clears her throat. "We need to talk to Jenna. Is she here?"

So, they *haven't* heard from Jenna?

"Nope. But I assume you already know that since Mrs. Kemp probably called you guys too?" Acting like I don't care has become my specialty, but at this moment, I'm actually worried. When her mom called earlier, I assumed Jenna might have slipped out for a run without saying anything or that she was with one of these girls or that asshole Dustin. But now I'm beginning to wonder where she is and if she's okay.

"Look," Delaney says, marching up onto the porch next to Keeley, "we all know she's been hanging out with you every weekend lately. If you were a *real* friend, you'd admit she's inside sleeping off a hangover." She narrows her mascaraed eyes at me.

I narrow my eyes right back at her, irritated that even on a Saturday, she makes herself look like a cover model and seething at the irony of her last statement. At least I know a friend's ex is off limits. I'm about to fire back at her, but then I remember the point of their visit and go back to looking like I don't give a fuck. "Like I told her mom, she's not here. I haven't seen her since last night."

I close the door a little, eager to get back to Sticks to tell him I need a ride to the grocery store and possibly someplace else now. But the way Keeley and Delaney look at each other and then back at me, their expressions matching how I feel on the inside, causes me to pull the door wide open. "Come in and look for yourselves if you don't believe me."

Keeley walks right in but Delaney hesitates.

"Are you coming in or waiting out there? I don't care either way."

She hustles past me without a word. I close the door and turn to find her standing hip to hip with Keeley in the middle of my living room. Hip to thigh, rather, since Keeley is about a foot taller than Delaney. "See?" I say, raising my hands. "She's not here."

They both scan every visible area, which includes an adjoining dining room, part of the kitchen, and a hallway that leads to the garage. These girls live in the privileged kind of neighborhood I used to live in with both of my parents, so I'm sure they probably think our townhouse is nothing special, but I don't give a flying fuck. I'd rather live in a cardboard box in a ditch than in a five-thousand-square-foot house in a neighborhood where everyone has perfectly manicured lawns if it means I don't have to sleep under the same roof as my dad. In the meantime, I take a seat on the furthest corner of the sectional from where they're standing. The soft black leather makes a crinkling sound as I slide back onto the deep cushion, my eyes trained on them and their contradicting features—Keeley with her dark brown everything and Delaney with her blonde hair, blue eyes, and flawless porcelain skin. If Jenna stood between them, with her chestnut brown hair and olive complexion, the trio would look like they belong in an ad promoting interracial friendships.

Keeley sighs, begins pacing the room, and says, "So, if Jenna isn't here, then where is she?" She stops and looks from me to Delaney then back to me. "You said you haven't seen her since last night. Where were you guys?"

"Here."

"Where was she going when she left?"

"Look, I don't feel right telling you two Jenna's business. If she wanted you to know where she was going, she would have told you herself."

"Excuse me?" Delaney takes three quick steps in my direction, causing Keeley to grab her pint-sized friend's shoulder, likely preventing her from doing something she'll regret. I'm shocked as hell by this sudden outburst, but there's no way I'll show it. Instead, I pick at the frayed hole in the left knee of my jeans and wait for the right moment to tell these bitches to leave.

"We've been friends with Jenna since grade school! You? You show up THIS YEAR with your stupid hair, weird gauges, and depressing wardrobe. And, of course, Jenna befriends you because that's her—always wanting to be nice, always wanting to help—or at least that *was* her." She sniffles, causing me to impulsively glance up at her. A single tear trails down each of her cheeks as she continues her tirade. "And then, BAM, all of a sudden, she starts acting like a completely different person. And I blame you, Leighton!"

Me? She blames me? Any bit of sympathy I may have been feeling for her has just gone out the window. "Fuck you. You're clueless. And I'd like both of you to get the fu—"

"Leighton. Wait . . ." Keeley pleads, her hand falling from Delaney's shoulder when Delaney collapses onto the couch and plants her face in her hands. "Can you just tell us where she went? Or even who she was with?"

I should. I really should. Because the more I think about where Jenna went last night, the more sick to my stomach I feel. But there are still explanations for where she could be now, so I can't. "Sorry," I say, shaking my head and pulling a lighter and one-hitter out of my hoodie pocket. "She can tell you herself." I maintain eye contact with Keeley as I bring the pipe to my lips, light up, and inhale deeply.

"Wait, what are you—"

Delaney gasps, interrupting Keeley. "You've got to be kidding me! You have no idea where your supposed friend is and you're smoking weed?" she shouts.

I chuckle to myself as I recall Jenna telling me Delaney was the one who wanted the three of them to try smoking pot together for the first time. She's even the one who bought the weed from Lou. But now that I'm doing it, apparently it's a mortal sin.

"Let's just go," Keeley says, shaking her head and motioning for Delaney to follow her to the door.

As soon as both girls are out on the porch, Keeley turns, still holding the screen door open as if she means to say something. But I'm done, so I close the inner door before she has a chance. Ignoring the angry chatter from outside, I pull up the messages I have going with Sticks and type as I head upstairs.

ME: NEED FOOD.

STICKS: WHERE YOU WANNA EAT?

I enter my bedroom and take a seat on my bed as I tap out a response.

ME: NO MAN, GROCERIES. MOM WANTS EGGS AND MILK.

STICKS: YEAH OF COURSE. AROUND 12 OKAY?

STICKS: WHY CAN'T SHE GET THAT SHIT HERSELF?

ME: DUNNO :/ YEAH THANKS.

I glance across the room at the bag Jenna has been keeping here for the past month or so. She said it was stuff for when she wanted to crash, but I've only seen her dig around in it once, and she's spent the night a bunch of times. The pink and gray stripes have become a comforting fixture in my room, sort of like Jenna has in my life. This realization makes me wish I'd never allowed myself to become friends with her in the first place.

For the third time since Mrs. Kemp called this morning, I try Jenna's phone. And for the third time, it goes straight to voicemail. I contemplate sending a second text, but I don't want to blow up her phone like Keeley and Delaney probably are so I decide against it. She'll get back to me soon.

But what if he didn't like what she had to say? *Damn it, you should have gone with her and watched from a distance.*

I do a quick Google search, and the first result gives me the information I'm looking for.

I send Sticks one more text.

ME: MIGHT NEED TO STOP ONE MORE PLACE TOO . . .

chapter six

SATURDAY, JULY 22, 2017
THREE MONTHS BEFORE JENNA'S DISAPPEARANCE

Jenna slowed her pace to a light jog, prompting Keeley to do the same. Cross country practice would start in less than a month, so they'd been conditioning since June and had just run three one-mile loops through Jolliet Park. Now they were heading home.

Keeley and Jenna knew there was a heat advisory in the forecast so they'd made plans after their run the day before to meet in their spot at six a.m. But Jenna texted Keeley just as she was heading out the door to see if they could meet at eight instead. Now they were both huffing and puffing, the hot sun causing beads of sweat to roll off the tips of their noses.

"I told you . . . we should . . . have done this earlier." Keeley caught her breath as she spoke. She raised the bottle in her right hand and squeezed a stream of water into her mouth, followed by a squirt to Jenna's face.

"Hey!" Jenna laughed. "I know, but . . . I had trouble sleeping last night."

"Why? Wait, don't tell me. You can't stop fantasizing about Dustin." Keeley wrinkled her nose as if the thought grossed her out.

The girls came to a stop on the corner of Jenna's street, just a few blocks shy of Keeley's house. They both leaned forward to stretch their hamstrings.

"Funny, but no," Jenna said, glancing over at the long, coarse curls of Keeley's ponytail as they fanned over her left shoulder. "I was late again last night . . . my mom freaked."

"Well, how late were you?" Keeley asked as they both switched legs.

"Almost an hour, but it was totally innocent. We fell asleep in the back seat of his parents' car."

"Umm . . . and what were you doing in the back seat? Wait, don't answer that." Keeley stood upright, her eyes squeezed closed, and motioned with her hand for Jenna to forget she'd asked the question. The girls had been friends with Dustin since third grade, so the thought of Jenna and Dustin doing anything more than holding hands made Keeley queasy.

"Nothing really. Just . . . kissing." Jenna pulled her left foot up behind her until her heel touched her butt. Keeley made a concerted effort not to picture her childhood friends making out as she mimicked Jenna's pose. "So even though I told the truth, my mom is still pissed and thinks we were having sex. You know, because everyone our age *must* be having sex."

The girls switched legs.

"I don't know, Jenna. My mom and dad would be suspicious too. If I had a boyfriend to break curfew with, that is . . ."

Jenna sighed. "But it's *Dustin*. And it's not like I'm some out-of-control teenager."

"True," Keeley said with a shrug. "So now what? Are you grounded? Did they take your phone?"

"I don't know yet. Guess I'll find out when I get home."

"Well, call me later and let me know. Maybe if you don't get grounded, we can hang out tonight. We could watch a movie or have a bonfire in my backyard."

"Yeah, that would be fun. Would you mind if Dustin joined us?"

"Um . . ." Keeley paused long enough for Jenna to know how she really felt. Then she cleared her throat, smiled, and said, "No, of course not."

Jenna knew she'd been spending a lot of extra time with Dustin but still felt bad turning him down when he asked her to hang out. She'd have to figure out a happy medium because now that they were dating, it was different having him around all the time, especially when it was just Keeley and Delaney with them.

On her way home, Jenna prepared herself for another argument with her mom. But when she entered the house through the back door, her mom was preoccupied with a phone call. *Thank God,* she thought. She missed the days when the biggest issue between them was deciding what movie to watch or why Jenna had such a hard time remembering to keep her phone charged.

"Hey, Mom," Jenna whispered as she made her way into the kitchen and headed straight to the sink to splash some water on her face.

Bonnie acknowledged her daughter with a distracted nod as she poured herself a cup of coffee, her cell phone pinned between her shoulder and ear. Two cups of coffee in the morning and tea at night. Those were two of her many daily rituals.

After lifting her T-shirt to dry her face, Jenna got herself a glass of ice water and a yogurt. Then she took a seat opposite where her mom was leaning her elbows on the counter.

"In three weeks? Really? This is great news!" Bonnie said into her phone. She smiled, briefly raising her eyes to meet Jenna's.

As Jenna eavesdropped on her mom's conversation, dread began to well up inside her. And by the time her mom hung up the phone, being grounded for breaking curfew or Dustin losing interest in her were the least of Jenna's concerns.

"Jenna! Your Uncle Greg accepted the lead pastor position at church! They're moving back! And Thomas and his family too! To help with the youth ministry!"

"Oh. Wow. That's . . ." Jenna tried to force a response, but she was hoping there were things she'd misheard.

Oblivious to Jenna's change in demeanor, Bonnie continued, "You know, it's so true what they say about things just working out for the best. I've been missing them so much since they all moved." Then she repeated all the details of her conversation with her sister that had her brimming with excitement. "So, in three weeks . . ."

They can't all be moving back, Jenna thought. She nodded at her mom, but the sound of her heart pounding in her ears made it difficult for her to maintain the illusion that she was listening.

". . . asked if I could help find some houses for sale in the area. But I suppose they could rent for a while too. Then . . ."

I must have misheard that part.

". . . get your cousins registered for school. Can you believe Elijah will be going to your school? You two were so cute together when you were little. This is so exciting!"

This can't be happening.

"And we finally get to meet Thomas's wife and their little one. Maybe you can babysit for her the way Thomas used to babysit for you when you were little."

Wife? Little one?

By the time Jenna realized she'd knocked over her ice water, her mom was already diving for the glass as it rolled over the edge of the counter.

"Jenna!" Bonnie juggled the glass before finally getting a firm grip on it and setting it back on the dripping counter.

"I'm sorry . . ." Jenna uttered, shocked by the incident, and still nowhere near recovered from hearing the news of her Aunt Lenore's family moving back to town. She had a feeling she might never recover.

"It's okay. It's just water," Bonnie said as she retrieved a handful of dishtowels from a drawer. "But what happened?"

"I just . . . I suddenly felt light-headed. Probably because it was already so hot out when Keeley and I ran." Jenna closed her eyes and squeezed the bridge of her nose.

With a sideways glance and a sigh, Bonnie tossed the spilled ice cubes into the sink. Then she finished sopping up all the water. "Well, I better get you another glass of water then."

"No. No, it's okay." Jenna slid off her chair and stumbled toward the hall. "I think I need to lay down."

"Okay," Bonnie called after Jenna, "but when you're done resting, we're going to discuss last night!"

Jenna allowed Lulu to slip into her bedroom before she closed the door swiftly behind them. Then she leaned against the door and stared vacantly out the window for a few seconds before sliding down to the floor. Lulu immediately rushed to Jenna, thinking it was a great opportunity for snuggles, or better yet, playtime. Instead, when Lulu attacked Jenna's face with slobbery kisses, all the dog got was a mouth full of tears.

"Okay, okay, that's enough, Lulu," Jenna said as she hiked herself up off the floor.

She headed to her nightstand, tossed Lulu a treat, and sank to the floor next to her bed with her diary.

July 22, 2017

Dear Diary,

Surprise. Me again. Yeah, I know. What kind of surprise is that? Anyway, I'm not back so soon for anything good. Just the opposite. It's HORRIBLE. My mom just told me they're coming back. Of course, she's over the moon excited that they'll be living here again, but you know how I feel. After ALL this time, why do they have to come back? Why now? Why when I still have to live here? I'll be forced to see them, not just on holidays either. That saying "out of sight out of mind" is the only thing that sort of seems to have helped me since they left. But it gets worse. Uncle Greg has accepted the senior pastor position at our church. Knowing my mom, she'll probably start volunteering even more, not because she necessarily loves serving others (honestly, sometimes it seems to be more about keeping up appearances) but because then she can hang out more with Aunt Lenore. But it gets even WORSE. He's coming back too.

How could God let this happen?

I feel sick.

So fucking sick. :(

~Jenna

chapter seven

DUSTIN BOCK
SATURDAY, OCTOBER 28, 2017
ONE DAY AFTER JENNA'S DISAPPEARANCE

"Dustin?" My mom's voice is accompanied by several light knocks on my bedroom door. "Are you up yet?"

"Yeah," I croak. As she opens the door, I clear my throat and quickly pull my phone underneath my down comforter. Not that I have anything to hide. I'm just confused about all the calls and texts since last night and don't feel like discussing any of it with my mom.

"Well, good morning, sleepy head," she says with a grin as she peeks into my room. "I know you don't get to sleep in very often, but eleven is kind of pushing it, don't you think?"

I drag myself into an upright position and rub my eyes with my fists. "Sorry," I say, yawning. "I've been up for a while . . . just laying here."

She opens the door wide and takes a few steps toward my bed. "Everything okay?"

"Yeah, fine," I say, plucking a piece of lint off my comforter and tossing it to the floor. "I just stayed up too late, I guess."

She nods twice and then a third time toward my window which overlooks our backyard. "Your father and I just got done trimming all the bushes out back. Could you please bag it all up and put the bags at the curb while we're at your sister's basketball game? We're heading out in about ten minutes." She's already turning to leave, which means there's only one possible response to her request.

"Yeah, sure. What time will you be back?"

"Around one," she says, peeking back at me from the hallway. "We'll probably stop at Panera for lunch. Do you want us to bring you something?"

"No, thanks. I'll make myself something here."

"All right. See you when we get home then."

As soon as she's gone, I flip my comforter back and pick up my phone. I listen to the distant sounds of my family as they prepare to head to the middle school for my little sister's basketball game, and I scroll through the missed calls and message notifications from Delaney and Jenna's mom. My dad asks my mom if I'm going to take care of the trimmings out back, and my sister complains that her ponytail is too tight. When the house finally goes silent, I navigate to my texts and click on the second name on the list. This is the last time I'm going to read the conversation before I delete it.

JENNA: CAN WE PLEASE TALK? NOT BY TEXT, ON THE PHONE OR EVEN IN PERSON.

I wanted to delete her first message from last night before I even read it, but of course I didn't. Then after I saw what it said, I wanted to delete it even more—not because I didn't want to talk to her but because the thought of how things used to be between us still makes my insides ache. Instead, I kept it and obsessed over whether to respond while at a movie with Delaney and some other friends. The third time I pulled my phone out of my pocket to read the message, Delaney squeezed my thigh. I can still feel the searing flash of guilt that shot through my chest as I lowered my phone just before she was able to catch a glimpse of it.

This message was the first time Jenna had reached out in over a month, and no matter how upset I was—still am—with her, I couldn't bring myself to ignore her. So, I ducked out about five minutes into the movie to "use the bathroom" and texted her back.

DUSTIN: WHY?

Her responses came through in quick succession.

JENNA: I NEED TO TELL YOU SOMETHING IMPORTANT.

JENNA: SOMETHING THAT WILL HELP YOU UNDERSTAND.

JENNA: I'M SO SORRY FOR EVERYTHING . . .

I was a goner. I had to talk to her, but I figured it would be best if I didn't sound too eager.

ME: I'M AT A MOVIE SO CAN'T TALK NOW. CAN I GET BACK TO YOU IN ABOUT AN HOUR?

JENNA: SURE.

I'm so sorry. Seeing those words from her didn't make me feel better the way I thought they would. Instead, they made the flash of guilt I'd felt when Delaney squeezed my leg return with a vengeance. If only Jenna had been willing to help me understand what was going on with us—with her—back when everything started to fall apart. Then maybe I wouldn't be faced with hurting someone the way she hurt me. And maybe I wouldn't feel like throwing my phone across the room.

As I scan through to the last few texts in the thread, I promise myself I won't respond the next time she contacts me. If there is a next time.

I exit the thread between Jenna and me and press down on her name. *Delete this conversation?* my phone asks. I hold my breath as I follow through. For a few seconds, I stare at the spot where Jenna's name had been, then I navigate over to my list of contacts and delete her from my phone altogether. It's time to move on, starting with calling Delaney and owning up to what I did last night.

Hi! You've reached Delaney . . .

My heart rate increases as the rest of her greeting plays, and I'm still considering whether to leave a message or not seconds after the beep. *Damn it.*

". . . Um, hey, Delaney. Sorry I'm just getting back to you now . . . I hope you're not pissed. I just . . . I'm still not feeling . . ." *FUCK! Quit lying!* "Look, we need to talk. So, just . . . call me back when you can . . . Bye."

Now, I need to take care of the missed call and message from Jenna's mom. I navigate to my call log and promptly press down to delete the missed call. Then I press down on the next notification, but curiosity gets the best of me before I follow through with deleting the unplayed message. I'd bet my baseball signed by Ryan Braun that Jenna snuck out last night and told her mom she was with me when she got caught. That would explain Jenna's texts. She probably just wanted to have something to back up her lie, and Mrs. Kemp is probably just calling to verify Jenna's story. Well, I won't lie for her, and I'll never let her get my hopes up again about the possibility of us getting back together.

I play the message.

"Dustin, this is Mrs. Kemp . . ."

She sounds like she has a cold or like she's been crying.

"We're looking for Jenna and wonder if you might have seen her or spoken to her since last night."

As I suspected, Jenna must have left her house again after I drove by last night. But now they're looking for her? Does that mean she never went home?

"I know you two aren't dating anymore, but . . . about whatever Jenna might have told you after that whole diary incident . . . well, I apologize. I know in my heart you would never hurt Jenna, and I shouldn't have jumped to conclusions. Anyway . . . Could you please give me a call back when you get a chance? Thanks."

Diary incident? What would make her think I hurt Jenna? I have no idea what Mrs. Kemp is talking about.

Confused, I instinctively open my call log and scroll to Jenna's name, but of course it isn't there, and I don't know the last four digits by heart. So, I go back to Mrs. Kemp's message. But before I call her back, I need to decide what I'm going to say.

Should I tell her I don't know about the diary incident she's talking about?

Should I ask why she thought I hurt Jenna when Jenna was the one who hurt me?

If I tell her I was supposed to meet up with Jenna, will she believe Jenna never showed?

chapter eight

SUNDAY, JULY 23, 2017
THREE MONTHS BEFORE JENNA'S DISAPPEARANCE

"So, what did you end up doing last night?" Jenna asked Keeley as they took a seat on one of the wide window ledges in the gathering area of His Grace Community Church. She immediately bit into the slice of cherry Kringle she was holding on a napkin. Since she was still upset with her mom for grounding her the night before, she hadn't eaten breakfast. In fact, she hadn't even emerged from her room until it was time to leave for church. She'd remained silent during the entire ride, even when Joseph made a few tacky dad jokes to lighten the mood. Shaina giggled, of course.

"Nothing much. Tina had people over last minute, so I waited for Delaney to get done babysitting for the Johnsons, then we went over there for a while. Played pool . . . listened to music . . . watched YouTube videos. . . you didn't miss much." Keeley nibbled on one of Mrs. Kimble's raisin bran muffins. Her legs were spread wide, and she was leaning forward slightly, elbows resting on her knees in an "unladylike fashion," as Jenna's late grandma would put it. Jenna smiled to herself at the sight of her tomboyish friend, whose cluelessness over her own beauty made her appealing to everyone.

"Who was there?" Jenna asked before shoving the last of the Kringle into her mouth.

"Uhhh," Keeley said as she sat upright and stretched her long, lean legs out as she reclined back against the window, "Lisa, Jordyn, and the Harvey brothers. Oh, and *Corbin* was there too." Her voice took on a timbre of annoyance when she said Corbin's name, which made Jenna laugh. "So, of course Delaney spent most of the time flirting with him and practically forgot I was there. Dustin's lucky he didn't go because it felt like a couple's thing, which made it super awkward for me, of course. Luckily, Corbin had to get his parents' car home by ten, so Delaney and I left when he did, and I got home a little after ten."

"I bet Delaney talked your ear off about him the entire way to your house." Jenna squeezed the napkin she was holding into a ball and turned to face Keeley, leaning her back against the window frame.

"Nope," Keeley said shaking her head and rolling her eyes. "It was worse than that. Corbin called her as soon as we pulled away from the curb, and they talked the entire way to my house. So even though he wasn't with us, I still felt like a third wheel. That's probably why she isn't here today. She must have been up all night talking to him." Keeley and Jenna both laughed. "I'm so glad you don't obsess over Dustin the way she obsesses over guys she isn't even officially dating."

Jenna smiled in agreement over Delaney's tendency to overdo it when she had a crush on someone. She would never choose a guy over Keeley or Jenna, but she saw no harm in flirting even if it meant ignoring her friends. What Jenna didn't agree with was Keeley's assessment that she wasn't obsessed with Dustin. Actually, she was, but it wasn't over wanting to be near him all the time. Jenna was obsessed with figuring out a way to feel close to him without shutting down. But now that the demons from her past had returned, she felt she might be on the verge of closing herself off completely—not just with Dustin, but with everyone close to her. Suddenly she felt an urgency to share with Keeley.

"So, my mom just found out—"

"I have to go to the bathroom," Keeley interrupted Jenna as she stood. "Can we walk and talk?"

"Sure," Jenna said with a shrug as she stood and followed Keeley toward the hallway where the nearest bathrooms were located. She took a deep breath before she proceeded to fill Keeley in on the news of her uncle's family moving back to Briarwood, pausing whenever someone walked near them. Jenna was unsure when the news of her uncle's and cousin's acceptances of positions with the church would be announced, so she didn't mention any of that. When Jenna finished dishing out what little she knew about the timeline of their relocation and was on the brink of confiding in Keeley, Keeley gave her a shy, goofy grin.

"So, I guess that means Eli will be going to our school?"

"Um, yeah. I'm pretty sure they want to live close to church. So somewhere in Briarwood . . . Hey, mind if we go outside?" Jenna pointed at the back entrance as Keeley was about to return to the gathering area.

"Yeah, sure. For a little bit anyway."

When they stepped outside, Jenna was relieved to see no one else was out there. Not that she expected anyone to be since it was almost as hot as it had been the morning before when she and Keeley ran together. As soon as they settled in at one of the picnic tables and Jenna was about to unload her deepest, darkest secret on Keeley, Keeley jumped in.

"I wonder if he's dating anyone."

"Who? My cousin Eli?" Jenna asked, dumbfounded. She knew Keeley thought Eli was cute back when he used to live in Briarwood, but that had been years ago.

"Yeah," Keeley said with an apologetic shrug. "Have you talked to him? Do you know? Or . . . wait, does it bother you that I'm wondering? I don't want to—"

"No, of course not." Jenna shook her head and forced a smile. "I remember how quiet you always were around Eli when we were little." Jenna recalled the time when they played Truth or Dare at a sleepover in fourth grade and Delaney asked Keeley who she would choose to have her first kiss with. After Keeley admitted her choice would be Jenna's cousin Elijah, Delaney started making kissing sounds whenever Eli was around. And then Delaney developed a crush on Eli too. Of course, it only lasted until the next guy caught her attention. Jenna didn't have the chance to bring that up, though, because Keeley interrupted the memory.

"Phew," Keeley exhaled the word and then laughed as she continued. "Yeah, I was actually nervous around Eli and Thomas because I thought they were both so cute." She wrinkled her nose. "Especially Thomas. I bet his daughter is adorable." She smiled over at Jenna and waited for a response, but it didn't even seem like Jenna was listening anymore.

Little did Keeley know that Jenna's unresponsiveness wasn't because she wasn't listening. In fact, it was the opposite. Jenna had heard every word Keeley had said, squashing her desire to share with her best friend how scared and panicked she felt and why. Just like the few times in the past when Jenna had tried to work up the courage to tell her friends what had happened to her, she decided once again to deal with it on her own. What good would it do to tell anyone anyway?

"Jenna?" Keeley finally said after an extended silence.

"Huh?"

"Nothing," Keeley shook her head, suddenly embarrassed for even bringing up the childish crush she used to have on Jenna's oldest cousin who was a teenager when they were in elementary school and was now a grown man with a family. "I think your parents are ready to go. Probably means mine are too."

Jenna looked up and followed Keeley's gaze to where Jenna's mom was sticking her head out the door, waving them back inside. As the door slowly closed behind her, she said to whoever was within earshot, "Geez is it hot out there! I can't believe those girls . . ."

Jenna and Keeley stood and made their way toward the back door of the church.

"So, you're grounded for one more day?"

"Yep," Jenna said with a nod. "No phone either. All for being honest."

Keeley laughed. "Can you imagine if Delaney's mom grounded her for breaking curfew? We'd only get to see her every other week."

"Right?" Jenna agreed. "I actually wish I was grounded for breaking curfew."

"What do you mean?"

"I wish it wasn't because of Dustin," Jenna said, lifting her hands and bringing them down with a slap on her thighs. "You know what?"

"What?" Keeley asked, her hand gripping the door handle.

"Her not trusting me makes me *want* to do the things she doesn't want me to do, the things she *thinks* I'm already doing." Jenna looked to the ground with a huff, then mumbled, "Not that I would, but you know what I mean."

"Yeah, I know," Keeley said as she pulled the door wide open, releasing a wave of cool air. But her response was given with little thought about what Jenna had just said. After all, Jenna had always been a rule follower and a people pleaser who always considered the consequences of her actions.

July 23, 2017

Dear Diary,

I've been trying so hard to not let it bother me, but it's just too hard. I can't help it. When we get hurt, aren't we supposed to try to protect ourselves from the same hurt happening again? I've been telling myself it's over for years, that I'm safe and it will never happen again, and I was almost starting to believe it. Now, I'm not so sure.

I almost told Keeley today, except I chickened out like I've been chickening out since the first time I almost told her and Delaney at my ninth birthday party. Do you remember? They slept over and we were in our sleeping bags in the family room. My parents had just gotten a new cable box and forgot to set the parental controls. That one click brought me so close to telling them, but then I saw the looks of disgust on their faces. They didn't look away, but it was obvious they'd think twice about being my friend if they knew I'd done things like that. At least that's what I thought at the time. But why can't I tell them now? Why do I have to feel so ashamed?

Actually, I know why. Because I'm perfect. The perfect daughter. The perfect sister. The perfect friend. The perfect niece of a pastor. The perfect student. And I have a perfect family too, right? Ha! Just because that's what everyone sees doesn't make any of it real.

What I'm perfect at is pretending.

I'm the perfect pretender.

Jenna

chapter nine

"Kind of ironic how she looked us up and down from head to toe when she's the one who looks like she belongs in a circus. What. A. Bitch!" Delaney says as she kicks a landscape rock back into its bed.

It feels like we're walking at twice the pace we did on our way to Leighton's.

"Yeah," I mumble, looking at my phone. "Shit."

She glances over and emits an exaggerated sigh. "Oh my God, Keeley. Why don't you ever charge your phone?"

"I just did," I say, shrugging as I shove the device into my pocket. "For like five minutes anyway. So, do you think she's telling the truth about not seeing Jenna since last night?"

"I don't think we should believe anything that comes out of her mouth. I mean, if she knows who Jenna met up with, then why can't she just tell us? Why is it such a big secret?"

I have no answer for Delaney but agree that we probably shouldn't believe anything Leighton told us. Are Delaney and I any better, though? Haven't we kept secrets for Jenna over the last couple months too? As much as I don't like Leighton, I can't help but respect and appreciate her loyalty to Jenna. "I agree, but we've been keeping secrets too, Delaney."

Delaney responds with a sigh.

"Seriously. Maybe Leighton just doesn't want to get Jenna into trouble. Or maybe she really is trying to be a good friend to her."

This time, Delaney scoffs, which doesn't surprise me. Between the two of us, she's much better at holding a grudge.

"Look, why don't we just forget about Leighton for now? Who else should we talk to?"

"I don't know . . . Tina? Lisa? Jordyn? We could send a group text asking if anyone has seen or heard from her."

"Yeah, right. Everyone in our entire school would know Mrs. Kemp is looking for Jenna if Tina found out. And if Lisa or Jordyn know something, you know Tina will find out too." I sigh. "Maybe we should just wait. Why start even more gossip about Jenna when she'll most likely show up at home soon?" I swallow hard when I realize that, once again, I've suggested Jenna isn't missing, that she's probably just off somewhere doing who knows what. Hopefully, I'm right.

"What about Eli?"

My breath hitches when Delaney mentions Jenna's cousin who started hanging out with our circle of friends shortly before Jenna started distancing herself. "Good idea. Maybe he overheard something about Jenna when he was working at the theater last night."

"Well?" She eyes my pocket. "Are you going to call him?"

As I take my phone out of my pocket, I remember the battery is at only four percent. "Actually, can you call him?"

"Seriously? Don't tell me you still feel like you need to avoid Eli." I can hear the eyeroll in her tone.

Looking over at her, I say, "I'm not avoiding him. I was never avoiding him. It's just . . ." I turn my gaze back to the sidewalk in front of us. "My phone's almost dead."

"Fine. What's his number?"

I pull up Eli's contact info on my screen, and Delaney punches in the numbers as I read them to her. Then she puts the phone to her ear. "Hey, Eli, it's Delaney . . . Nothing much. What's up with you?" She laughs. "Anyway, we're wondering—oh, Keeley is here with me. That's how I got your number . . ."

She giggles again, causing a twinge of jealousy to invade my belly. I know flirting is the farthest thing from Delaney's mind right now, but her tone and demeanor always change when she talks to guys. *Any* guy. It's been that way since we started wearing training bras.

"Hey," I whisper, interrupting. I stop walking and face Delaney. She stops too.

"Hang on a sec, Eli." Delaney keeps the phone near her ear but moves it back over her shoulder. "What?" she asks me.

"Can I talk to him?"

She shrugs and hands me the phone. I bring it to my ear, and we start walking again.

"Eli?"

"Keeley?" There's a hint of anticipation in his voice.

I can't help but smile. "Hey, sorry to call you so early."

"That's okay. What's going on?"

"Not much . . ." I say, pausing when our last real conversation comes to mind. Sometimes I wonder how things would be different if we had gone to homecoming together instead of deciding it wasn't worth upsetting Jenna. Funny thing is, she probably wouldn't have remembered anyway since she was so wasted that night. I clear my throat. "Delaney and I were wondering if you know where Jenna is. Or did you maybe hear anyone mention her last night when you were working?"

"No . . . Why?"

"So, your aunt hasn't called to talk to you or anyone else in your family this morning?"

"Umm . . . not that I know of. Why, what's going on? Did something happen to Jenna?" He sounds concerned now.

"No. I mean, we don't really—" I begin, but Delaney's phone beeps. "Can you hang on a sec, Eli?"

Without waiting for a response, I pull the phone from my ear and see a picture of Dustin on a basketball court and the words *Incoming Call* above it. Delaney looks over too.

"Just decline it," she says, shaking her head. "Now he can wait for me to call *him* back."

I do what she asks and return to my conversation with Eli.

"Sorry. Delaney was getting another call."

"So? What's up with Jenna? I mean besides the fact that she's a mess lately." The lack of concern in Eli's voice doesn't surprise me. He and Jenna used to be close when they were younger. This added to mine and Delaney's confusion when her uncle's family moved back to town this summer. We thought she'd be excited Eli would be going to our school, but she wanted nothing to do with him and what's even odder is she didn't want us or any of our friends to have anything to do with him either.

"Could be nothing. We don't really know. But your aunt—" Delaney's phone beeps with a message notification. "—called my mom this morning to find out if I'd seen Jenna. She called Delaney's mom too. I guess the car Jenna drives was in its usual spot this morning, but Jenna wasn't home, and she isn't answering her phone."

"Oh, so now they're worried?" He huffs quietly. "She probably just went for a run—if she even cares about running anymore—or maybe one of her new *boyfriends* picked her up to take her to breakfast or something." He sounds disgusted when he mentions the revolving door of guys Jenna is rumored to be spending time with lately.

"Yeah, that's pretty much what Delaney and I were thinking too. But your aunt doesn't think Jenna even slept at home last night . . ."

He huffs air through his nose again. "My parents were talking about how my aunt and uncle seem to be letting her run loose lately. And I'm sure you've noticed she hasn't been to church for the past few weeks. That's what really gets to my dad." He huffs again. "It's so weird. She never did anything wrong when we were kids." He sighs deeply. "Never even ratted out the rest of us when we did stupid shit . . ."

It's obvious Eli misses the old Jenna just as much as Delaney and I do. And now I know for certain that I need to squash the thoughts I was having earlier about reconsidering being just friends with him, even if it's only out of respect for the bond he and Jenna used to have as kids.

"Delaney and I don't get it either, Eli," I say, matching his sigh.

"So now what?" he asks. "I should really tell my mom and dad. Maybe—"

"No, don't. There's no reason to get everyone worried when she's been gone for less than a day, as far as your aunt knows anyway. I don't even think she's positive Jenna didn't sleep at home last night. Delaney and I probably shouldn't even have called you. We just feel like we should do *something.*"

"Yeah, when she gets home, I'm going to force her to tell me why she's being such a jerk lately. My mom and dad told me to give her time to get used to me being around again, but I think it's been long enough. They seem to think she was so upset when we moved away that she's probably just still hurt. Girls make no sense like that, I guess . . . No offense."

"None taken," I say with a laugh.

"Not that I can fix whatever's up with her," Eli continues, "but if I can fix things between us, maybe other things will get better too."

"Maybe." I hope he's right. "Well, if we hear anything, I'll let you know."

"Yeah, same here. Otherwise—" He pauses, probably not wanting to even consider the alternative. I totally get it. "See you at school on Monday and maybe at church tomorrow?"

"Yeah, sounds good. Bye, Eli." I end the call and hand Delaney her phone. "I think Dustin left a message."

She pokes her phone screen a few times and then brings it to her ear. We've arrived at the point where we need to go our separate ways, so I stand and wait as she finishes listening to Dustin's message. She seems worried when she lowers her phone and puts it back in her pocket.

"Did he talk to Mrs. Kemp? Or Jenna? What's wrong?"

"He didn't say anything about Mrs. Kemp or Jenna," she says, shaking her head, "just that he needs to talk to me."

"About what?" I ask. But I've seen this look on my friends' faces before. It's that doomed, worried-about-a-breakup expression, the one I can't relate to because I've never really dated anyone before.

"I don't know." She takes a deep breath. "But I'm going to head over to his house now, so I'll let you know when I find out. You know, I kind of hope it's about Jenna—like maybe he saw her this morning. Then again, I hope it's not because, well, you know . . ."

I nod and give her a hug. Then we part ways, and the distance grows between us as we begin walking backwards. "Call me when you're done," I call out. "We should do something tonight. Like make strawberry banana smoothies, put on avocado masks, and paint our nails." That avocado masks and nails bit was just an attempt to brighten her mood. Delaney loves that kind of stuff.

"Yeah," she says, smiling and nodding, but I can tell she's still distracted, wondering what Dustin has to say.

With a wave, I turn and jog the rest of the way home.

chapter ten

"Jennaaaa!" Hannah Steele squealed as Jenna entered her aunt and uncle's rented home on Birch Lane. Having already seen her Aunt Bonnie, Uncle Joseph, and Shaina two days ago when her family first arrived in town, Hannah bypassed them and rushed straight to Jenna. Uncle Greg had moved back to Briarwood two weeks ago to find a home and fill out paperwork with the church while Aunt Lenore and the kids stayed in South Dakota to pack. Then Uncle Greg had flown back to South Dakota on Tuesday to help drive their things to Wisconsin in a U-Haul.

"Hi, Hannah." Jenna smiled as she hugged her adoring cousin. "I'm sorry I'm just seeing you now. I've been busy." She had been busy, but not with anything she couldn't have gotten out of. This made Jenna feel guilty for lying to Hannah. The truth is Hannah was the only person in Aunt Lenore's family Jenna wanted to see. Everyone else had let her down, and just seeing them (even in pictures over the years) made her feel paranoid and betrayed.

Jenna took a large step back to get a good look at her twelve-year-old cousin, whom she hadn't seen in over three years. "You've gotten so tall!"

"Yeah, but look at this," Hannah said with an eye roll before displaying a toothy grin that sparkled with braces.

"Oh, you'll have those off in no time," Jenna encouraged. She couldn't believe how grown up Hannah looked. She was only about six inches shorter than Jenna, and puberty had clearly set in.

"Hey, I said the same thing, Brace Face," Eli said as he emerged from the basement. He playfully nudged his little sister out of the way so he could give Jenna a hug.

"You're so annoying," Hannah said as she headed toward the kitchen where the rest of Jenna's family was visiting with Uncle Greg and Aunt Lenore. The smell of pizza permeated through the open-concept area separating the two rooms.

As Elijah squeezed Jenna, he could have sworn he felt her stiffen. Then she surprised him with a rather formal greeting.

"Nice to see you, Eli."

"Yeah . . . it's pretty awesome to be back." Eli backed a few steps away from Jenna and proceeded with small talk even though he felt something was off between them. "Living in Buxton was boring as hell." Eli's eyes shot toward the kitchen as he covered his mouth.

Jenna knew him well enough to know he was only trying to make her laugh by acting worried his mom or dad might have heard him curse.

Jenna allowed the right corner of her mouth to curl up a bit causing Eli to beam. He'd always tried to make her laugh. As Jenna opened her mouth to respond, she was cut off by Aunt Lenore.

"Oh, it wasn't so bad!" Aunt Lenore said as she rushed past Eli to give Jenna a hug. "How are you, my dear?" She kissed Jenna on the cheek and gripped Jenna's hands as she took a good look at her niece. "So beautiful. It's no wonder why your mother is going bonkers with worry over the boys chasing you." Aunt Lenore released Jenna and gave her a wink before picking up a toolbox off the floor.

Jenna's cheeks pinked up as she cleared her throat and called after her aunt, who was already heading back to the kitchen. "It's only one boy, and . . . it's Dustin Bock, my friend since . . ." Her voice trailed off into a whisper. ". . . grade school."

"Hey, I remember that kid," Eli said with a laugh. "He's the one your friend Delaney had a crush on. You had a bunch of people over for your twelfth birthday, and we all played Spin the Bottle in your basement. Delaney nudged the bottle when Dustin spun to make it land on herself." Eli continued to laugh at the memory.

Jenna couldn't help but laugh too. Dustin sometimes made jokes at parties when Delaney was busy flirting with guys. He'd say things like "I guess she's over me" and "Now you're stuck with me, Jenna."

"So, you two are dating now, huh?"

Jenna nodded, a hint of a smile still on her lips.

"That's cool. What about your friend Keeley? Is she dating anyone?"

Keeley would be excited if she knew Eli had asked about her, but there was no way Jenna planned to facilitate anything between the two of them. That would just be too awkward. "Nah, Keeley doesn't date."

"Oh." Eli's chest deflated a little.

"But Delaney does," Jenna said with a bratty grin, remembering several instances when Eli had complained that Delaney was annoying.

They both laughed, and for a second, it felt like they were eight years old again.

Eli glanced around the room. "You want a tour?"

"Sure, I guess so."

As Jenna followed Eli through the split-level ranch his family was renting, a flurry of memories rushed back to her at the sight of certain furnishings. The grandmother wall clock hanging at the base of the stairs leading to the upper level reminded Jenna of her Grandma Charlotte. The oversized velvet wingback chair in Aunt Lenore and Uncle Greg's bedroom took Jenna back to heated games of hide-and-seek. She always used to hide behind this chair, and Eli always found her within minutes. There was also the familiar collection of crosses lining the walls of the upper hallway. They had been given to Uncle Greg as gifts from parishioners throughout his fifteen years of servitude. In her aunt and uncle's old house, the crosses adorned the solid wall of a sunroom and rainbow streaks would shoot in all directions across the room at certain times of the day. The colorful beams made the sunroom Jenna's favorite room in their house. One good memory after another—memories of things she hadn't thought about for years, things she never even realized were good memories—were helping to calm Jenna's nerves.

Eli took a shot at the mini basketball hoop that hung on his closet door then immediately rebounded it and chucked it to Jenna. She took the shot and smiled when she made it. Eli cupped his hands around his mouth and hissed to mimic the roar of a crowd.

"Jenna! Eli! Time to eat!" Aunt Lenore called from downstairs.

Eli picked up the mini basketball and tossed it at the hoop one last time as he followed Jenna out of his disheveled room. Neither of them looked back to see if he made it or not. Jenna smiled to herself as they headed down the hall toward the stairs, her hesitance about seeing Eli after all the years that had passed beginning to fade. She'd forgotten what a comfort he'd been to her during those days, and she began to reassess the conclusion she'd come to over the years: That Eli must have known what was going on.

"Oh, hey, there's one last room I forgot to show you," Eli said as he opened a closed door to the right of the stairs. "It's no big deal, just going to be my mom's sewing and craft room."

At first glance, all Jenna saw were a few towers of boxes. But then she saw Aunt Lenore's old sewing table, and her knees buckled.

"Whoa! Careful," Eli said as he stepped between Jenna and the stairwell. When he was sure she wasn't going to topple down the stairs, he immediately scanned the floor thinking she must have tripped on something. When nothing was found, he laughed as his eyes skirted across Jenna's ashen face, and he closed the door. "Clumsy as ever, huh?"

The chaotic scene in the kitchen made everyone oblivious to Jenna's change in demeanor. It didn't surprise her one bit either. Jenna's mom was busy arranging and rearranging the buffet of pizza, fresh-cut veggies and fruits, chips, and dips across the counter. Aunt Lenore was looking for the box that contained wine glasses so they could open the bottle of chardonnay Jenna's parents had brought. Joseph and Uncle Greg were finally done hanging up Aunt Lenore's floating wooden butcher block shelves. And Jenna's little sister, Shaina, and cousin Hannah were filling plastic glasses with fresh squeezed raspberry lemonade. Shaina had seen a video the day before on how to make it and had begged Bonnie and Joseph to stop at the grocery store on the way so she could get the supplies to make it for everyone. That left Jenna and Eli who entered the kitchen unnoticed.

Jenna felt like her family never noticed things when it really mattered, dating back to when she was three and her mom often scrambled to find someone to watch her. Sure, family stepped in to help after her biological father abandoned them, and Joseph showed up two years later, but the adults in her family had always been more wrapped up with their own drama and careers to bother noticing what was happening to Jenna. And even on the few occasions when she worked up the courage to confide in her mom, nothing ever came of what Jenna revealed. Maybe it was because Jenna hadn't correctly explained the things that had happened to her, or maybe it was because her mom was so busy working and attending night classes that she didn't want to disrupt the flow of their clockwork-like schedule. After all, Jenna's cousin Thomas had been her primary babysitter for years, and removing him from the equation would have halted the entire system her mother had worked so hard to achieve. Thomas had also been perfect in everyone's eyes—still was. So those conversations were always laced with doubt on her mother's part, and in the end, Jenna always ended up feeling guilty for bringing up something that could ruin so many lives.

Eli made a beeline for the stack of paper plates and worked his way through the spread on the counter, loading his plate with everything except black olives, which he hated. Shaina and Hannah followed behind Eli.

Her stomach still in knots, Jenna wasn't hungry at all, so she took a glass of lemonade instead and sipped it quietly while everyone else went on about their business.

"Are you going to eat?" Bonnie asked Jenna as she held her plate out for Aunt Lenore to spoon a dollop of ranch dip onto it.

"Not yet. I'm just thirsty right now." Jenna held up her cup.

Bonnie shrugged and turned back toward the food.

Jenna glanced into the adjacent room at her sister and cousin who were sitting with Eli at a card table set up where a dining table would eventually be. "Good lemonade, girls."

"Needs more sugar," Eli said, scrunching up his nose and smacking his lips.

"Did you hear that, Shaina?" Hannah asked. "I think Eli said he wants more lemonade." She stuck her tongue out at her brother, and Shaina giggled as she took a bite of cheese pizza.

This exchange made Jenna smile, and she could feel the knots loosening. Then she made the mistake of tuning into her mom and aunt's conversation.

"So, Thomas's family arrived this morning then?" Bonnie asked.

"Yes! And thank heavens they made it. They should have been here last night, but Stella had enough of being in the car. So, they stopped at a hotel just outside of Rockford."

"That's a long drive for a little one." Bonnie accentuated her statement with a nod of approval. "I can't wait to meet her! It's been so long since we had a baby in the family."

"Yes, she's certainly adorable. A bit of a handful—still not sleeping through the night yet—but Audra is so incredibly good with her. That woman," Aunt Lenore said, followed by a sigh of admiration, "we're so blessed Thomas found someone who complements him and his values so beautifully."

"Well, we can't wait to meet her and Stella. And I can't wait to give that nephew of mine a squeeze. It's been so long!"

Having heard enough, Jenna hastily dropped her cup on the counter and rushed out of the kitchen and down the hallway to where she assumed there had to be a first-floor bathroom. She left so fast that she didn't realize her cup had tipped, spilling the last bit of lemonade. Nor did she hear her mom calling after her and telling Aunt Lenore how Jenna hadn't been herself lately. *Moody teenager drama?* Aunt Lenore had asked. *Something like that.* Bonnie had responded, not wanting to reveal anything about Dustin or how Jenna had been breaking curfew lately. Bonnie was still ashamed of her own actions as a teen and would be damned if Jenna followed in her footsteps, but this wasn't something she wished to discuss with her saintly big sister, the wife of a pastor.

Jenna was lucky she'd guessed right about the bathroom because the second she fell to her knees, everything she'd eaten that day spilled into the toilet. After that, she sat on the floor, wiping the uncontrollable tears from her face.

A few minutes passed before there was a knock on the door. Jenna remained silent and stayed put, hoping whoever it was would go away.

"Hey, Jenna?" Eli knocked again.

Jenna slowly rose to her feet and plucked a tissue from the Kleenex box on top of the toilet tank.

"You almost done in there? I have to pee."

Ignoring Eli, she dried her eyes, then stared at herself in the mirror as she composed herself. In the past, whenever she'd been faced with the memories of what happened to her, she always did her best to stuff her feelings, often even trying to convince her inner child that none of it really happened. But something different was happening within her this time. This time she was filled with anger.

Fucking Eli. Leave it to him to make me think maybe I could handle this. His presence is no comfort. All it is is a reminder of what happened when we were kids. He was there. So many times. He was there.

Another knock. This time Jenna threw open the door and shoved right past Eli.

"Geez, Jenna. What's up with you?"

August 11, 2017

Dear Diary,

I'm not doing so well right now. Yes, it has to do with that. Can you believe seeing a piece of furniture made me freak out?

I finally saw Eli and Hannah today. There wasn't any avoiding it really. If I said I wasn't feeling well like I did on Wednesday when they arrived in town, it would have given my mom a reason to not let me hang out with Dustin tomorrow night. I haven't missed curfew in over two weeks now, but she's still treating me like she doesn't trust me. She says she does, but then why are there so many questions whenever I go somewhere, especially when I tell her Dustin will be there? It's to the point where sometimes I don't even mention him, hoping she won't ask. But she always asks.

It was great seeing Hannah. She's grown so much! As for Eli . . . things with us didn't start or end well. I know it wasn't his fault, but he was there so many times, so I can't help but associate what happened with him. Hannah was too little to know anything. But for some reason, I feel betrayed by Eli. Like he should have known, and he should have helped me. Would he have, though?

What made me freak out was Aunt Lenore's sewing table. I remember staring at the underside of it as I laid on my back on the floor of the extra room in their old house. It was where Aunt Lenore did her sewing and where they kept all their books and board games. That was the day he'd shown me the pictures. Some of them were kids, and some of them were doing things to each other. God, I feel like I'm going to barf just thinking about the images, not just because the people were naked but also because of the guilt I feel about it. I could have looked away or closed my eyes or told him I didn't want to see them. Instead, I looked because I was curious. It was the first time I'd ever seen pictures like that, my first introduction to all the different ways people could have sex. Then remember in sixth grade when they split up the boys and girls into separate groups and we learned all about our bodies? We learned everything about puberty, and body odor, and hormones, and our reproductive organs. I don't know about the boys, but us girls also learned about our periods and how we are in control of our bodies and who touches them. That's when I realized just how wrong and disgusting those pictures were. I can't remember if they were real, you know like pictures someone took with a camera, or if they were cut out from magazines. But what kind of magazines have pictures of naked kids with naked adults? I've wracked my brain over this a few times trying to figure out where those pictures could have come from or if I'm simply remembering them wrong. Maybe some of the people just looked young but were actually adults? The worst thing about this memory is that when I was lying on the floor after he'd talked me into doing something in one of the pictures, Eli started knocking on the door. He'd been sick that day and fallen asleep watching the movie Spiderwick. (I don't even remember where the grown-ups were.) Eli's knocking snapped me out of the dark place I was in, and the first thing I saw was the sticker on the bottom of Aunt Lenore's old sewing table, which used to belong to my grandmother. There was a big S on it along with some smaller words and an image of a tiny threaded needle. I don't remember what happened after that, but the next thing I knew Eli was in the room asking what we were doing and why the door was locked. He'd been told that we were just playing Uno and didn't realize the door was locked. Eli believed the lies, of course, and I remember feeling so afraid that he'd hate me if he knew I lied to him. We were only eight at the time, so the thought of being caught in a lie scared me to death simply because lying was wrong and 'do unto others' was always being pushed on us.

Now, after lying for so long to everyone, including myself, I'm more terrified of telling the truth. Maybe keeping my distance from Eli will make it much easier to keep my memories and secrets locked away.

Jenna

chapter eleven

I approach Sticks' car in the grocery store parking lot and smile when I see him tapping on the steering wheel like a madman. He's a drummer—not in a band or anything—but he's always tapping out a beat with his fingers or hands or whatever happens to be nearby. And he'll tap on anything. He once used tampons and a box of Hot Tamales when we were listening to old-school rock by Led Zeppelin and Rush in my bedroom.

Sticks gave band a try when we were in middle school and always had drumsticks in his hands or sticking out of his back pocket, which explains his nickname. By ninth grade, he was tired of band directors reprimanding him for throwing his own beats into rehearsed performances. In his defense, the spontaneity did make school concerts a lot less boring.

I open the passenger door, expecting to hear a metal or rock song. Instead, it's something I never expected Sticks would be into: upbeat music with what sounds like an accordion at the heart of it.

"Dude, what *is* this?" I yell, arranging three full plastic grocery bags at my feet.

"Zydeco!" He reaches to turn the volume down.

"No, don't," I say, resting my hand on his for a second. "I kind of like it."

As the music plays on, Sticks starts the car. After he pulls out of the parking spot, he starts dancing and tapping his fingers and thumbs on the steering wheel. I stare out the window and remain still because I don't dance.

When the song ends a few blocks later, Sticks turns the volume down low so all we can make out is the faint rhythmic tapping. "My mom chaperoned a field trip to the performing arts center for my brother's class. She got me this CD. It's mostly a mix of Cajun and jazz, but it reminds me a little bit of reggae too." He smiles and nods to himself, eyes still on the road.

"Cool," I say.

"So? How's school?"

"Fine."

This is where I would normally ask Sticks about his friend Ross, who Sticks has been slowly feeling out to see if they could possibly be more than friends. Last time we talked, Ross had asked Sticks how he knew for sure he was gay and that led to an exciting line of questioning for Sticks because he'd been waiting for a reason to talk to Ross about his sexuality. I told Sticks to just come clean and tell Ross he likes him, but Sticks is acting like a wuss about it. I'm just not in the mood for relationship drama today.

He comes to a stop at a red light and looks over at me. "What about your mom? She still clueless as ever?"

"Yep," I say with a brief chuckle, not because what he just said is funny but because sometimes it's just easier to laugh. Besides, I ran out of tears years ago.

"What about Jenna?" He gives me a concerned glance. "Is she okay?"

I'm tempted to tell Sticks what Jenna did the night before. After all, he knows a little about her past. But just like with Keeley and Delaney, it isn't my place to tell anyone Jenna's business. "Yeah, dude. She's fine."

He nods as he accelerates into the intersection, immediately moving on to talking about how fucking stupid most of his co-workers at Chipotle are. This is what I love about Sticks. He'll talk my ear off if I let him, making him the perfect friend for me since I prefer to listen.

"Hey," I say, straightening my posture and leaning forward, "can you turn right?"

"Sure," he says, glancing over at me curiously. "Where to?"

"There's a church up here on the left. Grace Community or some shit like that. There." I point.

"You mean His Grace Community?" Sticks side-eyes me again as he turns on his left blinker and eases into the left turn lane.

"You been here before?"

"No. We're Catholic. Not that it matters. My parents both work most weekends, so we hardly ever attend mass. I just drive by here sometimes on my way to a music store on the east side."

I nod, but I'm hardly listening anymore because I'm focused on two figures walking along the pathway toward the front door. Well, three figures really, but one is a baby.

"Why are we here? Do you want me to park?" Sticks asks as he slows to a stop in front of the church walkway.

Thomas Steele glances over his shoulder at us as he holds the door open for his wife and child. There's no recognition in his eyes, but he assesses us for a few seconds before raising his free hand in greeting.

"Never mind. Let's go," I bark. I still sense Jenna's cousin's eyes on us as Sticks punches it, causing his tires to squeal a little.

Damn it. Why didn't I just get out of the car and ask him if he knew where Jenna was? It's not like he'd do anything to me with Sticks watching.

"What was that? Did you know that guy?"

"No, I just . . . feel like I need to talk to someone, but there's no way I'm going back to that therapist my mom made me see last year." The words tumble out way too easily, and I feel bad for lying to Sticks. He's pretty much my only friend—besides Jenna.

Sticks looks relieved and says, "Yeah, maybe an exorcism would do you some good. I told you that old Ouija board you used to mess around with was bad news."

"You're such a dick," I say with a laugh.

Sticks smiles and then gets serious again. "You know you can always talk to me about anything, right?" he asks as we pull up in front of my townhouse. "I mean . . . you're not thinking about hurting yourself again, are you?"

"No," I say, shaking my head rapidly. "It's nothing like that."

He nods and says, "Cool."

"Thanks for the ride, dude."

We fist bump, and Sticks has the Zydeco music blasting before I even close the passenger door.

As soon as I get inside, I dial Jenna.

"Come on, come on, come on," I whisper as I slip off my shoes and the call connects. I feel a flutter of anticipation during that short pause before hearing either a ring or a voicemail greeting. I immediately feel pissed off when the default greeting on Jenna's phone kicks in. "Damn it." It beeps, and I disconnect.

As I put the groceries away, I can't stop thinking about the way Thomas Steele stared at us. His expression seemed inviting, kind even, which pisses me off even more than Jenna not answering her phone. If I didn't know who he was and what he was capable of, I might mistake him for a good guy or a real man of God.

Finally, I admit to myself that if Jenna doesn't turn up soon, I need to say something. But before I do, there's something else I need to look into. Jenna's cousin Thomas isn't the only guy I'm concerned about when it comes to Jenna.

After I finish putting the groceries away and eat a few spoonfuls of peanut butter out of the jar, I go to the office and turn on our computer. Jenna used it to log into her ChillChat.com account a couple of times, and I know there was one guy in particular she'd been talking to.

chapter twelve

". . . It'll be fun, just us girls," Bonnie said as she plopped a hot pancake onto Shaina's plate. Then she turned back to the stove and slipped the spatula under the next one. "Are you ready for another, Jenna?"

"What?" Jenna asked, looking up at her mom.

Bonnie glanced down at her daughter's untouched breakfast. It was unusual for Jenna to not gobble up pancakes, but Bonnie shrugged it off since Jenna had been complaining of not feeling well lately. "Never mind." As she slid the pancake onto an empty plate, she turned her attention back to Shaina, who was adding even more maple syrup to the puddle already surrounding her food. "Seriously, Shaina? I think that's enough."

Shaina shrugged and looked over at Jenna. "Why aren't you eating?"

"Not feeling well," Jenna said, poking at the pancake and strawberry chunks on her plate.

"Is it still your stomach?" Bonnie asked, trying to sound oblivious. But she wasn't entirely certain it was Jenna's physical health that had her claiming not to feel well over the past couple weeks. Something was going on, and she was concerned it had something to do with Dustin. She thought Jenna was just too young to be depressed over a boy.

Jenna nodded despite not wanting to be questioned. Then she forced herself to take a bite, even though her stomach was still in the same knots from the day before. She had to snap out of it. "I'll be fine."

"Well, good, because Aunt Lenore and Hannah are really looking forward to spending time with us. Like I said, it'll be fun."

"What'll be fun?" Jenna asked, confused.

Bonnie stared blankly at Jenna for a moment and then glanced at Shaina who appeared to be just as perplexed. "Jenna, weren't you listening to a word I just said? We're going shopping with them to get everything for the party tomorrow. Then we're going to take everything over to the church to get things set up. Others have volunteered to help with food prep after the service so we just need to make sure we have everything ready. It shouldn't take too long. Then maybe we can have lunch somewhere."

Jenna nodded robotically, holding eye contact with her mom and debating whether or not to protest. She decided on the latter because she sensed one false move could ignite an argument. Tiptoeing around her mom had become exhausting, especially with so many other things weighing on her lately. *Was dating Dustin really that important?* she wondered.

"So," Bonnie checked the clock on the microwave, "if you both could be ready to leave by nine, that would be great."

Shaina nodded and continued eating while Jenna shrugged and continued poking.

Bonnie continued talking as she poured the remaining batter onto the griddle, making one giant pancake. "What are your plans for tonight?" She snuck a quick glance at Jenna before turning the burner flame down as low as it could go.

"Dustin and I were thinking of going mini golfing."

"Just the two of you?"

"Not sure yet," Jenna said with a shrug.

"Well, you and Dustin have been spending an awful lot of time together lately. Wasn't it just the two of you when you went to the movie in the park on Tuesday and then to the lakefront last night? Maybe it would be a good idea to invite some of your other friends tonight."

Jenna inhaled deeply in an attempt to keep her cool. She knew exactly where this conversation was headed. Before she could respond, Bonnie continued.

"You know, one thing I wish I'd done when I was your age was spending less time worrying about boys and dating and more time just being a teenager and hanging out with my girlfriends." Bonnie chose her words carefully, knowing that other recent attempts she'd made to dissuade Jenna from making the same mistakes she'd made had led to unintentional arguments.

"Mom," Jenna said with an edge to her tone, "Dustin is my friend just like Keeley or Delaney, and it's not like I haven't done things with them too. Remember? Keeley, Delaney, and I went to the mall and out for gelato." Dustin and a few others had met them for gelato too, and then they'd all gone to Jolliet to hang out in the woods, but her mom certainly didn't need to know about that. "And I ran with Keeley three times this week."

"Jenna, it doesn't matter how long you and Dustin have been friends. A childhood friendship with a member of the opposite sex changes when you reach a certain age."

"And I haven't broken curfew for weeks," Jenna went on, ignoring what her mother had said. "So, can you please just trust me to decide how and who I spend my free time with? It's not like I'm ditching my friends for some random guy—not even close."

Shaina had gotten used to her mom and sister arguing more and more lately and was beginning to feel invisible at times. She took advantage of her mother's current distractedness and drowned another pancake in syrup. The chocolate sauce and whipped cream went unnoticed too.

Bonnie rubbed her temples then slid both hands down the sides of her face. She knew Jenna had a good head on her shoulders, but she was also fully aware that teens usually didn't disclose the full extent of their activities to their parents. "Jenna, I don't want to argue with you," she said with a sigh. "I'm just trying to do my job as a parent here, and part of my job is to make sure you don't do things you're going to regret. I remember what it was like to be young and caught up in my emotions. That's what it was like with me and your father."

"Are you three talking about me behind my back again? Is that why my ears are ringing?" Joseph gave Shaina's earlobe a gentle pull as he entered the kitchen and headed straight for the coffee maker.

Shaina giggled and said, "No, *they* were talking about Jenna's *other* dad."

Joseph paused for a beat with his hand on the handle of the coffee pot, then sprung back into action. He turned, holding a full mug of coffee, and smiled. "Everyone having a good morning so far?"

"Yep," Bonnie said with a smile that screamed *we'll talk later.* "Do you want some pancakes?"

"I'd love some, thank you," Joseph said, kissing Bonnie on the cheek and then rounding the island to take a seat next to Jenna. He opened the news app on his phone and sipped his coffee. Moments later, Bonnie slid the giant pancake in front of him then began cleaning up the kitchen. Jenna slid the syrup and bowl of quartered strawberries across the counter so her dad could reach them. Shaina delivered her dirty dishes to the counter and rinsed her sticky hands.

"Hey, Dad?" Jenna asked.

"Yeah?"

"Is it okay with you if I go mini golfing with Dustin tonight?"

Bonnie spun around and gave Jenna a hard stare.

"Other people will be there too," Jenna quickly added. Whether it ended up being true or not, Jenna didn't care anymore. It wasn't likely her mom was going to follow her around spying on her. The thought initially made Jenna laugh to herself, but her amusement quickly morphed into an overwhelming sense of disappointment, because maybe if her mom had been a little more vigilant when Jenna was little, she wouldn't be scared to death to see her cousin Thomas at the party the next day.

"Ahh . . . I don't see why not. But you know the deal. Just make sure you're home by eleven." He smiled at Jenna and began eating.

"And would it be okay with you guys if Dustin goes to the party tomorrow afternoon?" Jenna blurted.

"Sure, I don't see why not," Joseph shrugged at Bonnie, hoping she would just go with it. He knew from the research he'd done online lately on how to deal with hormonal teens that it was better to say yes whenever possible, and this request seemed completely reasonable to him.

Bonnie was caught off guard by the question and by her husband's hasty permission, so she said the first thing that came to her mind and immediately regretted the absurdity of her response. "But . . . is Dustin's family even Lutheran? Do they even go to church?"

"Um, Bonnie . . ." Joseph shook his head at her.

"Not every week . . . but they go on most holidays. Why? Does that matter?" Jenna asked.

"No, of course it doesn't," Joseph said as he scrolled through a news article on his phone, conveying that he hoped they were done with the conversation.

"Keeley and Delaney will be there too," Jenna added, a final plea for her mom's approval.

"Yes, I suppose it would be fine," Bonnie said.

By the end of the shopping and lunch excursion, Jenna was bursting with anxiety. She was certain that if she heard Thomas's name one more time, her eardrums would explode. Sure, her mom and aunt had a way of chattering on and on about all sorts of things when they were together, as if breathing wasn't even necessary for them, but Jenna couldn't believe how much of their conversation revolved around Thomas. Or maybe it just felt that way to her since hearing his name sent shockwaves through her bones.

You must be so proud of Thomas . . . His wife must be quite a beautiful soul for him to have chosen her . . . I wish we could have been at their wedding . . . He must be the most wonderful father to little Stella . . . I knew from when he was a teen that Thomas would make a great leader someday . . . Thomas has always been such a great role model . . . Our church sure is fortunate that Thomas has agreed to join our congregation.

The next day, Thomas and his family would make their first appearance at church since being back in town. Jenna almost threw a teacup against a wall in the kitchen at church when they were there setting up because she was scared to death about how she was going to cope when she saw him. She wondered if she would be able to hold herself back from screaming out the truth. She also wondered if she'd even be able to breathe.

Her only consolation had been knowing that her friends would be there, including Dustin. She hoped to draw strength from their presence.

As soon as she saw Dustin pull up to the curb in his parents' car, she was out the door.

"Don't forget, eleven o'clock on the dot!" her mom called out so loud that the reminder carried through the front door.

"Hey," Dustin said with the crooked smile Jenna had always found adorable. Jenna smiled back and buckled up as the car pulled away from the curb. "Ready to get your butt whooped? I brushed up on my skills with my dad's electric putter today." He quirked an eyebrow in her direction.

"That's cheating," Jenna said, trying to match his playful tone.

She knew she'd failed, though, when Dustin glanced over at her and said, "What's wrong?"

That was the thing about dating a childhood friend. It wasn't always so easy to hide when you weren't feeling yourself. Although, Jenna had hidden her demons behind a lot of fake smiles over the years, leaving her to often wonder who her true self really was.

Jenna self-consciously crossed her arms. "Would you mind if we skipped mini golf and just drove around for a while? Or maybe we could park somewhere? I don't feel like being around people."

"But what about Keeley and Delaney? You said earlier you were going to invite them too."

Jenna sighed. "I only said that because my mom was right there when you called. I'm sorry."

"Okay?" He ran his left hand through his hair. It was a habit he'd always had, a tic that would appear when he was confused or nervous.

"My mom is still being a pain about us spending time alone. That's all." Jenna put her hand on Dustin's thigh, immediately making his pulse race. That was the effect any physical contact with her had on him since around eighth grade. It was out of his control.

"Oh," he said, glancing down at her hand on his leg. He wasn't happy that Mrs. Kemp seemed to have changed the way she felt about him when she found out he and Jenna were becoming more than just friends, but he couldn't help but be excited about the prospect of parking with Jenna. As far as activities went, it ranked right up there with watching a Brewers game from field level right behind first base. "So where do you want to go?"

"Can we just drive for a while first? Maybe down by the lake?"

After cruising around for about an hour while listening to an alternative rock station, Dustin and Jenna parked in a small, seldom-used lot at Jolliet Park. It abutted the entrances to several walking trails, one of which led to the old playground where they'd played as kids. There was a new bigger lot located smack dab in the middle of all the action—a newer playground, a splash pad, a community building where they held nature classes, a pond, a pavilion for birthday parties, and a brand-new restroom/changing room. This smaller lot was tucked away and barely used, so it was ideal for a teen couple looking for some privacy.

"So," Dustin said, offering Jenna a piece of the gum he'd purchased when they stopped for gas. She declined. "What are we going to do for the next three hours?" He popped a piece of gum into his mouth and took hold of her hand.

They both leaned into their seats and turned to face each other.

"Do you want to walk some of the trails?"

Dustin wanted to groan because walking the trails wasn't at the top of his to-do-with-Jenna list, but he grinned, not wanting to be *that* guy. "Yeah, sure. Whatever you want."

Jenna knew the trails at Jolliet like the back of her hand since she'd been running them for years. So out of habit, she went a little faster than Dustin was expecting. When they exited the wooded path into the clearing next to the old playground, he was huffing.

"Wow, Dustin. A little out of shape?"

"Yeah . . . well, I don't run every day like you."

"Maybe you should start test riding the bikes you fix up at work around the block instead of around the parking lot. Otherwise, you're going to be totally out of shape for the basketball season."

Dustin laughed as he removed his palms from his knees and stood upright. Then he put his arm around Jenna, and they walked toward the rusty old merry-go-round. It was like they were walking backward in time toward their childhood.

"So, I was wondering . . ." Jenna said, taking a seat on the merry-go-round she knew so well. ". . . and it's no big deal. You can say no . . . Will you go to the party at our church tomorrow afternoon?"

"Uh, yeah sure," he said, grabbing a bar of the merry-go-round and giving it a slow push, "if you want me to. But is it okay with your mom? Isn't it sort of a family thing to welcome your aunt and uncle back to town?"

When Jenna told Dustin about her family moving back, she'd neglected to mention anything about Thomas.

"Kind of, but not really. It's more like a congregation thing."

Dustin shrugged. "As long as it isn't going to make your mom mad."

"Good," Jenna said, feeling a bit relieved that Dustin would be there along with Keeley and Delaney.

When the merry-go-round spun Jenna back to where Dustin was standing, he hopped on next to her and leaned over to kiss her. He had no idea if she would move to kiss him back or not because she still wasn't acting quite like her usual talkative self, but there was no way he was going to miss the opportunity to try. To his relief, Jenna leaned toward him, closing the remaining gap between their lips, and gave him a quick peck. *I'll take it*, Dustin thought, feeling triumphant. Then Jenna grabbed his hand, and they both laid back and looked up at the sky.

Dustin continued to slowly spin the top with his foot. It was something they enjoyed doing as kids. Only, when they were kids, going as fast as possible was the ultimate goal. Now that they were older, going slow seemed like the right thing to do.

chapter thirteen

Mrs. Kemp picks up on the first ring.

"Dustin," she says breathlessly, as if she'd been staring at the phone waiting for my call and lunged for it. "Thank you so much for calling back."

"Hi, Mrs. Kemp. No problem. I—"

"Dustin, have you seen or spoken to Jenna?"

"Um, no, not today, but . . ."

"When was the last time you spoke to her?"

I take a deep breath and contemplate how much to tell her. I can hear Mr. Kemp's muffled voice in the background. *What's he saying? Has he talked to her?*

"She texted me last night."

"What time? What did she want?"

The urgency in her voice startles me, and now I'm second-guessing my earlier assumption that Jenna must have left her house again last night and told her parents she'd be with me.

"Last night, around . . ." I wrack my brain trying to remember what time her first text came through.

"When? When was it?" She pauses, then lowers her voice and speaks more slowly. "Dustin, this is really important."

"Okay . . . I'd just gotten to the movie theater, so it must have been around eight forty-five. She asked if we could talk . . . in person."

"And? Dustin, did you see her?" she practically yells, and I finally realize something is wrong.

"Wait, when was the last time *you* saw Jenna?"

"Yesterday *morning* before school. As far as we know, she went to Leighton Pierce's house right after school and stayed there until around nine, but then we have no idea where she went, and we don't think she ever came home last night. So, if you saw her . . ."

This makes no sense. Mrs. Kemp has always kept tabs on where Jenna was going and who she'd be with. I want to ask how it was possible they didn't know if she went home last night, but it's really none of my business.

"No, I didn't see her, but I saw her car—well, your car—parked on the slab in back of your house. So, I thought she was home and that she stood me up."

"Stood you up? So, you made plans to meet? Where?"

"At Jolliet. But I got there around—I don't know for sure. I replied to Jenna's text around ten, and I was about fifteen minutes away." Suddenly I wish I hadn't deleted our entire text conversation. "But when I got there, she wasn't there. So I drove past your house just to . . . I don't know what I was going to do. But when I saw the car there, I figured she'd changed her mind about wanting to meet me, so I left."

She exhales the way people do when they've heard bad news. Then she finally responds to Mr. Kemp, but she must have covered the phone because I can't make out what's being said.

"Dustin?"

"Mrs. Kemp, I'm so sorry. I wish I knew where she was."

"Don't be. It's not your fault. It's mine. Maybe if I'd trusted her . . . and you . . . I'm the one who's sorry." I have no idea if she's apologizing to me again like she did in the message she left or if she's just sorry for the way Jenna's been acting lately, but I don't get the chance to ask because she continues. "Dustin, we're going to be calling the police if Jenna doesn't turn up by this evening. So if you hear from her, or if you hear anything at all *about* her, please let us know."

"I will."

"Thank you."

"Yeah, of course."

"Oh, and Dustin?"

"Yeah?"

"Did Jenna say what she wanted to talk to you about? I mean, you don't have to tell me, but . . . I'm just curious because . . ."

"No, all she said was it would help me understand."

"Understand what?"

"I don't know, Mrs. Kemp."

"Well, again, I'm sorry," she continues. There's a brief pause and then, "Bye, Dustin. Please remember to call if you hear from Jenna."

"I will."

Before Mrs. Kemp hangs up, I hear Mr. Kemp mutter his thanks too.

I sit and stare at my phone long enough to talk myself out of calling everyone I know to find Jenna because this really has nothing to do with me.

I head out to the backyard to work on the clippings, hoping the task will dilute my thoughts about Jenna. Instead, the mindless work makes me think about her and us and what she wanted to tell me even more. I know from some good sources that the rumors about all the guys are true, so maybe the drug rumors are true too. Maybe that's why she contacted me out of nowhere and then flaked out on me last minute. Maybe she was high on something other than weed and didn't know what she was doing. Or maybe she was just messing with me to get back at me for being such an idiot and hooking up with Delaney.

"Dustin?"

I turn, startled. I was so lost in my thoughts that I didn't hear Delaney open the gate to our backyard. She comes to a stop about five feet shy of me and my brush pile. For the past week or so, she's been giving me a hug or stealing a kiss whenever we see each other, so the distance tells me she must suspect what I want to talk to her about.

In all fairness, I've told her several times that I wasn't sure what we were doing was right, and she even wavered once too. But our discussions always seemed to circle back to the fact that Jenna had abandoned friendships with both of us and had even said in front of dozens of kids at school that she couldn't care less if Delaney and I dated. So, we both had our reasons for taking things too far, the main one for me being how betrayed I felt by Jenna. But now, guilt is eating me alive.

"Hi," I say, dropping the black lawn waste bag I'm holding and running a hand through my hair. Jenna's voice echoes through my brain. *I love how you run your hand through your hair when you're nervous. It's so cute.* I quickly shove both hands into my pockets, even though Delaney has no idea touching my hair is a nervous habit of mine.

"Hey." She shifts from one foot to the other and folds her arms around herself, void of her usual confidence that borders on arrogance at times. "I got your message."

"Do you want to sit?" I ask, gesturing to the crimson Adirondack chairs surrounding our fire pit.

Without responding, she walks toward the chairs, and I follow. I immediately regret choosing the chair next to the one she chooses because I'm terrified to be so close to her right now. I've broken up with girls before, but never a girl who was a childhood friend or a girl who used to be best friends with the first and only girl I've ever felt like I loved.

"Have you heard from Jenna?" Delaney asks at the same time I say, "I have to tell you something."

"What?" we respond in unison and both laugh.

I run my hand through my hair again as Delaney perches her elbow on the armrest and leans closer to me, making me wonder if the small bit of laughter we just shared has made her think things with us are going to be fine.

"You go first," I say.

"Mrs. Kemp called Keeley and me looking for Jenna."

"Yeah, she called me too."

"Oh . . . what did you tell her? I mean, did you mention any of the stuff Jenna has been doing lately? The drinking? The drugs? The *guys?*"

When she mentions *the guys*, her tone sours. I can't help but wonder if it's because she's upset with Jenna for hurting me or if it was meant as a reminder to me.

"No," I say shaking my head, "I didn't mention any of that. Why would I? All she asked was when I last talked to Jenna."

"What did you say then? When *was* the last time you talked to her?"

I inhale deeply, examining Delaney and wondering if it would be easier to not say anything and just start distancing myself from her. *No, that would be a dick move.* "That's actually what I wanted to talk to you about."

Delaney pulls both hands into her lap and leans away from me.

"She texted me last night. Right when we got to the theater, when we were in line for popcorn."

"So that's why you kept looking at your phone."

I nod and continue. "She said she had something to tell me, something that would help me *understand*. But she said she wanted to tell me in person."

"Understand what? Why she turned into such a shitty friend?"

I don't even bat an eye at the anger in Delaney's voice. She's entitled to it as much as I am, and Keeley too.

"I have no idea exactly what she meant."

"You didn't ask?"

"No, but I agreed to meet her, and that's why I lied to you about feeling sick and went home right after the movie—so I could wait for Jenna to text me back, to tell me where to meet her. Then, when she finally told me to meet her at Jolliet, I went and waited but she never showed up." I pause to take a breath only because I feel a twinge of anger when I think about how I felt when Jenna didn't show. Delaney shakes her head with an irritated huff. "Then I drove past her house just to see if her car was there," I say, embarrassed.

"But Mrs. Kemp said Jenna never went home last night," Delaney protests.

I shrug. "I'm telling you, the car she drives was there. So, who knows? Maybe she dropped it off after deciding to ditch me, and someone picked her up. Or maybe she never planned to meet up with me at all. I feel like I don't even know Jenna anymore, so . . ."

Delaney nods and gives me a sympathetic smile. Then she reaches over and wraps her hand around mine. "I can't believe she had the nerve to pull that. Thanks for telling me the truth."

"Delaney," I say pulling my hand out from under hers, "that's not all I wanted to talk to you about."

"Oh." Delaney pulls her hand back into her lap, and her gaze falls to the ground. She knows.

"The way I lied to you the first time I heard from Jenna after all this time . . ." I shake my head, a whole new level of shame welling up inside me. "It was totally wrong, and it confirms two things. One, I'm an asshole. And two . . . I'm not ready to date you or anyone else. I can't pretend I don't still have feelings for Jenna and move on just like that . . . even though she had no problem doing that to me." I pause, letting that last realization sink in deep. Jenna burned me, then I burned her by messing around with one of her best friends, and now I'm burning said best friend. My parents would be so proud. "Anyway, that's why I ignored your texts last night and this morning because I felt bad about what I'd done."

Delaney finally looks back up at me. "It's okay, Dustin. I get it. You even told me you didn't think it was a good idea for us to . . . well, you know. I'm sorry I pushed this on you." She stops talking and stares at the ground, a haunted look in her eyes. "I'm a terrible friend."

I feel bad for Delaney because I can relate to the guilt she's feeling, so I share something with her that I never intended to tell anyone. "You know, I didn't tell Mrs. Kemp this, but another reason I drove to their house is because I wanted to see Jenna face to face and tell her to never call me or speak to me again. So, if it makes you feel any better, I'm a terrible friend too. Because I obviously thought hurting Jenna would make me feel better . . . that's why I let things go so far with us. And that's the whole truth."

We sit in silence for a minute or so, watching as the wind blows stray leaves through the yard. Then, the next thing I know, Delaney is helping me finish bagging up the clippings. Sure, she keeps avoiding eye contact with me and isn't as chatty as usual, but I know there's no way her solemnness is only about us because the last thing we talk about before she leaves is Jenna. Our conversation has nothing to do with either of our relationships with her. Instead, we both wonder where she is and when she'll be home.

I suppose it was only a matter of time before our anger toward her morphed into concern. Too bad it took her disappearing for that to happen.

chapter fourteen

Bonnie had woken up earlier than normal for a Sunday morning. It was the day of the welcome party for the new pastors of His Grace Lutheran Community Church, her brother-in-law Greg and her nephew Thomas. Up until now, she'd only volunteered a few times a year to greet people at the door or help set up special events during the holidays, but since this party was for family, she'd devoted a lot of extra time and effort into helping plan everything.

Jenna had been lying in bed, staring out the window and listening to her mother complete her Sunday morning rituals. She envisioned her mom brushing her teeth and running down to the kitchen in her robe to pour her first cup of coffee and take care of Lulu. Then her mom returned to the bathroom to blow dry her damp shoulder-length hair before getting dressed and asking Jenna's dad if he was going to get up anytime soon, her best smart-aleck tone in full effect. Then she'd eventually made her way into Shaina's room and sang the special wake-up song she also used to sing to Jenna when she was younger.

Jenna continued to stare out at the billowy clouds in the sky as she listened to her mom finish the song. The giggles and chatter that followed registered in her brain as nothing more than a low hum of background noise.

Up until now, she'd avoided seeing her cousin Thomas. But today, there was no getting out of it.

Earlier in the week, there had been rain in the forecast, so she reached for her phone to check if that had changed. She needed to know what type of shoes to wear. Partly cloudy throughout the day with a high of eighty-one degrees and a one-hundred percent chance of thunderstorms by late afternoon and into the evening. Summer days could be baffling the way the sky often started out so blue and scattered with billowy beauty but then morphed into the darkness of a thunderstorm.

People can be like that too, Jenna thought. They might start out looking one way on any given day—perfectly happy, content, *normal*—but have the capacity to be the complete opposite in the blink of an eye. All because of a slight change in pressure.

"Heyyy, Jennaaa," Bonnie sang softly as she knocked and peeked inside her daughter's room. "Time to get up, sweetie. We need to be there a little early today so I can turn on all the slow cookers, get the coffee brewing, and double check that we have everything we need."

"You've already checked everything at least ninety billion times," Jenna said without diverting her gaze from the window, her tone emotionless.

"Very funny, teenager," Bonnie said, opening Jenna's door wide before she headed downstairs. "Please get up."

Jenna groaned and thought about calling her mom back to tell her she didn't feel well. It would be easy to send a group text to Keeley, Delaney, and Dustin letting them know she wouldn't be there. Keeley's family would go anyway, but Dustin and Delaney hardly ever attended church, so they probably wouldn't be going if she hadn't asked them to be there. But Jenna knew the claim (real or not) would be met with zero sympathy from her mother as she had been warned that last Sunday was the last time she'd be skipping church that month.

When Jenna finally sat up and threw her legs over the edge of her mattress, Lulu raced into the room and hopped onto the bed. The dog seemed to have a sixth sense about when her owner was getting up.

"Hey, girl," Jenna said, placing her forehead against the side of Lulu's face. In response, Lulu planted a slobbery kiss on Jenna's cheek, but even that wasn't enough to make Jenna smile.

By the time Jenna made her way to the bathroom, the rest of her family was already downstairs eating breakfast. Jenna's stomach was in knots, though, so there was no way she would be able to eat anything despite actually being hungry.

After she'd finished brushing her teeth and smoothing out her bedhead with some sea salt detangling spray, she applied some liquid foundation to the bags under her eyes. They'd appeared overnight, and she barely recognized herself. As she placed the spray back in the cabinet, a bottle of Tylenol PM caught her eye. She'd taken the over-the-counter drug a few times in the past for painful cramping during her period. Not only did it fix the pain in her abdomen, but it numbed a lot of other things too. Before she could talk herself out of it, Jenna opened the bottle and popped one into her mouth, forcing it down without water.

The Kemps arrived at His Grace Community forty minutes before the nine o'clock service was to begin. Normally, there were two services, one at eight and one at ten, but today there would only be one because of the party to follow.

Even though the only cars in the parking lot belonged to the pastors and several volunteers, Jenna's dad parked in one of the furthest corners of the main lot. He always did this when they went to church. He said there were many others who needed the closer spots more than they did, and someday, they'd all look back and wish they could walk the full distance of a parking lot. Shaina groaned, and Mr. Kemp asked if she had a broken leg. Everyone except Jenna laughed as they got out of the car.

"Jenna," Bonnie said, sticking her head back into the car and snapping her fingers a few times. "What are you doing? Let's go."

It wasn't until the passenger door closed that Jenna snapped out of the daze she was in, finally realizing they'd arrived. By the time she caught up to her mom, dad, and Shaina, they were already in the kitchen with Aunt Lenore, Hannah, Lisa Ballering, and Jeff and Betty Kimble. Mrs. Ballering had been Jenna's Sunday school teacher for years, and the Kimbles had played roles in the confirmation classes she'd attended almost every Wednesday night during the three years she was in middle school.

Hannah gave Jenna a quick hug and promptly went back to making cute labels for the desserts people had dropped off. It appeared to be a self-imposed job.

"Well, aren't you a sight for sore eyes? Aunt Lenore said to Jenna with a wink from across the room where she was unwrapping paper plates and napkins and placing plastic utensils into fancy baskets. "We were starting to worry about you. Glad you're feeling better."

"Thanks, Aunt Lenore."

"Jenna!" Mrs. Ballering said, giving Jenna a tight squeeze. "Mm, you smell like the beach, my dear."

"That's my leave-in conditioner," Jenna said with a smile she didn't have to force. She'd always liked the retired school teacher, who used to bring her pet tortoise, Sully, to Sunday school sometimes. She also used to slip Jenna those little pastel colored mints that melt in your mouth. Jenna never saw her give them to anyone else, and Delaney had confirmed once that she'd never received any from the kind old lady.

Mrs. Ballering released Jenna and took a step back to examine her. "We've missed seeing you these last couple of weeks. Are you feeling one-hundred percent yet, my dear? Because you look like you could use some sleep and perhaps a shot of whiskey." Jenna's dad chuckled from across the kitchen at the serving counter where he and Shaina were stacking coffee cups, teacups, saucers, and all the condiments for hot beverages. "In a hot toddy, of course."

"Oh, Mrs. Kimble, she's fiiine," Jenna's mom said as she adjusted the heat on a slow cooker. "Tell you what, though, it might do her some good to stop texting her friends at all hours of the night so she could get more sleep, especially since she's been running almost every day lately."

Mrs. Kimble smiled and gave Jenna's upper arm a gentle squeeze before retrieving serving spoons from a drawer. Then she removed the aluminum foil from the batch of raisin bran muffins she'd baked for the party and held the tray out to Jenna.

Jenna glanced over at Bonnie to make sure she wasn't looking before she accepted a muffin. Mrs. Kimble grinned as she set the tray of muffins down on the counter and ran her thumb and forefinger across her lips as if sealing them.

"Getting ready for cross country, Jenna?" Mr. Kimble asked.

"Yep. Keeley and I both," Jenna said with a nod.

"It's a good sport. Our son Zack used to run cross country. Of course, he's grown now and out in Arizona selling for Big Pharma." Mr. Kimble scoffed and refilled his cup of coffee.

"Oh, Jeff," Mrs. Kimble scolded, "someone has to sell the stuff. He's making a good living."

Jenna smiled politely as she quietly exited the conversation about Zack. She glanced around the kitchen and didn't see anything that needed to be done so she slipped into the hallway where there was a set of bathrooms and a drinking fountain. She could hear voices coming from the chapel— one sounded like Eli's, but she didn't recognize the others. She'd begun to feel woozy and took a seat on a bench, checking her phone for the time. It was eight thirty-five. Keeley's family and other parishioners would begin arriving soon. On the way there, she'd texted Dustin to tell him to be there by eight fifty if he wanted to attend the service too, or around ten fifteen if he only wanted to attend the party.

Jenna leaned her head back against the wall and closed her eyes, suddenly realizing how relaxed she felt. *Tylenol PM to the rescue* she thought. Maybe seeing Thomas wouldn't be as horrible as she thought it would be after all.

"Jenna?"

When Jenna's eyes snapped open, she was looking up at a smiling, blonde woman in a knee-length coral dress.

"I'm Audra," the pretty young woman said, briefly placing her free hand against her chest, "your cousin Thomas's wife."

Audra Steele smiled a smile that Jenna couldn't imagine anyone not returning. However, hearing Thomas's name paralyzed her for a moment despite her dulled senses.

"Oh, um . . . hi." Jenna reached to shake Audra's outstretched hand. Then she glanced down at the baby in the infant seat at Audra's side. Her smile melted on the inside at the sight of Thomas's child, and she couldn't help but wonder if the little girl was safe.

"I'm so glad you made it today," Audra continued, her ethereal friendliness confusing Jenna because she wanted to hate the woman who'd married Thomas. "Stella and I have been looking forward to meeting you." Audra paused, waiting for a response from Jenna that never came. She continued, assuming her husband's cousin was still feeling ill. In fact, she didn't look so well. "We've heard so much about you." Audra looked down at Stella, who had an entire fist in her mouth and was emitting loud suckling noises. "Haven't we, sweet pea? Yes, this is Jenna, Daddy's cousin whom he used to babysit for when she was a little girl." Audra refocused her gleaming smile on Jenna, who thought she might gag. "Are you okay?" Audra asked.

"Yeah, I'm fine," Jenna said. "I'm just . . . still feeling a little sick."

Audra gave Jenna a sympathetic frown. "Well, I hope you feel better soon . . . Now, I need to feed this little one a quick snack before the service starts." Audra nodded toward one of the empty Sunday school classrooms. "It was so nice to finally meet you, Jenna."

With that, Audra disappeared down the hall, leaving Jenna in a daze.

During the service, Jenna sat in the second pew of the center section. It had been the first time she'd been in a room with Thomas since he visited her family four years ago, and his presence made memories from that day swirl through her brain like shards of glass, damaging her ability to focus on the service. The only things her uncle said that registered with her had been how honored he felt to have been called by God to lead His Grace Community Lutheran Church, and his announcement that his son Thomas had agreed to serve as associate pastor and take on a leadership role to help develop youth services.

Youth services. Jenna replayed those words over and over until Dustin tickled the skin of her forearm with his pinky. She glanced at him, but he continued to stare straight ahead, pretending to be focused on the slideshow Thomas had put together to introduce himself to the congregation. As photos of Thomas serving the Lord through preaching and mission and charity work flashed across the screen, all Jenna could see flashing through her mind's eye were all the times he'd hurt her.

For the rest of the service, she went through all the motions—The Lord's Prayer, communion, the offering—but it was as if she was floating above the chapel, a bodyless presence lingering on the outside of an invisible bubble looking in.

"Jenna?" Dustin said.

She looked up to find him standing and waving his hand in front of her face. Then he gestured toward her family members who'd been seated on the other side of her. They were now exiting the row into the aisle.

Shocked by her loss of time, Jenna stood quickly and scurried out into the aisle squeezing in behind Shaina just before the next row was about to exit. Dustin had to say excuse me in order to claim the spot behind Jenna.

"Hey, are you okay?" he whispered over her shoulder. "It feels like you're . . . not even here."

Jenna glanced back, forcing a small grin. "Yeah, I'm fine," she whispered, the grin disappearing the moment she turned forward.

Luckily, Jenna's Uncle Greg was greeting parishioners at the door Jenna and Dustin were exiting, so she didn't have to figure out a way to sneak over to the other side of the chapel.

"Jenna!" Uncle Greg exclaimed, giving his niece a hug. "Thank you for being here today. I know you haven't been feeling well. And thank you for bringing your friend."

Dustin accepted Uncle Greg's outstretched hand. "It's nice to meet you, Pastor Steele. Welcome back to Briarwood."

"Good to meet you too, son," Uncle Greg said, nodding his head. "I hope to see you here again soon."

With that, Jenna and Dustin found themselves immersed in the crowd that was streaming into the gathering area where people were already holding cups of coffee, tea, or juice. Shaina was already off in a corner with Hannah and a few other girls their age, and Jenna's parents were nowhere to be seen, which meant they had probably gone straight to the kitchen.

Keeley and Delaney appeared as Jenna and Dustin were grabbing beverages.

"Hey, you two," Delaney said, placing a hand on each of their backs. "I can't believe how many people are here. There aren't even this many on Christmas Eve. Must be the free food."

"Or maybe people want to start off on the right foot with the new pastors," Keeley offered.

"Um, I'm not an expert or anything," Dustin said, "but don't people come here to praise God and pray and all that jazz?"

Keeley snorted as she poured herself a decaf coffee and added two sugar packets and cream just like Jenna did to hers. She glanced at Jenna expecting her to say something smart in response to what Dustin had said, but Jenna was blowing on her coffee as she stared at the floor.

"Hey, what's wrong?" Keeley asked Jenna as the four friends wandered away from the beverage table, Delaney and Dustin trying to remember the last time either of them had attended church.

"Oh, nothing," Jenna smiled. "I'm just tired." She took a sip of her coffee.

Keeley studied Jenna for a second and noticed faint bags under her eyes. Over the past two weeks, Jenna had said she was either tired or not feeling well several times. She even canceled their running date one morning. But this was the first time Keeley noticed the bags.

"You think you'll be okay to run tomorrow after conditioning? I think the email from Coach Wells said we're supposed to do two to five miles."

"It said *three* to five. And, yeah, I'll be fine," Jenna snapped, causing her friends to take pause. It wasn't like her to talk like that to anyone, especially Keeley, and she immediately felt bad. But before she had a chance to apologize, Eli showed up.

"Hey, guys." Eli smiled and looked from face to face as Jenna's friends welcomed him into their circle. When Jenna didn't return his smile, he rolled his eyes at her and proceeded to make conversation with her friends who were all perfectly fine with his presence, especially Keeley who was beaming. No one seemed to notice that Jenna wasn't happy.

While they talked about various things like the drive from South Dakota, the small-town school he'd attended the past two years, Eli's sports of choice, and what he'd been up to since arriving in town, Jenna scanned the room, honing in on groups of kids around their age. There were several, and she was tempted to pull Eli aside and suggest he choose a different group to socialize with. It was either that or she had to figure out a way to explain to her friends that she didn't want Eli hanging around them. Neither option seemed like a solution at that moment so she bit her tongue and dealt with the anxiety that Eli's presence was causing her.

Then it got worse.

Keeley blushed as Eli inched closer to her. *No, you can't like each other,* Jenna thought. Then she nodded when Dustin told her he had to use the bathroom, and smiled when Delaney made a comment about how cute Jenna and Dustin were together, but ninety-nine percent of Jenna's attention was focused on Keeley and Eli and the fact that they were flirting with each other.

Then it got even worse.

"Hey, guys. We're so glad all of you could be here today." Jenna froze and imagined Thomas's hand burning a hole right through the flesh of her shoulder where it rested. How dare he touch her. She wanted to scream and tell everyone who he really was and what he'd done to her. She wanted him condemned to hell.

"Hey, bro," Eli said. "Great speech and awesome pictures. I never knew you did mission work in India."

"Oh, yes," Audra said, her voice dripping with adoration. "Your brother has done so many amazing things, yet he keeps most of his good deeds to himself."

Thomas laughed, finally removing his hand from Jenna's shoulder and looking directly at her. "Enough about me. Jenna, it's been so long. Look at you all grown up." He held out his arms a little as if he was offering a hug, but that would never happen. Jenna could barely make eye contact with him let alone stomach the thought of willingly touching him. "I hear you've met my wife, Audra, and our daughter, Stella. I'd love to meet your friends."

Jenna glanced at Delaney and Keeley. The way they were both smiling at Thomas and his little family made her angry. She knew it was irrational, but she couldn't help it. She wanted them to hate Thomas as much as she did. "Um . . ." was all she managed to say before Dustin reappeared.

"Hi," Dustin said, reaching out to shake Thomas's hand, "I'm Dustin. I remember you from way back when we were kids." He looked over at Jenna and smiled, hoping he was making a good impression on her family.

Not Dustin too, Jenna thought.

From that point on, her world continued to crumble as Delaney introduced herself to Thomas and Audra, and Eli introduced Keeley to them. While everyone around her exchanged pleasantries and laughed, she was stuck inside her head with all the horrible memories from her childhood that had been slowly returning in full color and sound ever since she learned Thomas was moving back.

Thomas shared how he used to babysit for Jenna when she was "yea high" and how they used to love watching reruns of Looney Tunes cartoons together. He'd left out how he sometimes used to place her hand on his crotch as they watched. Jenna glanced over at Eli who had watched cartoons with them. She wondered for the millionth time if he ever saw anything. If so, he'd chosen to ignore it or convinced himself it wasn't what he thought it was. Either way, Jenna felt like he had betrayed her.

By the time Bonnie announced that people should start lining up for food, Thomas had solidified himself as someone to look up to in the eyes of her friends. He'd told them how grateful he was to have been called upon to serve the youth of His Grace Community. Then he'd wrapped up his infiltration of Jenna's circle with these words: "I'm always available to lend an ear to each of you. Or even a shoulder to lean on in times of need. Always. Feel free to reach out anytime."

August 13, 2017

Dear Diary,

My life is ruined, and I don't think there's any way to fix it. He tricked my friends into liking him, and now that I've seen him, I can't get his face out of my head. That smile is seared in my memory forever. It was as if none of it ever happened and he was genuinely happy to see me—and not in a disgusting kind of way. For a second, I even wondered if I've been remembering things wrong all these years. But I KNOW that can't be true because when he put his hand on my shoulder, it actually hurt. It was like a million razor blades were digging into my flesh and releasing more poisonous memories into my body.

The only thing that keeps me from completely losing it now is the possibility that he feels bad for what he did. Is it possible that since he wasn't an adult when it all started that he honestly didn't know what he was doing was wrong? Would it matter? Or is it possible that I did something to make him think I was okay with what he was doing, that I wanted to be doing it too? NO. That's a stupid thing to think. Right?

Whether he's sorry or not, it tears me apart to wonder if he's done what he did to me to anyone else. Have I let other girls down by not telling someone?

Would he hurt his own daughter?

And what about his wife? She's SO pretty and SO sweet. How did he find someone like that? Then again, maybe he chose her for a reason. Maybe it's because she IS so sweet and would never suspect he's capable of doing anything so horrible. He probably has her fooled just like he's fooling everyone else. Would he hurt her?

The funny and sick thing is, he and I are kinda alike the way we both pretend to be people we aren't. I shield myself with a fake smile, good grades, and being as nice and helpful to everyone as possible. I aim for perfection, so no one looks too closely at me. He shields himself with that fake smile of his too, his church upbringing, all of his missionary work, and a family that others strive for.

It's all a load of crap.

Jenna

chapter fifteen

"I just can't believe no one but Leighton has seen or spoken to Jenna since last night," my mom says, shaking her head. "And Leighton is sure she doesn't have any idea where Jenna went after she left her house?"

Lying makes me nervous, so I hesitate, swallowing hard.

My mom briefly glances over at me as she turns the car into the grocery store parking lot. "Keeley? That's what she said, right?"

"Yeah," I say, nodding. "She said she thought Jenna was heading home."

"Keeley, I swear . . . if you *ever* disappear this long without telling me where you're going . . ." She puts the car in park and grips the steering wheel, her chest heaving. "Well, I don't know what I would do." She looks over at me, her eyes glistening with an array of emotion.

"I know, Mom. I wouldn't . . . Promise."

"I never thought Jenna would either. Something has to be wrong." She cuts the engine and gets out of the car without another word.

My mom barely talks to me while we're in the grocery store. I can't tell if it's because she's worried about Jenna, suspects I might not be telling her everything I know, or if she just wants to get out of the grocery store as fast as possible. By the time we leave, I decide it's probably a combination of all three. She speed walks to the car and glances over at me several times as if she's about to say something while we transfer the bags from the cart to the car.

The first question she asks me when we get in the car confirms one of my three suspicions.

"Keeley," she says, again gripping the steering wheel, "in all the years I've known her, Jenna has never exhibited an ounce of rebellion. And you just don't seem as concerned as you should be right now." She looks over at me with narrowed eyes. "So what's going on?"

"I don't know," I say, focusing on the windshield to avoid eye contact. "She's just not herself."

"It just doesn't make sense," she says as she starts the car. Then she cranks up the air conditioner and doesn't speak again until we've driven a few blocks. "What about Dustin? Did he get back to anyone yet? He must know something. Or maybe he's with Jenna. Those two are inseparable, right?" She seems to relax a little after bringing up Dustin, as if she's just finished the border of a puzzle and now it's just a matter of filling in the rest of the pieces.

I bury my face in my hands and take a deep breath. I can't lie about Dustin too, not when she's asking me outright if they're still inseparable.

"Keeley?"

"Actually . . . Dustin is dating Delaney now."

"Wait, what did you say?" she asks, turning the fan down low so she can hear me better.

"Dustin and Jenna broke up."

"What? When did this happen?"

"The week before homecoming."

"Huh, well, that's a surprise," she says, turning the air back up a few notches. "And what was it that you said about Delaney?"

"Dustin is dating her now."

My mom's hand jets to the fan knob, and she turns it off completely this time.

"Did you say *Delaney* is *dating* Dustin?"

She glances at me, and I respond with a nod.

"Well, that's . . . that's just not part of the girl code, Keeley. How did all of this come about? Is this the real reason Jenna hasn't been hanging out with you and Delaney lately?"

"I don't know," I say with a sigh. Sure, it's a teeny tiny lie. But Dustin and Delaney really have nothing to do with whatever is going on with Jenna. I've been against it from their initial flirtations, but what's going on between them really has nothing to do with me either. Mr. Hines, the world history teacher at our school, would call me Switzerland.

The first thing I notice when we pull into our driveway is Delaney sitting in one of the chairs on our front porch.

"Speak of the devil," my mom mumbles.

"Mom," I say, looking at her wide-eyed.

"Sorry." She puts the car in park and throws her hands in the air for a second. "I won't say another word."

We get out of the car and head to the back to unload the groceries.

"Hi, Delaney," my mom says as Delaney heads down our front steps.

I breathe a sigh of relief because there's nothing in her tone to suggest she knows Delaney has broken the unwritten girl code she referred to earlier.

"Hi, Mrs. Simon," Delaney responds in the cheery default voice she reserves for parents. Then she looks at me and grabs a grocery bag. "Hey." Her cheery tone has been cut in half, and the look in her eyes is a dead giveaway that something is wrong.

"Hey," I whisper, furrowing my brow at her to convey I know something is up. "As soon as we bring this stuff in, we can go up to my room and talk."

She nods.

The three of us get the groceries inside in one trip, and my dad greets us at the door. I can tell from his old paint-stained clothing that he's decided to work on one of his ongoing basement remodeling projects—custom-made bookshelves, fresh paint, and some drywall to enclose the utility area in the basement.

"Any word from Jenna yet?" he asks as he holds the door open for us.

Delaney and I shake our heads, and my mom says, "Unfortunately, no. But I plan to give Bonnie a call soon. Just to touch base."

"And you girls called everyone you can think of who may know where Jenna is?" my dad addresses Delaney and me. We both nod as we set the bags down on the island. I make eye contact with Delaney and nod toward the hallway, indicating we should make our exit, but my dad continues. "Well, what about Dustin? Hard to believe he'd lose track of his girlfriend."

My mom coughs, and then the room remains silent long enough for Delaney to catch on to the fact that my mom knows about her and Dustin.

"What? Why are you all staring at each other? Did they break up or something?" My dad sighs and takes a sip of cold coffee from his Northwestern University mug.

"About a month ago," Delaney says, staring at the ground. "Jenna broke up with him."

"Oh, well . . . it happens," he says, looking from Delaney to me and then to my mom. When he gets to my mom, he shrugs and turns his palms upright. "Well, I should get back to it. The basement isn't going to renovate itself." He leans toward my mom over the corner of the island to give her a peck on the cheek and whispers, "You'll let me know what Bonnie says?" She nods as their eyes meet, somber expressions on both of their faces. My dad grabs his mug and heads to the basement.

Delaney and I go to my room.

"I can't believe you told your mom about me and Dustin," Delaney groans.

I follow her into my bedroom and close the door. I can't help the irritation that tickles at my chest because Delaney didn't try to hide it when she suddenly became interested in Dustin, but I don't think I can handle losing her too, so I don't bring it up. Not directly anyway. "I'm sorry, but . . . is it really that big of a deal? It's not like it's a secret. And . . ."

"Keeley, Dustin broke up with me," she says, wrapping her arms around herself and taking a seat on my bed.

"Oh." I sigh, feeling sad and guilty at the same time—sad because I can tell *she's* sad, and guilty because I'm glad. They never should have been dating in the first place. I turn my desk chair to face her and am about to sit when she sniffles. "Delaney? Are you crying?" I abandon the chair and sit next to her on the bed instead.

"I'm so embarrassed," she says, covering her eyes.

"Don't be," I say, placing my hand on her back. "People break up all the time."

"Keeley," Delaney says, looking over at me with mascara-coon eyes, her voice already nasally, "that's not why. I'm embarrassed for being such a shitty friend. Instead of trying to figure out what's been going on with Jenna, I stole her *boyfriend*. Oh my *God*, how can I blame her or Leighton or anyone else at school for hating me? I was just . . ." She looks up at the ceiling and takes a deep breath, clenching my comforter into her fists. ". . . so angry with her. She said some pretty mean things to me that night at Tommy's party." Dark tears begin to drip from her chin, so I grab a couple of tissues from the box on my nightstand and hand them to her. She takes them, but she's so wrapped up in her grief that she doesn't bother to wipe her face or blow her nose. This is the first hint of emotion other than annoyance, anger, and indifference she's shown regarding the "new" Jenna since the night of homecoming.

"You're not a shitty friend, Delaney, and you're not the only one who let Jenna down. We both screwed up, and now . . ." I shake my head, not sure which of my muddled thoughts to finish with.

"Now she's gone," Delaney chooses for me.

"But she'll show up," I respond quickly, standing and walking over to the wicker storage box on my desk. I reach in and grab the photo booth strip from homecoming I'd stuck in it earlier. "And when she does, we'll force her to tell us what's going on with her and why she's so mad at us."

Delaney nods. Then she cleans up her cheeks and eyes and blows her nose. "Is that from homecoming?"

"Yeah." I sit back down next to her, and we co-exist in silence as we look at the photos for a few seconds.

"Look at her," Delaney says. "She was already wasted by then, wasn't she?"

"I think so. That's the only reason I can think of that she would do the things she did that night. You know what, though?" I ask, standing and retrieving the old photo of the three of us on the merry-go-round.

"What?" Delaney keeps her eyes on me until I'm sitting next to her again with both pictures in my hands.

"The look on her face . . . it's the same look she used to get sometimes when we were kids. That vacant stare she'd get sometimes out of nowhere. Do you remember?"

Delaney shrugs, taking both pictures from me to examine them closer. "Maybe you should ask your dad what he thinks."

Delaney hands the photos back to me.

"No," I say, shaking my head and then tacking both photos back up on my corkboard, side by side this time. "He'd need more details than just the photos, and whatever I tell him, he always tells my mom. And—"

"Wait, I thought it was illegal for therapists to share private details with anyone."

"Yeah, but that's only with patients. Everything else is fair game for what my mom and dad call 'spousal privilege,'" I say with air quotes.

Delaney nods. "I'm starting to think that whatever's up with her is way more serious than we thought, more than just a rebellious streak."

"Why do you say that?"

"I didn't tell you what else Dustin and I talked about after he dumped me." She pauses and we turn to face each other in the middle of my bed, crisscrossing our legs.

"Did he talk to her last night?"

"No, but she texted him . . . around the same time she texted us."

"You mean, when we were at the movies? Is that why . . ."

She nods and continues before I even finish the question. "And he texted her back."

"Well, what did she want?"

"To talk to him in person because she said she wanted to tell him something . . . something that would explain everything."

"So, did they meet up? Wait, is that why he said he wasn't feeling well? Did he lie?" I ask, shock building as the pieces begin falling into place.

"Yeah," Delaney says with a huff, "he lied all right. But then when he waited at Jolliet where she told him to meet her, she never showed."

"So, then what? Didn't he text her to find out why?"

Shaking her head, Delaney says, "He drove to her house to tell her he was pissed, but then he changed his mind. The car she drives was there, so at some point after she texted Dustin, someone must have picked her up."

I sigh and rub my eyes. "She could be anywhere, with anyone."

"Right, and would you ever have guessed in a million years that Jenna would just leave without telling anyone where she's going or who she's going with?"

"No, but she'll be back soon, I'm sure. Do you want to hang out here tonight? Then when she gets home, we can go over there. I'm sure my mom will let us use her car."

"I can't. I'm babysitting for Stella tonight. Audra just called me while I was waiting for you to get home."

"Well, did she say anything about Jenna?"

"Nope, and I didn't want to bring it up because we don't even know if she's really missing. Plus, Eli had no idea her mom and dad were looking for her, so I'm guessing they might not either. Maybe they don't want to worry the whole family before they're sure something is up?"

"Maybe," I say, doing my best to ignore the nagging sensation in my gut that keeps making me second guess that Jenna will be home soon.

"Actually," Delaney checks her phone, "I need to be there in an hour, so I better get going. Thanks, Keeley."

"For what?"

"For not hating me for what happened with Dustin . . . for not judging me for being so stupid. I know you thought it was wrong."

"Neither one of us is perfect."

chapter sixteen

August 17, 2017

Dear Diary,

I ran so bad again today that Coach Wells suggested I skip tomorrow's conditioning and take a few days off from running altogether. If I don't figure out how to dig myself out of this black hole I've been in lately, I'm worried I might not be able to compete when school starts. All the hard work I've done all summer long could be all for nothing. But I can't sleep unless I take the Tylenol PM (and now I need two in order for it to work), but then when I wake up after taking it, I feel groggy. So I've either been running on no sleep or in a Tylenol PM induced haze. I don't feel like eating either, so that makes my foggy brain even worse, and I don't really feel like talking to anyone or doing anything either, not even Dustin, Delaney, or Keeley. Everyone thinks it's still because of the stomach bug I said I had a few weeks ago, but a stomach bug can't last forever. I know my mom is going to force me to go to the doctor soon if I don't start acting more like the Jenna they're all used to, though, so I forced myself to go to the beach with Keeley and Delaney on Tuesday after practice, and with Dustin for a bike ride after he was done working last night. Doing things I usually love and being with my friends didn't help at all the way I was hoping it would.

I need to talk to someone. But who?

Jenna

chapter seventeen

"No, still nothing. And we're out of ideas for who to call." I lay my head down on my forearm on the kitchen counter. Joseph is standing next to me with his hand on my back. He'd rushed into the kitchen when he heard me answer my phone because of my deceptively optimistic voice, I'm sure. I couldn't help it. Seeing Leslie Simon's name on my caller ID gave me false hope that she was calling to let me know Keeley had heard from Jenna, or better yet, that Jenna was at their house right now. This is the longest I've ever gone without talking to Jenna. The first thing I'm going to do when she shows up after disappearing without a word of warning for an entire day is hold her in my arms.

It's impossible not to think the worst when you don't know where your child is.

"Oh, Bonnie, we're so sorry," Leslie sighs. "The girls—Keeley and Delaney—they called around, and they stopped over at Leighton's too just to make sure Jenna wasn't there."

As if that's supposed to make me feel better.

"Please thank them for us," I say politely.

I stand and begin pacing the kitchen, and Joseph takes a seat at the island and taps the tip of a pen against the pad of paper we've been jotting things down on all day.

"Is there anything at all we can do? Maybe drive around looking for her?

Make some flyers to hand out tomorrow? I don't know. I just can't imagine . . ."

"No, not yet . . . We've called all the hospitals, checked all her social media accounts, and tried to locate her phone, of course. But she hasn't posted anything for weeks, and her phone must be off or . . ." *Not dead. Don't say dead.* ". . . out of juice because it goes straight to voicemail." I leave out how we know from Jenna's phone records that she sent texts to Keeley, Delaney, and Dustin last night because I don't understand why the girls didn't say anything about receiving texts from Jenna. The fact that Dustin was the only one who responded to her is also grating on me. I also don't share that the last place Jenna's phone had a signal was Jolliet Park. "We've also just informed family that we're looking for her . . . just in case . . . and we're getting ready to call the police. I honestly don't know what else to do at this point."

"Well, I think calling the police is best because . . . well, you just never know."

I know Leslie means well, but "you just never know?" I can't help but resent the fact that she's said this but realize she probably has no idea what to say. I'd probably say something similar if our roles were reversed and it was Keeley who was missing.

"Right, well, Joseph and I have a few things to discuss before we make the call, so I better get going. Thanks for checking in, Leslie."

"Of course. We'll be thinking of you. Please call if you hear from her or need to talk. No matter how late it is."

"Thank you. I appreciate that." I end the call and join Joseph at the island.

"That was nice of Leslie to call," he says, wrapping an arm around me and pulling me close.

"It was," I say, sitting upright and dragging the pad of paper across the counter so that it's in front of both of us.

We sit in silence as I examine the bulleted list, pondering if there's anything else we can do that isn't already on it.

Contact friends and family.
Check hospitals.
Check social media.
Track phone.
Alert authorities.

Each item on our checklist includes notes about who we've talked to and the last time each person saw, spoke to, or heard from Jenna; the hospitals we've called and who we spoke to; the dates of Jenna's last social media posts and what they were about; and the timeline of her incoming and outgoing texts as well as the last time a cell tower picked up a signal from her phone.

The only item we haven't seen through is the last one: *Alert authorities*. Beneath that item are reporting tips I pulled from a website for missing and exploited children.

> *Provide a detailed description of the person.*
> *Provide a recent photo.*
> *Keep a record of every law enforcement employee you talk to (including case numbers).*

Joseph waits patiently until I'm ready to make the call. He's wanted to call them since mid-afternoon, but for some reason, I kept telling myself that as soon as we informed the police, she'd probably come waltzing through the door, ready for another argument.

Now I can only hope that will be true.

I take a deep breath as I flip the page to things that might follow a call to the police.

> *Contact the National Center for Missing and Exploited Children (NCMEC).*
> *Call school/notify teachers.*
> *Organize a search party.*
> *Put up fliers.*
> *Maintain a call log.*
> *Call local newspapers and TV stations.*
> *Social media posts about Jenna being missing.*

"Bonnie," Joseph says, flipping the first page back over to cover the things nightmares are made of. "It's time to call the police."

chapter eighteen

On the last night before Labor Day weekend, Dustin and Jenna went to dinner at a new gourmet burger restaurant a few blocks away from UW-Milwaukee on Oakland Avenue. After dinner, they had plans to meet up with friends for a bonfire.

"So, this is it," Dustin said, following Jenna to an empty booth. "The end of our last summer as high schoolers. Man, I wish we didn't have to go to my cousin's wedding. Are you sure you don't want to ask your mom if you can go with us? My mom will talk to her."

"Dustin, she doesn't even like us hanging out alone after dark. Do you really think she'll let me go with your family to Door County for three nights?"

He shrugged as he sipped his iced tea. "Hey, my dad's side of the family and my cousin's fiancé's family are both super religious. They're Catholic, so . . . Anyway, maybe if your mom knew that . . ."

Jenna rolled her eyes. "Do you really think calling people "super religious" will make my mom feel better about it? And what, being surrounded by Catholics will ensure we wouldn't even think about touching each other? Seriously, Dustin. You said yourself that your cousin Joe is only marrying his girlfriend because he got her pregnant and her brothers threatened to beat him up if he didn't."

"Shhh," Dustin said, placing a finger to his lips. "No one is supposed to know about that."

Jenna chuckled. "Well, why did you tell me then? And how did you find out?"

"My aunt can't keep anything from my mom," he said, shaking his head. "And my mom can't keep anything from my dad. I overheard them talking about it when I had my earbuds in, and they thought I was listening to music. I wasn't listening to anything, though—just had the buds in so they wouldn't talk to me." He shrugs. "I don't see how it matters whether they're married or not, though. They've been dating for like five years."

"Her family probably just doesn't want to be judged, I guess," Jenna said. "I think it's stupid, too, the way people cover things up with religion."

Dustin nodded as they both removed their arms from the table when their food arrived. "Thanks," they said in unison to the waiter.

They dug into their burgers and switched to talking about how much they liked their food and how they'd definitely return to try different items on the menu. Dustin fed Jenna one of his sweet potato fries, and she offered him a bite of her bacon avocado ranch burger, which he accepted.

"So, what's your family up to this weekend? Are you going to hang out with your Aunt Lenore, Uncle Greg, and the rest of them?" Dustin chuckled and shook his head. "I'd much rather hang out with Eli and Thomas than my cousins. Mine are all either way less cool, way older, or my sister's age."

Jenna tensed at the mention of her Aunt Lenore's family. It had been almost three weeks since the party at church, and so far, Jenna had been able to avoid Thomas. After services, she kept close tabs on his whereabouts, disappearing to the bathroom or sneaking outside anytime he was near. There were a couple of close calls when her family was invited over to Aunt Lenore and Uncle Greg's for dinner and to Thomas and Audra's for a game night, but she got out of both by saying her stomach was bothering her and that she was sore from all the strength conditioning and running she'd been doing for cross country. Neither excuse was a lie, but her stomach wasn't sore due to illness, and she didn't mind the muscle aches because they took her mind off the emotional pain she was suffering from. What she did mind was that her performance continued to decline, which meant she wasn't running with Keeley much anymore during practices. Keeley wanted to stick with her, of course, but Jenna didn't want her friend's performance to suffer too, so she insisted that Keeley go ahead without her.

Jenna faked a cough, took a drink, and cleared her throat before answering. "I'm not really sure." She cleared her throat again and drank more Diet Coke.

"Oh. Well, do you have plans to see Keeley and Delaney over the weekend? Or are their families dragging them out of town too?"

Jenna was relieved to move on from the subject of her extended family. "Delaney and her mom are going to Chicago for a girls' weekend. Shopping, haircuts, and makeup. You know—all that kind of stuff Delaney is into. But Keeley will be around because it's her mom's turn to work a holiday weekend at the pharmacy, so maybe we'll do something."

"Why maybe?" Dustin asks.

"Eh, she's all excited because Eli asked her to do something, but he just got a job at the movie theater, so he isn't sure which nights he has to train."

"But you and Keeley will run together, right?"

Dustin had been so busy picking up as many hours as he could at the bike shop for the past few weeks that he wasn't aware of how Jenna's running had declined. In fact, Jenna was surprised that *no one* seemed to notice anything was different about her even though she felt like her ability to cope with her secret was diminishing each day. Everyone was so busy with their own things that they just assumed Jenna was functioning as normal too.

"I don't know. I haven't been running too well, lately, so I don't really want her to have to slow down just for me."

"What? Since when?" Dustin asked as he crumpled up the liner inside the basket his burger and fries came in.

"I don't know," Jenna said with a shrug. "A couple weeks now. I haven't been able to go much farther than a couple miles for some reason." She pushed her basket and half-eaten burger toward the middle of the table.

"That's weird. Maybe you're coming down with something." Dustin mirrored Jenna's shrug. "Do you want a refill?"

She shook her head no, and Dustin wandered off to refill his tea, depositing their garbage and empty baskets on his way. Jenna stared after him, a hint of resentment causing her chest to feel heavy. She couldn't believe he shrugged off the fact that she was having difficulty running when he knew she could usually run at least six miles without getting winded.

Jenna closed her eyes and took a few deep breaths to chase away the unwarranted feelings toward Dustin that were brewing inside her. When she opened them, she almost vomited. Standing next to Dustin was the last person Jenna wanted to see.

Thomas.

Thomas had his hand on Dustin's shoulder, and they were both smiling. Jenna panicked when Dustin was about to look her way, but then Audra walked through the front door with Stella. When Dustin and Thomas looked their way, Jenna jolted out of her seat and headed outside through a back door by the bathrooms.

By the time Jenna calmed down enough to realize what she was doing, she'd already walked a block away from the restaurant. She looked back and saw Dustin standing on the sidewalk looking for her.

"Dustin!" she called.

As he walked to her, she contemplated what she was going to say to explain why she'd left. *Oh, I just freaked out when I saw you talking to Thomas. He molested me when I was a kid, by the way.*

No, she couldn't tell him. Not right now.

"What are you doing all the way over here? And why'd you leave?" Dustin asked, incredulous. He looked around as if expecting to see someone they knew and that had to be why Jenna had left without a word.

"I . . . I just felt sick to my stomach all of a sudden and needed air."

"Oh, oh no," he said, concern spreading across his face. He took Jenna by the hand and led her to a bench outside an ice cream shop. "Here. Let's sit. Do you think you'll be able to go to the bonfire?"

Jenna looked over at Dustin, still contemplating whether she should continue to hide the truth from him or if she should just tell him. Tell someone. Anyone. It was so much easier to hide from her demons when she didn't have to constantly be on edge, wondering if she'd come face to face with them.

"Jenna?" Dustin asked, pulling her from her thoughts. "Are you going to be okay to go to the bonfire?"

"Yeah," she nodded.

"We don't have to go."

"I'll be fine."

Dustin inched closer to Jenna and put his arm around her. She leaned her cheek against his chest. The tears that had been threatening to fall before had dried up, so she closed her eyes and took a few deep breaths, causing the side of her breast to press against Dustin's chest. In response, Dustin slipped his hand between Jenna's arm and side and slowly ran it down the length of her ribcage, causing Jenna to open her eyes and pull away at the sight of his swollen pants.

Jenna pressed her hands over her face.

"Jenna? What did I do?"

"Nothing," she said, dropping her hands to her lap. "It's just . . ."

Dustin's eyes followed Jenna's gaze to the shrinking bulge in his shorts. "Crap. I'm sorry," he mumbled as he looked away.

"Dustin, it's okay. I just wasn't expecting to see that when I opened my eyes."

"I honestly didn't even realize . . ." Dustin raised his hands slightly and looked around at the random people walking the sidewalks of the outdoor mall. "I mean, trust me, this isn't the ideal place to pop wood."

Jenna wanted to laugh. Normally she would have. But it was as if she was losing the ability to find anything funny these days. All she could muster was a forced half smile at one corner of her mouth. She was so tired of lying and pretending. "Let's just get going. Okay?"

They stood and started walking.

"Oh, hey, I saw your cousin Thomas and his wife and kid in there," Dustin said, pointing ahead toward the burger restaurant. "They wanted to say hi to you, but . . . do you want to pop in before we go?"

"No," Jenna said, quickening her pace as they passed in front of the restaurant. "Corbin said people could go over any time after seven, so we should go."

"Are you sure?" Dustin scrambled to keep up.

"Positive . . ." And then it slipped out before Jenna could reign it back in. "I don't want to see Thomas. Not now or any other day."

"What?" Dustin looked over at her, shocked. "Why do you say that? I thought he babysat for you when you were younger and you two were tight."

"He was actually kind of mean," Jenna said, her voice quavering the slightest bit, but not enough for Dustin to notice with cars driving by.

"Really? But he's so . . ." Dustin searches for a word. ". . . friendly. And he's, like, a youth pastor."

"Yeah, well, appearances can be deceiving."

"Well, what—"

"We should stop and get marshmallows," Jenna said, cutting Dustin off. She was done talking about Thomas, and all she wanted to do was get out of there.

chapter nineteen

I wake up a little after eight to the smell of coffee and the sound of my mom unloading the dishwasher. I wonder if she'll make a big breakfast the way she used to every Sunday morning before we moved into our townhouse and she started working full-time. I dismiss the thought just as fast as it comes to me because I don't want to get my hopes up. Ever since my dad left, she's slowly stopped doing all the things most moms do. Once in a while, she'll finish a load of laundry I've put in the dryer, and sometimes she'll leave food in the microwave if she's made too much, but we rarely sit down and eat together anymore. It's total bullshit.

I decide it's too early to be up on a Sunday morning, so I pull a pillow over my head and close my eyes. I'm right at that point when you're about to fall asleep but you're still aware of your surroundings when my phone vibrates. *Jenna.* My eyes pop open as I throw the pillow off my head and search for my phone under my covers. The last thing I'd done before I crashed last night was text Jenna to let her know how messed up it is for her to not to let anyone know where she is, hoping that hearing something is messed up from me might snap some sense into her. Then I held my phone and waited, but I haven't received any texts until now.

Finally, I locate my phone.

Sticks: Whaaaaaat's uuuuuuuuuup? Me. And I think you should wake up too!

I roll my eyes and drop my phone on the bed next to me. Then I pull the pillow over my head again. It's best for me to not respond because then he won't stop. I have no idea how he wakes up early every day of the week no matter what time he goes to sleep. Nor do I know why he has to be so annoying about it. Sticks is one of the few people I've never been a bitch to in person, but when he texts me before nine on a Saturday or Sunday morning, all bets are off. I swear he just likes to get a rise out of me, and this is the only way he can do it.

My phone vibrates again, and my heart leaps again because I think it might be Jenna.

STICKS: WHAT TIME DO DUCKS WAKE UP?

Sighing, I navigate over to the last text I sent to Jenna.

LEIGHTON: NOT HEARING FROM YOU = NOT COOL. PRETTY MESSED UP THAT NO ONE KNOWS WHERE YOU ARE RIGHT NOW!

My phone vibrates, but I know right away it's not Jenna because a preview of the new text from Sticks pops up.

STICKS: YOU GIVE UP?

LEIGHTON: I'M SLEEPING.

STICKS: AT THE QUACK OF DAWN. *SLAPS KNEE*

I crack a smile even though I try not to. But then I have a flashback of what I found in Jenna's chat account the night before, and my lips fall back into a frown. The number of guys she's been in contact with is shocking because I never realized it was more to her than just a way to have some fun. Instead of lying to the guys she was talking to—like I do—she told them all a personal thing or two, including her first name. She'd also gotten close to a guy with the nickname Jake B, and they'd even moved to texting and talking on the phone. But the worst thing about Jenna's excessive chat room use is that I'm the one who introduced her to ChillChat.com.

"Leighton?" my mom says as she knocks.

I slide out of bed and open the door a crack. "Yeah?"

"What the hell is going on with your friend Jenna?" she whispers.

"Why?" I ask irritated. "What did you hear?"

"I didn't hear anything, but two detectives are standing in our living room right now, and they want to talk to you because her parents reported her missing." She pushes the door open and enters, closing it behind her. "Tell me what's going on right now."

"I don't know," I say as I lazily throw a hoodie over the Violent Femmes T-shirt I wore to bed.

"Then why do you think they want to talk to you? Wasn't Jenna just over here on Friday night?"

I nod but can barely hide my irritation. Just like back when she blamed me for my dad leaving, she's only worried about herself getting in trouble in case the police find out she hasn't been the most attentive parent lately. "Don't worry, Mom, I won't say anything about you leaving me alone so you can sleep at your boyfriend's house most nights."

"Leighton," she sighs, "that's . . . not what I'm concerned about. If your friend really is missing, then you need to be sure to tell the detectives the truth about everything they want to know." She sighs again and exits my room. "Let's go."

When my mom and I get to the bottom of the stairs, the man and woman standing in our living room turn to look at us.

"Leighton?" the man says. "Hi, I'm Detective Collins, and this is Officer Lange."

"Hi," I say as I take a seat on a far corner of our sectional. My mom stands behind me with her arms folded.

"Would you be okay with answering a few questions about Jenna Kemp?"

"Yeah, of course."

"Great," Collins says with a nod. Then he and the woman—Lange—take seats on the other side of our sectional so that we're facing each other diagonally. Collins opens a leather-bound notebook about the size of a paperback and unclips a pen from inside. He's about to talk again when a muffled voice comes through Lange's radio.

"Sorry about that," she says to no one in particular, as she adjusts the volume.

"Leighton," Collins says, "when was the last time you saw Jenna?"

"Friday night. She came over right after school—after she stopped home and asked if she could use her parents' car . . . It was supposed to rain that night. Anyway, she left around quarter to nine." I wonder if I should tell them where Jenna was going but decide it's too soon to steer the police toward Thomas, especially since I have no idea what happened when they talked—or even if they talked at all.

"What did you two do while she was here? Did you have any specific plans?"

"No, we were just hanging out—listening to music, talking—like we normally do."

"Why'd she leave?"

"I don't know," I say with a shrug. "She just wanted to go home, I guess." I examine their faces and can tell Lange doesn't believe me from the way she purses her lips and rubs them together. Collins just keeps jotting things down, expressionless.

"So, she said she was going home, then?"

"Well, no, but . . . she said she was heading out, so I figured she was heading home," I lie.

"Ms. Pierce?" Collins addresses my mom.

"Yes?" She's still standing behind me.

"Just to clarify, you said earlier you were at work?"

"That's right. I work variable second shift hours, so I usually leave here anywhere from four to six, depending on what day of the week it is. Some nights tend to be busier in the ER."

"And what time did you leave for work on Friday?"

"Oh . . . around five. The girls were here when I left, so I briefly saw Jenna." My mom begins pacing from the living room to the dining room and back.

Collins nods and flips back a couple of pages. Then he looks up at me. "Thanks for your help, Leighton. If you hear from Jenna or anything at all about her, you'll be sure to let the Kemps know?"

"Well, yeah," I say, nodding. "But . . . that's it? Do you have any idea where she is? Have you talked to anyone else?"

"You're the first of her friends," he says standing. Lange stands too. "But we have some other people on our list too."

Could Thomas be on their list? And what about the chat room guy? She said he seemed obsessed with her. What if she met him in person and didn't tell me about it? Suddenly I'm feeling panicked.

"Wait," I blurt as the officers are thanking my mom for letting me talk to them. They all look over at me from where they're standing by the door. "I need to tell you something."

My mom sighs and shakes her head at me as both officers return to their spots on the sectional.

"Whenever you're ready," Detective Collins says to me.

"So . . . I showed Jenna this chat room I mess around in sometimes." I look up from the floor to meet their eyes. "It's called ChillChat.com."

Both officers nod.

"What?" my mom interjects. "You've been messing around in a chat room, Leighton?"

"Mom," I say, looking at her, "can you just let me finish?"

She nods, and I turn back to the officers.

"Anyway, Jenna created an account too, and she started chatting with people. It was supposed to be just for fun. You know? Just making stuff up and pretending to be people we aren't." My mom emits a gruff sigh, but neither officer pays any attention to her.

"Go on," Lange says encouragingly.

"So, there's this one guy Jenna started chatting with—Jake B. She only talked to other guys once, maybe twice, but this Jake guy, she always seems to have an open conversation with him whenever we were messing around on the website."

"What types of things did they talk about?" Collins inquires.

I give him a hard stare as I contemplate how much to tell them. I know they're going to see everything, so there's really no point in telling them what I learned last night when I looked at Jenna's chat account. And there's probably no point in me telling them that Jenna hid all of it from me. I couldn't believe all the personal things she'd told these people, especially Jake B. He got more than just descriptions of what Jenna looked like, what she was wearing, or what some of her favorite things are. Jake B. knew details about Jenna's sexual experiences—some good, some bad, and some that she regretted horribly. (Thank God she left out that most of her experiences had been with her own cousin.) She also told him that she was a runner, that she was struggling with depression, that she felt alone, and that she was so tired of pretending to be someone she wasn't—even with people who are close to her. My mom doesn't need to hear these things.

"Just . . . a lot of personal things. I mean, you can look at her account, right?"

"We can. We just need to get permission from her parents," Collins says as he jots some things down in his notebook. When he's done, he looks back up at me and says, "Is there anything else you'd like to share?"

He says it like he knows I'm holding back.

"Yeah."

"Oh, Leighton." My mom's tone is laced with worry and disbelief. "I sure hope Jenna isn't with one of these guys."

I shake my head, wishing one of the officers would just tell her to zip it because nothing she's saying is helping.

"What is it, Leighton?" Lange asks.

"Jenna told me on Friday night that Jake B. was starting to creep her out."

"Did she explain why?"

"She said he kept asking her to meet him in person. So she'd decided to tell him she couldn't talk to him anymore. But I guess he wasn't happy about that, and he wouldn't stop bothering her. I thought she meant he was bothering her in the chat room, but . . ." They wait patiently until I continue. "But then I went into her account last night—she'd logged in once on our computer, so . . ." I shrug. "Anyway, her last message from Jake B. included a phone number, and it was sent a couple weeks ago. So, I'm thinking they upgraded their online chatting to phone calls and texts probably. I don't know for sure, though." I'm having flashbacks of Jenna checking her phone and smiling and sending texts to someone several of the times we've hung out lately.

Collins nods and jots more down in his notebook. Lange looks over at him and places her hands on her knees as if getting ready to stand. When they both finally stand, I stand too and follow them to the door.

"Thanks for your time, Leighton. If you think of anything else, please call the station, or you can give me a call directly." He hands my mom a card.

After they leave, my mom says somberly, "I hope you told the police everything you know because I have a feeling they have no idea where your friend is."

When I get back to my room, I grab my phone and take a seat on my unmade bed.

LEIGHTON: HEY THE COPS WERE JUST HERE ASKING ABOUT YOU AND I'M *REALLY* STARTING TO WORRY. PLEASE LET ME KNOW YOU'RE OKAY. I WON'T EVEN TELL ANYONE WHERE YOU ARE IF YOU DON'T WANT ME TO.

chapter twenty

Like most first days of school, Jenna's morning rushed by in a blur. She was bummed to not have Keeley, Delaney, or Dustin in any of her morning classes, but Tommy was in her pre-calculus class, and Jordyn and Emily were in creative writing with her. No one from her circle of friends was in economics or Spanish with her. She realized as she headed to lunch that it was the first time in at least a week that she was looking forward to seeing all of her friends.

As Jenna approached the area of the lunchroom where her friends sat last year, she spotted Keeley's dark curly hair. Then she saw Delaney talking a mile a minute to anyone within earshot. Jenna laughed to herself at the contrast between her two besties—Keeley with a high messy bun that probably took her less than a minute to throw up, wearing clothes Jenna recognized, and Delaney with her sleek honey-blonde hair that probably took her at least twenty minutes to flatiron, wearing a brand-new outfit she probably got in Chicago over the weekend. All the regular people they'd eaten with last year were already there too. There was Tina (who was known as the resident gossip queen), Lisa, Jordyn, Emily, Corbin, and Tommy. The only person missing was Dustin.

"Heyyyy," Delaney said with a wave when Jenna arrived.

More greetings followed, and Keeley smiled and scooted over to make room for Jenna between her and Emily. Jenna settled in and listened to the conversations already in progress as she bit into a Granny Smith apple. Delaney was telling everyone about her trip to Chicago, and Tommy was telling Corbin how much money he'd made driving a golf cart at the Mequon Country Club over the summer. Not wanting to interrupt either conversation, she scanned the lunchroom for Dustin instead of asking if anyone had seen him.

"Hey," Keeley said quietly, having heard everything about Chicago already, "how were your classes?"

"Fine," Jenna responded, "but I have a feeling pre-calc is going to be tough. I wish we had it together."

"I know. I can't believe we only have AP bio together. Do you have any classes with Dustin or Delaney?"

"Dustin is in U.S. history with me right after lunch, but no, not Delaney."

Keeley nodded and was about to speak when something caught her eye.

"Dude," Tommy said, standing and extending his arm over Emily's head.

Jenna turned just in time to catch the tail end of an elaborate handshake between Tommy and Dustin. Dustin smiled down at Jenna for a second before he introduced his new *friend*.

"Hey, this is Eli," he said. "He's Jenna's cousin."

Jenna made eye contact with Eli as everyone shifted to squeeze him and Dustin in. Eli smiled at her tentatively, unsure how she would react to him sitting with her friends. After all, she hadn't made any effort to talk to him since they last saw each other about a month ago. In response, Jenna faked a smile and broke eye contact immediately. This frustrated Eli because he didn't understand why she seemed to not want him around, especially when the rest of her friends had been so welcoming. Obviously, she hadn't shared whatever was bothering her with her friends.

Dustin greeted Jenna by squeezing her thigh under the table. This helped calm her nerves, but only for a little while because everyone started asking Eli questions.

Didn't we go to grade school together?

Where did you move from?

Did you like living in South Dakota?

Why did you move back?

Oh, so your dad and your brother are both pastors?

Are you glad to be back?

What grade is your little sister in? I wonder if my brother is in her class.

All the questions and conversations about Eli and the rest of Jenna's extended family made her head spin, and she started counting down the minutes until lunch was over. It wasn't until she heard Emily Davis whisper to Delaney how cute Eli was, that Jenna thought she might have to cut out of lunch early. Delaney's whispered response made it inevitable.

"Sorry, but I think Keeley already has dibs on him," she'd giggled. "You should see his older brother, though. I mean, he's too old for us—and married with a kid—but damn. He's just as hot. Actually, they look a lot alike." Then Delaney peeked over at Jenna, raising an eyebrow. "You have some good genes in your family, girl."

Keeley's cheeks pinkened, and Jenna responded with a fake chuckle and an eyeroll. When she glanced over at Eli for a second, she thought she might puke, because Delaney was right. He looked even more like Thomas than he did four years ago. And now she couldn't get the resemblance out of her head. It was almost as if Thomas—a wolf in sheep's clothing—was sitting there amongst her and her friends, and even worse, Keeley had a crush on him.

Dustin touched Jenna's thigh again, and everyone looked at her when she jumped.

"Hey, guys, we're eating. Keep it clean under there," Corbin said in his best adult voice, glancing pointedly at the table in front of Dustin and Jenna. Everyone except Jenna laughed, but she covered up her embarrassment by taking a long drink of water.

"What's wrong?" Dustin whispered in her ear, still smiling about Corbin's comment.

"Nothing," she said, shaking her head. "It just tickled a little." She lied. *Only ten minutes until the bell rings,* she thought as she stared into his eyes.

"Who's *that?*" Tina said loudly. Everyone stopped what they were doing and followed her gaze over to the new girl with funky-colored hair who was in Jenna's second-period economics class. She was dressed in black from head to toe and had just gotten up from a table where she was sitting by herself.

Right before she exited the lunchroom, she tossed a Coke bottle toward the garbage and missed but didn't bother to stop and pick it up.

"Real nice," someone commented.

Jenna figured she probably didn't even realize she missed the garbage.

"I think her name is Leah or Lisa—something like that," Tommy said.

"It's Leighton," Jenna said, hiding her irritation. She didn't understand the point in Tommy even saying anything when he didn't know for certain what the girl's name was. "She's in my economics class."

"Whatever," Tommy said, pulling everyone's attention back to him. "I think she's the one who used to go to Homestead High. My cousin goes there, and he told me she got expelled for beating the crap out of some girl."

A few people gasped, someone said, "Dayuuum," and another said, "That's badass." Jenna didn't know who said what, and she didn't care because she hated rumors.

"Wow, nice rainbow hair," Tina said sarcastically.

The laughs that followed made the idea of sticking around for the last five minutes of lunch unbearable to Jenna, so she got up to leave.

"I have to use the bathroom," she said for Keeley's and Dustin's ears only. She looked at Dustin, "I'll see you in a bit." Then she looked over at Keeley. "See you later."

Jenna slipped away quietly, walking slowly at first but then picking up her pace when she reached the hall. By the time she got to the bathroom, she was practically running. The next thing she knew, she was in a stall bent over the toilet, heaving up nothing but air. It wasn't until she stood and leaned against the door that she heard water running and realized she wasn't alone. Not wanting to see anyone, she waited until the water and the hand dryer stopped before picking her bag up off the floor and unlocking the door. But when she emerged from the stall, Leighton was at the mirror examining her left eye.

Jenna approached the sink two away from where Leighton was standing and wondered if she'd heard her dry heaving. Then as she pumped soap on to her hand and turned on the water, it occurred to her that Leighton may have already been in the bathroom at the mirror when she'd run in. She just couldn't remember.

"Do you see something in my eye?" Leighton turned and stepped in front of Jenna as she was about to leave the bathroom.

Surprised, Jenna jerked back and put her hands up in a defensive pose.

Leighton furrowed her brow at Jenna and then laughed. "My God. Why are you so jumpy?"

"You jumped in front of me," Jenna said with a shrug. "I thought you were gonna attack me."

"Okay, whatever. Just forget it." With one eye squinted closed, Leighton started turning back to the mirror.

"No, let me take a look," Jenna said.

This time when Leighton turned around, Jenna got a better look at her. Her drastic shoulder-length layers weren't really rainbow but more a mixture of pink, purple, blonde, and all the shades in between. She had gauges in her ear lobes and a small hoop hanging from her septum. And her dark clothing matched her dark eye makeup, which was smeared around her squinted eye, making it look like she had a black eye.

Leighton did her best to pull the skin of her irritated eye down so Jenna could get a good look.

"Don't move," Jenna said, as she carefully swiped across the lower inner skin of Leighton's eye with her pinky a few times. "Got it," she said, holding up a long eyelash.

"Thanks," Leighton said with an appreciative nod.

The bell rang, and Jenna started walking toward the door. "No problem. You might want to rinse your eye out and clean it up a little," she said over her shoulder.

As Jenna walked to class, she thought about the colors in Leighton's hair and how pretty she thought they were. She wished she had the guts to pull off a head of hair like that, but even if she did, her mom would probably freak out.

chapter twenty-one

The church parking lot is packed so my dad parks the car in the overflow lot across the street.

"You know, if you two weren't so lackadaisical about getting here on time, we wouldn't have to park so far away and rush inside," my mom jests.

"Oh Leslie, fifty feet . . . twenty feet. Does it really matter? Besides, you and I could probably use the exercise." My dad nudges me with his elbow as my mom grumbles about how maybe *he* could use the exercise.

My somber mood is lightened a little by my parents' banter, but there's no way anything will turn it around completely.

The first thing I did when I woke up was call Jenna's parents to see if she'd returned. Mr. Kemp answered in his deep soap opera voice. Delaney and I always joke with Jenna that her dad should quit his job as an electrician and become the voice behind those parental discretion announcements before shows intended for mature audiences. Either that or a radio show host. But Mr. Kemp's voice didn't entertain me at all this morning. It's normally smooth but has been replaced with gruffness as if he was either coming down with something or hadn't gotten any sleep. And all he said when I asked if Jenna had made it home was, "No. No, she still isn't home." Then, I'm sure for my benefit, he tried to lighten his tone. "Boy, is she in for a grounding."

All I could muster was, "Yeah, I'd be grounded too." Then he informed me that they wouldn't be at church today, and I told him we'd pray for Jenna's return. So, as of seven this morning, Jenna was still missing.

As we walk down the aisle to some open seats toward the front of the chapel, I scan the first few rows where Jenna's family normally sits. They usually arrive early to get seats in the front row, especially now that Mrs. Kemp's brother is the senior pastor. Jenna and I have been attending the same church since kindergarten, and our parents decided years back that us sitting together was not a good idea because we giggled way too much. Even if we weren't talking, just being near each other would set us off into a tirade of giggles that would embarrass our mothers. Of course, they aren't here today, but I picture Jenna turning to glance at me with a goofy look on her face, trying to make me laugh. The memory makes me feel cold and empty inside.

After we excuse ourselves past a family of six, we remain standing and join the congregation in singing the prelude hymn. My lips move, but no sound escapes. Instead, I'm busy scanning for Delaney on the off chance that she's here. The moment I spot her, a few rows back and to the right, our eyes lock. I'm still staring in her direction when my mom gently nudges me to pay attention. Some things never change, I guess.

I robotically participate when necessary and nearly fall asleep during Pastor Steele's sermon. It isn't until he mentions Jenna that I perk up.

"Many of you may have noticed the absence of Joseph, Bonnie, Jenna, and Shaina Kemp—the family that normally sits right up front here." A murmur travels through the congregation as he motions to the first few rows in the center section of pews. "Sadly, their absence is due to the fact that Jenna—my niece—has been missing since Friday evening." He pauses the way pastors often do for effect, only this time I don't think it's for effect, and he appears to be struggling to continue. "If you're new members of His Grace or if you're visiting or don't attend regularly enough to know what Jenna looks like, there are several pictures of her hanging in the lobby. Please, if you think you've seen her since Friday, contact the Briarwood police department. It's still the weekend, so we're hoping she'll arrive at home this evening, ready to get a good night's sleep for school tomorrow. Either way, Jenna's family—my family—could still use your prayers that she returns soon." Another pause, more scripted this time. "Let us pray."

While everyone's heads are bowed, I peek back at Delaney. Her eyes are squeezed shut, and her lips are moving. I bow my head and catch the tail end of The Lord's Prayer.

Two Pastor Steeles was confusing at first, so the congregation now calls Jenna's cousin Pastor Thomas. At the end of each service, Pastor Steele and Pastor Thomas each stand at one of the chapel doors while congregation members file out two by two, shaking the hand of whichever pastor is on their side.

"Good to see you, Keeley." I shake Pastor Steele's hand. Last week, my family exited through Pastor Thomas' door.

I smile and nod as I keep moving. It's not cool to be the talker who holds up the line. I can't help but wonder if the congregation prayed a little harder for Jenna than for all the others who received prayer requests today. I wonder how concerned each of her family members are, given how odd she's been acting lately. Although, I doubt any of them know the extent of how much she's changed. I also wonder who they'll blame if she never comes home—God or Delaney and me for not telling anyone about the things she's done.

A hand grabs at my elbow as I'm about to head off in search of Delaney. I glance back to find Pastor Thomas has stepped away from his post at the door opposite his father, causing his line to come to a halt. Still holding my elbow, he whispers, "Keeley, I'm so sorry about Jenna."

Why is he saying sorry to me? Jenna is his flesh and blood. Shouldn't I be the one saying sorry? Then again, we don't even know where she is at this point.

"No, I'm—" I begin, but he releases my elbow and returns to his post, shaking the hand of the next person in line. The way his voice immediately goes back to its usual boisterous tone surprises me, but as I move into the growing crowd of chatty parishioners, I reason that he's just doing his job.

After each service, there's coffee, juice, and an array of baked goods, which my mom always complains about. *Should we really be allowing all these children to get hopped up on sugar so early in the morning?* As a part-time pharmacist, she sees a lot of prescriptions for insulin and other medications for conditions she swears could be eliminated if sugar was removed from patients' diets. So my dad often refers to my mom as the sugar police, just never to her face.

Before I head over to see what's being offered, I scan the cheerful yellow room for Delaney.

My dad is hard to miss in his Green Bay Packers sweater. He reasons with my mom that after dressing professionally all week for work, he deserves to wear whatever he wants on the weekends, especially at church where God would want him to be comfortable. Nearly a dozen other men are gathered around the same table, most with a doughnut in one hand and steaming cups of coffee in the other. This is his group of middle-aged church buddies. They discuss sports, cars, lawn care—all the boring stuff younger versions of themselves probably never imagined they'd be talking about early on a Sunday morning at church. I hear a few names of NFL players and figure they must be talking about today's games. Pastor Steele shows up, and the group becomes even more lively.

My mom is standing at the serving window that connects the room to the kitchen. She's talking to Betty Lawry, the organist who always volunteers in the kitchen after the ten thirty service. When we were little, Jenna and I used to think Betty lived at the church because she was always there when we arrived and still there doing dishes when we left. She also organized the quilting group, which my mom is part of once in a while, usually during the fall months leading up to the holidays when the group makes quilts for homeless shelters and families in need. You'd think a woman like Betty who was always so involved with church and charitable activities would shun gossip, but she's the gossip queen. My ears ring as I imagine her probing my mom about Jenna. It irritates me that she's probably gathering tidbits for this week's quilting session.

Finally, I spot Delaney entering the room from the back hallway where some bathrooms are located. I return her wave, and we meet at the refreshment table.

"It's not Christmas today, is it?" I joke.

"Ha ha. Very funny."

We both laugh, but the light-hearted moment is short-lived.

"Seriously, though," Delaney says, glancing around the room, "my mom said we should be here today to pray that Jenna comes home soon. She's really freaked out about this, Keeley."

"Yeah, mine too." I look around, momentarily thinking about how inappropriate it was for us to be laughing when Jenna still hasn't shown up.

We both make sugary decaffeinated coffee, just like I do every week. My mom frowns at me from across the room, so I smile and wave. Delaney loads several mini cream puffs and a piece of coffee cake onto a paper plate. Then she follows me to an empty corner of the room where we sit on a window sill. I shake my head when Delaney holds her plate out to me. She sighs and sets the plate down on the ledge next to us. Normally, we would sit at one of the large circular tables in the center of the room, but I sense an unspoken understanding between us. There's only one thing people would want to talk to us about today, and neither of us feels like talking to anyone at church about where Jenna could be. The rumor mill around here is just as bad as, if not worse than, at school.

"People keep looking at us," Delaney says.

I steal a quick glance in the direction of the tables and spot Eli talking to a group of kids. There appears to be a larger group than usual. Nothing like drama to bring together groups of kids who usually don't socialize with each other. "Yeah, I know. Probably because they're all wondering if we know anything about Jenna. Just don't look at anyone." No eye contact should keep our private bubble safe until our parents finish socializing.

"Can you imagine if these people knew about the things Jenna's been doing?" she asks, eyes wide and glazed.

I shake my head in response, not wanting to encourage that topic of discussion. What if someone overheard us? "Did you talk to Dustin again last night?" I ask, changing the subject.

"No," she responds flatly, grabbing a mini cream puff and shoving the entire thing into her mouth.

I can tell she doesn't want to talk about Dustin, so I quickly say the first thing that comes to mind. "How was babysitting?"

"Fine," she says, still chewing. "Stella's a good baby. She can't crawl yet, so no chasing her around." Delaney chuckles softly as she picks off a corner of her coffee cake. She pauses just before putting it in her mouth. "So, the babysitting part was fine, but Pastor Thomas and his wife had a little argument in front of me." She wrinkles her nose and pops the cake into her mouth.

"What about?" Not sure why, but I whisper it.

She finishes chewing and swallows. "Well, before I left, Audra asked if I was free to babysit again next Friday. But before I could answer, Pastor Thomas told her they probably shouldn't be making any plans right now. She asked why, and he said just because. But she just shrugged him off and asked me again if I was free. So Pastor Thomas told her no again, and she asked if it was because he was worried about Jenna. Then he turned and stormed out of the room without even answering her." She pauses and stares at a crumb of coffee cake that has fallen on the floor as if remembering the scene. "It was super uncomfortable."

"Well, then what happened?"

"Audra just stood there for a second then turned her attention back to me like nothing happened. You know, with her usual plastered-on smile that I bet she was born with. She told me Thomas has been stressed lately what with still getting situated in his new position here. Then when she walked me out, she asked if I could please pencil them in and said she'd be in touch to confirm."

I shrug. "Audra was probably right. He's probably just worried about Jenna. I mean, she is his cousin so . . . Although, I guess it's kind of weird that he stormed out like he did."

"Well, there's more," Delaney says, raising her eyebrows at me.

"Oh, sorry."

"Anyway, as I was about to get in my car, Pastor Thomas came running out after me. He asked me a bunch of questions about Jenna." She pauses and reaches for her coffee, but instead of taking a drink, she just stares down at the cup as she holds it in front of her with both hands.

"Like what?"

"Like . . . did you or I talk to her last night? And when I told him no, he asked when the last time was that either of us spoke with her. He also mentioned how she hasn't been in church lately and wanted to know if I knew why."

"Huh. I'm sure he's just as worried about her as her mom and dad and all of us are."

"Yeah, but I've never gotten the impression that they're super close. Have you? I mean when they moved here, she never said much about it. Not to me, anyway."

"Right, but when we were younger, didn't Thomas babysit for her a lot? Before they all moved away? I mean, I have cousins who I was close with when we were younger, but we've just grown up and apart, so now we don't have much in common. But still, if any of them went missing, I'd be concerned."

"Yeah, I guess so. But it still seems weird that he ran outside to ask me all those questions instead of asking when I was still inside. I guess that's what struck me as odd. The way he ran out after me. And why would he ask me when we'd last talked to or seen her? Don't you think Jenna's parents probably told all their family members that you and I haven't hung out with her for a while?"

I ponder Delaney's questions for a second and consider telling her about how he'd just told me he's sorry about Jenna, but I don't want to make more of it than it probably is—just a concerned family member who's reaching out to Jenna's best friends—we are as far as he knows anyway. So instead, I'm about to tell her I have no idea, but another voice fills the brief silence.

"Hello, ladies," Audra Steele says warmly as she reaches out to give both of our upper backs a welcoming rub. She removes her hands and laces her fingers together. She sort of reminds me of the Snow White I met at Disney World when I was six.

"Hi, Audra," Delaney says.

"Hi," I say, returning her warm smile. I haven't figured out yet if I should call her Audra or Mrs. Steele. Delaney only started calling her Audra a few weeks ago when she first babysat for Stella.

Mrs. Steele looks at Delaney. "In case we don't see you here on Wednesday during youth bible study group, I just wanted to double check that you're available to watch Stella again on Friday night. I know Thomas was pretty adamant that we not make plans so far in advance, but I really don't foresee anything preventing us from going to this get-together we've been invited to, so . . ."

"Yeah, of course. I actually just set a reminder on my phone. Friday the fourth at six thirty, right?" Delaney looks down at her phone to verify.

"That's right. Thank you, Delaney. I'll be sure to give you a call right away if our plans change, but like I said, it's not likely they will." With a smile that never seems to leave her lips and a parting wave to both of us, Mrs. Steele excuses herself to visit with other members of the congregation.

"She sure doesn't seem too concerned about Jenna, does she?" Delaney asks, still staring after her.

"No, but . . . Jenna's not *her* cousin," I shrug, giving Pastor Thomas's pretty wife the benefit of the doubt. "Plus, she just recently met Jenna, and I highly doubt they've gotten to know each other since it was around the time they moved to town that Jenna started acting weird."

Delaney and I lock eyes.

"Keeley?" my dad says, interrupting the moment. He glances at Delaney. "Hi, Delaney. How are you this morning?"

"Hey, Mr. Simon."

He looks back at me. "It's time to get going. I need to get more work done on the rec room. How about if I rescue both of your mothers from gossip overload," he widens his eyes and raises his eyebrows in my mom's general direction, "and we'll meet you two by the door?"

I smile at the silly expression on his face, but Delaney is too fixated on Pastor Thomas to notice. She sighs and scrunches her eyebrows together the way she does whenever something is bothering her. I'm surprised she doesn't have eleven lines from all the eyebrow scrunching she used to do back when her mom and dad first separated.

"Do you think the way Jenna has been acting has anything to do with Thomas?"

"What do you mean?" I ask in a hushed voice.

She shrugs. But not a 'who knows?' kind of shrug. It's more of a 'yeah, that's exactly what I mean' or 'anything's possible' kind of shrug.

We stare hard at each other. My heart starts beating faster as I wonder if Delaney might be on to something.

"Keeley, sweetie, let's go." My mom waves from across the room. Dad is already walking toward the exit.

"Yep, us too, Laney," Delaney's mom says as she adjusts her designer handbag on her shoulder.

"Call me when you get home so we can talk more about everything." I try to be more specific by purposefully glancing at Pastor Thomas. "Or just come over."

"Should I just ask my mom to drop me off?"

"Yeah, good idea."

Just before I walk outside into the crisp fall air, I glance back into the room, my eyes landing on Pastor Thomas who's bouncing a little girl on his knee. On any other day, it would have been sweet to see him holding a little kid like that. Now I don't know what to think.

chapter twenty-two

Jenna and Dustin had just gotten done eating at a sub sandwich shop, and they were on their way to Jolliet Park. Jenna really wanted to stay in and watch a movie, but Keeley and Delaney had begged her to go. "C'mon. You're already skipping the football game, so you at least have to go to Jolliet. Everyone is going to be there," Delaney coaxed her. And then there was Keeley. She wasn't usually big on pressuring people to do things, but that night she'd done a little coaxing too. "Jenna, you can't leave me alone with Delaney tonight. She's all hyped up and talking about how Corbin and Tommy are bringing beer and stuff. I don't feel like babysitting her alone." Dustin was fine doing whatever Jenna wanted to do, but he would have preferred staying in too, even if Mrs. Kemp kept an eye on them. Since neither of them really wanted to go, they'd agreed to only stay for one hour. That would give them enough time to still go back to Jenna's and maybe watch an episode or two of *The Office* before Dustin's midnight curfew.

KEELEY: WHEN WILL YOU BE HERE?

JENNA: ON OUR WAY. WHO'S THERE?

KEELEY: THE USUAL AND A FEW OTHERS LIKE THE HARVEY BROTHERS. OH, AND HAYLEY TOMPKINS.

Jenna let out a soft chuckle at the eye roll emoji Keeley had used because she felt the same way about Haley Tompkins.

"What's funny?" Dustin asked, keeping his eyes on the road.

"Keeley's just funny. I guess everyone is there. She said Jamie, Tyson, and Haley are there too."

Now Dustin laughed. "I guess word got out about the booze Corbin's brother was buying for him."

"Are you going to have anything?" Jenna asked.

"Maybe a beer," Dustin said with a shrug, "but I'm driving, so . . ."

Jenna had sipped beer at parties before but never more than two cans or bottles in one sitting. She liked the numb feeling it gave her, clearing her mind a little and making her feel more carefree, just like the Tylenol PM she'd been taking, But Jenna had a hard time stomaching the flavor of beer.

"Maybe I'll try something different than beer tonight."

"Like what?" Dustin asked, a surprised grin appearing on his lips.

"I don't know," she said. "Maybe vodka or rum. Isn't that what Corbin's brother usually gets for him?"

"Yeah, but you can barely handle a few sips of beer. Not sure you should be drinking hard liquor, Jenna. Besides, aren't you running tomorrow morning?"

Even though Jenna knew Dustin was right, his response irritated her. It almost felt like he was trying to control her. But instead of telling him how she felt, she decided to simply ignore his advice.

It wasn't a secret to adults or even the Briarwood PD that kids would hang out at Jolliet, so when there were get-togethers, people would carpool so there were as few cars as possible near the park. Then anyone who drove made sure not to park their cars near each other. This is why Dustin looped around the neighborhood surrounding Jolliet a few times before choosing an inconspicuous place to park.

When Jenna and Dustin neared the clearing in the woods where everyone was hanging out, they could hear the faint sound of music, talking, and laughter. When they entered the clearing, they were instantly whisked into a corner of Briarwood's hidden world of teen rebellion. It was the type of gathering at Jolliet that would encourage copious amounts of nicotine and alcohol consumption.

"Jenna!" Delaney squealed as she threw her arms around her friend. Keeley wasn't far behind, but she offered a much less obnoxious hug.

Jenna smiled, genuinely happy to see her friends, but her smile instantly faded when she saw Eli huddled around a small fire pit with several other kids. The glare of the flames framing his smile instantly elicited images of Thomas. Disoriented and distressed, she turned and started walking back toward the path she and Dustin had emerged from only moments before.

"Hey, hey, hey . . ." Dustin said, confused. "Where are you going?" He caught up to Jenna and stepped in front of her.

Keeley and Delaney looked on, confusion splayed across their faces as well.

"What's going on? What happened?"

"Nothing. I just . . . think we should go."

"But why?" Dustin asked.

But Jenna didn't get a chance to answer him because Keeley and Delaney were already grabbing her and whisking her away to a group of girls.

"Oh, no you don't," Delaney said.

"You said you'd hang out for at least an hour," Keeley chimed in.

Dustin followed behind the girls until he veered to the right toward the group Eli was standing with. He figured it might have been the heavy scent that hit them when they entered the clearing that had spooked Jenna. Missing out on cross country because she'd been around people smoking pot was something he knew she would be devastated by. So he wanted to make sure to say hi to all of his friends just in case she decided it was time to head out before the hour was up.

Jenna was unsettled by the way Dustin had abandoned her, but what was even more unsettling was the fact that he was now standing shooting the breeze with all his buddies, who apparently were now Eli's buddies too.

She kept an eye on Dustin and counted down the seconds until it seemed like a good time to grab him and make their exit. And despite pretending to be engaged in the various conversations going on within her circle of friends, all she was really focused on was her own toxic thoughts. She wondered who had invited Eli. She was depressed that she didn't feel like herself. She was annoyed that Haley Tompkins was standing across from her, chatting away without a care in the world. She was angry that Dustin and Eli were getting along. She wished she had something to numb her anxiety.

"Hey, ladies, anyone want a drink?" Corbin asked, inserting his head in between Keeley's and Emily's. Then he wiggled his entire body into the circle and placed his open backpack on the ground. A few girls accepted cans of beer and Tina and Delaney did shots of citrus vodka. "What about you two?" Corbin asked Jenna and Keeley.

"Pfft. Whatever, Corbin." Keeley laughed off the offer because Corbin knew she and Jenna both ran cross country.

"Sure, why not," Jenna said, drawing several shocked stares from her friends.

"Really?" Corbin hesitated. But when Jenna held out a hand, he shrugged and poured her the shot.

"Are you joking?" Keeley asked.

Ignoring her, Jenna downed the shot. Then she handed the glass back to Corbin. "I'll take another one."

Corbin smiled and obliged.

"Jenna, seriously?" Keeley raised her voice this time, drawing even more attention to Jenna's uncharacteristic behavior.

"What's wrong?" Delaney asked.

"She's having more," Keeley said, her expression a mixture of disbelief and frustration. "Corbin, don't . . ." she said as he poured yet a third shot for Jenna, her protest falling on deaf ears.

"Hey, at least she'll get a good night's sleep tonight. She might be barfing every few feet when you two run tomorrow morning, though." Delaney said, earning a few laughs and a rare dirty look from Keeley.

"What's up, guys?" Dustin asked, arriving to see what the commotion was about.

Jenna looked at him, immediately zeroing in on the beer in his hand. She was about to tell him that he better drink up if he wanted to catch up to her, but then she noticed Eli, which made her clam up.

"Oh, Jenna's just getting her drink on," Corbin said with a laugh.

"What are you talking about?" Dustin asked.

"The three shots of vodka she just had," Keeley said.

Dustin's face hardened. He grabbed Jenna's hand and led her a few feet away from the group.

"Three shots? What's up with you tonight?"

"Nothing's up with me. And who are you to talk? You're drinking a beer," Jenna said as she pointed to his hand.

In response, Dustin poured what appeared to be an entire twelve ounces of beer on the ground. "Not anymore." He gave her a small grin, hoping to lessen the tension he sensed between them. "Should we get going?"

"It hasn't been an hour yet."

"But you wanted to leave right when we got here," he said, checking his phone. "And it's been almost thirty minutes. Close enough for me."

"Well, I want to stay longer now." Jenna turned her back on Dustin and showed no recognition when he sighed loudly and followed her. "Corbin," she said loudly when she got back to the group, "can I have a beer?"

Corbin turned to face Jenna, but his gaze fell on Dustin, who was shaking his head behind Jenna. "Uh . . . are you sure you—"

"Can I have one or not?" Jenna snapped, surprising everyone within earshot.

"Fine," Corbin said, bending down to retrieve a can from the duffel bag. He held it out to Jenna.

"Hey, I don't think that's a good idea." Eli grabbed the beer before Jenna could get a grip on it.

This pissed Jenna off, but something else pissed her off even more. Keeley was there next to Eli, and she whispered "thank you" in his ear after he swiped Jenna's beer.

"What the hell, Eli?" Jenna hissed.

"Now what's going on?" Delaney asked, just noticing the commotion.

"Apparently Eli thinks he needs to babysit me," Jenna replied. Then she looked at Eli and demanded, "Give me the beer, Eli."

Delaney gasped and covered her mouth, and Keeley quickly gripped Jenna's upper arms as she lunged for the beer. Whispers circulated as the news of Jenna Kemp losing it on her cousin spread throughout the clearing.

"No, Jenna, he's right. You don't need any more," Dustin said, grabbing her hand. "Come on. We're going. Keeley? Delaney? Need a ride?"

"Yeah, we better go too," Keeley said as Jenna pulled her hand away from Dustin's and stormed off. Keeley and Delaney hustled after her.

"Hey, man, thanks," Dustin said to Eli.

"Yeah, of course. I don't know what the hell is up with her."

"Yeah, me either. But, hey, can you do me a favor?"

"Sure." Eli shrugged.

"Don't tell your mom or dad about this, okay?"

"No, of course not. I never ratted her out when we were kids. Don't plan on starting now." Eli gave Dustin a nod and left.

<hr>

September 8, 2017

Dear Diary,

Why does Eli care about my well-being now? It's not enough that he's becoming friends with all my friends and I suddenly have to see his face everywhere I go? School. Church. Parties. And it's only the first week of school!

His face reminds me of one thing. Him. And all those times he was in the room, did he know what he saw? (I've never asked because I'm afraid to hear his answer.) Would he tell the truth anyway? Maybe not because he never said anything to Uncle Greg and Aunt Lenore. Why? I've wondered this so many times, and all I've got is a blurry memory of HIM saying Eli would get a bad report about his behavior if he told them I got to play games in Aunt Lenore's sewing room and he didn't. Sometimes instead of HIS eyes above me in my dreams, I see Eli's eyes staring at me from across the room, peeping through a crack in the door. I don't know if these memories are real, same with a lot of the others, but I've never been able to get them out of my head. Maybe I don't know what's real and what isn't because it's been so long. If my memories are real, then he had to know something was wrong, even if he was a stupid kid.

And now Eli wants me to be safe. Ha! What a load of shit.

And whose side is Keeley on anyway?

And as for Dustin trying to stop me from drinking a beer? Well, that's a load of shit too!

The only "friend" I have who wasn't a total jerk tonight is Delaney.

Okay, so I admit maybe all the vodka wasn't the best idea because my head is starting to hurt, but at least it numbed me enough that I didn't feel sad or depressed. If they had all just let me be, they would have seen. After another couple of drinks, I might have even been able to stomach Eli's presence.

~Jenna

chapter twenty-three

"I'm making a rustic pasta salad for lunch, but it won't be ready for another fifteen minutes or so. Do you girls want some?"

"No, we're fine for now," I say, eager to go to my room with Delaney to finish the conversation we started at church about Thomas.

"What about you, Delaney? Can I get you something?"

"No, thanks, Mrs. Simon. I had two of Mrs. Kimble's raisin bran muffins and a croissant after church. "Can I have something to drink, though? Thanks for the ride, by the way."

"No problem. No sense in your mom driving you when we were headed here anyway." My mom smiles at Delaney, and I feel relieved that she seems to have forgotten about the whole Dustin and Delaney thing. "So, what are you girls planning to do today?"

"We thought we might check social media to see if anyone mentioned Jenna since Friday night."

"Oh! That's a great idea. I'm guessing you've already taken a look at Jenna's?"

"Yeah, she hasn't posted anything in weeks," Delaney says.

"Huh," my mom says, going back to chopping the celery for her salad. "That's unusual isn't it?"

Delaney and I nod and glance at each other. "She's never really been into social media," I say.

"Well, why don't you girls go scan the media stuff, and I'll bring you both some fresh iced tea in a bit."

"That would be great," Delaney says.

"Thanks, Mom." I motion for Delaney to follow me out of the kitchen.

"Are you sure you don't want a little snack too? Maybe some celery and peanut butter?" my mom calls after us.

"Sure, why not," I holler back, knowing she probably won't stop pushing food on us until we accept something.

As Delaney and I head upstairs to my room, I think about how Jenna loved celery and peanut butter and how she used to bring ants on a log in her lunch when we were in grade school. She traded me one for a plum once, and it was the first time I'd ever had ants on a log. The memory causes tears to well up in my eyes. Jenna goes through a little rebellious rough patch, and what did Delaney and I do? We turned our backs on her. Who would have thought something as simple as celery and peanut butter could make me feel so guilty?

When we enter my room, Delaney heads straight for my dresser. She removes a tube of gloss from her pocket and applies a fresh coat, puckering her lips at herself in the mirror.

I stand next to her in front of the corkboard hanging above my desk, my attention again on the old group picture of Jenna, Delaney, and me from the summer before seventh grade. I touch the outer corner of my right eye, remembering the bruise I had for a week after the photo was taken because the camera slipped out of my hands after I snapped the shot. We're all lying on our backs with our heads in the center of the merry-go-round at Jolliet Park. Jenna was wearing her favorite floral headband. Delaney had on a sundress, and her hair was flowing in golden waves outstretched to meet mine and Jenna's heads. Jenna and I were excited to finally be able to join a cross country team, so we'd just run two miles.

"So . . . about Thomas. Do you think there's something up with him and Jenna?" Delaney asks, pulling me from the memory. She takes a seat on my bed and grabs the August 2017 edition of *Runner's World* magazine from my nightstand and begins flipping pages.

"I don't know what to think," I say, tacking the photo back up. "Maybe the weird feeling I got from him this morning was for no reason. I just can't seem to stop thinking up the worst possible reasons to explain why Jenna hasn't contacted anyone. You know?"

"Right, but what about how he ran out to ask me questions about her last night? And it's so weird how she started spiraling out of control when her family moved back to town. I mean, she hasn't seen them for years. And remember how much it used to irritate her when her mom would say what wonderful kids her cousins are—how perfect her Aunt Lenore's family is. Makes me wonder if Jenna's always been so hard on herself, wanting to be perfect at everything, just to keep up with that standard. Maybe them moving back made her feel pressured to be even more perfect and she just snapped."

These are some of the deepest thoughts I've ever heard from Delaney, and they actually make sense. "I don't know. Maybe you're on to something."

"I mean," she finally looks up from the magazine, "she traded in celery and peanut butter for weed. And she traded in those Kevita drinks she loves so much for booze. Oh, and her sweet, virginal girl next door reputation? Ancient history."

"Come on, Delaney. We don't know for sure if any of those rumors were true." I break eye contact with her because we both know there's usually some truth to a rumor.

"And you know what? The drugs and the sex aren't even the biggest issues to me. It's not like I'm all that innocent," she mumbles. "The thing *I'm* really pissed about is how she treated us—the way she yelled at us in front of everyone that night and then again in the cafeteria." She shakes her head as if shaking the bad memory away and looks back down at the magazine.

"Yeah, that was pretty shitty."

We sit in silence for a few minutes, Delaney flipping and me pondering for the hundredth time why Jenna was so angry with Delaney for babysitting for Stella and why she was so against Eli and me liking each other. I thought she'd be happy that I finally liked someone.

Delaney finally breaks the silence.

"I can't believe you still read magazines. Why don't you just use their website?"

"I got a two-year subscription for my birthday last year," I say with a shrug.

"Why do you have all of these places starred?" She holds the *Runner's World* up and turns it to face me for a second. It's open to a map of marathons and half-marathons voted best in the country in 2016.

"Those are the ones Jenna and I want to do someday."

"Hawaii?"

"You never know. Hopefully, Jenna gets back into her running groove soon. I don't know if I'd be able to do any of those without her." Instead of worrying about betraying Jenna by ratting her out for all the shit she's been doing lately, I'm starting to feel more like a traitor for not worrying much sooner about *why* she's been doing so much stupid shit. Suddenly angry with myself, I say, "We should have done or said something a month ago . . . two weeks ago . . . hell, even a week ago."

Delaney nods and studies me for a second. Then her eyes begin to tear up like mine. "Keeley, I need to tell you something, and you have to promise you won't judge me for it."

"Yeah, of course," I say, wiping each of my eyes with the back of my hand. "What is it?"

"So, we both know Jenna and I were never as close as the two of you were with all the running you've always done together. Hell, we all know I can barely run a mile without stopping to rest. Anyway, I have to admit . . ." She sighs heavily. "I've always been a little jealous because of it."

"Oh, my gosh, Delaney, why would I judge you for being jealous? I've been jealous of the two of you too, like when you've gone school shopping together. But it was something the two of you shared without me so . . ."

"No," Delaney says, shaking her head, "that's not what I'm worried about you judging me for."

"Okay, what then?"

"Well, after Jenna yelled at me and we stopped hanging out with her, I guess it felt good to not always feel like I was competing for your friendship. No, that isn't right. I don't guess; I know. It felt good. It was a load off. And now it feels like the load off has been reloaded times three, like the little bit of relief I felt that I didn't have to compete with her anymore weighs more heavily on me than all the times I felt jealous of you two put together." A tear trickles down Delaney's cheek and I quickly wipe it away.

"Hey, it's okay. I get it. No judgement here. I know it probably won't help much, but you weren't the only person she yelled at. Remember? She yelled at Dustin, Eli, and me too."

Delaney nods and sniffles. "All right," Delaney says, returning the magazine to my nightstand and picking up her phone, "should we scroll through social media?"

I'm a little surprised she's changed the subject already, but that admission must have been hard for Delaney, so I just let it go.

"You check Snapchat, and I'll check Instagram?" I say, grabbing my phone. Delaney nods, and I start scrolling through my Instagram feed. I click to view each friend's profile and quickly begin feeling overwhelmed. Looking at hundreds of posts and stories since Friday is going to take hours.

"Christ, this is going to take forever," Delaney voices my concern. "Maybe we should just think of the people most likely to have had contact with her and start by checking their profiles only?"

I stand up to grab a pad of lined lime green Post-it notes and a pen from my desk. Then I write *People Who Might Have Seen Jenna* at the top. "We could start with Matt Sanford," I say, adding his name to the list. "He works at Taco Mama's, and you know how Jenna loves their fajitas. Maybe she went there this weekend."

I click to view the list of Instagram accounts I follow, and Delaney opens her list of Snapchat friends. Then we reason aloud why various people might be worth contacting.

Twenty minutes later, we're sipping iced tea and staring at a list of four names. Matt Sanford, Jamie Harvey, Tyson Harvey, and Lou Tang.

"Four out of over a thousand?" Delaney laments. She sighs and rakes her fingers through her hair a few times, making it look disheveled. "Plus, Lou hasn't used Snapchat in over a year, and none of them hardly ever post pics of people on Instagram."

"Yeah, well, keep in mind that most of your friends list overlaps with my Instagram list, and the only person at school Jenna has really been talking to lately is Leighton so . . ." I realize what we're doing is pointless. "Anyway, I have Tyson's number, so how about if I call him and Jamie, and you message Matt and Lou?

Delaney sighs then says, "Fine."

I locate Tyson's number in my phone but don't call right away because I'm pondering exactly what I'm going to say. The Harvey brothers are a year older than us, and we've known them since grade school. We'd probably still hang out with them like we did in middle school if they didn't hang out with rougher crowds and party hardcore every weekend. Jenna and I used to talk about Jamie and Tyson's transformation over the years. In grade school, they were both model students. Jamie even played football freshman year, and Tyson is a really good basketball player. But they don't participate in anything anymore. No sports. No dances. Definitely nothing fun like spirit week activities or school plays or fundraisers. All they seem to do is get high, sleep in class, and go to the bathroom to vape. It's like the teachers have given up on them because I've never heard of them getting detention or suspended for anything. My dad says people are products of their environments, but I'm starting to disagree with him. Mr. Harvey is some bigwig at Miller Brewing Company, and Mrs. Harvey is a college professor. And then there's Jenna. Her family is wonderful. Her mom might be a little overprotective at times, but both of her parents are supportive and loving. So why are any of them doing the things they're doing?

"Hey . . . Matt says he didn't see Jenna at all this weekend, but he'll ask around, and Lou hasn't gotten back to me. I doubt he'll respond. Are you going to call Tyson or what?" Delaney says, throwing her palms up.

"Yep. Right now," I say as I press to connect the call.

Tyson answers after the second ring. "What's up?"

"Tyson? It's—"

"Nope. It's Jamie."

"Oh, hey, Jamie. It's Keeley. I'm calling to—"

"Keeley Simon? Wait, don't tell me. You've decided to take a walk on the dark side just like your girl, Jenna?

"Jamie, did you guys see Jenna this weekend?"

"Nah, but I saw her like two weeks ago at Leighton's."

"Really?"

"Yeah, she was pretty messed up."

"What's he saying?" Delaney whispers. I signal for her to wait a second.

"What were you doing there? I didn't know you hung out with Leighton."

"I don't, but a buddy from the south side asked if I'd drop some stuff off. He actually seemed pretty cozy with Jenna that night, which might have surprised me a couple months ago, but ya know . . . people surprise you sometimes."

"Yeah, tell me about it," I say. "Hey, do you know if your friend has seen Jenna since then?"

"Pft. I doubt it. He isn't exactly into dating one girl."

"Well, could you maybe ask him?"

"What? Why?"

"Jamie, you and Tyson might as well know because I'm sure word will get around, but Jenna hasn't been home since Friday."

"Yeah? Well, maybe she's partying."

"No, I don't think she'd party for two days straight without contacting anyone."

"Fair enough, but you never know, right? Who would have thought Jenna Kemp would be hanging out with losers like my brother and me?" He emits a self-deprecating chuckle.

"Whatever. You guys aren't losers."

"Yeah, okay, Keeley."

"So, will you please ask your friend if he saw her at all this weekend? And can you ask him today?"

"Sure. Hang on, I'll text him right now."

"He's texting a friend who he says was with Jenna a couple weeks ago," I whisper to Delaney.

"What friend?" she whispers back.

"Some guy from the south side. That's all he said. Oh, and they were at Leighton's."

Delaney rolls her eyes.

"Hey, Keeley."

"Yeah, what did he say?"

"He said . . . hang on, I'll read it to you . . . *Nah done with those girls.*"

"Oh."

"Yeah, that's Bob."

"Well, thanks for asking him, Jamie."

"Yeah, no problem. If Tyson and I see or hear anything about Jenna, we'll let you know. Don't sweat it, though. Jenna will make her way back to the bright side soon," he says with a chuckle.

"Well?" Delaney says.

I shake my head. "His friend hasn't seen her."

"Keeley?" my mom says as she opens the door a crack. "A couple of police officers are here, sweetheart."

"Oh . . . God, okay. Should we both—"

"Just you, Keeley. Delaney, I texted your mom. She's on her way. One of the officers said your mom needs to be present when they talk to you. But Keeley, they'd like to speak with you right now."

Throwing a sweatshirt over my head, I rush for the door. Why is my heart beating so fast? And why do I feel like I've done something wrong? *Maybe it's because the cops probably wouldn't even be here if you'd forced Jenna to tell you what's going on with her. Maybe whatever phase she's going through would have been nipped in the bud by now.*

"Keeley, come on." My mom waves me forward and starts walking down the hall toward the stairs.

My eyes meet with Delaney's just before I turn into the hallway. She looks just as scared and wracked with guilt as I feel.

chapter twenty-four

Jenna removed her diary from the second drawer of her nightstand and sat on her bed staring at it for a few minutes. The pill she'd taken before church had completely worn off, so she was debating whether to take another dose because she was starting to crave the numb feeling. She'd discovered on Friday night that alcohol mimicked the same sensation as the Tylenol PM, only it didn't make her feel like passing out, not right away at least. So, she decided that it would be best to take the pills only when she went to church or when she was staying home. She was sure she could get her hands on some alcohol to self-medicate for other occasions.

She glanced over at the digital clock on her nightstand. It was a little after noon, so she knew her mom would be calling up to her to come down and eat something. She'd already decided she wasn't hungry, though, and just felt like going to sleep. But first, she wanted to add an entry to her diary. Since she hadn't been running well lately, writing down her thoughts seemed like the only way she had left to vent her frustrations.

She opened her diary and began to write.

September 10, 2017

Dear Diary,

We went to church today, as usual, and it sucked. Even though I've upped the number of pills I've been taking to two, I still couldn't stop wondering which people at church have bad things to hide. I mean, I like to think most people are good, but what we think and reality are different a lot of times. Who's pretending to be something they aren't? Who's only there to hide who they really are? Who's cheating on their spouse? Who hits their wife or children? Who's a sick twisted pedophile?

My mom thinks going to church cleanses your soul. Does everyone need cleansing? What about me? Do I?

How can he claim to be a servant of God anyway? Does being at church and serving God cleanse HIS soul? Because if God allows that, I'd rather not go to church ever again. I don't need that kind of God.

What if there are more like him? What if he's done what he did to me to others? Did he harass anyone else while he was away? What about his wife? Is she a sicko just like him? How else is it possible that she can't see it in his eyes? Then again, no one can. He's good at hiding it. Like today when he was giving a speech to the congregation, saying how excited he is to serve the youth of our church community. The look in his eyes was so normal. The sickness I've witnessed so many times wasn't there. How does he hide it?

Even Keeley doesn't see it. She shook his hand, and he touched her back. How does she not feel the evil in him? I want her and Delaney to hate him just like I do. But they don't.

So, I continue to mask how I feel with fake smiles. It sort of feels like I'm trying to run away from the memories, but I can't move my legs. I'm stuck. And not only that, everyone is still moving around me, and they're all just waving as they pass thinking I'm still keeping up. Well, I'm not. I'm losing ground fast.

What am I going to do, Diary? I can't choose whether I see him or not. I'm stuck, and the only thing I can do to deal is pretend nothing happened. How am I supposed to do that?

~ Jenna

When Jenna put her diary back in the drawer and grabbed the bottle of Tylenol PM, her phone vibrated next to her. She immediately felt guilty for wishing everyone would just leave her alone because she knew she didn't really want that from her close friends. What she really wanted was to not feel ashamed every time she looked into their eyes. She felt like a liar for hiding her secret from them—from everyone—all these years. But she'd decided that telling someone now would only make her look like a fool. She also feared no one would believe her.

After popping another pill, bringing her total count for the day to three, she lay back and checked her messages.

DUSTIN: HEY, I NEED NEW B-BALL SHOES. WANT TO GO TO THE MALL WITH ME?

KEELEY: I'M GOING FOR A RUN LATER ON. YOU FEELING UP TO IT YET? (FRIENDLY REMINDER: VODKA AND XC DON'T PLAY WELL!) FIRST MEET ON TUESDAY!

Jenna definitely didn't feel like going to the mall, but she considered Keeley's running invitation since she wasn't able to run the day before and had skipped out on practice on Thursday. She began composing a response but ended up closing her eyes. It was supposed to be for just a moment, but almost instantly, she'd fallen into a deep nightmare-less sleep.

chapter twenty-five

This isn't happening. This isn't happening. This isn't happening. I repeat the thought over and over, my eyes closed and my forehead resting on our kitchen table. But then someone mentions her name again, and my thought pattern is broken. There's no more denying it or wishing it wasn't true. The two police officers leaving our house right now are proof that Jenna is missing.

The front door closes and the living room goes silent. The only thing I can hear is the sound of my heart beating in my ears, and my skull is pulsing to the beat. I sit upright and rake my fingers through my hair a few times before resting my head in my hands. The light streaming through our kitchen windows pierces the spaces between my fingers, making me feel even more disoriented.

"Oh, Dustin . . ." my mom laments when she enters the kitchen. My eyes are still closed, but I sense that my parents are standing on either side of me.

My dad clears his throat. "Hey, Buddy," he says, placing a hand on my back, "Detective Collins gave me his card, so . . . if you think of anything else that might be helpful, we can call him directly."

He removes his hand, and I hear the chairs on either side of me being pulled out.

I open my eyes but still don't make eye contact with my parents. Now that they know what's been going on with Jenna, I just can't. They listened as I told the officers how I drove to her house that night like a stalker and *left*. Why the *hell* didn't I ring the doorbell that night? Even if she wasn't home, her parents would have realized she was gone at that point. Now she's been gone for God knows how long. Then they asked if I'd noticed any changes in Jenna lately. I thought about telling them I wasn't aware of anything unusual, but they were staring at me like they already knew, like they were daring me to lie. So what choice did I have? I just wish my parents hadn't been there to hear all about Jenna's moodiness, drinking, and drug use.

"Dustin, why didn't you tell us what was going on with Jenna? Was your break up really a joint decision like you said? Or was it because of these sudden changes with her?" My mom sounds desperate for answers, but I don't have any for her. When I don't respond, she continues, her voice growing louder, possibly angry. "And what about Keeley and Delaney? Why didn't they say something? I just . . . I don't understand." She pauses for a second. "Do you believe this, Brian? Sweet little Jenna Kemp drinking and doing drugs?"

"No, no I don't. Do you think maybe we should reach out to Bonnie and Joseph? They must be going out of their minds. I know I would be."

"That's a good idea," my mom says as she begins to back her chair away from the table.

"Don't," I say, finally breaking my silence. I look from my mom to my dad and then back down at the table.

"Why?" my mom says, lowering herself back into her seat. Then she leans in close to me, craning her neck to make eye contact with me. "Dustin, do you understand how serious this is?"

Something about the accusatory tone in her voice makes me snap.

"You think I don't know that?" I yell, looking from my mom to my dad, no longer able to contain the slurry of emotions that have been building up inside me over the past several weeks. My mom starts to say something, but my dad holds up a hand to stop her. "I should have gone to the door and knocked and demanded to talk to her that night. If she was there, maybe that would have prevented her from going wherever she went. And if she wasn't there, then Mr. and Mrs. Kemp would have known much sooner that she was gone. And even before I went to her house, I should have called when she didn't show up. And even earlier that night, I should have agreed to see her as soon as I got her text, and I should have gone to see her immediately." My chest is heaving, and my eyes are becoming cloudy with tears. "I should have tried to figure out what's been going on with her *weeks ago*. I should have been there for her!" I abruptly back my chair away from the table and stand.

"Oh, Dustin . . ." my mom says, standing and moving toward me.

"No," I say, shaking my head and putting up a hand to keep her away. "I don't deserve any sympathy. Those are just some of the things I *should* have done. You don't know about the things I *shouldn't* have done, things that probably made whatever is going on with her worse."

"Dustin, should've would've could've. Son, you can't beat yourself up for the choices Jenna has been making," my dad says. "And there's no way anything you've done or didn't do had any effect on where she is now."

"Your dad is right. From what you told Detective Collins, it sounds like Jenna pushed you and her other friends away. There's only so much you can do in a situation like that."

"No," I say, shaking my head, "you're both wrong. I was wrong too." I turn and leave the kitchen, throwing over my shoulder, "I need to be alone for a little while."

When I get to my room, I send a group text to Keeley and Delaney.

DUSTIN: THE POLICE WERE JUST HERE. WHERE THE HELL IS SHE?

chapter twenty-six

"Hey, my mom is on her way. Maybe she could drop us off at the rec center so we can get some miles in on the treadmills." Keeley leaned against the locker next to Jenna's as Jenna put on her jacket. It was storming, so cross country practice had been canceled.

Jenna sighed. "Aw, man, I can't. I already said I'd go over to Leighton's to work on an economics project." She threw on her backpack and closed her locker.

"Oh . . . well, how long will you be there? Maybe we can go later. I'm sure my mom would drive us." Keeley was shocked that Jenna already had plans. They'd only found out an hour ago that practice had been canceled. Not only that, but Keeley hadn't seen Jenna outside of school or cross country since church on Sunday, and the time before that had been at the disastrous Jolliet party on Friday night.

"Uh, not sure. We just got the assignment yesterday, so we haven't really had a chance to figure out who's doing what. A couple hours, I guess," Jenna said with a shrug. What she didn't say was that she probably wouldn't want to go to the rec center even if she didn't already have plans to go to Leighton's. Her performance in their first meet the day before was abysmal, and now on top of being a mess emotionally, Jenna's self-esteem, which had always been connected to her performance as a runner, was suffering too. She was even thinking about quitting the team.

"So, I'm guessing you and Leighton were paired together?" Keeley asked as they started walking toward the stairs at the end of the second-floor hallway.

"Yeah, why?"

"I don't know. After what Corbin told us about her, I was just surprised to hear you're going to her house. Do you think what he said was true?"

Jenna shrugged. "Does it really matter? All I'm worried about is getting an A on our project, so as long as she'll put in some effort to help out, I don't care if it's true. Besides, you know Corbin. He's like the male gossip-queen version of Tina."

"Yeah," Keeley said with a laugh, "he kind of is, isn't he?"

Jenna spotted Leighton near the front doors as soon as she and Keeley exited the stairwell. Dozens of kids were standing around waiting for rides, but her hair made her easy to find.

"Well, I guess I'll see you later," Jenna said to Keeley. Leighton glanced over at them and then back outside without saying anything.

"Yeah," Keeley said, raising her eyebrows at Jenna. "Good luck with your project."

Jenna waved as Keeley walked out the door, then she turned to Leighton. "Hey, thanks for offering me a ride to your house. Hopefully, we can get everything figured out tonight, so we don't have to meet up after school again."

"Yeah, sure. My mom was coming to get me anyway . . . There she is now." Leighton shoved open the door with her elbow and slipped through so quickly it almost slammed in Jenna's face. Leighton slipped into the passenger seat of her mom's car and Jenna into the back. She felt awkward at first when Leighton didn't introduce Jenna to her mom, but Leighton's mom swooped in, putting Jenna at ease.

"Hi, there," she said, smiling at Jenna in the rearview mirror. "I'm Abigail, Leighton's mom."

"I'm Jenna. Thanks for the ride."

"Not a problem. I don't have to be to work until five, so plenty of time to pick you girls up so you don't have to get soaked in this downpour. Geez, it's been raining all day long." Abigail shook her head. She was wearing hospital scrubs, so Jenna figured she did something in the medical field.

"So, do you live close to school or . . ."

"Yeah, just a few blocks away, right over on Berkeley."

"Oh," Abigail said, glancing at Jenna in the mirror again, "nice area. Did you grow up around here?"

"Pretty much. We used to live in West Allis but moved here when I started kindergarten."

Abigail nodded, keeping her eyes on the road. "So, what do your parents do, Jenna?"

"My mom's the circulation supervisor at the Briarwood Library, and my dad is an electrician for Custom Concepts Homes."

Abigail continued to make small talk with Jenna, asking her what she did in her spare time, if she participated in any sports, if she had any brothers or sisters. The whole time, Leighton stared out the window. Jenna wondered what she was looking at because it was pouring. Then it occurred to her that maybe she wasn't looking at anything and just wanted to stay out of the conversation.

"Well, I'm glad Leighton is having you over. She could use some nice friends."

Leighton scoffed but stayed focused on the window.

At first, Jenna couldn't believe that such a friendly woman could have a daughter like Leighton, but then she reminded herself that appearances aren't always what they seem. There had to be a reason why Leighton acted the way she did.

When the car came to a stop in front of a townhouse, Leighton quickly opened her door and started getting out, but her mom stopped her. "Leighton."

Jenna gripped the handle of her door and watched as Leighton turned to look at her mom.

"I made some lasagna. It's keeping warm in the oven. Offer some to Jenna, okay?"

"Yep," Leighton said as she hopped out and closed the door.

"Nice to meet you, Jenna!" Abigail called after Jenna as she got out of the car.

"You too. Thanks again for the ride."

"So, what are we doing again?" Leighton asked.

Jenna stared at her from across the table, unsure if she was joking or not.

Leighton stared back, and Jenna took that as confirmation she wasn't.

"We're supposed to choose a product or service and create a poster that shows how the four factors of production influence the final good or service that's produced."

Leighton rolled her eyes and sighed. Why did teachers always have to make students work with partners? *People like me are way better off working alone* Leighton thought.

"So what product do you want to use?" Jenna asked, unaffected by Leighton's attitude.

Jenna's patience surprised Leighton. Any partner or group work she'd been part of since her freshman year had ended in disaster. She wouldn't deny it was her fault either. Maybe this time she should just do the work and get the stupid project done.

Leighton shrugged and was about to make a genuine suggestion when her phone buzzed. With a simple glance, she went from being in an okay mood to irritated as hell. She pressed both hands against the table and stood, causing her chair to almost topple over. Then she bent over and retrieved a pack of cigarettes from her backpack.

"Does your mom know you smoke?" Jenna asked, surprised to see someone her age smoking right in the middle of her own dining room.

Jenna's mom and dad would have grounded her for life.

Leighton scoffed and rolled her eyes again before she lit the cigarette and took a long drag. She exhaled all the smoke out in one long breath and repeated the process two more times before her phone buzzed again.

Jenna looked up from their assignment rubric, first at Leighton as she rushed over to swipe her phone off the table and then at Leighton's phone. Leighton wasn't fast enough to prevent Jenna from reading the text and the name of the person who'd sent it.

DICKHEAD: I MISS YOU, HONEY.

Leighton took another drag of her cigarette as she glanced at her phone. Then dropped her phone face down on the table and sat back down. She took one last puff before tossing her cigarette stub into a can of Diet Coke. It makes a little thud when it hits the bottom.

"Let's get to work," Leighton said, opening her econ folder and pulling out a copy of the rubric. "We need a product, right? Okay, here's a product."

She pointed to the can of Diet Coke. "Done." She made a checkmark next to *Decide on a product*, then jotted down *Diet Coke*.

Jenna mimicked Leighton's movements, checking off the first direction and writing *Diet Coke.*, but she couldn't stop wondering who the text was from. She glanced around the open concept dining area they were sitting in, over to the living room, and then over to the entryway. Next to the door was a shoe rack that was full of female shoes.

"Come on," Leighton said, tapping the table with her palm a few times, "now we need to decide who's going to do what."

"Oh, right." Jenna looked back down at her rubric. *Assign each member their task* was indeed up next.

"I suck at writing, but I can draw. So I'll do the poster if you don't mind."

"Yeah, sure, that sounds good," Jenna said, writing Leighton's name next to *Create the poster* and her own name next to *Write the one-page explanation*.

"Okay, good. So, should we just both research all this stuff," she said, pointing to the four factors of production, "or should we—"

"Who's Dickhead?" Jenna asked.

Leighton stared at her for a few seconds contemplating whether or not to tell Jenna to mind her own business. She decided not to because she liked Jenna's directness. "It's just my psycho dad."

"Is he really psycho?"

Leighton shrugged. "Anyway," she said, focusing on the rubric again, "I think this'll go a lot quicker if you research ingredients and processes, and I research people and production. Or however you want to divide it up. I don't really care what I research." She looked up at Jenna.

Jenna resisted the urge to ask another question. Clearly, Leighton didn't want to talk about why she was so upset over a couple of texts from her dad.

"No, that's fine. I'll take ingredients and processes."

As the girls dug their school-issued Chromebooks out of their backpacks, Jenna thought about how she'd never met anyone like Leighton before. For some reason, she felt drawn to this social outcast—as she'd been labeled by some of Jenna's friends. With all the pressure she'd felt lately to hide the emotional turmoil going on inside her, she felt free in Leighton's presence. Maybe it was because Leighton knew absolutely nothing about her so there weren't any expectations for Jenna to behave a certain way. This realization made Jenna take a deep cleansing breath.

"Are you gonna start working anytime soon so we can just get this research done and you can leave?" Leighton asked, giving Jenna a weird look.

"Yes, ma'am," Jenna said with a mock salute. Then she opened her Chromebook and smiled to herself. She could have sworn she saw a hint of a curl at the corner of Leighton's lips.

A few minutes later, Jenna's phone vibrated.

KEELEY: HEY, DECIDED NOT TO RUN. GOING TO A MOVIE AT 7 WITH DELANEY INSTEAD. WANNA GO?

Leighton eyed Jenna for a moment as she read Keeley's text.

"My friends are going to a movie at 7. Do you want to go with?" Jenna asked Leighton.

Leighton laughed. "I've seen your friends. No thanks."

"What's that supposed to mean?" Jenna asked, genuinely curious.

"So, the blonde with the perfect hair who always dresses all matchy-matchy?"

"Yeah?" Jenna said with a shrug. She knew Leighton was talking about Delaney.

"Well, don't turn your back on that one because she'll stab you in it. And the other one, the tall mixed one with the thick curly hair?"

Jenna nodded. She meant Keeley.

"That one's all right, but make sure you don't do anything she wouldn't do because she'll judge you for it."

Jenna wanted to tell Leighton she didn't know what she was talking about, but she couldn't because she wasn't sure Leighton's assessments were that far off. Instead, she said, "So you're sure you don't want to go then?"

Leighton rolled her eyes and went back to her Chromebook.

JENNA: SURE, I'LL GO.

KEELEY: WE'LL PICK YOU UP. WHAT'S THE ADDRESS?

chapter twenty-seven

My dad's voice and static from a police radio drift from the living room as I descend the stairs. All eyes turn to me when my mom and I enter the room. My dad and the two officers—a woman in a standard police uniform and a man in plain clothes—break away from a tight circle in the middle of the room. I know they're here to help, but the sight of them makes me want to throw up. My mom moves behind me and leads me to one of the paisley wingback chairs.

"Detective Collins, Officer Lang, this is our daughter, Keeley. She'd be more than happy to answer any questions you have. Anything to help locate Jenna," my dad says.

"Thank you, Dr. Simon," Detective Collins says, taking a seat on the matching chair next to mine. Lang remains standing and my parents sit on the sofa.

"Please, call me Jack . . . and this is Leslie," my dad says, motioning toward my mom.

Collins nods and directs his attention to me. "Nice to meet you, Keeley."

"Nice to meet you too," I say.

"Keeley, Mrs. Kemp tells us you've been best friends with Jenna since Kindergarten."

I nod.

"When was the last time you saw her?"

"Do you mean the last time we hung out or the last time I actually saw her? Because we've hardly spent any time together since late September."

"The last time you physically saw her."

I prop my elbows on my knees and cup my chin in my hands. I focus on the rug in the center of the room for several seconds, then I sit upright again and say, "I usually see her during lunch, but I don't remember seeing her Friday. I guess I've gotten so used to not sitting with her that I just haven't been making a conscious effort to look for her anymore."

And now she's nowhere to be found. Some friend I am.

"So, you can't remember the last time you saw her?"

"Well, I'm sure she was at school on Friday. Otherwise, Mrs. Kemp would have gotten a phone call, right?"

"Yes, we've confirmed that she was at school."

"Oh . . . then what difference does it make whether I saw her or not?" I even shock myself with this comment, but for some reason, I feel guilty for not seeing Jenna on Friday and angry because *someone* must know where she is. "We stopped talking regularly about a month ago. So why are you here questioning me? Why aren't you talking to the people she's been hanging out with? Like Leighton Pierce? And have you gone through her phone or her computer yet?"

My mom takes a seat beside me on the arm of my chair, probably because of the tears that have welled up in my eyes.

Detective Collins doesn't show the slightest reaction to my emotional outburst. He seems indifferent like he's talking to me just so they can say they investigated the call about Jenna. I wonder if they think Jenna's just some dumb teenager who's off having fun for the weekend. But then I look at Officer Lange and see that her forehead has become severely creased. "Keeley, we need to gather as much information as possible. We weren't aware that you hadn't done anything with Jenna since September. Mrs. Kemp didn't mention that. Did the two of you . . ." She flips back a few pages in her little notebook. "Or should I say the three of you? Delaney Burns, we understand she's close to Jenna too?"

I nod.

"Did the three of you get into an argument?"

"No, not an argument exactly. It was more like Jenna just . . . *changed* and stopped wanting to do things with us.

"How has she changed?"

I look at my mom. I'm not sure if I should tell them what I told her earlier because I don't want Jenna to get in trouble for the drinking and the drugs.

"Keeley, Jenna hasn't been in contact with anyone for almost forty-eight hours. You have to tell them everything you know." My mom gives me a reassuring nod.

"Okay . . . um . . . around the beginning of September, she started wanting to do things she'd never done before like drinking and smoking pot. I've also heard through the rumors that she's been at parties where there's other stuff too."

"Other stuff?" Detective Collins asks.

"Yeah. You know, like cocaine, oxy, ecstasy, and something called Molly." I glance at my mom and dad when I say this. My dad remains stone-faced, but my mom's jaw drops, so I quickly add, "But no one ever said they *saw* her do any of that stuff. People just assume."

Both Detective Collins and Officer Lange nod, but only Collins jots things down.

"Anyway, she also started staying home a lot and not answering our calls and texts. It was like she was trying to ditch us or something." I sigh. "Oh, and she stopped running with me."

"Running?" Collins asks.

"Yeah, we were both on the cross country team this year, have been every year. In fact, Jenna was the one who got me into running back when we were in sixth grade. This is actually the longest we've gone without running together and the first year she's ever missed more than one practice. So, there has to be something wrong."

"Did you ask her what was going on with her? Or did you discuss why she was neglecting things that are normally important to her?"

"No," I say, closing my eyes and thinking about the argument Delaney, Dustin, and I had after homecoming. We weren't sure whether to say something about the things Jenna was doing. Delaney thought we should, but Dustin and I were on the fence. In the end, we decided not to because we weren't sure who to tell, and none of us wanted to get her in trouble. And then we all just stopped talking to her, judged her, and ditched her. I can't tell the police all of that, though, not with my parents listening. They'd be so disappointed in me, especially my mom. I'm disappointed in myself. "I should have. But we figured she was just going through a rebellious phase, and it would end soon."

Collins looks up from his leather notebook but keeps his pen perched above it. "Thank you for sharing all of this with us, Keeley. Is there anything else you think that might be useful to us? Names of new friends she's been spending time with perhaps?"

I refuse to repeat anything I've heard about Jenna that has to do with sex. I'm sure she'd die of embarrassment if anyone else found out about what Tyson Harvey told me. In fact, I don't even think I should mention the Harvey brothers. "No," I say, glancing at my mom who narrows her eyes at me, "not that I can think of. But you do plan to talk to Leighton Pierce, right? Jenna has been hanging out with her a lot lately. She might know something."

"We've already spoken to her, Keeley," Detective Collins says, standing.

"Oh," I say, wondering if Leighton told them things she didn't tell Delaney and me. "You know what? I actually—"

The sound of the doorbell causes all of us to look toward the hallway.

"That must be Trish," my mom says scurrying left into the hallway.

Lange flips her notebook closed and pockets it along with her pen.

"Wait that's it?" I ask.

"No, we still need to speak with Delaney," Detective Collins answers. "Dr. Simon, would you mind stepping out of the room with your wife and your daughter?" He approaches Delaney's mom. "Mrs. Burns," Collins shakes her hand. "It's nice to meet you. Thank you for coming here on such short notice."

"Well, under the circumstances, I didn't see any other option. You need to find Jenna, and I certainly don't want you talking to Delaney without me," she sighs. "Can we please make it as quick as possible, though? I'm sorry, but I really need to get back to work."

"We'll do our best," Collins says, peeking over his shoulder. "Lange, can you please let Delaney know we're ready for her?" Then he moves toward me with his arm outstretched. I'm unsure if we're going to shake or if he means to help me out of my chair. Instead, when I take hold of his hand, he gives me something. "Here's my card in case you think of anything else or if you talk to anyone who might have seen Jenna after school on Friday."

"Actually, there is one more thing, and I'm sure Delaney will mention it too."

"Oh?" He gestures toward the chair I was sitting in, and we both sit back down. "Go ahead."

"Well, on Friday night when I was at the movie theater, Jenna texted me for the first time in weeks."

He nods as if he's heard this before, and he reopens his leather notebook. "What time was it?"

"It was before our movie started, so it must have been just before nine. I can get my phone if you want."

"No, that won't be necessary right now. We have access to Jenna's call log, and we should be able to identify the outgoing text to your number. What is it?"

I tell him, and he writes it down.

"Now, something we don't have access to is the content of Jenna's text messages, not without her phone anyway. So, can you please tell me what her message said?"

I nod. "She just said hey and asked if maybe we could get together this weekend."

"And what was your response?"

I swallow the guilt that's creeping up my throat, ready to choke me. "I didn't respond."

"Come on, Keeley. Let's give the officers some privacy with Delaney and her mom," my dad says, already walking hand in hand with my mom out of the room toward the kitchen.

Delaney and I brush shoulders as I make my way out of the living room and she heads in to take my spot in the chair. We make eye contact for a second, and again, I try to convey to her the remorse I feel over abandoning Jenna when she probably needed us most. Delaney shoots back a timid grin that could mean anything, making me miss Jenna even more. She always seems to know what I'm thinking. Wherever she is right now, I wonder if she can sense how sorry I am, and that I wish she would just come home.

Delaney and her mom only stayed for a few more minutes after the officers left because Mrs. Burns had to get back to work. She took Delaney with because she said she could use her help with stocking and reorganizing product shelves. From what we could tell, they pretty much asked us the same questions, but Delaney and I will compare notes more thoroughly later on.

I'm about to head up to my room to do some homework when my mom stops me.

"Hey, sweetie, I need to ask you something."

"Okay? What is it?"

"Near the end of your interview, I noticed you hesitated when Detective Collins asked if there was anything else you could think of. Can you tell me why?"

I nod, close my eyes, and take a deep breath. "People have been saying that Jenna has done things with a few guys." I open my eyes just in time to catch the tail end of a mortified expression on my mom's face. Luckily, she's smart enough to know what I mean, so I don't have to spell anything out for her.

Her eyes narrow at me. "What about you? Have you . . . done anything yet?"

"No."

She's visibly relieved. "Okay, good. Now, I'm not even going to pretend to not know you've tried alcohol, but have you tried pot or any other drugs?"

"Mom," I balk, "no. I mean, I didn't even like vaping."

"So, you've vaped?"

"No," I say, shaking my head. "Well . . . yes, but it was only once, and I didn't like it. But this isn't supposed to be about me. Remember?"

Taking a deep breath, she composes herself. "Right. So, Jenna has been smoking pot?"

"And drinking way too much at parties. Like to the point that she slurs her words."

"Why in the world didn't you and Delaney try to talk some sense into her? The three of you have been like three peas in a pod since grade school. Why would she all of a sudden start doing these things? And why would she alienate herself?"

"Mom, it wasn't all of a sudden. You know she started ignoring my calls and texts like two months ago. And we've tried to stop her from doing stupid stuff a bunch of times, but she just ignored us."

"So, what about this Leighton girl? How does she factor into all of this? Do you think she's the reason Jenna started experimenting with drugs?"

"No, I told you. She started hanging out with Leighton after she started acting weird."

"Keeley, why didn't you say something? I've asked you so many times what's going on with you girls. Why didn't you tell me Jenna was having problems?"

"Because . . . we were upset with her for saying some mean things to us and for ditching out on us and being weird and . . . I don't know. She was being a crappy friend, but she was still our friend, and we didn't want to get her in trouble."

"Well, there has to be some explanation for the way she's been acting. And if this is all true, there's no way Bonnie and Joseph wouldn't have noticed. Why wouldn't they have done something about it? They could at least have had Pastor Steele or Pastor Thomas talk to her."

chapter twenty-eight

Leighton opened the door a crack at first and then a little wider when she saw it was Jenna. "Hey," she said, turning to leave. Jenna let herself in and closed the door behind her.

"What are you doing?" Jenna said as she approached Leighton at the dining room table.

"Just messing around."

Jenna leaned over Leighton's shoulder to see what was on her laptop screen. It wasn't the school's Chromebook, so Jenna knew whatever Leighton was looking at had nothing to do with their project, which was due on Monday.

Leighton glanced over at Jenna, their faces only inches apart. "Do you mind?"

Jenna shrugged as she pulled out the chair next to Leighton and started removing things from her backpack. "What's ChillChat?"

"It's a chat room site."

"Who do you chat with? And why can't you just text them?"

Leighton laughed. "Because I don't know these people, and a lot of times I hang out in group chats. You've never been in a chat room before?"

"No," Jenna replied, drawing out the "o" as if she didn't understand why it was so hard for Leighton to believe. "What's the point of talking to people you don't know?"

"Oh my God, Jenna, what's with all the questions? I don't always chat with people. A lot of times I just observe conversations. Like this one."

Leighton pointed to the screen, and Jenna scooted her chair over to have another look. "This group chat is called Devil Child because it's for families who are trying to figure out if their kids are possessed or have mental disorders."

"What? Is it a joke?"

"Nope. Some of the shit people talk about in there is super creepy. This one's pretty entertaining too," Leighton said clicking on a different group."

"Kissin' Cousins? Does that mean what I think it means?"

Leighton smiled and shrugged.

Jenna looked down at the table for a moment to compose herself. "So, do you ever just talk to one person?"

"Yeah, you can start personal chats if you want to. Like this guy," Leighton said, clicking on a conversation. "Hangman thinks I'm an aspiring actress living in L.A."

"Oh my God, Leighton, he said he wants to meet you."

"Yeah, it's time to end this thread." Leighton clicked to delete the chat and blocked Hangman, but Jenna noticed she had several other active conversations on her screen.

"Have you ever met anyone from this site in person before?"

"Yeah, a few times. And once I went to a huge group meetup at a concert. I couldn't even keep anyone's real name straight with their chat nicknames. Other than that, I just pop on here for fun sometimes. But I bet this is the only form of human interaction some of these people get. There's a group chat for everything."

"Weren't you worried that the people you met weren't who they said they were?"

"Is anyone really who they say they are?" Leighton asked in response.

Jenna shrugged and felt self-conscious that the comment was aimed at her even though she knew it wasn't.

"Seriously, though, I just don't tell anyone anything personal, and the times I've met up with people have been in public places. You can ask them to send a screenshot of a selfie with the date and time displayed too."

"Huh," Jenna said with a nod. She wondered if there were any chat rooms for people like her who'd been abused by a family member, and she made a mental note to check out the site sometime. "All right, we better get to work." Jenna moved her chair back to where it belonged.

"Do we really need to do this on a Friday night?" Leighton complained, closing her personal laptop.

"Well, it's due next week. When else would we finish the project?"

Leighton rolled her eyes.

"I told you," Jenna continued, "I don't have any other free time. I hardly have time to breathe with school and cross country."

"Fine," Leighton said. She slid the poster she'd started in front of her and surveyed the layout.

"It looks great," Jenna said. "I'll open the notes we took on Wednesday so we can see if everything important is on it."

A few minutes later, Leighton's mom emerged from the stairway. "Oh, hi, Jenna! What are you girls up to tonight?"

"Hi, Abigail. We're just finishing up a project."

"Wow, homework on a Friday night. I've never seen Leighton do that before." She gave Leighton's shoulder a squeeze as she walked past the girls toward the kitchen. Leighton rolled her eyes and kept working. Abigail continued to talk as she rummaged around in the kitchen. "Leighton, I'm going to stop at Blake's house after work tonight, but I'll be home before you wake up in the morning. Make sure you remember to lock the door if you go anywhere."

Leighton sighed. "Yeah, okay."

"Did you see you got a letter from your father? I left it on the counter for you." Abigail slid the letter onto the table next to Leighton as she breezed past on her way to the front door. "See you girls, later. Good luck with the project."

The entire time Abigail had been talking, Leighton didn't stop working on the poster, but as soon as her mom closed the door behind her, she was on her feet. She disappeared upstairs for a minute and emerged from the stairway holding a pipe to her mouth with one hand and lighting it up with the other.

"Leighton? What the hell just happened?" Jenna asked, her hands still poised on the keyboard of her Chromebook.

Leighton didn't respond. Instead, she set her pipe down on the table next to Jenna's things and picked up the letter from her dad. Then she lit the corner of it on fire as she made her way into the kitchen.

Jenna sprung out of her seat, unsure if she was seeing things or not. She turned the corner into the kitchen just in time to see Leighton holding the burning letter over the sink.

"Leighton, what are you doing?" Jenna asked, a sense of urgency in her tone.

Again, Leighton ignored her. When there was only about an inch left before the flames would reach her fingers, Leighton doused what was left of the letter under running water. She opened the cabinet under the sink and dropped the letter in the garbage, then she squeezed past Jenna and returned to the dining room for her pipe.

Jenna followed to find Leighton taking another hit from her pipe.

"Do you want some?" Leighton asked, holding out the pipe and lighter to Jenna.

"Are you serious?" Jenna asked, incredulous. "You haven't said a word to me since before your mom came downstairs, and that's what you're going to start with? How about telling me why you burned that letter from your dad and why you're always such a bitch to your mom?"

"Look, no offense, but I don't want to talk about it. Okay?"

Jenna nodded.

"So, do you want a hit or what?" Leighton held the pipe and lighter out to Jenna again.

"No," Jenna shook her head, "I can't. I have a meet tomorrow morning."

"Have you ever tried it?"

"Kind of," Jenna said with a grin.

"What do mean, *kind of?*"

"It was last year at Jolliet, the park not far from school. Delaney was the one who really wanted to do it, so she bought a joint for ten dollars from this kid at our school who sells everything."

"She got ripped off," Leighton interjected.

Jenna smiled and continued. "So, when it was my turn to take a hit, I pretty much just held the smoke in my mouth and inhaled as little as possible. I found out later that Keeley did the same thing, but Delaney really did it and was out of it. She barely said a word the rest of the night."

"Well, if you want to feel relaxed and get a good night's sleep, maybe you should try some for real. No biggie if you don't. That just means there's more for me," Leighton said, setting the pipe and lighter down on the table and sitting back down in front of the poster to finish up.

The thought of feeling relaxed and getting a good night's sleep appealed to Jenna. She liked that the Tylenol PM she'd been taking made her feel that way, but it also caused her to feel groggy in the morning, so it took her longer to get moving. "How do you feel in the morning . . . after you smoke?" she asked.

"I feel great," Leighton said, glancing over at Jenna for a second.

Jenna reached for the pipe and lighter and stared at them in her hands as she sat back down. Then she mimicked the way Leighton put the pipe to her lips and inhaled as she held the flame over the pot. Unlike the year before when she barely inhaled a thing, this time she allowed every bit of smoke possible into her lungs. It was only a few seconds before she erupted into a coughing fit, expelling the smoke in bursts.

"Geez, Jenna, take it easy. Don't inhale so much if you try it again," Leighton said, not even looking up from the poster.

Jenna's second try went much smoother, and within minutes, she was feeling calm and numb all over her body. Yet somehow, she was still able to focus on her work. She looked over at Leighton, stoned out of her mind, and secretly thanked her.

chapter twenty-nine

I'm jarred awake by something other than the daily alarm I have set on my phone. And it isn't the smell of the coffee that wakes me up. It's the sounds of my life. My two-year-old whining because he's hungry. My five-year-old arguing because he's been told to change into clothes that match. The dog barking to go outside. My wife hollering at the kids, the dog, and herself for forgetting about the wet clothes in the washing machine last night. The sound of dishes being unloaded and loaded into the dishwasher. The sound of the machine that helps my mother-in-law breathe. I wake up every morning to these sounds that are my life.

"Daddy!" my son Brady yells as he leaps into my arms. "I didn't know you were home."

"Yep. My flight got in late last night, so you were snug as a bug by the time I got here."

"Jacob, he needs to finish eating," my wife, Julie, says. She means no harm, but I still feel a twinge of resentment when she says it.

I nod and ruffle Brady's hair before he jolts back to the table to finish his Gorilla Munch. Then I adjust my tie because it feels a little tight, but it still feels constrictive even after it's loosened. I can't help but compare the feeling to my life in general.

"Oh no," Julie says, stopping to look up at the small flat-screen TV mounted above our refrigerator. Brady and I both follow her gaze because it's rare for her to take pause in the middle of our morning frenzy.

When I see the picture on the TV screen, I choke on the sip of coffee I've just taken. It's a picture of the girl I was supposed to meet on Friday night. I've only caught the tail end of what the newscaster was saying, but the caption underneath her picture is enough to make my tie feel like it's just come to life and plans to strangle the life out of me.

Missing 16-year-old Girl

Sixteen years old? No, no, no, no. She said she was nineteen.

When Jenna's picture disappears, Julie returns to her morning routine and laments over how sad the news is nowadays. Then Brady pipes in with several questions Julie couldn't possibly answer. *Why did they show that girl, Mom? Where did she go? Will the police look for her?*

Oh, God. What if they come here looking for her?

I quickly place the cap on my travel mug, grab a banana and my bag, and head for the back door.

"Jacob? The school bus will be here in five minutes. Don't you have time to walk Brady to his stop?"

"I, uh . . . I can't. I have to go," I say, rushing over to kiss Brady on the head. Then I stop at the Pack 'n Play and give my toddler son, Sam, a quick pat on the head.

"Uh, Jacob?" Julie calls out.

I look back from the door and find her tapping her cheek, so I rush back over and place a peck right above her freshly manicured nail.

When I'm finally alone in my car, I lean forward and place my forehead on the steering wheel. I think about all the things the police could find that would connect me to Jenna and realize the situation is hopeless. People are going to find out.

I lean back and reach into my bag for my phone but change my mind. Instead, I unlock the glove compartment and retrieve my other phone, figuring there's no sense incriminating myself with an Internet search to find out what they know already about Jenna.

I type in 'missing 16 yr old girl briarwood wi' and the first result is an article posted by the same local network that just aired Jenna's picture. The same photo is displayed above the article.

POLICE are seeking public assistance to help locate a 16-year-old girl

missing from Briarwood.

Jenna Kemp was last seen shortly before 9 p.m., Friday, October 27, near the 1600 block of Fairmount Avenue, and has not contacted family since.

Kemp has light brown hair and brown eyes. She's 5' 4", weighs approximately 130 pounds, and was last seen wearing black leggings and a gray Briarwood High Cross Country hoodie with navy blue trim.

Police are appealing for Jenna or anyone with further information to contact local authorities.

If you have information for police, contact the Briarwood Police Department directly at 414-555-0189 or provide information using the online form 24 hours per day.

You can report information about crime anonymously to Crime Stoppers, a registered charity and community volunteer organization, by calling 1800 222-TIPS or via www. crimestoppersusa.org 24 hours per day.

I take a few deep breaths, attempting to release some of the panic I'm feeling when I see that police are appealing for Jenna to contact local authorities. Could this mean they don't suspect anything has happened to her? Could it mean they think she ran away? I scroll down to see if there are any comments on the article and my stomach drops when I see there are already nearly a dozen. The most recent one sends me back into a crippling state of panic.

Dizzy Beaver says: When was the last time a teen from Briarwood ran away? I call FOUL PLAY. Someone knows where this girl is, and the lazy Briarwood PD is about to have a ton of pressure dropped on them if they don't find out who.

I jump and reflexively slide my burner phone between my legs when there's a knock on my window. Julie is holding Sam and peeks in at me with a hard stare. Brady smiles and waves. I wave back and then watch in my side mirror as my family walks down the driveway. This situation could turn our whole lives upside down, so I need to do damage control before it's too late.

I compose myself and then head back inside to wait for Julie.

"Jacob?" Julie hollers when she enters the house.

"In here," I say from the living room.

"What's going on? Why are you still here?"

"Can you please put Sam back in his playpen and sit down over here for a bit? I need to talk to you about something."

"Okay." She disappears into the kitchen to put Sam down to play with his toys. When she returns and takes a set next to me on the sofa, she says, "You have to make this quick, though. I need to give Mom her meds soon."

I nod and take a deep breath. "So, that missing girl they reported about this morning?"

"Yeah? It's very sad. What about her?"

"Well . . ." I turn my body a little more to face her. "I know her."

"What do you mean you know her? How's that possible?"

"Look, Julie, I did something stupid."

Julie stiffens, but she remains silent, her lips form a thin line.

"So . . ." I swallow hard and selfishly wish for a heart attack. "I've been feeling lonely. Because . . . we're always so busy with your mom and the kids, and the baby on the way. So I—"

Julie jumps up, causing me to flinch. "What are you talking about, Jacob? Just spit it all out," she says through gritted teeth.

"Okay, okay," I hold up my hands, a plea for her to calm down. "I started using this chat room a few months ago. It started out just as a way to pass the time when I was overnight for work, and then I started using it more and more and making connections with people. Jenna was someone I chatted with."

"You're having an affair with a sixteen-year-old, Jacob?" she screams.

We both look toward the kitchen where Sam fusses a little. When we hear him go back to playing with his toys, I continue.

"No, I'm not having an affair." *Not anymore.*

"Then what do you call chatting with other women—no, *GIRLS*—online? And do you know where she is? Did you have anything to do with her disappearance? Is that what you're getting at? Because I will turn you in so fast your head will spin."

"No. No, no, no." I stand and reach for her, but she recoils. "It was just innocent conversation and a sore lapse in judgement on my part. That's all. I never met any of them, and only talked to Jenna on the phone a few times."

"Ohhhh, my God, Jacob." She clutches her forehead and begins breathing heavily.

"I didn't know she was only sixteen. I swear."

"Wait, the news said she was last seen Friday night. Were you really out of town for work on Friday night?"

This is where things could turn very bad, so I don't know whether to tell her the truth this time. I need her as an alibi if it comes to that, so my answer to this question is crucial. "No. The truth is I was feeling stressed and just needed some time to myself, so I got a hotel room over in Brown Deer, just to decompress." *Thank God I paid cash.*

"So why are you telling me this?"

"Because they'll probably look into her social media accounts if she isn't located soon, which means they'll probably find out I was talking to her . . ."

"And what? You want me to lie for you? Say you were here all night?" She asks, tears now streaming down her cheeks. "How can I do that when you could be lying to me? When you could have had something to do with her disappearance?

"That's ridiculous. I wouldn't—"

"You wouldn't what?"

"I wouldn't hurt someone. You know that."

"Do I, though? I didn't know you were making connections with other people behind my back—behind our *children's* backs," she seethes. "Hell, I didn't even know you were lonely. I thought things were fine with us."

"Please, Julie. Think about how bad this will look if they find out I stayed in a hotel that night and lied to you about having to work. I swear. I just had to clear my head. Don't let this tear our family apart," I plead.

"You've done that all on your own, Jacob," Julie says as she storms off into the kitchen, leaving me by myself on my knees in the middle of the living room floor.

chapter thirty

"Hey, Corbin," Jenna leaned into him and whispered, "can I have some?" They were at Jolliet, and Jenna had been with her friends just moments before. She knew right away what Corbin was doing when she spotted him all by himself on a log on the outskirts of the tree line.

He exhaled all the smoke in his mouth and then looked over at her, their faces only a few inches apart "Dude, you're not gonna freak out like you did that one night, are you?" He looked around to make sure no one else was near them and then scanned their group of friends about twenty yards away to make sure no one was watching.

"Corbin, I'll be fine." She hoped he'd share his pot with her because she badly needed something to calm her nerves, and the two beers she already drank didn't seem to be helping at all. She knew right away when Keeley found her way over to Eli within minutes of their arrival that it was going to be a rough night. If she'd known Eli was going to be there, she'd have declined going to the outing at Jolliet or asked if she could use her parents' car. At least then she could have left whenever she wanted to, but now she was stuck watching Keeley and Eli flirt with each other.

Corbin handed her the joint, and she inhaled her first drag with caution. She didn't want to embarrass herself by hacking up a lung like she had the night before at Leighton's. Her second drag was much deeper and produced the effect she was hoping for. She handed the joint back to Corbin and stayed put next to him on the log. She wished she could just sit there in that spot for the next two hours until Delaney and Keeley were ready to go, but she knew that would never happen.

"So, where's Dustin?" Corbin asked.

Jenna exhaled a sigh. She hadn't seen Dustin the night before because he'd gone to a Brewers game with his dad at Miller Park, and that night, he'd agreed to work a late shift at the bike shop. "Working. Apparently. There's an indoor triathlon going on at Marquette next weekend so the bike shop is crazy busy."

Corbin nodded and passed the joint back to Jenna. She wondered if maybe two hits were enough for her, but she took it anyway. Just as she was passing it back to Corbin, Delaney and Tina approached, both giggling and walking erratically. Neither of them was drunk. It was simply the result of two silly girls high on life and being in their teens.

"What are you two doing over here all alone?" Tina asked in a sing-song voice.

"Yeah, what's going on here?" Delaney said in mock accusation.

Corbin laughed, and smoke from his mouth wafted toward the girl. Tina waved a hand in front of her face and made a fake gagging noise, which made Corbin chase her around blowing his weed breath in her face as the pair made their way back to the rest of the group.

Delaney took a seat next to Jenna and whispered, "Did I see you take a hit off Corbin's joint?"

"Maybe," Jenna responded dully, too stoned to lie.

"Jenna," Delaney scolded, "what the heck is up with you lately? Dustin is going to be pissed if he finds out."

"Then don't tell him."

"Pft. You know I won't. But I think Tina might have seen too."

If Jenna hadn't been feeling so relaxed, she might have been worried, but her train of thought had already switched tracks. "So, is Keeley still throwing herself at my cousin?"

Delaney laughed, and Jenna tilted her head slightly, wondering if her friend thought she was only pretending to be irritated by it. Or was it possible that she hadn't said it the way she thought she did? Her brain felt numb, so maybe that was it.

"Oh, it isn't just Keeley. Eli's putting on the moves too. Keeley probably wants to tell you this herself, but he just asked her to homecoming!"

"Wh—" Jenna began but never finished because Delaney started going on and on about homecoming. *Where do you and Dustin want to eat beforehand? Should we get a limo? I think Corbin is going to ask me, and I heard Tommy was going to ask Tina tonight too, so the ten of us can probably go in on one together. We'll need to go dress shopping either tomorrow or next weekend.*

The next two hours passed by in a blur for Jenna thanks to the fact that she was high as a kite and had managed to snag a fourth beer from some seniors who'd shown up. When Delaney and Jenna made it back to the group, Keeley and Eli immediately broke the news about homecoming to Jenna—Keeley did anyway while Eli stood next to her hoping Jenna wouldn't be a jerk about it. He had been walking on eggshells around his cousin since school started, and he was praying that she'd eventually lose the chip on her shoulder, whatever it was about. Jenna continued to ignore Eli but acted happy for her friend who'd never been to a high school dance with a date before, not because no one ever asked her but because she never wanted to go with anyone before. As sick as the thought of Thomas' look-alike going out with her best friend made her, she didn't want to steal Keeley's joy, so she stuffed her anger and disgust and acted like nothing was wrong—until her friends were ready to leave.

"Hey, you guys ready to go?" Keeley asked Delaney and Jenna. She was standing in front of them, holding Eli's hand. "I'm going to drop Eli off too. I hope you guys don't mind."

Delaney nodded and said, "I'll meet you over by the trail in a minute." Then she looked over at Corbin, whose lap she was sitting on. They made plans to go to the mall the next day and said their goodbyes. Apparently, he'd asked her to homecoming and Jenna had missed it, and apparently, Delaney was ditching Jenna and Keeley to go dress shopping with Corbin instead.

Jenna wanted nothing more than to go home at that point, but there was no way she was getting in a car with Eli. "Actually," she said, standing, "I want to stay a little longer, so I think I'll get a ride with someone else."

"Who?" Keeley seemed upset.

"I don't know." As Jenna looked around at the people who were still there, a senior named Jayson spoke up.

"I can give you a ride home, Kemp."

"I'm getting a ride home with Jayson," she told a flabbergasted Keeley.

"Well . . . why? I don't—"

"Come on, let's just go. If she wants to stay longer, let her stay longer," Eli said, giving Jenna a disappointed look and pulling Keeley to leave.

To Jenna's surprise, Keeley left without another word. Jenna knew if Eli hadn't been with her, there was no way Keeley would have left her like that. By the time Delaney found out Jenna had decided to stay, they were already well on their way back to the car. And shortly after her friends were gone, Jenna was on her way to a party on the East side with Jayson and his two friends.

The moment they walked through the door of the house on Hampton Avenue, Jenna wished she'd made Jayson take her home instead. Not only was the crowd a lot rougher than the one she normally hung out with, but she was starting to feel nauseous from the four beers she'd drank. As she looked around the dark, crowded, smoke-filled room, she wondered what the hell they were doing at a party like this anyway.

"Jayson!" she yelled above the hardcore punk music that was blaring throughout the entire first floor. "What are we doing here?"

He leaned into Jenna and was about to say something in her ear when Lou Tang appeared. Knowing that answered Jenna's question, Jayson backed away from her and greeted Lou. Then he turned back to Jenna and yelled, "Be right back!" before following Lou into a room just off the living room.

Great, Jenna thought as she looked around for the most likely place for a bathroom. There were way too many bodies blocking the hallway just past the room Lou, Jayson, and the other guys had gone into, so she decided to head straight up the stairs. There had to be a bathroom on the second floor. When she rounded the corner at the top, she came face to face with a tall guy with spikey black hair and gauges in his ears. Based on his appearance, she wasn't expecting the soft, medium-pitched voice that came out of his mouth.

"Whoa. Let me get outta your way, girl." He lengthened his body and held up his hands, careful not to bump into Jenna as she tried to move around him.

As Jenna squeezed past him, she heard her name. "Jenna?"

"Leighton? Oh my God! I'm so glad to see you." Jenna threw her arms around a stiff Leighton who gave her a few slow pats on the back and then pulled away.

"You smell like beer . . . I can't stand beer."

"Ahem . . ." the guy Jenna nearly collided with interjected, "Excuse me, but aren't you going to introduce me to your hottie friend here?"

Jenna eyed the guy, unsure whether she should be offended that he'd called her a hottie.

"Don't worry. He's gay," Leighton said, rolling her eyes. "Sticks, this is Jenna. Jenna, Sticks. Okay, can I use the bathroom now?"

Sticks surprised Jenna with a hug. "Nice to meet you, girl. I wasn't playing before. In case no one told you today, you're gorgeous."

"Thanks," Jenna said, smiling for the first time that night.

"Leighton, I need fresh air stat. Meet you at the car." With a parting peace sign, he headed down the stairs.

"What the hell are you doing here, Jenna?" Leighton said, leaning against the wall. She was third in line for the bathroom. Jenna stepped behind her and leaned too.

"I was wondering the same thing."

"Don't tell me the rest of your friends are here too?" Leighton raised an eyebrow.

"No, just me with a couple of seniors who are downstairs in a room with Lou Tang doing who knows what. I can't believe they're my ride home."

"Sticks can drive you home if you want. We're leaving as soon as I GET INTO THE BATHROOM!" Leighton screamed the last bit causing everyone in line to look back at her, but they were all too messed up to react.

Jenna laughed for the second time that night, but her amusement was short-lived because a text from Dustin came through.

DUSTIN: I STOPPED AT JOLLIET. WHERE ARE YOU? DID YOU REALLY LEAVE WITH JAYSON MORRIS??

"What's wrong?" Leighton asked, peeking at Jenna's screen. "Whoops. Your boyfriend sounds mad."

Jenna contemplated whether to respond to Dustin by text right then or call him when she left the party, but she became distracted when the first person in line for the bathroom started pounding on the door. Then the second person started pounding too. After about a minute straight of pounding, a guy with his pants half off and a girl holding her shirt against her naked chest stumbled out. "Get a room next time," the person in front of Leighton mumbled.

Jenna watched as they stumbled down the hall to a closed door right across from where she and Leighton were standing. The guy opened the door wide, revealing another couple messing around. "Ooops, sorry," the guy mumbled as he closed the door.

The sight of the couple in the room made Jenna feel even more ill than she already did. It was the same feeling she'd get when she thought about what happened to her or when she was at church and at risk of bumping into Thomas. Jenna cupped a hand over her forehead and squeezed her temples.

Leighton stopped laughing at the clumsy couple making their way farther down the hall when she noticed Jenna's change in demeanor. "Why are you all pink and sweaty?"

"It's nothing. I just . . . they were . . ." Jenna glanced up at the closed door across from her and Leighton.

"Getting it on? Yeah, that's what people do at parties like this. Are you telling me you and What's His Name have never—"

Jenna shook her head.

"Well, how long have you been dating?"

"Officially, it's been about a year. Unofficially . . . three years I guess."

"Well, he's not going to wait for you forever."

"What do you mean by that?" Jenna asked, knowing full well what Leighton meant. It was something Jenna had been paranoid about, especially with her issue with being physical with Dustin.

Leighton shrugged and entered the bathroom. It was finally her turn.

While Jenna waited, she decided that Leighton was probably right. Then she wondered if she smoked a little pot the next time she and Dustin were alone if maybe she'd be relaxed enough to go through with it. And then maybe as soon as she replaced the horrible memories that had plagued her all these years with a good one, she'd be better able to forget what happened to her. But would it ever be a good experience for her? Or would she never be able to be intimate with anyone and have it be an enjoyable experience?

Her phone vibrated again.

DUSTIN: WHAT'S GOING ON WITH YOU? DID YOU SMOKE POT AGAIN?

DUSTIN: DON'T BOTHER CALLING OR TEXTING ME TONIGHT.

Jenna quickly lowered her phone when the bathroom door opened. "You're up," Leighton said. "Make sure you hover."

September 17, 2017

Dear Diary,

The only good thing going for me right now is that I got out of going to church today. Everything else is a mess. Dustin and I are arguing. Keeley is dating Eli. My miles are taking longer and longer. I can't sleep without taking a pill, or drinking, or smoking. I just want to go back to the way it was before they moved back. Trust me, I know how crazy that sounds. But before I was at least getting along with my friends, I liked going to church, and I was still running strong.

Speaking of Dustin, he finally answered the third time I called him this morning. But the conversation didn't go well. He hates that I smoked pot (even though he's done it a bunch of times), he can't believe I went to a party with a bunch of "losers," and he thinks Leighton is a bad influence because she happened to be there. It didn't even matter that she's the one who rescued me and got me a ride home last night. And it didn't even matter that I admitted it was a bad idea for me to go with Jayson. He had the nerve to tell me that I need to start making better decisions. Who is he now? My father?! Or should I say my mother? He actually sounded a lot like her.

The thing that really pisses me off is that Dustin has no clue what's really going on with me, and the way he's acting is making it worse. I know it's kind of irrational for me to be mad at him, and Keeley for liking Eli, and Eli for wanting to hang out with my friends, but what am I supposed to do?

Gather everyone together and tell them exactly why I'm not acting like the Jenna they think they know?

You know what? I take back what I said earlier about the only good thing being that I didn't have to go to church today. There's also Leighton. At least she makes me feel like I don't have to pretend to be someone I'm not.

~Jenna

chapter thirty-one

The sky is the most brilliant shade of blue I've ever seen, and it's dotted with huge puffy clouds. Perfect for bunny rabbits, I think to myself. Wait, I'm not alone. I look to the right. Delaney is pointing to the sky and laughing, but there isn't any sound coming from her mouth. I look to the left. Jenna has a sad smile on her face. It must be one of those days for her. She's hugging her diary to her chest. I don't say anything to her because she'd rather just spin when she isn't feeling happy. And if there's anything I've learned over the years, it's that a good spin can solve any problem. I reach over to pat her hand, but there's nothing there. I look over at her again, and sure enough, she's still hugging her diary. I reach out again, keeping an eye on her hand to ensure I make contact this time. But when I should be feeling the warmth of her skin, I feel nothing. There's nothing there. I turn back to Delaney to ask if she can see Jenna, but all of a sudden, the merry-go-round picks up speed, and I'm forced to close my eyes to avoid getting sick. When I open them, I'm sitting at a table in the cafeteria at school.

"Stay away from my family!" Jenna's face is red, and specks of spit fall onto the table as she screams.

Everyone except Delaney, Eli, and I either pulls their lunch trays back to avoid further contamination or stands and backs away from the table.

"Jenna, why are you screaming?" Eli asks, his hands raised in a defensive pose.

"Why am I screaming? If anyone should know, it should be you, you . . . you disgusting piece of shit! Why, Eli? Why are you here?"

"Jenna, calm down. Otherwise—"

"*Otherwise, what?*" *She hisses at me.* "*Otherwise, I'm going to get in trouble for making a scene? Well, guess what. I don't care!*" *She leans in close to me and whispers,* "*And you need to stay away from my family too.*" *Her expression is softer now and the tear that streaks down her cheek tastes salty. How is it possible that I can taste her tear? Wait, I'm tasting my own tears. I'm crying, and now everyone is looking at me instead of Jenna.*

"*See, I told you she was going crazy,*" *Delaney says. She stands and joins the crowd surrounding us. Then she looks at Jenna and says,* "*You're not my friend anymore. I don't have to listen to you. I can babysit for whoever I want, and I can be friends with whoever I want.*" *She holds out her hands, and in a blink, Eli is holding one and Dustin is holding the other.*

"*Come on, Jenna. Let's get out of here.*" *The crowd surrounding us, which is now five students deep, parts where Delaney, Eli, and Dustin are standing, and Leighton squeezes through.* "*These aren't your friends anymore. I'm your only friend now.*"

"*It's time to wake up, Keeley,*" *Jenna says as she slowly backs away from me. I look around and find that I'm the only person still sitting at the table.*

"*Jenna, wait.*" *I look back to where she was standing, but somehow, she's already standing next to Leighton and clutching her diary to her chest.*

"*You need to wake up,*" *she says.*

"*What?*" *I ask her, confused.*

"*WAKE UP, KEELEY!*"

"I'm already awake," I mumble as I open my eyes. "Oh, crap," I say, throwing off my covers and stumbling to my feet. I grab my alarm clock and squint at the flashing red numbers. "What time is it?" I throw the clock down on my bed and rush to my desk to check my phone. "Seven fifteen?" I yell.

"Keeley! Are you up?" My mom shoves my door all the way open and rushes to pull back my curtains. Sunlight pours into my room nearly blinding me.

I bring my fists to my eyes and stumble as I head to my dresser. That's when I notice the moisture around my eyes and cheeks. I also bump my nightstand, causing the scrapbook Jenna made for me for my fifteenth birthday to fall to the floor.

"The power went out last night. Hurry up. I'll drive you to school," she says as she scurries toward the door. "I don't understand why your father didn't wake me to tell me about the power or at least reset my clock before he left . . ." Her voice trails off as she heads down the hallway and continues to talk to herself.

I scoop up the scrapbook and place it back on my nightstand, wondering if looking at it before I fell asleep last night has anything to do with the dream I had. There's no time now, but I need to try to remember everything from the dream later. What if it meant something?

As I get ready for school, all I can think about is Jenna's diary. I'd forgotten about it until now, but she's always writing in one—ever since we were in third grade. Maybe there's a clue that explains what's going on with her or where she went. I make a mental note to ask Mrs. Kemp if she's seen the most current one. Of course, if she knows where it is, they've probably already thought to look at it or given it to the police. Or, if prayers really do work, maybe Jenna will be at school today.

As I head down the hallway to the bathroom, I cross my fingers on my left hand the way we used to when we were kids and I don't uncross them until I hop into my mom's car. That's another thing we used to do, cross our fingers for as long as possible in hopes that the longer we had them crossed, the more powerful the effect would be. It worked when we hoped we'd end up in the same fifth-grade class and when we hoped Delaney would make the cheerleading squad last year and a whole bunch of other times. I know these thoughts are childish, but I don't care. It has to work this time too. Then again, maybe the magic of crossing our fingers only works when all three of us combine our efforts.

I have never been late for school before, but I guess there's a first time for everything. When my mom pulls her Nissan to the curb, I debate telling her I don't feel well and asking if she could turn the car around and drop me off at home. Except for when I'm running, having the attention of a lot of people scares me to death, so the thought of walking into first-period psychology has my stomach in knots.

"Looks like we weren't the only ones who got a late start this morning. Maybe others had their power go out last night too." She nods toward the main entrance where several others are straggling in. I stare at the front door and watch as they all disappear inside. "What's wrong?"

The words 'I'm sick' are on the tip of my tongue, but then a vision from my dream pops into my head. I see Leighton standing next to Jenna, and I have a sudden urge to talk to her again, to press her for anything she might have neglected to tell Delaney and me on Saturday. I open my door a crack as I look over at my mom. "Nothing. I'm fine."

She leans over and gives me a hug and a kiss on the cheek. "Have a good day, honey." She turns and places her hand on the shifter, ready to leave.

"Thanks," I whisper, diverting my gaze out the window at the large brick sign in front of our school. *Not unless Jenna's here. God, please let her be here.*

"Keel? You okay?" I feel her eyes on me again.

"Mom?"

"Yeah?"

"Do you think she's in there?" I know she doesn't know the answer, but I ask anyway because the little girl in me will always believe my mom has all the answers, that she can solve any problem.

"You mean Jenna?"

I nod and look over at her just in time to see her face tense up.

She swallows hard. Then, as she breaks eye contact with me, she says, "I don't think so, sweetie. I'm sure Bonnie would have let us know if she turned up last night."

We sit in silence while the late bell rings, signifying I'll need to stop in the office for a pass.

I take a deep breath and open my door all the way. "I'm going to run the track after school, so I'll be home a little late. Thanks for the ride." I sneak a smile her way before hopping out of the car and hustling up the stairs to the front doors.

I appreciate the way my mom isn't one to sugarcoat things. But maybe, just this once, she could have made an exception.

The atmosphere in my first-period psych class feels different today. In fact, the entire path to the office for my late slip, to my locker, and then to class seems off. I shrug the feeling away, thinking it's probably because I'm disoriented from being late. Or is it possible the news that Jenna is missing has already spread to all our classmates?

When I walk into class, people are arranged in groups scattered around the room—some standing, some sitting—all too preoccupied to notice me. Even Mr. Sartorius is busy tapping away on his laptop. I place my late slip on the corner of his desk. "Sorry I'm late."

He looks up quickly but doesn't say anything, which is uncharacteristic of Stickler Sartorius. He stares at me for so long, I begin to wonder if there are crumbs from the breakfast bar I ate in the car on my face.

I sweep the back of my hand across my lips and then say, "For some reason, our power went out, so our alarms didn't go—"

"Oh, don't worry about it, Keeley," he says as he waves off my excuse. I don't think I've ever heard him speak this kindly to anyone before.

"Okay, well, should I just . . ." I begin backing away slowly. ". . . join a group and find out what the assignment is?"

"Hold on." He waves me forward, so I backtrack to where I had been standing beside his desk.

Whispering, he says, "How are you doing?"

So, he knows.

"Um . . ." I feel eyes on me now. "I'm fine."

"Well, if you need to talk, just know that I'm here. Okay?"

But what exactly does he know?

"About?"

"About Jenna. We were informed of her disappearance at an emergency staff meeting this morning, and a couple of police officers are interviewing teachers and students in Coach Jeffries' office. I know the two of you are close. Don't let it get you down. You're a good student." With a lazy grin, he goes back to clicking away on his laptop.

His intentions might be good, but I want nothing more than to knock the mug of coffee into his lap. Don't let it get me down? Well, thanks for bringing it up.

"I won't." I turn and quickly walk to the nearest group, praying that Sartorius doesn't call me back for anything and never offers me another pep talk again.

Aside from talking to Tina for a few minutes, I spend the remainder of class avoiding unnecessary eye contact with anyone and doing my best to focus on my group's task at hand—to come up with an argument for rehabilitation as opposed to prison for non-violent drug-related offenses. It's hard for me to concentrate, though, because I sense a lot of staring in my direction and off-task whispering going on within the other groups. It makes me anxious. Could *everyone* know Jenna is missing? There's no way they would have already announced it to the entire school. Has she been gone long enough for them to do that?

The rest of the morning drags. I get some of the same long, piteous stares from a few more teachers but still no direct questions or comments from anyone besides Tina, who wanted to know if I'd been interviewed by the police already.

When lunch finally rolls around, I'm dying to see Delaney. I wonder if teachers are treating her weird too. As I approach our table, the glance we share gives me my answer. Delaney looks tired, and her expression is flat, unlike her usual chipper self. Dustin is sitting on the other side of the table as far away from Delaney as possible. The only person talking is Emily Davis, which is no surprise at all. Whenever she snags a spot next to Eli, no one can get a word in edgewise with him. But it is unusual for the rest of the table to be so quiet.

Delaney waves and picks up her bag to make room for me between her and Emily.

Great.

As I make my way around the circular table, everyone greets me with a hey or a nod.

Eli glances over his shoulder at me before I pass behind him and Emily. Emily ignores me, leaning in closer and talking louder to Eli, eager for him to turn his attention back to her.

At least *she's* acting normal today.

I sigh quietly when I maneuver into my seat because I notice the way Eli and Emily are sitting hip to hip. I know Eli will always be off limits to me, but I still feel a twinge of jealousy. I'm also still irritated that Emily moved in on him so fast after Jenna's outburst when she made it clear to everyone within earshot that not only was she not cool with Eli "weaseling his way into our group" but she also didn't want Eli and I having anything to do with each other. It was a week after Eli had asked me to homecoming, so now I've still never been to homecoming with a date.

Emily looks over at me, and I hope the piece of chocolate she's just popped in her mouth results in a big pimple on her nose.

"Why is everyone so quiet?"

Delaney stares at me for a second then asks, "Keeley, haven't you heard the rumors?"

"What are you talking about?"

"The cops have been here talking to kids all morning, and now there are even more stupid rumors flying around about Jenna." She narrows her eyes and glances around the table at everyone.

"Sartorius told me about the cops, but what rumors?" I ask.

"That maybe Jenna overdosed on something. Or maybe she witnessed a drug deal gone bad and is buried in a cornfield somewhere. Maybe she ran away . . ."

"Well, I was late this morning, so this is the first I'm hearing any of it. I sure hope people aren't telling the police that junk, though." As I unscrew the cap from a bottle of water and take a drink, I glance around the table. Everyone diverts their eyes, even Dustin.

Delaney is looking at me, but instead of agreeing with me, she takes a bite of a granola bar.

"Wait, does anyone here think any of those rumors could be true?"

"Well . . . she was doing drugs," Tina says, glancing over at Corbin who's staring at the table.

"And she was drinking a lot too," Lisa adds.

"Right, but she got most of the alcohol and drugs she did from Corbin. So . . . are you aware of anyone ever overdosing on pot? Were you recently involved in any drug deals gone bad? I mean, give me a break."

"Well, she still could have run away," Delaney says.

I don't even have time to convey my disbelief to her with a look because then Dustin adds his two cents, which shocks me even more.

"Come on, Keeley, how can you blame anyone for wondering if those things are possible with the way Jenna has been acting?"

Almost everyone nods their agreement, and suddenly I find myself nodding too. Because after what Tyson told me, I guess anything is possible now with Jenna.

"You're never late. What happened?" Delaney asks loudly, changing the subject.

I can sense everyone's relief.

"Our power went out last night, so no one's alarm went off. Well, except for my dad's because he uses his phone."

"Yeah, ours went out too," Tommy pipes in.

"Ours too," Eli says, making eye contact with me, holding my gaze a little too long for my liking considering the audience. Everyone knows we liked each other before Jenna made it clear that she wasn't okay with us dating.

"Hm, wonder why," Delaney shrugs.

"Who knows. They're renovating that gas station over on Silver Spring. Maybe workers hit a power line," Tommy offers.

"They don't build gas stations in the middle of the night, doofus,"

Delaney jokes, and everyone laughs. Even me. Except I'm just going through the motions.

The banter prompts several side conversations. Plans are being made for the upcoming weekend. Basketball game. Party at Emily's. That's when I see Leighton toss her tray in the trash and head for the door.

"I have to use the bathroom. Be right back," I say to Delaney as I hop up to chase after Leighton. Delaney's disappointed voice follows me, but I don't have time to stop and explain what I'm really doing, especially not in front of everyone. Eli is staring at me again when I glance back. I don't have time to worry about that either. I'm desperate to catch up to Leighton.

When I turn the corner, the hallway is empty, so I cross over to the girls' bathroom. The door squeaks when I pull it open, like it always does, except the silence amplifies it. No one is at the sinks, so I crouch down and scan for feet. Nothing. I'm about to turn and head back to the lunch room when footsteps approach.

I stand and turn around at the same time, putting up my forearms in defense.

"What the hell? Wait . . . did you think I was attacking you or something?" Leighton laughs.

Dropping my arms, I exhale my panic. "No. No, I . . . you snuck up on me." I roll my eyes and cross my arms. "What were you doing hiding in the corner, anyway?"

Her smile fades. "Why are you following me?"

"What are you talking about? I wasn't. I had to go to the bathroom."

"Yeah, okay," she says with a scoff as she moves to step around me.

"Wait," I say, putting both of my hands up, hoping to temporarily eliminate the passive-aggressive barrier that divides us.

"What do you want?"

"Did the police talk to you yet?"

"Yeah. So?"

"Well, what did you tell them?"

"I told them Jenna had been meeting people in a chat room, and one of the guys was starting to creep her out."

"Why? What did he do?"

"She just said he wouldn't stop messaging her and kept asking to meet her in person."

Delaney bursts through the door. "There you two are." She walks over and stands next to me so we're both facing Leighton.

"Oh, great," Leighton mumbles.

"Well, was she talking to other guys in this chat room? And why didn't you tell Delaney and I about this when we talked to you on Saturday?"

"Wait, what chat room?" Delaney asks. "And yeah, why didn't you tell us about it on Saturday?"

"Just stop, both of you. Because it wasn't any of your business. It still isn't."

"Well, I'm glad you told the police. Will you tell us where she was going when she left your house now?"

"Again, not your business," she says, shaking her head.

"Are you kidding me?" Delaney snarls, but Leighton acts like she didn't even hear her.

"Leighton, do you not care at all that Jenna still hasn't shown up? Do you even care about her at all? Are you capable of caring about anyone?" My voice gets louder and louder until I practically scream the last question.

Leighton's nostrils flare and, for a second, I'm afraid she's going to slap me. I take a step back. But to mine and Delaney's surprise, her shoulders slump, and she backs away until she's up against the wall. Then she slides down onto the floor. "Yes, I care."

Delaney and I look at each other, both of us stunned. Then we move closer to Leighton and crouch down in front of her.

"Then if there's anything else you haven't told us or the police already, you really need to."

Leighton closes her eyes, grips her temples, and sighs heavily. Suddenly her eyes snap open. "I saw her writing in a fancy notebook a few times, on the nights she slept over."

"Oh my God. That's so weird. I had this dream, and Jenna was holding her diary in it. And she was with you," I say, looking at Leighton.

"So, do you think we should try to find her diary?" Delaney asks.

"That's actually a good idea," I say.

"Don't you think they would have already checked her diary or handed it over to the police?" Leighton asks, sliding her back up the wall until she's standing. Delaney and I follow suit and stand too.

"Maybe," I say, realizing Leighton is probably right. "But we should still take a look, just in case."

"Okay, so where is it and how do we get it?" Delaney asks.

"Well, it must be in her room somewhere, so we could go over and talk to Mrs. Kemp today after school. Then maybe one of us could sneak into her room and grab it?"

"Wait, but if the police haven't already seen it, don't you think they'd want it?"

"Yeah, you're probably right, but I still feel like we should look at it first. Just in case there's something in there that'll help us figure out what's been going on with her, something the cops and her parents might not understand."

"Okay, then I'll ditch out of cheer practice, and we'll go tonight," Delaney says. Then she looks at Leighton. "Do you want to go?

"Sorry, but you guys are on your own if you plan to snoop around in Jenna's room."

chapter thirty-two

After the argument Jenna and Dustin had gotten into the weekend before, things had been strained between them. He was taking longer to return her texts, he skipped walking to history class with her twice, he didn't make an effort to sit next to her during lunch, and he seemed distant the night before when they'd watched a movie at her house. She knew it was because she'd been drinking carelessly and smoked pot at Jolliet, but she also wondered if he was beginning to tire of having a girlfriend who tensed at his touch and never seemed to be any closer to taking their physical relationship any further. So Jenna swore to herself she'd do her best to fix things. She couldn't risk losing Dustin because of her past. She'd try harder to pretend nothing was wrong, that she wasn't riddled with anxiety and fear. She'd make it all up to Dustin somehow, starting with accompanying him to Tommy's second annual pre-homecoming bash. To prepare, she'd smoked some of the pot she'd purchased from Lou after school on Friday.

Two hours into the party, things were going great. Dustin had driven Jenna, Delaney, and Keeley, and the four had a blast playing an intense game of Tippy Cup, a popular party game among their classmates. Jenna tried to show Dustin that she had taken his suggestion to start making better decisions to heart, so she drank water when their team lost a round and didn't give in to the hecklers encouraging her to switch to beer. For the first time in weeks, it seemed like things were getting back on track, minus the pot she'd consumed earlier without anyone's knowledge.

"Hey, I need to use the bathroom," Jenna said to her friends who were now gathered near the Tippy Cup table as spectators.

"Oh, I'll go with you," Keeley said.

"Me too," Delaney added.

"Well then, I'll just stay here and save our spot in line." Dustin leaned over, meaning to kiss Jenna's check, but she surprised him by turning to catch his lips with hers.

"Boom chicka wowow," Delaney mumbled, making Jenna laugh.

When the girls returned, Dustin was no longer watching Tippy Cup, so they went looking for him.

As they circulated, Jenna and Keeley lost track of Delaney in the kitchen where a group of girls were talking about making appointments to get their hair and nails done for homecoming the following weekend. Delaney had to do her best to send some business her mom's way. Then Jenna lost track of Keeley in the living room when someone in her psych class asked her about something. When Jenna turned the corner to the back hallway leading to the basement, she ran into Eli who happened to be holding a beer that spilled down the front of her shirt.

"Oh, man. I'm so sorry," he said, quickly setting down his half-empty red Solo cup and dabbing the front of Jenna's shirt with his sleeve.

Mortified, Jenna stumbled backward and tripped over someone's shoes. Whoever it was caught her clumsily, and she felt hands touching her breasts as they both fell to the floor.

"Jenna, I'm sorry. I didn't realize that was you," Eli said, moving forward and extending a hand to help pull her off of the person she'd fallen on.

But Jenna didn't want to touch Eli, nor did she want to be in the lap of the person who'd just groped her, so she ignored the apologies that were coming at her, crawled her way past Eli, and stumbled to her feet. She staggered a few feet and disappeared down the basement stairs. When she emerged into the rec room, she smelled pot and knew right away she needed more. She scanned the room, and when she spotted Corbin, she took off in his direction.

The next thing Jenna knew, she was leading Dustin upstairs.

"Jenna, where are we going? Slow down."

She heard his voice but nothing he said registered because she only had one thing on her mind.

"What are we—"

Jenna leaned up and pressed her lips to Dustin's as she closed the door of the room they'd just entered with her foot. Dustin continued trying to talk for a few seconds, but then he gave up and started kissing Jenna back. Then next thing Jenna knew, they were on the bed. Then her shirt was off. Then Dustin's shirt was off. Then she was unbuttoning his pants.

"Whoa . . . Jenna, hang on . . . Jenna, *stop*," he finally demanded.

But Jenna was lost in a pot-induced haze, and just below that haze was the memory of Eli wiping the front of her shirt and an unknown person grabbing her breasts. She didn't know if either incident was an accident, but she didn't care anymore. Lurking even deeper was Leighton's warning that Dustin wouldn't wait much longer for her, and even further below that was Thomas. She was determined to do what she had to do to take as much power away from her memories of him as she could, and the thing that made sense that moment was having sex with Dustin. It seemed like the only solution to her problems.

"Dustin, I'm ready," Jenna whispered in his ear.

"No, Jenna, we can't. Not like this. Not here."

"Come on, Dustin. Yes, we can."

"Jenna," Dustin forcefully grabbed and pulled her hand from inside his boxers, "stop. Why are you doing this? Just stop."

Stunned by his rejection, she looked him in the eyes and what first felt like sadness morphed into anger.

"Wait, are you high?" Dustin shot to his feet, zipped his pants and grabbed his shirt off the bed where Jenna remained glaring at him. "This is ridiculous, Jenna. What the heck is going on with you?" He threw on his shirt and walked toward the door.

"Dustin, wait . . ." she called after him. He turned back to face her but remained silent. "I thought this was what you wanted."

Dustin shook his head. "Trust me, it is, but what I want even more is you and for you to want me back. But apparently you need to be high or drunk in order to feel that way. This is just . . . I think we need a break."

When Dustin turned and left the room, Jenna ran after him, yelling as she followed him down the stairs.

"You're breaking up with me? *You're* . . . breaking up . . . with *me*? Dustin, wait! Fine . . ." Jenna looked around at the faces staring up at her, among them were Delaney, Corbin, Tina, and Haley Tompkins. Then when she looked to the right into the living room, there was an additional sea of faces looking at her, including Keeley and Eli.

"This is all your fault," Jenna yelled, pointing at Eli. Then she ran down the rest of the stairs and got in his face. "Why do you have to be here? Why are you trying to steal my best friend? Why, Eli? Haven't you done enough to me? Why do you protect your brother?"

"Jenna, I don't know what you're talking about." Eli tried to grip Jenna's upper arms, but she jerked away from him.

"Keep your hands off me."

"Jenna," Keeley pleaded, "why are you so hysterical? What happened up there?"

"Shut up, Keeley, just shut up, and stay away from my cousin," Jenna mumbled under her breath. Her hurtful words were met with Keeley's wide devastated eyes, but Jenna didn't care. She had reached an emotional breaking point that wouldn't be easy to return from.

Done with Eli and Keeley, Jenna rushed to the kitchen where she knew there was a keg. Moments later, Dustin entered the room along with Keeley, Delaney, and Eli. Delaney lunged forward to rip the beer from Jenna's hands as she was poised to take a drink. For the second time that night, beer spilled down the front of Jenna's shirt.

"You're such a bitch, Delaney. And you wonder why girls sometimes seem like they don't want to talk to you. I'll tell you why. It's because you're a bitch and you have to flirt with EVERY guy you meet."

"Okay," Dustin held up a hand to Delaney preventing her from responding to Jenna's horrible words, "Jenna, you don't need anything to drink. You just need to go home."

"Well, I'm not going home with you. You dumped me, remember?"

"Fine, then find someone else to drive you home, but if you don't do it soon, I'm calling your mom to come and get you."

Jenna glared at him, not believing his threat, and one by one Dustin and the rest of her friends exited the kitchen. She was left standing there, her shirt soaked with beer, and people awkwardly distancing themselves from her. Embarrassed and disoriented, she made her way into the first-floor bathroom just off the kitchen and texted the only person she could think of who hadn't let her down.

JENNA: CAN YOU PLEASE COME AND GET ME?

LEIGHTON: SURE. WHERE ARE YOU?

JENNA: ONE SEC.

Jenna went into Google Maps and retrieved her location, then texted it to Leighton. Then she left the bathroom and snuck out without anyone noticing. Before she scurried past the living room, she peeked around the corner and spotted Delaney whispering in Dustin's ear. The sight made her want to puke as she recalled how Delaney always used to say how cute Dustin was and what a catch he was. Now the door was wide open for her to have him for herself.

When Jenna entered the kitchen the next morning, her mom walked over from where she was standing at the sink and embraced Jenna in a hug. "I'm so sorry honey. So, so sorry."

"About what?"

Her mom studied her face for a moment. "About you and Dustin."

"Oh, right," Jenna let her head fall back down onto her mom's shoulder and started to cry. She suddenly remembered everything, starting with getting home last night and breaking down into tears and telling her mom about how Dustin had dumped her. Her mom wanted to know why, but Jenna wasn't about to tell her any part of the truth, so she said she didn't know.

"Do you think you'll still go to homecoming?" Bonnie asked, still holding her daughter, wishing she could erase the pain she was feeling over her first breakup.

"I don't know." Jenna couldn't believe her mom was already thinking about next week and how easy it was for her to just accept that she and Dustin had broken up. It almost seemed like she'd been waiting for it to happen.

"Well, you already have your dress and shoes, so maybe you can go with some friends. You certainly don't need to decide right now, though."

chapter thirty-three

"Doughnut."

Delaney points to an oblong-shaped cluster of clouds that doesn't look anything like a doughnut. I respond by pointing to nothing in particular and say, "Cotton candy."

"You can't say cotton candy. It *all* looks like cotton candy."

We slowly propel the merry-go-round with our legs.

"It's almost four thirty. We should go. Mrs. Kemp will be home soon," I say.

My sneaker drags across the ground for a few feet until the merry-go-round comes to a stop. We continue to lay and look up at the sky until the spinning sensation wears off.

"So, how are we going to get Jenna's diary without her mom knowing? I mean, we can't just waltz into her bedroom and grab it out of . . wait, do we even know where it is?" Delaney asks as we start walking along the path away from the old playground.

"I'm pretty sure she just keeps it in her nightstand. The last time I slept there—the night before our meet in Delafield—she'd written in it."

"Okay, well, if it's in there, what's the plan? Are we just going to walk straight to Jenna's room and grab it? Don't you think Mrs. Kemp will want to know what we're doing?"

"I don't know," I say, feeling overwhelmed with uncertainty about pretty much everything. "Let's just figure it out when we get there."

We walk in silence for a few minutes. Somehow, Delaney finds a rock to repeatedly kick ahead the way she always does.

"Hey, remember when Jenna used to keep her diary under her mattress?" I ask, smiling to myself.

"Yeah," Delaney laughs. "She acted like there was top secret information in there." She stops laughing and looks over at me, suddenly serious. "Who knows? Maybe there was." She refocuses on the path and gives the rock a kick.

It hadn't occurred to me until now that maybe we should grab Jenna's older diaries too. Reading any of her personal thoughts is a total invasion of her privacy, but maybe she wrote things that will help us understand what's going on with her. "Hey, do you think maybe we should try to find her older diaries too?"

Delaney shakes her head. "I can't even believe we're on our way to find her current diary."

"I know, but what if there's something in them that might help us figure out what's going on with her?"

Delaney sighs. "I don't know, Keeley. It's your call. I don't think Jenna and I will ever be close like we used to be, especially if she finds out we did this. She'll forgive you, though." I don't respond because I have a feeling Delaney might be right, and I get the sense she's beating herself up again over the whole Dustin debacle. "Do you have any idea where her old diaries could be?"

"Actually, I do. She keeps them in one of the shoe boxes in her closet. Second row, third from the right—unless she rearranged the boxes. Charcoal gray and hot pink Saucony Hurricanes."

"How do you even know that?"

"We went through her shoes a few months ago, and I opened that box. A stack of her old diaries was inside. Not sure where the shoes are," I say with a shrug. "Even if the box isn't in the same spot—which I doubt—I'll be able to find it."

"Wow. I can't believe your shared obsession with Jenna over running shoes might actually come in handy."

The walkway to the Kemps' front door is covered with leaves from the two maple trees in their front yard. This isn't normal for Jenna's house because her dad is *that* neighbor who's always meticulous about outdoor maintenance. And Mrs. Kemp provides the same attention to detail inside their home. Everything with the Kemps is usually perfect, even Jenna, up until a few months ago. It might seem like no big deal to most people, but an unkempt walkway means something is up with the Kemps.

We're just stepping foot on the large front porch when the front door flies open. "Keeley? Delaney? What are you girls doing here? Please tell me you heard from Jenna," Mrs. Kemp leaves the door wide open and steps outside in bare feet.

"I'm sorry, Mrs. Kemp," I say, annihilating the hopeful look on her face. "But, no, we haven't."

Delaney offers a sad shake of her head in apology.

"Oh." She looks from me to Delaney. "Well, what are you girls doing here then?" Normally perky with a smile bright enough to light up a room, she stands before us looking like she hasn't slept for weeks.

"We just wanted to see how you're doing. Maybe talk a little."

"That would be great," she says, opening the door wide for us to enter. "Please come in."

We know Jenna's house rules as well as we know our own, so as soon as we enter, we place our shoes on the mat just inside the door and hang our jackets in the hall closet. Doing so makes me think of several times when Jenna was upset with her mom for wanting everything to be perfect. Mrs. Kemp would never be the same if she knew how imperfect Jenna had been lately. It occurs to me for a moment that all the pressure to be perfect is what may have finally pushed Jenna over the edge, but then I shake the thought away because as much as Jenna stressed about the expectations her parents placed on her, she'd grown to expect the same of herself. And when she wasn't striving for her own perfection, she was pushing Delaney and me to be the best at whatever we were doing.

After nearly two decades of being Holly Homemaker, even worry and sorrow aren't enough to dash Mrs. Kemp's desire to keep things orderly. The house still looks spotless. The only noticeable change is that instead of the bowl of potpourri and framed family photos that are usually kept on the hall table, it's now covered with a small shrine to Jenna consisting of last year's school picture, a photo of her from when she was a baby, the medal she won at our first track meet freshman year, and a baptismal cross with her name engraved on the base. There are also lighted candles and a set of car keys with a big purple ribbon on them.

"Why don't we go into the kitchen and I'll get you girls something to—"

"Actually . . . um, excuse me for interrupting . . . but would it be okay if we talked in Jenna's room? It's just that . . . I miss her." It's not a lie. "And I wonder if it would make me feel better to just be around her stuff for a little while. You know?"

Mrs. Kemp wraps her arms around me and kisses the top of my head. While she does so, Delaney gives me a suspicious look. "Oh, sweetie, I know. Trust me, I know." Then she leads the way to the stairs.

Jenna's room is not what you'd expect of a sixteen-year-old girl's room. It looks more like a dude's room with the dark mahogany colored wood furniture and turquoise and gray bedding. The girliest thing would have to be a poster of the soccer pro Cristiano Ronaldo, but I imagine the same poster is probably hanging in a lot of guys' bedrooms too. Besides Cristiano, there are framed pastel paintings of runners. She'd been receiving one every year for her birthday from her parents. Mrs. Kemp's best friend owns an art gallery in downtown Milwaukee, so she has them custom-made for Jenna.

Mrs. Kemp takes a seat on the edge of Jenna's bed. Then she scans the room slowly. "It feels like she's gone off to college or something." She leans over to grab a fuzzy turquoise pillow and hugs it to her chest.

Delaney and I stand awkwardly next to each other until she takes a seat at Jenna's desk, leaving me standing in the middle of the room. I cross and uncross my arms while Mrs. Kemp fills us in on all the phone calls they've received from neighbors, teachers, and members of the congregation. She talks about how they have enough casseroles in the deep freezer to last a year, how no one in the Kemp house is getting enough sleep, how Mr. Kemp can barely concentrate on work.

After about ten minutes of crossing and uncrossing my arms and shifting from foot to foot, I inch my back to Jenna's closet, eventually sliding into a sitting position on the floor. I can almost hear her diary calling to me, and my back feels oddly warm. It makes me think about the hotter and colder game when you're looking for something and you know when you're close to it because someone tells you you're hot and vice versa. Then there's warm. If you're warm, you're close enough that if you keep looking around where you are, you're sure to find it, but if you veer too far out of the warm pocket, you find yourself cold once again. Jenna's diary might not tell us anything, but maybe, just maybe, it will contain a hot spot. If we're lucky, it'll contain many.

The sunlight streaming through the windows is beginning to fade, so I know it must be close to five. Time to act. Clearing my throat, I ask, "Mrs. Kemp, may I please have some water?"

Delaney pipes in. "Yeah, me too, please." I look at her with wide eyes. How am I supposed to have time to snag Jenna's diary in the amount of time it takes her mom to walk downstairs for a glass of water and return?

Mrs. Kemp stands. "It's about time for me to finish making dinner anyway. Come on down to the kitchen, and I'll get the two of you bottles to go."

"Actually," I say, clutching my head. "I'm feeling a little dizzy. Probably wasn't smart to run right after school and not replenish my fluids right away."

"I'll bring you some." Delaney to the rescue. "That way you can work on dinner, Mrs. Kemp."

Mrs. Kemp nods. "All right."

The moment I hear their footsteps on the stairs, I throw open the first drawer of Jenna's nightstand and panic when there's no diary. Then I remember it had been in the second drawer and am relieved to find it there. As soon as I shove it into my backpack, I open her closet doors and search the rows of boxes. I sigh with relief when I find the correct Saucony box exactly where I remembered it being, except the box is empty. As I contemplate searching every box, the sound of someone clearing her throat sends me into panic mode, and I scramble to my feet.

"What are you doing?"

"Shaina! Hi!"

She hands me a bottle of water. "What are you doing in Jenna's closet?"

"I was just . . . she had borrowed a pair of flip flops from me over the summer and I was just—"

"Flip flops?"

I can't tell if she's just confirming what I said or questioning my honesty. Desperate to change the subject, I say, "How was volleyball practice?"

She emits an exasperated sigh. "The same as everything has been ever since Saturday morning when my parents realized Jenna never came home. It sucked."

"I'm so sorry, Shaina." I don't know what else to say. I don't know Shaina that well, but she's always gotten along with Jenna. Never any of that bratty little sister stuff I hear some older siblings have to put up with. I wouldn't know because, according to my big brother, I'm the bratty little sister. Shaina's blank stare makes me wish I knew what else to say. But if I'm being honest, I'm starting to lose hope. That's why I'm here for the diary. Maybe it will provide some hope that Jenna is just off doing something she shouldn't be doing or that she ran away the way I heard the police think she did.

When we get downstairs, Mrs. Kemp is sitting at the kitchen table. Her head is down, and she's sobbing. Delaney is patting her back.

"Mom." Shaina rushes to her allowing Delaney to step back.

I pat my bag and nod toward the front door. I feel bad for Mrs. Kemp because there's nothing we can do or say to make her feel better, but I ask anyway, "Is there something we can do to help?"

"No, you guys just go," Shaina says as she cranes her neck in an attempt to look our direction while she hugs her mom's shoulders.

We retrieve our coats quickly and rush outside. Mrs. Kemp's crying can still be heard from the porch, but by the time we step off the Kemps' property, their house looks perfectly normal in the dim dusk lighting.

"So, two things. Why didn't you warn me that Shaina was bringing water up for me? And why was Mrs. Kemp crying?"

"Hey," she throws her hands up in the air. "It all happened so fast. Shaina walked in. Mrs. Kemp tossed the water to her and asked her to bring it to you. Then she immediately dropped a serving platter into my hands and started piling beef and potatoes and other junk from the slow cooker onto it."

We stop and wait for a red light. "Yeah, well, she walked in while I was digging around in Jenna's closet. I made up the stupidest excuse. And what about Mrs. Kemp? Did the food not turn out?"

"That's not funny, Keeley."

"I know, that was a dumb thing to say . . . So, what made Mrs. Kemp snap? Why was she crying?"

"I'm not one-hundred percent sure. All I know is she got a call from the police, but I have no idea what they said to her. When she hung up, she started crying. That's pretty much when you and Shaina walked in."

As soon as we get to the privacy of my room, I remove my backpack and retrieve Jenna's diary. Then we sit on my bed, and I start reading the entries aloud.

October 2, 2017

Dear Diary,

School was so-so today. I felt so tired in first period that I kept dozing off. You know, when your head bobs a few times and it wakes you up? Finally, I asked if I could stand at the back of the room for a few minutes to get my blood pumping. That worked . . .

"Skip ahead. This entry doesn't say much of anything," Delaney says.

So, we skip to an entry on the fourth, then to an entry on the eighth. Then we jump ahead a couple pages to the twelfth but still don't find much of anything.

"What the heck? She didn't mention anything about any of us or about homecoming. She doesn't even say anything about Leighton in here. What kind of diary is this? Go to the last entry. When was it written?" Delaney sounds equally as confused as I am.

October 25, 2017

Dear Diary,

I'm so tired. And I miss my friends. I think it might be time for me to tell everyone the truth.

~Jenna

Delaney and I look at each other, more confused than ever.

"The truth?" I say, shaking my head.

Delaney shrugs. "I don't understand the point of keeping a diary like this. It's just a bunch of unimportant stuff. I mean, except for this last entry. But no one will know what it means."

"Unless Leighton knows about a secret she was keeping," I say.

"I don't know. Maybe the chat room was the secret. Maybe she met someone in there and ran off with him. Maybe the rumors about her running away are true." Delaney sighs. "Well, this was a waste of time."

"At least we know she misses us."

My phone vibrates. "It's Leighton," I say to Delaney as I open the text.

LEIGHTON: DID YOU GET THE DIARY?

"When did you give her your number?"

"Right after school. She stopped at my locker at the end of the day so we could exchange. I guess maybe she does really care about Jenna. She wants to know if we got the diary."

KEELEY: YEAH, IT'S USELESS. LOOKED FOR HER OLD ONES TOO BUT COULDN'T FIND THEM.

"Hey girls?" my mom says, knocking.

"Yeah?"

She opens the door when I respond. "How was school today? I heard Detective Collins was there interviewing kids?"

Delaney and I both nod, and my mom sighs, probably because she has no idea what else to say. None of us do.

"Delaney are you joining us for dinner tonight?" she finally asks. "Wait, don't you usually have cheer practice on Monday nights?"

"Um," Delaney looks at me, and I widen my eyes at her because we both know she's terrible under pressure, "not tonight I don't."

"Oh, okay, well we have plenty of taco fixings if you'd like to eat with us."

"Thanks, Mrs. Simon."

"So, what are you girls doing?" I snatch Jenna's diary off the bed when my mom glances at it, piquing her curiosity. "What's that?"

"It's . . ."

"It's Jenna's diary," Delaney says, making my jaw drop.

"What?" my mom exclaims. "Why on *earth* do you have her *diary* and how did you get it?"

"Really, Delaney?" I say, ignoring my mom for now.

"What? There's nothing in it, so what does it matter?"

"I don't care if there's nothing in it. How did you get it?" my mom asks, closing the distance between us and outstretching her hand until I hand it to her. "*How* did you get it?"

"We went over to the Kemps' house after school today."

"Oh, so Bonnie knows you have it?"

I shake my head.

"All right, let's go. You girls are going to return this, and you're going to apologize for taking it without permission. How do you know the police won't need to see this?"

"Honestly, there's nothing important in it," Delaney says.

My mom looks from Delaney to me, undeterred. "Up. Both of you. Let's go."

"Keeley, Delaney, you're back." Mrs. Kemp pulls the door open wide, and we file inside.

"Hi, Bonnie," my mom says, giving Mrs. Kemp a hug as soon as she's inside.

"What' going on? Wait, did you—"

We all shake our heads, so she doesn't finish her question.

"Bonnie, the girls have something to return to you."

My mom nods me forward, so I pull Jenna's diary from my bag and hand it to Mrs. Kemp.

"Where did you . . ." Her eyes light up with recognition. "You girls took Jenna's diary earlier? Why?"

"Because we thought maybe there was something in it to give us a clue. Something to help us find her," I say, glancing over at Delaney. "But it's—"

"Useless," Mrs. Kemp says, finishing my sentence. "Joseph looked at it on Saturday. I just couldn't bring myself to, though," she says, shaking her head. "Not after I betrayed her trust and read an entry in it the night of homecoming. I'm sure she told you girls about that."

"Actually no," I say, confused. "She never mentioned it. Then again, homecoming was the last time either of us talked to Jenna."

"Oh, I . . ." Mrs. Kemp's eyes become cloudy, and she winces. "I didn't know. She even told me the two of you would be where she was going most nights when she went out. After that night, I didn't ask a lot of questions. I just wanted her to feel like I trusted her, and I wanted her to trust me again. I screwed up," she says, covering her face with her hands. "I screwed up so bad."

"Oh, Bonnie." My mom puts an arm around Mrs. Kemp and leads her into the living room where they take a seat on the couch. Delaney and I follow and sit too.

"Mrs. Kemp?" I ask. She looks up and dries her face with a tissue my mom has handed her. "You said you read an entry in her diary on the night of homecoming but based on the dates in the one we just returned to you, it couldn't have been that one. Do you know where the one you read is?"

"Jenna . . ." Mrs. Kemp says, shaking her head and looking up at the ceiling as if trying to contain more tears, ". . . threw it away that night. She was so angry with me. But I only looked because she'd broken curfew and you girls were already home asleep and . . . I wondered if maybe she'd gotten back together with Dustin and didn't tell me. It was wrong, and I'll always regret breaking her trust like that."

I sigh, frustrated that the plan to get useful information from Jenna's diaries has fizzled.

"Girls?" Mrs. Kemp asks, her tone nasally, "have either of you ever heard of ChillChat.com?"

Delaney and I look at each other, and we both nod. Delaney answers, "Leighton told us Jenna was supposed to meet someone she was chatting with on there. They were supposed to meet on Friday night, but Jenna canceled."

Mrs. Kemp's face goes pale. "I wasn't aware of that . . . But, Detective Collins called today—while you girls were here actually—to let us know that they've tracked down a man named Jacob Bickers. Jenna had been chatting with him on that site. I wonder if he's the man she was supposed to meet."

"Oh, God," my mom whispers, clasping her hands together the way she does when she's nervous. Delaney stares at the floor with her mouth agape, and my heart begins to race. None of us say it, but this could either be a good thing or a bad thing. Good because maybe this Jacob guy knows where Jenna might be. Bad because maybe he had something to do with her disappearance. Or maybe he knows nothing, and we're all tensed up for no reason.

"Do you know if they've interviewed him yet?" my mom asks.

Mrs. Kemp shakes her head. "The police stated he wasn't available today but has agreed to go in first thing tomorrow morning." She lowers her face into her hands, and her body shudders. My mom places a hand on her back, and I rush to sit on the other side of her. "I have a really bad feeling about this," she says through her hands. "I don't know what will be worse—if he knows where she is or if he doesn't. This is all my fault. Maybe if I hadn't been so hard on her after she started dating Dustin, and maybe if I hadn't invaded her privacy . . ."

"No one is to blame, Bonnie," my mom says.

I can't help but think she's wrong.

chapter thirty-four

Monday, September 25, 2017
Four Weeks Before Jenna's Disappearance

September 25, 2017

Dear Diary,

I may have had the most miserable day of my life today.

Walking through the doors this morning was one of the hardest things I've ever had to do. I felt like everyone's eyes were on me, and most of them really were. Lunch was horrible with everyone trying to pretend nothing happened at the party on Saturday, but I knew it was the only thing on everyone's mind. Dustin didn't even sit with us today, so of course neither did Tommy. I'm not sure why they didn't take Eli with them! (Corbin was fine—he was actually the only person who looked me in the eyes on purpose.) I wanted to get up and leave within the first few minutes, but I couldn't move. I was paralyzed by the fear of getting up and having people look at me, walking away from the table and having more people look at me, and then even more people would have been looking at me as I walked out the door. Then there'd be more people. It doesn't matter if people were at the party or not, everyone has heard some version of me standing on the stairs and screaming at Dustin that night. Jenna Kemp, 2016 homecoming princess, has lost her mind. And I did—on Saturday night and then AGAIN today at lunch when I heard Delaney talking about babysitting for Stella again. I honestly can't even remember how it all happened because I was so angry, but I told

*Delaney I couldn't believe she would still babysit for them even after I asked
her not to, and then while I was gathering my things to leave, I thanked Eli
and Keeley for even bothering to ask me how I felt about them going to
homecoming together or how I felt about them dating each other at all.
Keeley and Delaney thought I was just drunk or high on Saturday night,
none of them took me seriously. So, I made it clear and told them to STAY
AWAY from my family. Made it real easy for them and everyone else in the
cafeteria to understand. After I left, Dustin showed up out of nowhere, and
the first thing out of his mouth was "What's wrong with you?" I couldn't help
but think is it me or is it all of you? So I asked him back, "What's wrong
with you?" And he told me he's tired of the roller coaster I've put him on and
he's tired of feeling like I don't feel the same way about him as he does about
me. When I tried to walk away, he grabbed my arm, and after what
happened on Saturday night, I'm done. We're done.*

*Closed off. Scared. Dying inside. That's how HE'S made me feel. And now
nothing in my life is going right.*

~Jenna

---

*You started out as my friend.
You kept me safe and promised our fun times would never end.
But then you changed and wanted more.
I didn't know any better, so I just laid there on the floor.
It hurt more than any feeling I've ever known.
Physically and emotionally broken, I'm all alone.
I don't want you near, yet here you are.
But the pain is the same whether you're near or far.*

chapter thirty-five

KEELEY: YEAH, IT'S USELESS. LOOKED FOR HER OLD ONES TOO BUT COULDN'T FIND THEM.

Sighing, I fall back onto my pillow and place my phone face down on my chest. Even though I didn't think it was a good idea for Keeley and Delaney to steal Jenna's diary, I was hoping it would reveal something—anything that might help us figure out where she is.

I've gotten to know Jenna pretty well over the past three weeks, and there are two things I know for sure.

One, she's tired of pretending to be something she isn't. This is a direct quote from her and the reason why I've never tried to tell her what she should or shouldn't do. Some people might say that's being a bad friend, but I disagree. I just realized she didn't need another person telling her who to be.

Two, she wouldn't run away like some idiots are saying she did. She'd just decided to expose what her sicko cousin did to her, so there's no way. I feel like punching a wall when I wonder if Thomas, Jake B., or some other chat room guy had something to do with her disappearance. My hope is that my tip about Jenna using ChillChat will help the cops figure something out. But what kind of hope is that? What are the odds anything they'd find out would be good?

For the first time since my dad ruined my life, I cry sad, hopeless tears.

The kind of tears you cry when your dog dies or you lose a best friend. As I walk over to my dresser for a tissue, Jenna's bag catches my eye. I've gotten so used to it hanging on the hook on my wall that it's begun to blend in. She brought it here the first time she spent the night and hasn't taken it home since. I reminded her about it once, but she asked if it was okay if she just left it here because all it has in it is a change of clothes and a toothbrush in case she sleeps over again. Only, now that I think about it, the bag has never moved, and I've never seen her touch it.

I crumple the soggy tissue and toss it on my dresser, then I grab Jenna's bag and sit down with it on my bed. Something is telling me to open it, but I'm struggling with the idea of invading her privacy. I contemplate for a few minutes, wondering if the fact that she hasn't called or texted for three days is reason enough to defend going through her things. Finally, I flip open the flap and unzip the large canvas pouch. My shoulders drop when I look inside and see a Briarwood High sweatshirt. I reach inside and pull it out expecting to find more clothes underneath, but instead, I see a stack of notebooks like the one I've seen Jenna write in a few times. The moment I pull out the tattered stack, I realize what I've found.

Jenna's old diaries.

I stare at the stack of Jenna's private thoughts, and a flurry of questions run through my mind. What should I do with them? Should I give them to the police or Jenna's parents? Should I tell Keeley and Delaney about them?

Should I read them?

Jenna said she's been having nightmares about her cousin for years, so I'm guessing she wrote a lot about him and what he did to her. So, if I give them to Jenna's parents, and they find out about Thomas, what if they don't want to make what happened public? What if Mrs. Kemp wants to protect her nephew? What if they decide not to tell the police even though her cousin might have had something to do with her disappearance?

I need to find out how much she's written about what happened to her.

Before I can change my mind, I open a random page of the diary on top of the stack.

August 25, 2013

Dear Diary,

Today me and my friends went to the beach again. It was so much fun! We jumped off the end of the pier and made designs in the sand. Then Mom took us to get ice cream. I wish summer could last forever, and I hope I can be happy like this forever.

~Jenna

The next couple of entries are similar. Jenna sounds like a normal twelve-year-old. I skim a lot of a really long entry because it's all about her dog and all the tricks she can do. Just as I'm beginning to wonder if maybe Jenna didn't mention anything about Thomas, I flip to the next entry.

August 30, 2013

Dear Diary,

What's wrong with me? What's wrong with my parents? Why would they leave me alone with him?

You're right. It's not their fault. Maybe it's my fault. But what am I supposed to do?

I thought it was over and sometimes I even thought I dreamed it all. Or nightmared it. (Is that a word? It should be.) I thought maybe all the memories were fake. My teachers always say I have a great imagination. Or maybe I've watched too many movies on the Lifetime channel with my mom. I always pray, asking God to make sure it doesn't happen again or to erase the thoughts from my head. I'm starting to think he can't hear me.

I can only remember bits and pieces from this time, just like all the other times. After, it's always like I was a stranger, watching from outside. (So maybe it is all in my head? I can't figure it out.) I jumped when he knocked and said he'd picked up a DVD copy of Pitch Perfect and would I like to watch it. I thought, "say no . . . tell him you're sick. Whatever you do don't let him in!" But he came in before I had a chance to move, and then my brain screamed at me to get out! Leave the room! Then I realized I'm old enough now to leave the house too. But where would I go? I don't remember what I said to him as I rushed past him to get out of my room. His smell makes me sick, and I'm scared I'll never get it out of my nose. Even shoving cotton balls up my nostrils doesn't work. I still smell him. I could smell him following me. But there's never any way for me to escape. When we first sat down, he acted normal and I thought maybe since he's a grown-up now he wouldn't touch me. He asked questions. How's school? Are you still running a lot? Have you taught Lulu any new tricks? I started thinking maybe he wanted to forget too, and I answered his questions. Then the movie started, but after a few minutes, he asked more questions. Questions that made me feel sick because I knew he was the same. Have I been on a date yet? Do I have a crush on anyone? Have I gotten my period yet? That's when I thought talking to him might make him think I'm okay with everything he's done to me. So I told myself to go back to my room. To run. Close the door. Push something in front of it so he can't get in. Just don't talk to him. Don't even look at him. And I was about to run. But then he asked about Shaina. She was at a sleepover, so I knew she was safe. But I still felt like I had to protect her, to make him not think about her. So I froze like all the other times.

I can hear his voice right now like he's next to me whispering in my ear, but I don't know what he's saying because I try not to listen. I can feel his clammy hands on my face and neck. And I can feel him petting my hair like I'm a dog. Sometimes he does it too hard and rips out strands of my hair. I think this is what crazy people feel like.

The next thing I remember is staring at the TV and the sound of water running in the bathroom. When he came back, he grabbed the package of Twizzlers off the coffee table and sat down next to me. Then he restarted the movie. I didn't really watch, because I couldn't see anything. It was like when you close your eyes and all you can see is black, except my eyes were wide open. I think my brain was rebooting or something, sort of like at school when a computer freezes, and you have to turn it off and then back on to unfreeze it. I wish my brain could restart like that.

When Mom and Dad got home, Dad paid him for babysitting, and Mom wanted to know why I looked so pale and if I felt sick. I can hear them talking and laughing downstairs. I don't know what they're saying, but every time I hear his voice, I want to scream. I hate you! And every time I hear my mom's voice, I want to scream. Do you know what he did to me? And every time I hear my dad, I want to scream. How could you let him do this to me?

I wish I could go down there right now and tell them everything I can remember. But what would I say? Where would I start? With the time he showed me the pictures? They'd probably wonder if I was sleepwalking again or if I was confused from a bad dream. Or why I never said anything before. And he would just say he didn't know what I was talking about. And everyone thinks he's so wonderful, so who would believe me?

Now the best summer ever is the worst. Why did he have to visit?

~Jenna

And after that, her entries in this diary all seem darker for weeks. Sometimes there are pictures instead of words. There are a lot of sad faces and hearts with cracks down the center. Finally, around November, she stops writing mostly about nightmares and memories and wondering if it was her fault, and more of the entries are about school and her friends and her dog and how much she loves running.

I skim random pages of all six diaries, and even though the entries seem to be about normal stuff, there are some about Thomas scattered throughout. She never says his name, but I know they're about Thomas. The last entry in the final diary in the stack is dated June 2, 2017, so right around the end of last school year. So the one Keeley and Delaney read must be the next one in line, and Keeley said it was useless? How is it possible that there's nothing in it that would freak them out even a little bit? Jenna never went an entire diary without random depressing entries.

I sigh and scrub my eyes with my fists, and then place the notebooks back inside Jenna's bag. I'm even more confused about what to do with them now that I've seen what they contain.

If Thomas did something to Jenna, then the police will need to see these diaries. The problem is can they prove it's Thomas she's talking about? They'd have to question the entire family. And I know enough to know that not all family members are willing to go against their own, even if their own happens to be a worthless piece of shit. And plenty of people live in denial, much like Jenna described doing at times, even when the truth is staring them in the face. And those are my same issues with giving the diaries to Jenna's parents. What if they don't want people to know what Thomas did to Jenna? From what Jenna has told me, her mom is extremely close to her Aunt Lenore. So even if Mrs. Kemp wanted to expose Thomas, who's to say her sister wouldn't talk her out of it. *Beg* her out of it.

And what if Thomas doesn't know where Jenna is? What if he never even saw her on Friday night? Would turning the diaries over to the police now hinder their search for her? Maybe I should just hold on to them until the police are done looking into Jenna's ChillChat account.

Maybe my best bet is to share the diaries with Keeley and Delaney since they've known Jenna longer. Maybe they'll know which of Jenna's family members can be trusted to help her.

As I slide Jenna's bag under my bed, my phone pings.

KEELEY: WE WENT BACK TO JENNA'S BECAUSE MY MOM FOUND OUT ABOUT THE DIARY AND SHE MADE US RETURN IT . . .

Dumbasses. Another text comes through.

KEELEY: WE FOUND OUT SOMETHING BIG . . .

Something big? Then why the dot dot dot? I begin a reply asking what it is when another text comes through.

KEELEY: THE POLICE ARE GOING TO INTERVIEW A GUY NAMED JACOB (CAN'T REMEMBER HIS LAST NAME). JENNA MET HIM THROUGH THE CHAT ROOM, AND THEY WERE TALKING ON THE PHONE TOO. DO YOU RECOGNIZE THE NAME?

My heart starts racing.

LEIGHTON: THAT'S THE GUY SHE WAS SUPPOSED TO MEET ON FRIDAY.

As soon as I send the text, I smoke a cigarette to calm my nerves. But there's nothing I can do about the guilt I feel for being the one who introduced Jenna to ChillChat.com.

chapter thirty-six

Jenna sat at one of the fall-themed homecoming tables, making patterns and shapes with the fake leaves. She'd smoked and drank some vodka she'd been keeping stashed in her closet in a unicorn Pillow Pet before Keeley picked her up. The first slow dance of the night had just started, and she was already wishing she hadn't agreed to attend. Tommy ended up going alone too, so he'd asked Keeley to dance. As far as Jenna could tell she was only one of about a dozen people not on the dance floor.

After her blowup at lunch on Monday, she figured that was it for her and her friends. Why would they want to talk to her after the way she'd yelled at them? But for some reason, Keeley acted like nothing had happened when they saw each other at cross country practice, so Jenna just went with it. Then late Wednesday night, Keeley called Jenna to let her know that she wouldn't be dating Eli anymore, which meant she'd be going to homecoming alone for the third year in a row. As determined as Jenna was to keep Keeley and Eli apart, she couldn't help but feel bad for ruining things for Keeley, so that was the only reason she agreed to go.

Delaney was a different story. She hadn't said a word to Jenna the entire week, despite Keeley urging Jenna and Delaney to work it out. Delaney's stubbornness was expected and fine by Jenna. She had too many other things on her mind to worry about Delaney's feelings.

When the slow song ended, "Party Rock Anthem" came on, and Jenna's first reaction was to smile. In fifth grade, she'd choreographed a dance to the song for Keeley, Delaney, and her to perform at the talent show. Their performance was a hit, and any time the song came on when they were together, they'd break out the old routine. Her smile faded quickly when she realized several people were calling her name and waving her out to the dance floor. She shook her head, but they wouldn't let up, and then Corbin was sent to get her on the floor. Despite her inebriated protests, moments later, she found herself next to Delaney and Keeley who were doing the dance, surrounded by all their friends. Since she'd been put on the spot, she did her best to remember the moves but had a hard time focusing through the haze she was under. She couldn't tell if people were laughing because they loved seeing the old routine or because Jenna, who'd always been a great dancer, was a mess.

When the song ended, the crowd dispersed, and Jenna was left standing with Keeley and Delaney.

"You okay, Jenna?" Keeley asked.

"Yeah, why?"

"Because you seem tired or something. You've never forgotten the moves before, and you're the one who made up the routine," Keeley said with a shrug.

Delaney remained silent with her arms folded.

"I'm fine. I just don't really feel like dancing and probably shouldn't have come."

"That makes sense considering this is a dance," Delaney said in a snooty tone. Keeley delivered her a knock-it-off look, but Delaney ignored her. "In fact, why are we even on the dancefloor when we aren't dancing anymore?"

"Great question," Jenna said. "I'm just going to go back to the—"

"Hey! Keeley, Delaney, Jenna! Get over here so we can get a group shot!" Tina called from one of the rented photo booths.

Delaney headed over immediately, always ready for a photo op, but Keeley hesitated when Jenna didn't appear to be interested.

"Are you coming?" Keeley asked.

"No, I—"

"Give me a break, Jenna." Keeley grabbed Jenna's hand and started pulling. "You're going to be in the picture!"

"Hurry up, you guys!" Tina stuck her head out of the booth and yelled.

Keeley and Jenna slid into the booth just as the first shot was being taken. Then everyone quickly resituated for the second and then for the third.

When Jenna slipped out of the booth, her gaze fell on Dustin, and she froze. He was on the dancefloor with a girl named Phoebe. Jenna liked Phoebe, but Dustin had revealed once that he thought Phoebe was the second prettiest girl in their grade, right after Jenna. Suddenly, Jenna wanted to find someone with pot or alcohol to help take her mind off the jealousy and anger she was feeling.

"Hey," Keeley said, "that's nothing. You know that, right?"

"Dustin and I aren't together anymore, so I don't care."

"What do you mean you don't care? You and Dustin are going to get back together. I know it."

"Yeah, okay," Jenna said, tearing her eyes away from Dustin and Phoebe and turning to Keeley. "Hey, I'll be right back. I have to use the bathroom."

Keeley nodded. "I'm going to dance," she said pointing both fingers at the dancefloor.

It didn't take long for Jenna to find some kids who'd snuck outside for a drink, and even though they were shocked Jenna asked for some of their stash, they were happy to share. As Jenna made her way back to the dance, her phone buzzed.

LEIGHTON: ARE YOU DONE WITH THE DANCE YET?

JENNA: NOT YET. WILL PROBABLY LEAVE SOON. WHY?

LEIGHTON: WANNA GO TO A PARTY?

JENNA: CAN KEELEY GO TOO?

LEIGHTON: IF THAT'LL GET YOU THERE. :)

JENNA: I'LL GET BACK TO YOU.

For the rest of the dance, Jenna blended in like she always had, laughing and smiling at the right times. She even danced a little but decided she was done when she almost tripped over her own feet. After that, any lucidity she still had was devoted to counting down the minutes until she and Keeley could leave.

"There you are," Keeley said when she found Jenna exiting the bathroom. "Are you still up for going to Corbin's party?"

"Who's going to be there?" Jenna already knew that even though Eli wasn't at the dance, he'd be at the party. She knew Dustin would be there too.

"Well, everyone," Keeley said with a shrug.

"Hey, I have an idea," Jenna said. "Leighton told me about a party that's going on in Glendale. I guess there's a hot tub. Can we maybe go there instead?"

Keeley folded her arms across her chest. "I don't know, Jenna."

"Come on, Keeley. You know it's going to be all couples at Corbin's, besides Eli and Dustin."

Keeley sighed. The idea of being around Eli and not being able to really talk to him since Jenna would be there didn't sound like fun. And since Jenna's argument with Dustin had only been a week ago, she finally decided skipping Corbin's party might be a good idea.

"Fine." Keeley smiled, glad that at least she'd be with Jenna at the party. "But don't forget I need to have the car home by midnight, so we can only go for like an hour."

"Yay!" Jenna pulled out her phone to ask Leighton for the address. "We can change in the car."

As Jenna stumbled her way up the walkway to her front door later that night, all she could think about was the burning sensation between her legs. Her inebriated brain did the best it could to keep Jenna's hand steady as she tried to insert her key in the door, but it was hopeless.

"Jenna Kathleen! Where have you been?" Bonnie yelled as she pulled open the door.

"I'm sorry . . . my key wouldn't . . ." Jenna mumbled the rest of her sentence as she staggered into the kitchen for some water.

"Are you drunk? Joseph! Joseph, she's home!"

When Jenna lowered the water bottle, she'd guzzled over half of, her parents were standing at the counter staring at her.

"Sorry, I'm—"

"Sorry? You're sorry?" Bonnie yelled, circling the counter and stopping in front of Jenna. Then in a measured voice, she said, "It's two o'clock in the morning. Where the hell were you?"

"I went to a party. Keeley was—"

"Don't you *dare* lie to me. I've already called Keeley's and Delaney's parents who've confirmed that your friends are asleep in their beds."

"But . . ." Jenna's brow creased. "Keeley *was* at the party with me. She just left earlier than I did." Jenna tried to walk around Bonnie, but Bonnie blocked her path.

"Where was this party and who have you been with?"

"Leighton and some kids she knows who go to a school in Glendale."

"Well, who drove you home? And were they even sober? And what have you been doing this whole time? My God, Jenna, I figured now that you and Dustin are broken up that we wouldn't have to worry about you anymore! But now this and . . ." Bonnie's voice trailed off, and she walked back to the counter where Jenna's dad was squeezing the back of his neck, a pained expression on his face.

Jenna stared at her mom, stunned that she'd brought up Dustin. She wanted to laugh when she thought about all the arguments they'd had over the summer about her and Dustin spending too much time alone together because her mom was worried they were having sex. Little did Bonnie know, Dustin had been helping Jenna maintain her innocence. Jenna could only imagine what her mom would do if she found out Jenna's own cousin had stolen that innocence a long time ago, or that she'd just made out with a senior from Glendale High School who she'd probably never see again.

"Jenna," her dad said, "we're extremely disappointed in you for coming home so late, but we need to talk to you about something else right now. Can you please come over to the table?" Her mom and dad turned away from the counter and took seats at the table themselves.

Confused, Jenna walked over, and when she saw what was lying in the center of it, she gasped and rushed forward to grab it.

"No," her mom said sternly, moving to swipe Jenna's diary before she could get her hands on it. But Jenna was too fast, and now she stood there gripping all of her secrets to her chest.

"How could you read my diary?" Jenna yelled, eyeing the bottle of Tylenol PM still on the table.

"It's two in the morning, and your friends all went home at midnight! What else were we supposed to do?"

"That doesn't even make any sense! How about NOT invade my privacy?! I can't believe you would do this!"

"Okay," Joseph stood, "*this* isn't going to help. Jenna, *sit* down, and *both* of you stop yelling."

Jenna sighed as she pulled out a chair to sit. Bonnie and Joseph found it peculiar the way Jenna eased her bottom onto the seat.

"Jenna, are you okay?"

"Yeah, I just . . . slipped on the stairs at school tonight and hurt my butt bone."

"Well, after we talk, maybe you should put some ice on it."

Jenna nodded and looked up at her dad. She did her best to hide the panic she felt thinking about what they might have read in her diary. Did they read any of the entries about Thomas? If so, would they know she was talking about Thomas? Suddenly she couldn't remember if she'd ever written his name in any of the entries. Did they know she'd started smoking pot?

"Jenna," her dad said calmly, "your mom was extremely worried. We both were. So, out of desperation, she read one entry from your diary. But—"

"But then I stopped," Bonnie said, her eyes falling to the table, "because, yes, it was an invasion of your privacy. *But* we need to talk about what I read."

Oh, God. What was the last thing I wrote about? Jenna tried to remember. "Jenna, the mention of you doing pot and drinking excessive amounts of alcohol is disappointing . . . and so is this bottle of Tylenol PM we found in your drawer. But that's not the most concerning thing to us right now." Bonnie looks at Joseph before continuing. "We want to talk about the poem that was in your last entry."

Jenna wracked her brain. *The poem.* It was about Thomas, and she'd written it after she wrote all about the arguments she'd had with Dustin and her other friends at Tommy's party and at school on Monday.

"Jenna did Dustin hurt you?" her dad asked.

"What?" Jenna looked up, confused.

"You came home so upset last Saturday night when you and Dustin broke up. Then you wrote that he grabbed your arm at school. And then in your poem . . . did Dustin force himself on you? Is that why the two of you broke up?"

"No," Jenna breathed the word instead of saying it. She was still a little drunk and high, and on top of that she was now angry because of her mom's betrayal and disoriented because of the accusations against Dustin. How could her parents mistake a poem she'd written about Thomas as being about Dustin? Dustin would never hurt her the way Thomas did.

"What was that poem about then?" her mom asked.

"It was just a poem, Mom. That's it. I write a lot of stuff like that."

Bonnie and Joseph looked at each other again, neither of them sure what to believe. Finally, Bonnie said, "Okay, then what about the drinking and the drugs, not just the pot, but this Tylenol PM too? Why are you taking this?" Bonnie asked, picking up the bottle and giving it a little shake.

Jenna rubbed her eyes with her fingers to afford herself some time to think of an answer. "I haven't been running well because my knee was bothering me a couple weeks ago, and I didn't want to say anything because I was afraid you'd make me go to the doctor and that I'd end up having to stop running for a while. Those pills helped with the pain better than ibuprofen." Jenna laid her head on the table and mumbled, "I guess I should have sat out instead because I've been running like crap anyway."

"I think this is enough discussion for tonight. It's late," Jenna's dad said. "How about we get some rest and revisit all of this in the morning?"

Jenna sat up and looked from her dad to her mom. "What's there to revisit? I broke curfew again, I've tried pot, I've been drinking at parties, I like to write emotional poetry, and you invaded my privacy by reading my diary. So, what's *my* punishment going to be?"

"Hand over your phone," her dad said, reaching his hand across the table.

But instead of placing her phone in his hand, Jenna removed it from her bag and dropped it on the table. Then she picked up her diary from her lap and stood. "I guess it's pointless to keep one of these around here," she said, tossing her diary in the garbage and walking out of the kitchen.

chapter thirty-seven

JACOB
TUESDAY, OCTOBER 31, 2017
FOUR DAYS AFTER JENNA'S DISAPPEARANCE

"For the record, do you know who this girl is?" Detective Collins asks, sliding a picture of Jenna in front of me. In addition to Jenna's picture, he also has a leather-bound notebook and a manila folder.

I know it's Jenna without even looking at the photo, but I lean forward and examine the picture before answering. "Yes. Her name is Jenna."

"And you're aware that she's been missing since Friday evening?"

"Yes, but I have no idea where she is," I offer.

"Mr. Bickers, how did you meet Jenna Kemp?"

"We met on a chat room site called ChillChat.com."

Detective Collins remains expressionless, but I note a twitch at the corner of his left eye. If I were him, I'd be wondering why a married man with children would be chatting with young girls on a site like ChillChat. "I imagine there are thousands of users on this site. How did you and Jenna happen to find each other?"

On my way to the police station, I told myself to stay calm—tell them only what they ask, offering no additional information, and be careful not to show any emotion. But now I wonder if that's the best approach to take. After all, I don't want to make myself look guilty of something. Don't guilty people act like nothing is wrong? Maybe I need to rethink my strategy.

I break eye contact with him and sigh heavily. "We were both in this group called *Lost and Alone, Looking for a Friend*. Her nickname—Runner

"

Girl—jumped out at me, so I sent her a chat request. That's how we started chatting."

Detective Collins nods. "Mr. Bickers, we've read through your ChillChat conversations with Jenna, and . . ."

I panic, wondering how they accessed our conversations since I deleted my account shortly after finding out about Jenna. Who am I kidding, though? Nothing really disappears from online. Plus, they could easily have accessed Jenna's account by now, or maybe ChillChat gave them access.

". . . Actually, we'll get back to your conversations. Could you first explain how you ended up on this site? How did you find out about it?"

I draw my eyebrows in, leery about the way he backtracked. Is this some sort of mind game? Did he want to see how I'd react to the mention of my private conversations with Jenna? I'm also perplexed as to why they need to know how I found the site.

"This information might help us determine how Jenna found out about the site," he adds as though he read my mind.

I nod and pause to decide exactly how much I should tell him.

"I found it one night when I was browsing the Internet. I was overnight somewhere for work . . . I think I was in Eau Claire that night—I'd have to check my calendar. Anyway, I don't remember what site I was on, but an ad for ChillChat popped up. I actually didn't even mean to click it, but you know how tricky those pop-ups can be." I shrug, and Collins nods. "Then one thing led to another and . . . well, you see I've been feeling stressed about a lot of things in my personal life, and . . ." *No, stop rambling.* "Anyway, I created an account and ended up browsing chat rooms for a couple hours. The next day, I logged in intending to delete the account, but I'd received a couple of chat requests, so . . . I started using the site." I leave out how the requests were from women offering live nude footage. "About a week later I started frequenting that Lost and Alone chat room, and I kept seeing Jenna's nickname pop up, so I sent her a private chat request."

"Mr. Bickers, did you have any idea how old Jenna is?"

"No. She told me she was nineteen."

Detective Collins opens the folder in front of him and rummages through the papers inside. They appear to be transcripts of our chats. "I'm glad you mentioned that because my next question was going to be if you've ever had communication with Jenna outside the ChillChat site." He places a piece of paper in front of me and points to my last chat message to Jenna when I gave her my phone number.

"Yes, we spoke on the phone and exchanged some text messages after I sent this last message," I say, handing the paper back to him. He places it back in its spot and closes the folder. Then he folds his hands atop of the folder and leans forward.

"Why is that? Why move communications off of ChillChat?"

"I don't know. Partly because I'm not the best typist, have always been a hunt-and-peck kind of guy, and partly because it seemed like a natural progression. We'd become close, and I thought it would be nice to hear her voice. I was a shoulder for her to lean on, a confidant. She seemed sad and lost, and I felt bad for her. And she filled a void I've been feeling lately in my life . . . in my marriage." I sigh, wondering if I've said too much or anything to incriminate myself. "But now that I know how old she is, I don't feel that way. I mean I would never . . ."

"Are you willing to provide us access to your phone records?"

"Of course, but it was just some cheap disposable phone I purchased at Walmart, and . . . I don't even have it anymore."

"Hmm," Detective Collins says, eyeing me. "So, you purchased a burner phone for the purpose of talking to Jenna?"

"Yes, but not just Jenna. I was talking to a few others as well. And I got the phone because I knew what I was doing was wrong, okay? I was doing all of this behind my wife's back, and she has access to my phone records."

The detective's eye twitches at the corner again, and this time he also narrows both eyes slightly. "When and where did you dispose of the phone?"

"Yesterday, at a Kwik Trip gas station up in the Madison area. I was up there for work. I refueled before heading home." I deserve the stupefied look he gives me. "I know what you must be thinking, but it was before I knew Jenna was missing. I've been doing some soul-searching, and I know I have to stop what I've been doing behind my family's backs."

Collins opens his notebook and jots this down. Then he continues questioning me. "Do you recall the last time you spoke with Jenna?"

I hesitate because there's a good chance they already know the answer to this question. "It was on Thursday. And then—" I'm about to provide further explanation for the next few calls from my phone to hers on Friday morning, but he interrupts before I have a chance.

"What was your last conversation with Jenna about?"

I think about how frustrated I felt when she told me she had to cancel our plans to spend the night together on Friday and how I tried to reassure her how great it would be for us to meet in person. How I took things way too far by trying to entice her to change her mind with all the things I'd do for her and to her. "Like I already told you, I realized I needed to stop communicating with other women behind my wife's back. So, saying goodbye was the main focus of our conversation. I felt terrible cutting ties with her, especially since she'd confided in me that she was feeling down that day. She'd recently been dealing with some family issues, and a good friend of hers had recently started dating her ex-boyfriend. I wish I could continue to be there for her, and I hope she's okay, but I have to clean up my act."

"Mr. Bickers—"

"Oh, there's one more thing, just so you know I'm not trying to hide anything," I put my hands up in apology for interrupting him. "I tried to call Jenna a few times the next day, just to see if she was feeling better. But she didn't answer and never returned my calls."

"Okay," Detective Collins says, jotting a few things down in his notebook. Then he checks the wall clock. "I just have a few more questions for you, and then we should be able to wrap this up."

I nod. "I'll do my best to answer any questions you have."

He peeks inside the manila folder again. "Can you tell me about Cynthia Morris and Faith Perkins? Their corresponding nicknames on ChillChat are Sassy Sweet and Perky One."

Holy shit. This question catches me off guard, and I do my best to hide a hard swallow. I swear he can see and hear my heart trying to beat its way out of my chest. If they talk to either of these women, they will likely wonder why I have not cut ties with them the way I said I cut ties with Jenna.

"Um, as you know, I met them in chat rooms on ChillChat, and I had relationships with both of them."

"And what was the nature of these relationships?"

I shift in my seat and fold my hands on the table in front of me. "I met up with Cynthia a few times in person. Faith and I have spoken on the phone a number of times and have also communicated through Facetime, but our plans to meet in person fell through a few times."

"So is Cynthia the only woman from ChillChat who you've met in person?"

"Yes."

"So, you never met Jenna in person?"

"No."

"Did you ever make plans with Jenna to meet in person?"

"No."

"Did you ever ask her to meet you in person?"

"No."

"Mr. Bickers, do you have any idea why Jenna would have told a friend of hers that you'd asked several times if she would meet with you. Our source says it made Jenna uncomfortable."

Shit.

"No." I know I'm shaking my head too quickly, but I can't seem to stop. What else did Jenna tell this *source*? Suddenly, I realize it doesn't matter because my conversations with Jenna about meeting at the hotel were all verbal. We never texted about anything like that. Finally, I stop shaking my head. "I never asked Jenna to meet with me in person."

Detective Collins opens the damn manila folder again and flips to near the back of the pile of papers inside. I wait uncomfortably while he scans a few pages. Finally, he looks up as he closes the folder and says, "Just one last thing, Mr. Bickers. Where were you on Friday night?"

"Well, I worked until around six, then I stopped at a Chasers Pub over on Brown Deer Road for a couple drinks. Then I went home and didn't leave until Saturday afternoon to take my son to swimming lessons."

"Well, I think that covers all of my questions for now," Detective Collins says, stacking his notebook atop the picture of Jenna and the folder. "Is there anything else you'd like to add? Perhaps something Jenna may have mentioned when you spoke with her on Thursday? Something that might indicate where she might have gone on Friday night?"

"No, I can't think of anything. But . . . I'm just wondering . . . is *everything* I've told you unrelated to Jenna confidential?"

"Yes, Mr. Bickers. Your indiscretions will stay here at the station." He shakes his head and stands. Then he reaches across the table after I've stood too. "Thank you for coming down here today. We'll be in touch if we have any more questions for you."

"I'm happy to help," I say, shaking the detective's hand.

chapter thirty-eight

Sunday, October 1, 2017
Three Weeks Before Jenna's Disappearance

Jenna woke up a little after five in the morning. Her head was much clearer than it had been when she got home three hours earlier, but her eyes were still swollen from crying, and her mouth felt like it was full of cotton. As she downed the remaining water in the bottle on her nightstand, visions from the night before swarmed her. The way she'd smoked pot before the dance. The sadness and jealousy she felt when she saw Dustin dancing with Phoebe. The vodka she'd stupidly downed behind a dumpster at school. Making a fool of herself and her friends on the dance floor. Ditching out on the party she was supposed to go to. More pot and alcohol. Making out with the guy from Glendale. Was his name Nick or Nathan? She couldn't even remember. Stripping down to her bra and underwear and going in a hot tub in front of guys and girls she didn't even know. Telling Keeley to just leave without her. Having sex with the guy whose name she didn't even know for sure and whom she'd probably never see again.

Overwhelmed with guilt and panic, Jenna stumbled to her feet and rushed into the hallway, nearly tripping over Lulu. "Get out of the way," Jenna whispered harshly. Then, there in the dark hallway, she crumpled to her knees and buried her tear-soaked face in the dog's fur. What was wrong with her? Now she was even being nasty to her most loyal friend? "I'm so sorry," she whispered. Then she stood and tiptoed downstairs. She needed to text an apology to Keeley.

After she snuck into her dad's office and grabbed her phone off his desk, she stopped in the bathroom for tissues to dry the uncontrollable tears still streaming down her cheeks. Then she went to the kitchen to get another bottle of water. As she was about to exit into the hallway, she froze next to the garbage can, remembering her diary. She stepped on the lever to open the top and retrieved it.

Her tears slowed to a trickle as she recalled the conversation with her parents from the night before. How dare Jenna's mother read her diary, and how dare she accuse Dustin of hurting her. Maybe if her mom had thought a little harder about the entry she'd read, she would have realized that Jenna couldn't possibly have made up the poem without having experienced something traumatic, and that it had to be about a real person in Jenna's life. Now on top of embarrassed and ashamed, she was angry. All three were emotions Jenna was so tired of feeling.

When Jenna returned to her room, she invited Lulu in with her, and she got back into bed with her phone and her diary. She picked up her phone to text Keeley but found herself staring at text notifications from Dustin and Leighton. When she clicked to read Dustin's message, which had been sent around three a.m., her tears returned.

Dustin: Heard you had quite a night . . .

No. What did he hear? And who did he hear it from?
Jenna tried to recall if she saw anyone she knew other than Leighton or Keeley at the party, but she just couldn't remember. So, she skipped Leighton's text and opened the thread she had going with Keeley. First and foremost, she needed to apologize, but she also had to find out if there was anyone at the party who might have known Dustin. Surely, Keeley wouldn't have told him what happened? But would she have told Delaney, and then would Delaney have told Corbin?

Jenna: I'm sooooooooooo sorry, Keeley. For EVERYTHING. Please call me as soon as you get this.

Jenna sent the message and then began typing another right away to ask what Keeley remembered about the crowd at the party, but she realized she had to patch things up with Keeley before worrying about her own pride. Whatever Dustin heard about Jenna and whomever he'd heard it from didn't really matter because the fact was he knew. The thought overwhelmed Jenna and sent her into another fit of tears.

Out of habit, she threw open her nightstand drawer and reached for the Tylenol PM bottle that was no longer there. Without the ability to self-medicate, she did the only other thing she could think of. She opened her diary and started writing.

October 1, 2017

Dear Diary,

You're probably sick of hearing about me doing stupid things. Sorry. I can't seem to help it anymore. I feel like everything is spinning out of control, and I'm at the center watching it all happen. I know I could have skipped the party last night and prevented what happened, but I felt so jealous and angry when I saw Dustin with Phoebe, and I wanted to erase those feelings, just like I've been trying to erase all of my memories of Thomas. So tonight I made the decision, somewhere between beer pong and the hot tub that I was going to do something about it once and for all, and I let a boy I barely know have sex with me. I didn't enjoy it. In fact, I felt numb and thought about Dustin the whole time. When it was over, I felt nothing but empty, which actually felt good. Because it was so much better than all of the messed up emotions I've been feeling for the past couple months. But the feeling of nothingness was only temporary, and now I'm in an even worse state than I was before I found out Thomas was coming back to Briarwood because I think Dustin found out what I did, and I don't know if Keeley will forgive me for being a terrible friend to her again.

~Jenna

Jenna closed her diary and out of habit, leaned over to put it away in the second drawer of her nightstand. But just as she was about to let go of it, she realized she had to find a new place for it. She placed her current diary on her nightstand, hopped out of bed, and retrieved a shoebox from her closet. She brought the shoebox back to her bed, set it on her lap, and opened it. The sight of the eight tattered, old diaries almost caused another fit of tears, but she took a few deep breaths and was able to keep them at bay. She looked around her room, contemplating where else she could ensure the safety of her secrets. There wasn't anywhere.

Then she caught sight of the old pink and gray canvas bag she used to use for sleepovers at her grandma's house. It was big and sturdy with a waterproof lining. She rushed over to her open closet with the shoebox full of her old diaries and grabbed the bag off a hook. Then she transferred all the diaries into the bag before adding her old Briarwood High sweatshirt on top and zipping it up. She then forced the bag into her backpack along with her schoolbooks. It barely zipped but she was feeling desperate to protect her secrets, so she'd carry them around with her until she figured out a better solution. The empty shoebox went back in its place in her closet. Then she stood, staring at her current diary and wondering what to do with it. She couldn't bring herself to stow it away with the others because she wanted to continue using it. Jenna glanced over at her desk where she had a medium-sized storage bin full of craft supplies. She picked up her diary and took it to her desk where she opened the craft bin and pulled out an extra strong Velcro fastener—the kind her mom used to secure a power strip to the wall under Jenna's desk. She fastened one side to the back of her diary, and then crouched next to her nightstand and secured the matching side to the flat surface underneath. Finally, she secured her current diary in place, out of sight under her nightstand. No one would ever find it.

The sun streaming through Jenna's blinds woke her at ten the next morning. Her first thought when she opened her eyes was that it looked like a perfect day for a run. But when she rolled over, the desire to lace up her sneakers dissipated.

She glanced over at her phone and wondered if her dad had noticed it was gone yet. Then she reached for it, certain Keeley would have responded by now and hoping they could straighten things out before she was forced to give her phone back to her dad. But when she looked at her screen, her heart dropped. The only notification she had was the one for Leighton's text from the night before.

LEIGHTON: HEY. THAT WAS SOME PRETTY HEAVY STUFF WE JUST TALKED

ABOUT. I HOPE YOU'RE OKAY. I'M HERE FOR YOU ANYTIME YOU NEED TO
VENT.

Jenna didn't have any memory of venting to Leighton about anything, so instead of texting her back, she called.

"Hey, you okay?" Leighton asked.

"No. God no. I'm the furthest thing from okay."

Leighton responded with a sympathetic sigh.

"Leighton, I ditched Keeley, and even worse, I lost my virginity to a guy I don't even know."

"What are you talking about Jenna?"

"What do you mean? You were there."

"I know, but . . . first of all, you didn't *ditch* Keeley. She wanted to leave, and you didn't, so she left without you. So, technically, she ditched you. We're lucky Sticks was able to pick us up and take us home. And then what do you mean about losing your virginity?"

The mention of Sticks made something click in Jenna's brain. There was a gap in time Jenna hadn't realized she'd lost. Suddenly she remembered, and she was stunned speechless.

"Jenna? Are you there?"

"Yeah," she whispered, now cognizant of the breakdown she had in Sticks' car and of what she'd told them. "You know about my cousin, about what he did to me all those years."

"You don't remember telling us?"

"I didn't a few seconds ago, but I do now . . . I'm sorry for telling you that."

"What are you talking about? Why would *you* apologize? He's the one who should apologize. He should go to prison for what he did to you, Jenna."

"Leighton, please don't tell anyone about this. No one—"

"I would *not* do that to you, not unless you wanted me to. But if I ever see your cousin, I can't promise I won't hurt him," Leighton says with a protective fierceness in her tone.

"Thank you."

"Of course. I don't tell my friend's secrets to anyone."

The silence in Jenna's house made her think her family had gone to church without her, but when she entered the kitchen, they were all eating breakfast.

"Good morning." Her dad was the first to break the ice.

"Good morning," Jenna said as she made her way over to get a glass for juice.

"By the way, as soon as you're done with breakfast, I'm going to need your phone back," he said, raising his eyebrows at her. She nodded.

"How are you feeling today?" her mom said, looking over the cup of coffee she was holding.

"Not great." Jenna took a seat next to her little sister and whispered, "Hey." But Shaina kept her eyes on her bowl of cereal and didn't respond.

"You need to eat something. I'll make you some eggs," her mom said, standing.

"No that's okay. Juice is enough."

"No, I'll make you eggs, and you'll eat them."

Jenna glared at her mom, resentful of her controlling nature and still pissed about her diary.

"Jenna," her mom said, as she fired up a burner, "your dad and I are concerned about you, and it isn't necessarily about you breaking curfew last night. That's just part of it. We've been talking this morning, and we've realized you seem down lately. Is there anything going on that you want to talk to us about?"

"I think you found out everything you need to know from my diary," Jenna shot back.

"Jenna, I apologized for that."

Jenna shook her head, not interested in her mom's apology. She didn't trust her anymore because she knew that once someone crosses a line, it seems to be much easier to cross it again.

chapter thirty-nine

"Excuse me. Excuse me. Mr. Bock!"

I look up. Everyone in class does.

"I thought I made it clear that phones are not allowed during tests," Mr. Beauchamp taps an index finger on the class rules posted at the front of the room. "Number five, Mr. Bock. Absolutely NO phones during exams. Hand it over."

"But, Mr. Beauchamp, they found—"

"We don't have time for this, Mr. Bock. *You* don't have time for this." Beauchamp holds his upturned palm in front of my face. "Unless you'd like a zero on this exam, that is."

I hand it over with a loud slap against Beauchamp's hand. One by one, heads lower as everyone gets back to solving problems about logarithms. I lower my head but keep my eyes on Mr. Beauchamp because the stocky, rosy-cheeked man has stopped dead in his tracks and is looking at my phone screen.

At the end of class, I head up to Mr. Beauchamp's desk to get my phone. While I wait for him to finish talking to another student, I notice Keeley standing outside the room. I return her wave.

"Mr. Bock," Beauchamp says, handing back my phone. "I'm so sorry. Rules are just rules." He grips my shoulder and gives it a sympathetic squeeze.

"What was that about?" is the first thing out of Keeley's mouth. "He's even more of a hardass than Stickler Sartorius. Why did he touch your shoulder like that?"

I motion for her to follow me as we weave through the horde of students rushing to class or lunch.

"What is it? Can't we walk and talk?" Keeley asks.

I ignore her and keep walking because it's pointless to talk with all the noise around us. When we get to a less hectic landing at the top of the stairs, I look down at Keeley and hand her my phone. "Here."

"What?" She stares at Jenna's school picture from this year. It's displayed at the top of a short article in the *Milwaukee Journal Sentinel*. After a few seconds, she scrolls past it to read the article.

Teen Jenna Kemp (16) was reported missing by her parents on Saturday evening. Kemp, who is a Junior at Briarwood High School was last seen by a classmate on Friday evening just before nine.

A police department representative has confirmed that a 43-year-old man has been interviewed by a police detective. He is believed to have information that may lead to the whereabouts of the missing teen.

According to police reports, the man is associated with Kemp via a popular online chat room. Authorities are now looking into the screening protocol used by this particular site to ensure that users adhere to legal age requirements and are who they say they are.

Anyone who may have information about the whereabouts of Kemp is encouraged to call the Briarwood Police Department. Kemp is 5'4" and weighs approximately 130 pounds.

Keeley hands back my phone and says nothing. Her mouth just hangs open, and she stares at the floor.

"Do you believe this?" I ask. "Forty-three frickin' years old. What the hell was she thinking?" I ask, angry and hurt by Jenna all over again. "At least that asshole from Glendale was our age."

Keeley looks at me, but she still doesn't say anything.

"And this guy is *believed* to have information? What does that even mean?" I ask.

"I don't know," she says, shaking her head and lowering her face into her hands.

The bell rings, and when it stops, we're standing in complete silence.

"This chat room . . . Did you know she was using it?"

Keeley looks up at me and barely nods.

"What? Are you kidding me? And you didn't *bother* to tell me?" I glance through the windows of the doors to the second-floor hallway, worried that someone might have heard me.

"I just found out yesterday, and I was going to tell you today."

"Ever heard of this nifty thing called texting?" I shake my phone at her.

She crosses her arms. Her lips start to quiver, and I realize I'm being kind of a jerk.

"I'm sorry. I'm just . . . freaked out by this," I say, running a hand through my hair. "So how did you find out she was using it?"

"Well, Leighton is the one who told us about it first. She also told us about this guy who wouldn't stop messaging her, but she never said anything about him being forty-three. Then my mom, Delaney, and I went to see Mrs. Kemp last night because . . . well, that's a long story so never mind. Anyway, Mrs. Kemp said the police called her and told her about this guy Jenna met on ChillChat. When I texted his name to Leighton, she confirmed it was the same guy she knew about, the one mentioned in the article."

"My God, Keeley, this is bad. What was she thinking?" I ask.

"I don't know," she says, shaking her head. "But we better get to lunch."

I cringe at the thought of being around everyone because all they're going to be talking about is this man Jenna has been "chatting" with, and I'm sure everyone will have an opinion I don't want to hear.

When we arrive at the table, it's clear that the cat is out of the bag. No one is eating. Instead, everyone is looking down at their phones. As Keeley and I maneuver into empty spots, I scan a few of the surrounding tables to find the same scenario playing out at each, only some eyes are beginning to set sights on our table. Lara Stapleton is whispering in Rita Spangler's ear, and they're both staring at me. I shake my head at them and look away. Then I clear my throat, prompting half of the kids at our table to look up. Delaney glances at me but breaks eye contact right away. I wonder if it's going to be awkward like this with us forever.

"Oh my God, did you guys see?" Tina holds her phone up.

We both nod, and Keeley glares at Tina, probably not in the mood for her gossiping.

"We did," I say quickly scanning our table and nodding politely to anyone who looks up at me. *No Eli. That's weird.* "Hey, has anyone seen, Eli?" I get several head shakes and a couple nos. I'm sure he and his family have heard about this, and I hope he's okay.

"His family is probably really upset about this, so maybe they all stayed home today. You know, to pray or something?" Tommy offers.

Corbin shrugs. "All I know is if my sister was dating a forty-three-year-old, my parents would be pissed as hell."

"Corbin, that's not really the most disturbing thing about that article," Delaney says.

"Yeah, you're right. Sorry." He looks over at me and then at Keeley. "Sorry, guys."

"It's okay, man. It's hard to know what to say or think about any of this," I say.

"What I think," Tina announces to everyone, "is that we *all* should have seen something like this coming."

"Something like *what?*" Keeley asks.

"Oh, come on, Keeley. Everyone knows Jenna has been out of control since school started. I mean, she went from being a homecoming princess last year to being the sad drunk girl at every party."

"I can't even believe you just said that, Tina," I say, shaking my head and looking around the table. But to my surprise, everyone except Keeley has this look on their faces that tells me they all agree with Tina. I can't handle any more, so I stand, grab my backpack and leave.

"Where are you going?" Keeley calls after me.

I'm too upset to answer, so I just throw my arms up and keep walking. A few seconds later, I hear footsteps behind me. I glance over my shoulder and see Keeley and Delaney catching up to me. It feels like everyone is watching us leave, but then there's a commotion to our right. All three of us stop and look.

Leighton has her hands on her hips, and Haley Tompkins is yelling at her. Leighton is holding an empty Coke bottle, and the front of Haley's shirt is stained brown. When Leighton turns to leave, I catch her eye, and she acknowledges me with a nod. I nod back, wondering if the confrontation we witnessed had anything to do with Jenna.

chapter forty

Jenna almost didn't make it to school Monday morning. She couldn't fathom the idea of walking into Briarwood High because she knew what the hot topic of the day would be. Her.

To make matters worse, Keeley had never responded to her apology text from early Sunday morning. That wasn't like Keeley, who always checked her phone throughout each day. As for Dustin, Jenna never got a chance to respond to his cryptic text because she had been forced to hand over her phone, and she wouldn't be getting it back for at least a few days.

She could feel eyes on her from the moment she walked through the front doors, and the suffocating sensation stayed with her even after she got to her first class. When she walked through the door, she could have sworn she heard one of the guys who sat near the door whisper her name, and then other whispers followed. Desperate for some sort of friendly connection, she took a chance and glanced at Jordyn and Emily when she walked past their desks. They both gave her the same indecipherable smile, fueled by either embarrassment or pity. Jenna couldn't tell which, so she decided it was probably both. Either way, it was definitely a bad sign.

After their creative writing teacher finished explaining the paired writing activity for the morning, everyone scattered to pair up. Jenna just sat there, hoping she'd be the last person without a partner so she could join an already formed pair. That would make it much easier for her to participate as little as possible. But to her dismay, someone must have been absent because there was an even number of students that day, and the last person left without a partner was Haley Tompkins.

"So, Haley and Jenna, you two can pair up then. Sound good?" Mrs. Holbarth asked. But both girls knew it wasn't a question she wanted them to answer.

Haley pulled an empty desk next to Jenna's with a huff. "This sucks," she said under her breath.

Jenna glared at her but didn't care enough to respond. She had enough going on without worrying about their feud that had started in eighth grade.

After a few minutes of working on the writing exercise, Jenna began to relax and figured as long as they stuck to only talking about the assignment things would be fine. But there were other things Haley wanted to talk about.

"So, I heard *you* had fun after homecoming."

Jenna knew there was no way she'd make it through the day without having to hear what people knew about homecoming night, but of all people, Haley was the worst to hear it from. "Who did you hear that from?"

Haley smiled. "I don't remember to be honest because I heard about it in a group text on Sunday." She shook her head. "Poor Dustin. I'm glad he at least had Delaney to lean on while you were at that party."

The mention of Dustin infuriated Jenna, making it impossible for her to keep her cool. "What are you talking about?" she hissed.

"Oh, you don't know?" Haley asked, genuinely surprised.

Jenna clenched her teeth and glanced around the room. Even though everyone appeared to be working, she was certain they were all listening in on her conversation with Haley.

"Corbin had a little too much to drink and passed out pretty early, so Delaney ended up talking to Dustin the whole night. I guess he even drove her home." She shrugged. "I figured you heard about it already. I mean, they are two of your closest friends, right?"

Jenna felt like slapping the smug expression off Haley's face. Instead, she didn't even give her nemesis the satisfaction of a response, which squashed the topic.

By the time lunch rolled around, Jenna was eager to talk to Keeley. Leighton suggested maybe it would be better for her to wait until after school, but Jenna was done waiting. Comforted by the fact that Leighton was watching from across the cafeteria, Jenna approached her usual lunch table. She scanned for only two people: Dustin and Keeley. Dustin wasn't among them. Wide eyes, whispers, and a gasp or two greeted her when she got there, but she didn't bother addressing anyone except Keeley.

"Hey, can we please talk?" Jenna asked, crouching down next to Keeley.

Keeley looked over at Jenna, her eyes appearing darker than usual due to the circles around her eyes. Jenna instantly recognized the effects of excessive crying. "I guess so."

"How about somewhere private?"

As Keeley slid out of her seat, Delaney said, "I'll save your spot." Then she looked at Jenna, but Jenna couldn't bear to meet her gaze.

Jenna led Keeley across the cafeteria and took a seat near Leighton.

"I thought you wanted privacy?" Keeley asked, staring hard at Leighton.

Leighton nodded at her and said, "Hey." But Keeley just shook her head and sat down next to Jenna, turning her back away from Leighton.

"Keeley, I'm so sorry for not going home with you on Saturday night. I don't know what I was thinking." Jenna knew her last statement wasn't true, but it seemed like the right thing to say.

"Yeah? Why are you sorry? Because of what you ended up doing after I left? Because you were late getting home? Or because someone from our school happened to be there, and now everyone knows what you did?"

"I . . ." Jenna wanted to know so badly who from Briarwood was there that night, but she knew it wasn't the time to ask. "I'm sorry about all of it, but I'm especially sorry for telling you to leave without me. Not because any of the other stuff that happened after you left, but because I know it probably upset you."

"Okay," Keeley said, shaking her head. Jenna knew it didn't mean she was forgiven, but it was something.

"Keeley, I need to ask you something else."

"What?"

"Do you know what Dustin knows? And what happened between him and Delaney?"

Keeley scoffed. "Jenna, everyone knows *everything*. If you didn't want people to talk about how you stripped down to your bra and underwear in front of a bunch of people you don't even know, then maybe you shouldn't have done it. And if you didn't want people talking about what you did with that guy, then you *shouldn't* have done that *either*. And as for Delaney and

Dustin, I think you and Delaney should talk about it . . . or you and Dustin . . . or maybe all three of you." With that, Keeley stood and was about to leave, but then she turned back and said, "I just . . . I just need some time to cool off. And maybe you need some time to figure out what's going on with you."

But at that point, Jenna was barely listening to Keeley. She was too overwhelmed with her feelings of embarrassment and abandonment. First Dustin had abandoned her, and now Keeley was about to as well.

"You have got to be kidding me," Leighton said with disdain. "Those are *some* friends you've got." When Jenna didn't respond, she tried again. "Screw them." Still, Jenna sat there unresponsive, staring after Keeley.

chapter forty-one

"Leighton. What are you doing here?"

"Hey, I need to talk to you."

I step to the side and hold the door open wide for her to come in.

"Keeley?" my mom calls. "Who is it?" I hear her footstep approaching so I don't answer just yet. When she rounds the corner from the living room, she pauses. "Oh," she says pleasantly.

"Mom, this is Leighton." I look at Leighton, who's already stepping forward to shake my mom's hand. "Leighton, this is my mom."

"It's very nice to meet you, Leighton." My mom smiles at her and then at me. "Keeley, I forgot we need olive oil and parmesan. I'm going to run to the store. Do you need anything?"

"No, thanks."

"Bye, girls."

"Bye, nice to meet you," Leighton says.

"Come on," I say to her. "My dad is in his office working, so we can talk in my room."

When we walk into my room, Leighton looks around as she sets her backpack on my bed. "Nice room."

"Thanks. Hey, what was that commotion at lunch about?"

"Oh, that Haley girl likes to talk a lot of smack about people, so I was just setting her straight."

"Well, what did she say?" I ask, knowing just how right Leighton is about Haley.

Leighton shakes her head. "You don't want to know."

"Pft. Yeah, I do."

She sighs. "Fine. I overheard her talking about Jenna and the night of homecoming . . ."

Maybe she's right, maybe I don't want to know.

". . .She said something about the guy from Glendale and called Jenna something not so nice. So, suddenly I wasn't thirsty for my Coke anymore, and I needed a place to pour it."

Despite what a sour memory the night of homecoming is for me, I can't help but laugh at Leighton's choice of words. She laughs too.

"So, what's up? What did you need to talk to me about?"

Leighton's expression turns grave, and she grabs her backpack. "I found something."

"What?" I'm not sure I want to know what she has.

Leighton walks over to my desk and places her backpack on top. Then she unzips it and pulls out a bag that looks familiar. It takes me a second to realize it's Jenna's. I watch as Leighton raises the flap of the pink and gray bag and unzips it. I feel like I might pass out wondering what's inside. I'm confused for a second when Leighton pulls out Jenna's ratty old Briarwood hoodie, but then I see what's still inside the bag. *Jenna's diaries*.

"Where did you get those?"

"Jenna brought this bag to my house the first time she slept over and left it there. I reminded her about it a couple times, but she asked if she could just leave it there in case she slept over again."

"Did you read them?"

"Parts," Leighton says, glancing at the floor.

"Well, is there anything revealing in them?"

"Yes . . . but—"

"Then maybe we should give them to Mrs. Kemp. Because maybe the police can—"

"Keeley," Leighton says, shaking her head vehemently. "You need to read them first." She lifts the stack of journals and holds them out to me.

"Why?" I ask, carefully taking Jenna's diaries and transferring them to my bed. "Just tell me what you read."

"I can't. I promised Jenna I wouldn't, and I'm not breaking the promise. So I need you to read them and see for yourself."

"Wait, so you knew about whatever it is *before* you read them?"

"Yeah." Leighton starts pacing my room.

"I don't understand," I say taking a seat on my bed next to the diaries. What would Jenna share with Leighton, someone she'd only known for a couple months, that she wouldn't share with me or Delaney?

"Just read some of the entries," she pleads. "Just pick one and start reading. Trust me, you'll understand."

"Okay," I say, splaying the diaries out in a line across the width of my bed. I open each one to see when they start then put them in chronological order. Leighton glances at me every few seconds as she continues to pace. "Are you sure this is all of them?"

"Yeah, why?"

"Because the last one ended in June, so where's the one . . ." Suddenly, I remember where the next one in line is. "Never mind."

"Why never mind? Leighton asks.

"Because Mrs. Kemp said Jenna threw it away the night of homecoming when they got into a huge argument."

"That sucks," Leighton says with a sigh. "So, are you going to read or what?"

I nod, grab the most recent diary which appears to cover our sophomore year, and place it in my lap. Leighton takes a seat at my desk and pulls out her Chromebook.

I read a few entries and become anxious because I still don't know what Leighton wants me to see so bad. So far, it's all normal stuff like how excited Jenna was about cross country, how annoying her little sister could be, how lucky she was that a guy like Dustin liked her, how happy she was when I gave her a photo album for her birthday, and details about her runs. But then I read something weird about how she's not like other girls when it comes to liking guys . . . about how she was never like us.

October 5, 2016

Dear Diary,

I wonder if I'll ever be interested in guys the way "normal" girls are. Ever.

*He took that from me. And now I'm afraid that I'm scarred for life and
doomed to never be able to have a relationship because of everything that
happened. (All those things that my nightmares have been made of for
years.) I'm not saying I don't think a certain guy is cute. I just feel like it
wouldn't be fair to him to try to be more than friends.*

Do you think I'll ever be normal?

~Jenna

He took that from me. I read the line at least ten times. He took *what* from
her? Her ability to be interested in guys? And who is she talking about? I
read the entry to Leighton and ask, "What do you think she's talking about?"

"Just keep reading," she says.

So I do. I reread this same entry a few more times and obsess over the
part about Jenna wondering if *she's scarred for life and doomed to never be able
to have a relationship because of everything that happened.* I read this part at
least twenty times. At some point, my brain wanders back to seventh grade
when I clearly remember being into guys. Delaney and I must have been the
most boy-crazy girls in our grade. I thought Jenna was too. She talked all
about who liked who and helped us write stupid love letters. She even wrote
a few herself. Was it all an act? Was she pretending to be interested? It
makes me wonder how well we know Jenna.

None of the entries I read next raise any red flags. Jenna wrote about
things like which shoes she wore to go running, how far she went, and
which course she took. If I was with her, she wrote about how trying to
match my stride made her run faster one day but slower the next. She wrote
about how she felt while she was running, what she thought about while
running, what the temperature was, and what she ate before and after. Even
after reading all of it, I wouldn't say she's obsessed, but I would say she's in
love with routine and recordkeeping. She also mentioned conversations I
remember having at the merry-go-round. This was around the time when
we talked about the order in which we'd get our licenses and what colleges
we'd apply to. Of course, we all planned to apply to the same places and
would only agree to go somewhere that all of us could go. The only requests
Jenna had was that it couldn't be Northwestern because that's where her

dad went and that she wanted to go somewhere at least an hour away from home.

Frustrated, I grab the diary from when we were twelve and going into middle school and open it to a random page.

August 25, 2013

Dear Diary,

I have the best friends ever. They've been such an important part of my life ever since we met in kindergarten. Remember when we were The Three Little Pigs for Halloween? Now that I think about it, we always wore costumes that went together. Three peas in a pod, The Three Stooges, The Three Blind Mice—anything you can think of that comes in threes. I wonder if my mom and dad remember calling us a three-ring circus. Haha. Anyway, I haven't written in almost a week, so I figured I'd pop in and write something.

This year is going to be great. I can't believe we're going into middle school!

This entry makes me feel horrible, and I wonder if Leighton is playing some prank on me. Then I flip the page to an entry that sends chills down my spine and turns my entire world upside down.

August 30, 2013

Dear Diary,

What's wrong with me? What's wrong with my parents? Why would they leave me alone with him?

You're right. It's not their fault. Maybe it's my fault. But what am I supposed to do?

"What?" I whisper, glancing over at Leighton. She stops typing and turns in my desk chair to face me. I return my attention to the entry.

I thought it was over and sometimes I even thought I dreamed it all. Or nightmared it. (Is that a word? It should be.) I thought maybe all the memories were fake. My teachers always say I have a great imagination. Or maybe I've watched too many movies on the Lifetime channel with my mom. I always pray, asking God to make sure it doesn't happen again or to erase the thoughts from my head. I'm starting to think he can't hear me.

I glance up at Leighton again, my brow creased. She stands and walks over to stand beside me while I continue reading.

I can only remember bits and pieces from this time, just like all the other times. After, it's always like I was a stranger, watching from outside. (So maybe it is all in my head? I can't figure it out.) I jumped when he knocked and said he'd picked up a DVD copy of Pitch Perfect and would I like to watch it. I thought, "say no . . . tell him you're sick. Whatever you do don't let him in!" But he came in before I had a chance to move, and then my brain screamed at me to get out! Leave the room! Then I realized I'm old enough now to leave the house too. But where would I go? I don't remember what I said to him as I rushed past him to get out of my room. His smell makes me sick, and I'm scared I'll never get it out of my nose. Even shoving cotton balls up my nostrils doesn't work. I still smell him. I could smell him following me. But there's never any way for me to escape.

"Oh my God. Oh my God. Oh my God," I whisper, fearful of what's coming next. Leighton sits next to me but stares across the room.

When we first sat down, he acted normal and I thought maybe since he's a grown-up now he wouldn't touch me. He asked questions. How's school? Are you still running a lot? Have you taught Lulu any new tricks? I started thinking maybe he wanted to forget too, and I answered his questions. Then the movie started, but after a few minutes, he asked more questions. Questions that made me feel sick because I knew he was the same. Have I been on a date yet? Do I have a crush on anyone? Have I gotten my period yet? That's when I thought talking to him might make him think I'm okay with everything he's done to me. So I told myself to go back to my room. To run. Close the door. Push something in front of it so he can't get in. Just don't talk to him. Don't even look at him. And I was about to run. But then

*he asked about Shaina. She was at a sleepover, so I knew she was safe. But I
still felt like I had to protect her, to make him not think about her. So I froze
like all the other times.*

Like all the other times. I read it again, and tears well up in my eyes. I don't
know if I can stomach this anymore. Then I think about how Jenna must
have felt, and I press on.

*I can hear his voice right now like he's next to me whispering in my ear, but
I don't know what he's saying because I try not to listen. I can feel his
clammy hands on my face and neck. And I can feel him petting my hair like
I'm a dog. Sometimes he does it too hard and rips out strands of my hair. I
think this is what crazy people feel like.*

*The next thing I remember is staring at the TV and the sound of water
running in the bathroom. When he came back, he grabbed the package of
Twizzlers off the coffee table and sat down next to me. Then he restarted the
movie. I didn't really watch, because I couldn't see anything. It was like
when you close your eyes and all you can see is black, except my eyes were
wide open. I think my brain was rebooting or something, sort of like at
school when a computer freezes, and you have to turn it off and then back on
to unfreeze it. I wish my brain could restart like that.*

*When Mom and Dad got home, Dad paid him for babysitting, and Mom
wanted to know why I looked so pale and if I felt sick. I can hear them
talking and laughing downstairs. I don't know what they're saying, but
every time I hear his voice, I want to scream. I hate you! And every time I
hear my mom's voice, I want to scream. Do you know what he did to me?
And every time I hear my dad, I want to scream. How could you let him do
this to me?*

*I wish I could go down there right now and tell them everything I can
remember. But what would I say? Where would I start? With the time he
showed me the pictures? They'd probably wonder if I was sleepwalking again
or if I was confused from a bad dream. Or why I never said anything before.
And he would just say he didn't know what I was talking about. And
everyone thinks he's so wonderful, so who would believe me?*

Now the best summer ever is the worst. Why did he have to visit?

~Jenna

"Oh my God . . ." I climb off the bed, and start pacing, "Holy shit . . ." My breathing is labored, and my chest hurts so bad. "I can't . . . I just can't . . ." Leighton steps in front of me and grips my shoulders.

"Keeley, calm down. I know. I know." She pulls me in for a hug. "It's okay. You're okay."

I don't know how long we stay that way because all I can think about is the things I just read. Jenna's tortured words. Words that represent memories of actual torture. When Leighton loosens her arms, I pull back slowly and say, "Okay, I'm okay. I mean . . . I'm not okay, but we need to figure out what to do next."

She nods supportively and steps over to my dresser to grab me a few tissues. As I'm wiping my eyes, my phone rings. Leighton peeks at it where it's charging on my desk. "It's Delaney," she says, handing it to me.

I sniffle and clear my throat before answering. "Hello."

"Hey, Keeley, hang on a sec . . ." Mumbling . . . *too loud . . . math homework . . .* "Hey," she says. "I'm almost to my room. . . Okay, I'm here."

"Why's it so loud in your house?"

A door slams. "Ugh! My mom invited some of the ladies from her salon over for tacos and margaritas. Fiestas are loud. I'm so pissed at her. Jenna's missing, and she's acting like everything is fine and dandy. It's like she couldn't care less that I don't exactly feel like being around so many cheerfully clueless women. Sheesh. So, what are you doing?"

"Well," I glance at Leighton, who's looking at the pictures on my cork board, "Leighton is here, and she brought something with her."

"Excuse me. Did you say Leighton is there?"

"Yes, and this is serious. She has all of Jenna's old diaries."

"And she brought them to your house?"

"Yes."

"Why didn't you call me to let me know?"

"Because she just got here a little while ago, and . . . I wasn't sure there was anything in them worth telling you about, but . . . Oh my God, Delaney," I burst into tears again. "The one I just read is horrible."

"What do you mean? Why is it horrible?

I blow my nose and compose myself before answering. "Can you just come over?"

"Keeley, I *can't*. I have to babysit for our neighbor's kids in like twenty minutes. Just tell me what's horrible."

"I . . . I don't think I can . . ." I glance at Leighton, who's staring at me sadly. "I'll just read it to you. It's from the summer before we started seventh grade."

"Okay, go ahead."

I read the painful entry, pausing every time Delaney freaks out. When I'm finished, she's speechless. "Delaney?" Nothing. "Hello?" Still nothing. "Are you okay?" I hear sniffling and then nose blowing so I wait until she's ready.

Almost a minute later, she says, "It's Thomas."

"Yeah, I think so too. Hey, is it okay if I put you on speaker so Leighton can hear?"

"Yeah, of course."

Leighton sits back down in my desk chair as she and Delaney exchange brief, somber greetings, and then Delaney says, "Oh my God. Maybe Jenna did run away. What Thomas did to her would give her plenty of reason. We need to give the diaries to Mrs. Kemp."

"But do you think Mrs. Kemp will want to share them with the police when she finds out what Thomas did to Jenna? Will she be okay with basically turning in her nephew? Jenna told me how close her mom is to Thomas's mom. Will she be okay with turning in her sister's son?" Leighton asks.

I'm speechless because it never even occurred to me that Mrs. Kemp would protect Thomas.

Delaney sighs, "Well, we need to tell someone."

"I agree," I say, "but I hear what Leighton is saying too. Plus, maybe we should read more to see if she actually ever mentions Thomas's name. I mean, to us and to anyone who knew Jenna's family back then, it's obvious who she's talking about, but it might not be for other people."

Leighton chews on her lip, considering what I've said, and Delaney sighs through the phone.

After a few seconds of silence, I continue. "You know, after reading those entries, Jenna's transformation makes perfect sense. She did start acting weird after Thomas moved back. Maybe all the drinking and drugs was the way she was coping with having to see him again."

"Yeah, and on a regular basis too," Delaney says. "It's not like it's easy for her to avoid him when he's part of her family." Delaney gasps. "It's probably hard for her to be around her aunt's entire family. I mean, Keeley, you and I have always talked about our aunts and uncles and cousins and about how much we look forward to family gatherings during the holidays. Jenna only talks about her dad's side of the family, but never her mom's, not until recently when she told us they were moving back. It never even occurred to me how odd it was that she never mentioned them after they moved."

"That might explain why she didn't want Eli around," I say, feeling guilty for ever even liking Eli and putting Jenna through that stress without even knowing what I was doing. Then my stomach turns sour because I wonder if Eli might know what Thomas did to Jenna. I can't bring myself to share these thoughts with Delaney and Leighton, though. Instead, I say, "I wonder why she never told us."

"Maybe she was afraid no one would believe her, or maybe she was afraid it's been so long that he wouldn't face any consequences. Or maybe she thought she was fine after he was out of the picture for so long," Leighton says. "Like you said, all of her issues started when he moved back."

"But why did she tell you? I don't understand. Why not Me or Delaney . . . or Dustin even?"

"Wait, when did she tell Leighton?" Delaney's frustration is crystal clear.

"She told me the night of homecoming, but she was kind of messed up, so I'm sure that had something to do with her telling us. She had a breakdown in the car when my friend Sticks and I were taking her home. It was heartbreaking." Leighton rubs her eyes hard with her fingers as if trying to erase the memory.

"If she told you way back on the night of homecoming then why didn't you say anything?" Delaney practically yells.

"Because I promised her I wouldn't," Leighton yells back. She stands and starts pacing again.

"You guys, this isn't helping," I say.

"Look, I probably should have tried to convince her to tell someone, but . . . I didn't want to push her. I just wanted to be there for her. But now I realize I could have handled it differently, and . . . I have to tell you guys something else."

Delaney and I both remain silent. The only sound is Leighton's footsteps on my carpet.

Leighton stops at the foot of my bed where my phone is lying. Then she folds her arms across her midsection and takes a deep breath. "That night—the last night I saw her—she told me she was tired of not facing shit, tired of stuffing her feelings all these years and tired of self-medicating the way she has been lately. So, she'd decided to confront Thomas, and that's where she was going when she left my house."

chapter forty-two

Jenna had just done horribly at a home cross country meet, so instead of getting dropped off at home by her teammate Sonia's mom, she asked to be dropped off at Leighton's saying they had homework to do together. For the past few days, she didn't communicate much with anyone in her family—just muttered greetings and fake pleasantries at mealtimes. Her dad had just returned her phone that morning, but after three days without it, she had no desire to even use it. She'd told herself she didn't care if there were messages from Keeley or Dustin when she turned it on, so when there weren't, she shrugged it off.

"So, how was cross country?" Leighton asked.

"Eh, it sucked. I ran horribly and ended up in the bottom quarter. I think I'm just going to quit."

"Didn't you say you trained all summer and you've been running, like, since birth?"

"Yeah, but I'm just not into it anymore . . . Can I have one of those?" Jenna pointed at Leighton's pack of cigarettes.

"Yeah, sure," Leighton said with a shrug. She wondered why all of a sudden Jenna wanted a cigarette when Leighton had never seen her smoke one before, but she fought the urge to ask. Instead, she satisfied other curiosities. "How's everything with your mom? Is she still walking on eggshells around you?"

"It's so annoying. And she's trying to be super nice to me by making my favorite foods and buying snacks I like." Jenna said. She lit a cigarette, mimicking how Leighton held the flame of the lighter to the edge and inhaled. She only coughed a little as the smoke rushed down her throat, but she enjoyed the instant numbness she felt in her head. It was nothing compared to drinking or smoking pot, but it was something.

"I wish my mom would cook dinner more often for us, but I don't even think she knows what my favorites are anymore."

"Right, but at least your mom doesn't invade your privacy by going through your personal things."

"True, but my mom has other issues," Leighton said, grabbing her laptop off the coffee table and opening it.

Jenna was in the middle of taking a puff, so she didn't respond to the comment Leighton had made about her mom, but she did make a mental note to ask her again what was up with her hostility toward her mom. "What are you doing over there?

"I was chatting with a few people before you got here."

Jenna stood and moved next to Leighton on the loveseat. She leaned back and into Leighton so she could get a good view of the laptop screen. "Let's Taco 'Bout It?" she asked.

"Yeah," Leighton laughed. "It's exactly what it sounds like. These people love tacos and talk about all sort of crazy new combinations they've tried. Sometimes I get bored eating macaroni and cheese or tuna from a can."

Leighton waved the smoke from the Jenna's cigarette out of her face.

Jenna wasn't really smoking it anyway, so she put it out.

"So who were you chatting with?"

"What?"

"You said you were chatting before I got here."

"Oh, right." Leighton clicked out of the taco chat and showed Jenna a list of people she'd been privately chatting with.

"What are you talking to all of them about?"

"I don't know. Just random stuff. This guy, Spoonman, is like the founder of a Soundgarden fan club, and he messaged me because of my nickname."

"Black Hole Daughter," Jenna said. "That's creative."

"The thing is I'm not really even a Soundgarden fan. I told him that, but he just won't stop talking to me about the band. He keeps asking me trivia questions."

Jenna laughed.

"This is Hobs. I met him in a Breaking Bad chat group, and he has some pretty interesting theories about the show. And this one, Stacy P., is from a group for kids considering running away. I told her it was a bad idea, and then she started telling me why I was wrong, and I changed my mind."

"Huh,' Jenna said. "Maybe I'll open an account."

"You can do it right now if you want." Leighton logged out of ChillChat.com and placed her laptop on Jenna's lap. "Just click right there on Register. I have to go pee."

When Leighton returns, Jenna is so immersed in browsing the chat rooms, they don't talk for a good thirty minutes. Leighton spends the times playing Candy Crush on her phone.

"You weren't kidding. This is kinda fun. And addictive," Jenna said without looking up from the screen.

"Right?' Leighton responds. "Just remember not to share anything too personal."

Jenna nodded and clicked on a chat room that came up in her search results for the word *alone*. Her only thought when she then clicked to join the group *Lost and Alone, looking for a Friend* was that maybe hearing about other people's problems might make her feel better.

"Hey, do you wanna sleep over tomorrow night?"

"Sure, but my mom will probably want to talk to yours." She rolled her eyes but still didn't take them off the screen.

Leighton laughed. "My mom will say she's going to be here after she gets done with her shift, but I guarantee, she'll go to her boyfriend's house right after instead. And she usually doesn't even come home."

chapter forty-three

Before Leighton left and I disconnected the call with Delaney, I read one more entry aloud at Leighton's urging. It wasn't as descriptive as the one that gave Thomas away in mine and Delaney's minds, but it was equally disturbing because Delaney and I remember that day like it was yesterday. Leighton and Delaney both say it's up to me to decide whether we should hand the diaries over to Mrs. Kemp or not because I've known her the longest and my mom talks to her mom more than Delaney's mom does. So now I'm sitting here, looking at the scrapbook Jenna made me for my fifteenth birthday and trying to decide what to do next.

The scrapbook is filled with running-related photos of Jenna and me. The first two pages are from grade school. The next set of pictures are from various fun runs we've done over the years. That section is followed by middle school track meets and selfies we've taken while out on practice runs together. The last photo in the book is from our most recent spring break. After admiring the photo for a few seconds, I remove it from the scrapbook and use it to mark the page of the *Runner's World* magazine that Delaney was looking at the day before. The next time I see Jenna, we'll decide where our first out-of-state running event will be. I know she's going to pick Hawaii.

I close the scrapbook, grab Jenna's diary from 2013, and flip to the last entry I read out loud to Delaney and Leighton.

August 31, 2013

Dear Diary,

I didn't really feel like going to Jolliet today, but Keeley and Delaney wouldn't quit texting me. Where are you? What are you doing? Tell me you're not ditching us on the last night of summer vacation . . . so I went. My mom wasn't happy about it since I didn't go to church and spent the morning hiding out in my room, but my dad agreed that some fresh air would do me good since I've been "cooped up all day."

Anyway, getting to the park was hard. My feet just didn't want to move. It felt like I was walking in sand. But I forced myself to keep going. When I was close enough to see them on the swings, it got a little easier.

I did my best to act normal, but they could tell I was having a bad day. I knew they would be able to tell. They've always been able to tell. And like always, they kept asking what was wrong. You know how I sometimes wish I could tell them everything, right? Well, today was one of those days, so I almost spilled my guts—right in the middle of Delaney's story about her dad agreeing to let her mom open a beauty salon. I kept looking from Delaney— who was describing her parents' argument from the night before—to Keeley —who was being a good friend and actually listening to Delaney. I imagined the way they would probably look at me if I told them what's been going on. What if they tell people? What if they ask why I've never said anything before? What if they don't believe me? Worst of all, what if they do believe me and think it's my fault? What if it is my fault?

So I didn't say anything. And when we got the merry-go-round going, I closed my eyes and wished it would all just spin right out of me. The anger. The shame. The pain. His warm breath making stray hairs tickle my cheeks. His weight suffocating me. I used to pray for it to stop, but when it didn't, I switched to praying to forget. Praying never worked.

~Jenna

This was the last day she met us at the merry-go-round. She didn't want to go to Thomas's going away party before he left for graduate school. She begged us to go, but we were tagging along with Delaney's mom to a wedding in Minneapolis. Delaney and I thought Jenna was just upset that she couldn't go with us to the Mall of America.

Now that we know why she didn't want to be anywhere near Thomas, we need to do something about it.

"Mom?" I whisper, knocking lightly on my parents' bedroom door. My dad's rhythmic snores become louder as I gently push the door open.

"What's up, honey?" She slides her glasses to the tip of her nose as she glances up from the book she's reading. "Trouble sleeping?"

Clutching Jenna's diary from the summer before seventh grade to my chest, I glide over to the chaise lounge situated next to her nightstand and sit.

"What do you have there?" She dog ears her book and places it on the nightstand. Then she wriggles upright and adjusts the pillows behind her.

"Do you promise you won't be upset with me?"

Turning to face me, she throws the covers off and swings her legs over the side of the bed. "Keeley. What is it?"

"Do you promise?"

Sighing, she says, "I promise . . . but only if it's not something illegal. Now what is it?"

I release Jenna's diary from the death grip I have on it and lay it gently on my lap. "We found Jenna's old diaries. Well, Leighton did."

"Oh, Keeley, not ag—"

"Mom," I plead, "you have to read something. Something horrible that happened to her when we were twelve. And I'm positive it wasn't just the one time."

"What are you talking about?" she says, standing.

"You have to read it for yourself, Mom. I don't even think I can stand to read it again," I say. I wipe my eyes with one hand and hold the diary out to my mom with the other. She slowly reaches out and takes it from me. "Read the entries dated August thirtieth and August thirty-first."

"Keeley, I can't read Jenna's diary," she says, shaking her head and placing it on her nightstand. "But I'll go with you tomorrow to return it to

Bonnie. Then she and Joseph can decide whether to read it or not. Now please—"

"Pastor Thomas assaulted her."

"Excuse me?" She places a hand on her chest.

"That's why she's been having so many problems lately. I think it all happened when we were younger, before he left for college. And now he's back, and she can't handle it. And Delaney and I should have known." Tears form, and my face heats up with anger and regret. I feel like I've let Jenna down.

"Oh, my . . . Are you sure?" she stammers. "What exactly does it . . . are you positive about this?" She snatches the diary from her nightstand, sits on her bed, and places it on her lap. Then she flips to the entry from August thirtieth and reads as I look on. A few moments in, I already have to get her some tissues. When she's finished, she stares straight ahead, a blank expression on her face. And I just sit there and wait for her to say something, anything. Instead, she flips to the next entry.

"Mom?"

She puts a hand up to silence me. So, I lay back on the chaise lounge and wait while she reads a few more entries. I get her new tissues when her eyes well up with fresh tears. Then I get some for myself too because seeing her cry makes me cry.

"Oh, Keeley," my mom says, closing Jenna's diary. "Oh, honey." She joins me on the chaise, and we hold each other until our sobbing ceases.

"Who else knows about this?" my mom asks, standing and getting new tissues.

"Just Delaney and Leighton."

She nods as she hands me a tissue and then blows her nose.

"So, what should we do? The three of us talked about giving all the diaries to Mrs. Kemp, but we're afraid she might not want to turn them over to the police because she'll want to protect Thomas."

"No," my mom says shaking her head. "Absolutely not. When Bonnie finds out, she will do everything in her power to make sure Thomas pays for what he did to Jenna. Trust me," she cups my chin, "I know."

For the first time since I found out about Thomas, I breathe a sigh of relief.

"Mom?"

"Mm-hm."

"There's something else."

"What is it?"

"The night Jenna disappeared, Leighton says she had plans to confront Thomas. She was going to tell him that she was going to the police about what he did to her unless he turned himself in."

"Oh, Keeley," she says, gripping her forehead. "We need to give these to Bonnie and Joseph as soon as possible."

I stand and pick up Jenna's diary. "Is it okay if I put this with the others?"

"Of course. Get some rest, and we'll deal with this tomorrow. Goodnight, sweetie." She kisses me on the forehead.

"Goodnight."

As I pull my parents' bedroom door closed, I hear my dad's groggy voice. "What's going on?" I hear the bits and pieces of my mom's response. "Keeley's . . . upset . . . back to sleep . . . morning."

<hr>

Before I go to sleep, I call Jenna's phone, even though I know it'll probably still go to voicemail.

"Hey, Jennaboo. It's me Keeley. I miss you. We all do. And we need you to come home. I'm so sorry for not responding to your text last Friday. Turn your phone on, and you'll get so sick of me because I'll text you every day for the rest of your life . . . Jenna, are you there?"

When I disconnect, I can barely see through my tears.

chapter forty-four

"So, what do you feel like doing tonight?" Leighton asked Jenna as they walked up the stairs to Leighton's bedroom. Jenna took a seat on Leighton's bed. She was clutching a pink and gray bag to her chest. "You can put that down if you want," Leighton said, motioning to a chair in the corner of her room.

"I don't know," Jenna said, walking over to the chair and placing her bag on it. "What do you want to do? Thanks for having your mom call my mom, by the way."

"Sure," Leighton said with a shrug. She looked down at her phone when it pinged. "I was going to suggest a party on the East side Sticks heard about, but I just got a text from this guy I met at a Red Hot Chili Peppers concert at Summerfest. He says he and a buddy are looking for something lowkey to do tonight. Do you want me to invite them over? Or would you rather check out the party? Or we could just watch movies. It's up to you." Leighton held her phone, poised to respond to the text one way or the other, depending on Jenna's response.

After two weekends in a row of parties, Jenna figured staying in would be better. "Invite them over. Maybe we can all watch movies," she said with a shrug.

Two hours later, the girls were playing drinking card games like Asshole and Bullshit with Aaron and Trey, the guys Leighton had invited over. Aaron was the guy Leighton had met at the Chili Peppers concert. They'd texted and hung out a few times after, but this was the first time they'd seen each other since school started.

As the minutes ticked by, the guys spent less time focusing on playing cards and more time focusing on playing the girls. Leighton was keen to the moves that were being made, but Jenna didn't seem privy. She didn't react at all when Aaron put his hand on Leighton's thigh or when he leaned over and bit her earlobe playfully. Nor did she react when Trey slid close to her so that their thighs were touching. Maybe it was the rum and Cokes they'd been drinking, or maybe she didn't mind.

When the cards had been abandoned and *The Breakfast Club* turned on, the four sat in pairs—Aaron and Leighton on the loveseat and Jenna and Trey on the couch. Aaron was just about to put the moves on Leighton when Trey said, "You got any pretzels or something?" He swiped his fingers around the edges of his mouth bringing them down into a V at his chin. Jenna recalled seeing him do this a few times throughout the evening and wondered if it was a nervous habit like the way Dustin always ran his fingers through his hair. Then she scolded herself for thinking about Dustin.

"No, but we have some pickles and cheese curds."

"What about Doritos or something? Something crunchy." Trey asked.

"Pickles are crunchy," Leighton said, giving him a look.

Trey gripped the couch cushion and pushed himself up. "Aaron, gimme your keys. I'm gonna run and get something. You all want anything?"

"I'll just go with you. I need cigarettes," Aaron said. "You two wanna come?"

When they got to the gas station on the corner of Hampton and Santa Monica, Leighton and Jenna decided they were too cozy in the backseat of Aaron's car to make the trek inside. "Get me a Coke," Leighton said, as they got out of the car.

Trey leaned his head back inside. "Jenna, you want anything?"

Jenna shook her head then continued swaying to the song that was playing. She smiled a thanks at Trey, and he smiled back. When he stood to leave and closed the door, a couple walking out of the Italian restaurant next door caught her eye and then her breath.

"What?" Leighton asked, catching the stone-cold expression on Jenna's face. She followed her gaze out the window then moved her body to block

Jenna's view. "Don't worry about them, Jenna." But Jenna didn't so much as blink. "Hey," Leighton said, shaking Jenna's knee.

"Huh," Jenna finally met Leighton's eyes.

"I said don't worry about them."

"I'm not," she lied. But she wasn't just thinking about how close Delaney and Dustin were walking next to each other or how happy they looked. She was also thinking about how she could use another rum and Coke and a cigarette or two.

By the time eleven o'clock rolled around, Jenna was feeling nice and toasty inside. She was hoping Trey might kiss her, but he only seemed interested in having his arm around her as they sipped their drinks, smoked their cigarettes, and watched end credits of the movie. Leighton and Aaron were another story. Jenna tried not to watch as they made out, but she couldn't help stealing a few peeks. She looked over at Trey and was about to lean over and kiss him, but his phone rang.

"Hey," he said, standing and walking to a far corner of the room. Jenna sighed and watched as he talked and nodded to whoever was on the other end. "Hey, Leighton," he called out.

Leighton didn't respond so he walked up next to the sex-crazed pair and leaned in close. "Leighton, what's your address?"

"Why?" Leighton and Aaron both looked up at Trey, unfazed by how close he was to them.

"A buddy of mine is in the area and needs to stop by," Trey said, standing.

Leighton rattled off her address, and within minutes, the doorbell rang. Leighton looked over and saw Trey was already moving toward the door, so she went back to kissing Aaron, who'd never stopped kissing in places other than her mouth.

"Hey, man," Trey said, opening the door.

Jenna thought she was imagining it at first when she saw Jamie Bock walk through the door. When she realized it was him, she quickly set her drink down on the table and pushed the ashtray she'd been using as far away from her as possible. She didn't need any more rumors about her circulating at school.

"Jenna Kemp? What the hell are you doing with this guy?" Jamie said as he gave Trey a dude handshake. He glanced over at Aaron and Leighton on the couch. Aaron raised his arm and did some kind of symbol with his fingers in greeting. Leighton ignored Jamie.

"I'm just hanging out . . . Leighton knows them."

"Hope you're behaving yourself," Jamie said with a nod before he and Trey turned their attention back to each other. From what Jenna could tell, Jamie was there to do some business with Trey. She saw them make an exchange but couldn't tell who had given what to whom. Then Jamie was gone, and Trey was back next to Jenna rolling a joint.

"Be careful. This stuff is strong," Trey said to Jenna.

Jenna didn't listen, and the next thing she knew, the room was dim, and a hand was stroking her arm. It took her a few seconds to get her bearings. "Trey?" she said.

"Shhh," he said back. Then he kissed her neck, and she froze.

By then Jenna's eyes had adjusted to the dark, so she was confused when she saw blond hair. Wasn't Trey's hair black? When she realized what was happening, she tried to push herself up, but she was trapped under Aaron's weight.

"Get off of me," Jenna said, but either Aaron hadn't heard her, or he was too messed up to care. Jenna struggled and pushed and squealed, suddenly reenacting what she imagined herself doing when she was twelve years old. And just when she was about to start punching and pulling hair, the lights turned on.

"What the fuck are you doing?" Leighton said, rushing down the last few stairs. All she had on was an oversized T-shirt. "Get off of her, you asshole!"

Jenna's eyes flicked from Leighton's wild eyes as she approached, to Aaron's glazed eyes, to Trey on the loveseat. He was beginning to stir.

Within seconds, Aaron was on his feet, shirt in hand, and Leighton was shoving him toward the door with her body. "Jenna, throw me his keys," Leighton said without taking her eyes off Aaron. When she heard the keys rattle, she looked over her shoulder and caught them when Jenna tossed them. "Get out of here, and don't ever contact me again," Leighton said, shoving Aaron's keys into his pocket.

Aaron mumbled obscenities as he put his shirt on. "Yo, Trey, wake up."

"I'm up. What's going on?" Trey stood and glanced around the room, blinking a few times. When he saw Jenna's unbuttoned shirt and the way Aaron was practically pinned to the door by Leighton, he seemed to understand they'd overstayed their welcome. He gathered up his belongings off the coffee table and met his friend at the door.

Within minutes of Aaron and Trey's exit, Jenna had returned to the groggy state she'd been in before she realized Aaron was touching her. Leighton took a seat at the other end of the couch and covered herself with a blanket. She sat there staring at the front door and smoking a cigarette.

"Thank you," Jenna whispered.

"That guy is an asshole," Leighton responded.

"Why did you burn that letter from your dad?" Jenna didn't know why she was asking that question at that moment, but it had been on her mind ever since the day she witnessed it. Plus, she figured she'd shared her own dark secret with Leighton the weekend before, so it seemed only fair for Leighton to share a secret of her own in return.

Leighton caught Jenna's eye and stared at her for a second as she took a drag. After she exhaled all the smoke, she started talking.

"The last time I had friends sleep over, I was in ninth grade. It was Sasha, who I'd been best friends with since kindergarten, and this new girl Candy, who'd moved to our neighborhood that summer. My mom was working late at the hospital like she always does, so my dad was home with us. We'd just removed our charcoal masks and brushed our teeth. At that point, we were all going to take turns in the bathroom to change and do whatever. Anyway, while Sasha and Candy were taking their turns, I went downstairs to get my phone charger and bottles of water for everyone. When I got back upstairs, I caught sight of Candy walking back into my room.

I figured I'd drop the water bottles off in my bedroom before using the bathroom. So when I got in there, Candy was standing just inside the door like she was frozen. Sasha was sitting on my bed reading a magazine. I held a bottle over Sasha's shoulder, but she didn't reach back for it, so I lowered it and squeezed by her so I could get all the way into my room. As I did Sasha looked up and asked Candy if she was okay. Candy raised her electric toothbrush cap as she raised her eyes to meet mine and said she'd forgotten it, so she'd gone back to get it. I shrugged, tossed a water bottle onto the bed next to Sasha, and tried to hand one to Candy again but again she didn't take. She looked up at me and said she didn't feel well and had to go home. I asked her what was wrong, but she just repeated she had to go, so her mom picked her up, and when I asked my best friend if she thought the new girl was really sick, she said she didn't know. Then I asked if she wanted to watch a movie, but she said she was tired, so I lay there watching TV by myself and wondering why Candy had to leave so suddenly. Monday at school just didn't feel right. I had the sense people were whispering behind my back, and it kept happening day after day. Within a week, I felt like a total outcast, so I asked Sasha, who had also been acting weird toward me, if she knew anything. She told me Candy had told her that my dad had exposed himself to her, and then she told me that my dad had done the same thing to her a few times. I was pissed and called her a liar, which made things worse, of course. School became a daily hell for me because everyone seemed to think I must have been defending my dad. My mom never believed it was true, and even after she found out he'd gotten a twenty-year-old pregnant and was leaving us for her, my mom still wanted him to stay. Can you imagine what it was like when that got added to the Leighton Pierce rumor mill at school?"

Leighton paused, listening for a response from Jenna. When all she heard was slow rhythmic breathing, she stood and tossed the blanket over Jenna. Before she went up to bed, she said, "So, anyway, yeah, the rumors you've probably heard about me ripping Candy Sloan's hair out might have some truth to them."

———

October 7, 2017

Dear Diary,

I finally figured out a way to escape. Leighton. Her mom will tell my mom and dad whatever they want to hear. She set my mom's mind at ease last night, telling her that she'd be home all night long to monitor Leighton and me. Well, here's a secret. She really wasn't. It's not that her mom is a deadbeat parent or anything. She just works nights and likes to sleep at her boyfriend's on weekends.

Some of her friends came over and drank and played some drinking games I'd never played before. It was actually a lot of fun, and I thought maybe it would continue that way. But then we took a drive to a gas station, and I saw Dustin and Delaney walking out of a restaurant together. I told myself it wasn't them at first, but my mind just doesn't seem to like when I try to block out things that bother me, so yep, it was them. When we got back to Leighton's I tried to drown out how upset I was over seeing them by drinking more, but that didn't really work. And then one of the guys who was there (Trey) he offered me some really strong weed, so I took it hoping that would put Dustin and Delaney out of my head. And it did. And things would have been great after that if I hadn't woken up to the other guy Aaron all over me, groping me, and trying to kiss me. Thank God Leighton stopped him.

But you know what? I fought him. I did things that I'd always thought about doing to Thomas. And you know what? It felt good.

~Jenna

When Jenna finished her entry, she closed her diary and secured it with the elastic band around its center. She crouched down on the floor and slid it underneath her nightstand, securing the Velcro in place. Then she crawled back up on her bed and logged into her ChillChat account.

chapter forty-five

I've just returned from walking Brady to his bus stop, and Julie already has more tasks for me.

"Now I need you to change two burnt out lightbulbs—one in the basement and one in my mom's room. Then, while you're in Mom's room, why don't you go ahead and administer her meds? I need to clean up Sam."

I hold in my irritated sigh. This isn't what I meant when I said I would make it up to her after she'd told the police I was home with her last Friday night. I didn't really have anything specific in mind, but none of this was it. I help plenty on the weeknights when I'm home and on weekends, so all this extra stuff before I leave for work is a pain in the ass. "Okay, but those are the last two things I can do because I have an appointment at ten."

"Fine," she says as she wipes the kitchen table clean then moves over to Sam in his filthy highchair.

In fact, she hasn't been looking at me much since I told her about Jenna. How does she expect us to work things out when she's being so cold and distant?

When I get down to the basement, I pull my phone out of my pocket and check a local news app I downloaded for the sole purpose of checking for new articles about Jenna. I almost drop the lightbulb I'm holding when I see a new headline.

Person of Interest in the Jenna Kemp Case Identified

"Crap, how the hell did the media get my name?" I say to myself. Then I reason that I might be jumping to conclusions. There could very well be another person of interest at his point. Maybe Jenna was talking to other people on ChillChat. Or maybe that relative of hers who assaulted her when she was a kid has something to do with it. The thought makes me nauseous. Most of the chat room conversations I've had are shallow and only about one thing, but it was different with Jenna. I really enjoyed my chats with her and wish she was still around. I'm tempted to click on the article, but I know if I do, I'll never get out of here on time, so I pocket my phone and finish the tasks Julie assigned me.

After I finish pouring water into my bedridden mother-in-law's GI tube, I tidy up her blankets and turn on the TV for her. She can't watch it, but Julie says she likes to listen to it.

I need to get going if I want to make my appointment in Oconomowoc on time. When I enter the kitchen, Julie is standing at the counter staring at her phone screen. The dishwasher is open but still not unloaded, and Sam is clean and in his playpen, but his highchair is still a little dirty. I need to get out of here before she asks me to help with any of it.

"I should be home around—"

"Why . . . is your name . . . in the *paper*," she growls. "And how are you still a person of interest?"

I close my eyes and wish I was anywhere other than standing in my kitchen.

"Jacob, my sister forwarded me the link to this article. Do you have any idea what that means?"

I take a seat at the kitchen table, set my bag on the floor, and lower my forehead onto my hands.

"No? You don't have anything to say? Fine. I'll spell it out for you. It means everyone we know is going to know that you were using a filthy chat room to pick up women! And some of them might even wonder if you did something to that girl."

"I'm not a person of interest anymore, because I did *nothing* to Jenna," I say, not even bothering to look up at my wife. "And I have no idea why the press would say that."

"Oh, but you are a person of interest. To everyone who reads the *Milwaukee Journal Sentinel* this morning. Have you seen this yet?" Julie slides her phone across the table, and it lands directly under my nose. I close my eyes again, though, because I don't even want to see it anymore. I don't have to either because I'm sure Julie will tell me what's in it.

"And just FYI, Sienna Carter, the woman you went on a few dates with in college, has informed the whole world, including me, about your porn fetish." This gets my attention, so I finally look up at her. Big mistake. She's looking at me like she wants my head on a stake. "I guess there's still a lot I don't know about you."

"Come on, Julie. That was something from my college days. You know me."

She shakes her head with a smirk. "I don't believe you never met Jenna Kemp in person, and I don't believe you've never met up with any of the other women. Tell me the truth, Jacob. I know you lied to me, so just tell me the truth!"

"Julie, I swear I never met Jenna in person, and I also never me—"

"You're lying. I know you are. Tell you what, how about you tell me the truth, and I don't go down to the police station and recant my statement about you being home with me on Friday night?"

"Julie—"

"I swear to *God*, Jacob, I'll do it."

I sigh heavily and run my fingers through my wavy hair like a madman because Julie doesn't bluff. "Okay, Jenna and I had plans to meet on Friday, but I canceled them. I've also had plans to meet one other woman, but it was at a Starbucks, and she didn't show."

Julie narrows her eyes at me. "And?"

"And that's it, Julie. I *swear* on my mother's good name."

"And you swear you didn't know Jenna Kemp was a minor?"

"I swear it," I say, making an X on my chest with my finger.

She shakes her head and turns to the dishwasher. "Please pick up a rotisserie chicken on your way home from work."

I exhale a slow, silent sigh of relief because at least the article doesn't reveal the truth about my infidelity with women from ChillChat. If it did, Julie would be asking for a divorce instead of a rotisserie chicken.

chapter forty-six

Jenna's phone chimed. It was the sound she'd assigned for notifications for ChillChat. She glanced at the screen wondering if it was a response to her comment in the discussion about which sex offender levels should qualify for rehabilitation. Jenna's opinion was that there should be zero tolerance, and she was ready to defend her stance.

Instead, it was a response from a private chat.

Patty P.: But do you think he likes me?

Jenna typed her answer and immediately hit send.

Runner Girl: ABSOLUTELY. But even if he didn't, you'd still have to break up with Tim. No lying to each other, right? Okay, then . . . You've been stringing Tim along, waiting for Mario to make a move. That's not cool.

Then she went back to doing homework on her Chromebook. But she had a hard time concentrating because she couldn't ignore when someone responded to her on ChillChat.

She was obsessed with the site. The anonymity of it allowed her to express herself the way she was never able to before. At first, she did a lot of observing in chat groups, but over the last few days, she'd begun to type responses when a thought struck her. And the more she participated, the more comfortable she started to feel. Leighton kept reminding her to not trust people on there and to not share any personal information, but she didn't see the harm in sharing certain generic things like her favorite color or what her dog's name was. Patty P. was her first private ChillChat friend. They were in a chat room called *Relationships for Dummies*, and Patty and Jenna had bonded in a conversation about whether it's okay to date a friend's ex. Patty and Jenna both said absolutely not. Patty sent Jenna a private chat request the next day, and they'd been messaging back and forth ever since.

Besides Patty, Jenna had private chats going with a few others too. Duke was a dog lover she met in a chat room called *Let's Talk Dogs*, and he sent her an old comic called Marmaduke one day. Jenna figured that's where his nickname came from. So, Jenna responded with a Snoopy cartoon, and now they send cartoons containing dogs back and forth. Leighton saw the conversation once and told Jenna that Duke was probably a thirty-year-old guy who lives in his mom's basement and sending comics was his way of flirting. StoneFX found Jenna in a chat room about marathon training. He'd told Jenna he was a forty-eight-year-old divorcee just looking for a friend with similar interests. When he asked Jenna how old she was, she said she was twenty-six. The next day, he asked her if she'd like to meet for a run because she also said she lived in Chicago where he lived. She told him they needed to chat more first before meeting in person. Then there was Jake B. He'd only just contacted her privately on Tuesday night, but they spent hours chatting. It wasn't until Jenna realized it was after one in the morning that she said goodbye. The next day, Jake B. contacted Jenna again, but unlike the lighthearted getting-to-know-you conversation they'd had the day before, he asked if he could vent. She said sure, and they ended up chatting again for hours about how depressed he'd been lately. It was amazing how Jenna could relate, not to the exact life experiences he'd described, but to the way he was feeling in response to a life of pretending.

Jenna was finally able to finish her homework when she silenced all notifications from the discussions she was part of and closed out all but one of her private chats. She was still hoping to hear from Jake B. that night.

It wasn't until around ten after she'd gotten ready for bed, let Lulu out to use the bathroom, and made her lunch for the next day that he messaged her.

Jake B.: Know what I just realized?

Runner Girl: Hi! What?

Jake B.: We never properly introduced ourselves. I'm Jacob.

Jenna thought for a moment about whether to give him her real first name. She quickly decided it was harmless information. How would anyone track you down with your first name?

Runner Girl: So, is your nickname really a nickname in real life? My name is Jenna.

Jake B.: No. So that's just my way of staying anonymous on here. :)

Runner Girl: Are you feeling better today?

Jake B.: A little bit now that I'm talking to you, but I still have a lot on my mind.

Runner Girl: You can tell me anything.

And Jacob did. He told Jenna all about how stressed he felt about having to take care of his deceased wife's ill mother and how much it reminded him of his own mother who'd been bedridden due to an accident and died when he was just nineteen. That led to stories about his alcoholic father who'd abandoned them because he was unable to cope with his mother's health issues. Jenna was happy to hear that Jacob at least had kind and caring grandparents who'd stepped in to care for him and his mom after his father left. Jacob then went on to talk about how in debt he was after paying for the health bills and funeral expenses of his grandparents. He could have put them in a nursing home and walked away, but that wouldn't have been right after they'd cared for his mother when she was ill. They nearly went bankrupt having to pay for all the medical equipment and home health care nurses she required. And now he was going through the same ordeal with his mother-in-law. The only silver lining was that he stood to inherit a good chunk of money when she died, including a lot of land up north. Jenna listened, only asking relevant questions for things she wanted to know more about. Two such questions were how he met his wife and what happened to her. He told her all about how he and his wife met in college when they worked together at the student union bookstore. It had been a few months after his mother had passed away, and he'd moved into an apartment on campus. After he and his wife got married, they tried to have children but couldn't. So, they began fertility treatments during which they found out she had stage four uterine cancer. What started out as the hope of having a child turned into the hope that she would survive, but she didn't.

Somehow, Jenna and Jacob ended up chatting well into the early hours of the morning. In fact, it was so early that Jenna decided to not even go to sleep before school. Instead, she did something she hadn't done for a while. She went for a run. While she ran, she thought about Jacob's parting message that night.

Jake B.: Maybe the next time we chat, we can actually talk. I would love to hear your voice. Call if you feel comfortable. I'm busy this weekend, but Monday night works great for me. 414-555-2375 Bye, Jenna.

She wasn't sure what she was going to do. All she knew at that moment was that talking to Jacob was making her feel like she might be able to tell someone other than Leighton and Sticks about Thomas. After the things Jacob had shared with her, maybe she'd even feel comfortable telling him. She had three days to decide what she was going to do.

chapter forty-seven

"Hey, Mom. I'm home," I call out as Delaney and I enter through the back door. We rushed straight home after school because my mom had texted me that she'd been in touch with Bonnie. She was expecting us at four, so my mom had left work early and said she'd be waiting for us when we got home.

"I can't believe I would have been babysitting for Stella tomorrow tonight if we hadn't found out about Thomas."

"How did you get out of it?" I ask.

"I called Audra and told her a family emergency came up. I felt horrible talking to her and knowing what I know, especially when I heard Stella laughing in the background. That poor little girl."

"Yeah, poor Audra too. Did she ask what the emergency was?"

"Um, actually, yeah. So, I said my Grandma Shirley slipped in the bathtub and broke her hip and we had to drive to the hospital in Stoughton tomorrow after school to see her. She was very sympathetic and said she'd pray for my grandma. I felt even worse about lying to her then. To think she's going to pray based on a lie I told. I'm sure God will love that."

We hear my mom padding down the stairs, and we enter the kitchen at the same time, Delaney and I from the mudroom and my mom from the hallway. She's wearing the leggings, fuzzy knee-high boots, and a sweater I picked out for her the last time we went shopping together. The outfit screams comfy-cool mom.

"Hey, sweetheart. Hi, Delaney. I'm glad you're able to go over to see Bonnie with us."

"Hi, Mrs. Simon." Delaney gives my mom one of her signature angelic smiles reserved for parents.

"So, Keeley, I just got off the phone with your father, and he thinks—"

"You told Dad?" My voice is an octave higher than normal.

"Well, not everything. But, Keeley, you can't expect me to process all of this on my own. Your father has worked with clients who've been abused, so he has experience. You know? He thinks it's a good idea if we come right out and tell Bonnie what Jenna wrote about Thomas instead of just handing over the diaries and sitting there while she reads it for herself. After we find out how she's doing, of course. We can't just march in and start out by telling her that her nephew is a sick son of a bitch."

Delaney and I look at each other, eyes wide, then we both look at my mom and nod. She's right. He is a sick son of a bitch. And my dad *is* a good resource when it comes to issues like this. God knows he's seen it all as a therapist. I just don't like the thought of him thinking about what Thomas did to Jenna. Actually, I don't like thinking about it myself. I'm also worried that now he's going to psychoanalyze Jenna every chance he gets, the way he normally does whenever someone we know has anything traumatic happen to them.

My mom clasps her hands together. "Ready to go?"

"I don't think I'll ever be ready to talk about this with anyone," I say.

On the short car ride over, we talk about Jacob Bickers and the article that everyone at school was gossiping about today.

"I just don't understand it," Delaney says. "I thought he was questioned and released on Monday."

"Well, I imagine the media needs to report something about Jenna, and so far, Jacob Bickers is the only lead they seem to have." My mom turns down the volume of the radio as she talks.

"Is it legal for them to talk to a bunch of people who knew him a long time ago?" I ask. "I mean they interviewed people he went to high school and college with."

"I don't think there's any law about reporting on people's opinions of someone," my mom says with a shrug. "And those people's opinions got people talking. That's what news outlets want."

"I still can't get over the fact that Jenna was using a chat room to meet people. The police have to be able to find someone else they can question from there," I say.

"And how Bickers is a forty-three-year-old married father of two," Delaney adds. "I wonder what his wife thinks about him talking to a sixteen-year-old."

"He said she told him she was nineteen, though," I say.

"Girls," my mom says, "sixteen . . . nineteen, to a wife that wouldn't matter. The first thing I'd want to know is why my husband was using a chat room in the first place."

We pull up in front of the Kemps' house. Mrs. Kemp must have been watching for us because she's already holding the door open as we get out of the car.

We all give Mrs. Kemp a hug when we walk through the door. Then she leads us into the living room. As soon as we're all seated, Mrs. Kemp says, "Thank you, ladies, for checking in on me again." She eyes my backpack as she talks.

"Is there any new news from the police, Bonnie?" my mom asks.

"No," she says, her eyes glazed as if she's looking through us. "Nothing at all. Absolutely . . . nothing." She shakes her head and then looks out the window. "You know, they asked about the motion cameras at our front and back doors. They wanted to see the footage, thinking maybe they could narrow down the time when Jenna dropped off the car, maybe see if she was with someone. But the batteries got low in August, and we were just so busy all the time that neither Joseph nor I changed them." She looks at us. "Do you believe that? If one of us had taken five minutes to pop new batteries into even just the front porch camera, we'd probably know a heck of a lot more than we do." She leans forward in her chair, props her elbows on her knees with her hands folded, and stares at the floor.

I widen my eyes at my mom, imploring her to say something. I don't know how Mrs. Kemp is going to react to what we discovered, but at least it's something.

"Bonnie?" my mom says.

Mrs. Kemp looks up.

"The girls—Keeley and Delaney—"

"And Leighton," I add, to which Mrs. Kemp creases her brow.

"And Leighton," my mom says, "they discovered something you should know."

"What is it?" She looks from me to Delaney and back again.

I take a deep breath, unzip my backpack, and pull out Jenna's pink and gray bag. Mrs. Kemp eyes the bag curiously as if she knows she's seen it before but isn't sure if it's Jenna's or not. I unzip it and pull out Jenna's diaries.

"Keeley," Mrs. Kemp's breath hitches, "are those . . . where did you . . ." She stands slowly, shaking her head.

"Leighton. She said Jenna brought them over to her house about a month ago and she left them there."

"Oh my God," she says, bringing her hands to cover her nose and mouth for a second. "Thank you for returning them."

Delaney and I look at my mom. She sighs before looking at Jenna's mom. "Bonnie, there's something Jenna talks about in these that you should know."

"You mean, you've read them?"

My mom nods.

"So did I," Delaney says.

"We all did," I say.

Mrs. Kemp looks from me to Delaney to my mom. "Leslie? Is it bad?"

"Bonnie, your nephew Thomas . . . we think he sexually abused Jenna."

"What? What are you talking about? Thomas wouldn't . . ." She shakes her head in disbelief, and I think about making a run for it with Jenna's diaries. "Why would you say something like that?"

"Because it's true," my mom says. Then she turns to me and holds out her hand. I remove the diary on top and hand it to her. She opens it to the page we've marked as she stands, walks it over to Bonnie, and sets it on her lap. "Read this."

"No." Bonnie shakes her head and closes the diary. "I've invaded Jenna's privacy before. I won't do it again. No."

"Bonnie, you have to read it." My mom pulls the diary from under Mrs. Kemp's hands, reopens it and plants it back in her lap. But this time she doesn't let go. She holds it open until Bonnie looks down at the entry and begins to read.

After what seems like an eternity, Mrs. Kemp closes her eyes for another eternity. Delaney and I begin looking at each other and shifting in our seats. My mom puts her hands up, motioning for us to be still.

Then all of a sudden, Mrs. Kemp is out of her seat and heading for the kitchen.

"Bonnie!" My mom gets up and follows her.

Delaney and I tail both of them. When we get into the kitchen, my mom is standing between Mrs. Kemp and the door to the garage.

"Move out of the way, Leslie," Mrs. Kemp screams. She accidentally drops her keys, and my mom beats her to them. "Give me my keys!"

"Not until you calm down and tell me what you're going to do."

"I'm going to kill him," she says through gritted teeth.

"Mom?" We all look over at Shaina who's behind us looking on from the living room. "Who do you want to kill? Did someone hurt Jenna?"

Mrs. Kemp stands there staring at her youngest daughter, her chest heaving. "Yes. Someone hurt your sister very badly, and I'm going to make him pay for it." She holds her hand out to my mom and says very calmly, "Leslie, please give me my keys. You, of all people, should understand that I *need* to help my daughter."

As we pull away from the curb in front of the Kemps' house, I watch Joseph hugging and comforting Shaina. When he got home from work shortly after Bonnie left and asked where she was, Delaney and I took Shaina upstairs so my mom could explain what happened. His reaction wasn't much different from Bonnie's, but somehow my mom convinced him to stay with Shaina.

"Do you think Thomas will go to jail?" Delaney asks.

"I don't know," my mom says.

"What do you mean, you don't know? How could he not go to jail for what he did to Jenna?"

"Keeley, we can't assume everything in Jenna's diary is one hundred percent accurate. Those entries were from a long time ago, and . . . with the trouble she's been getting into the last couple months and the drug and alcohol abuse." She shakes her head. "I just don't know."

"Why would any of that matter?"

"I don't know, Keeley, because they could say she was a troubled child."

"But she wasn't a troubled child," I say.

"Yes, she was," Delaney says. "Just not in any way that would lead her to make up something like that. Remember the nightmares she used to have, Keeley?"

I nod, turning in the passenger seat to look back at Delaney. "She had them all the time, at almost every sleepover."

"And the way she would whimper and toss and turn in her sleep. Sometimes when I touched her to wake her, her skin would be all sweaty," Delaney says.

"Oh, girls. I had no idea. Jenna has always been such a sweet, polite girl. And she always seemed so . . . happy."

"That's how she was to everyone mom. Only Delaney and I saw her when she was sad."

"Well, no wonder she snapped. A person can only hold sadness and trauma in for so long."

We sit in silence the rest of the way to our house. When my mom stops at a red light by Jolliet Park, I think about how Delaney and I were just here on Saturday morning, right before we walked to Leighton's, but it feels like it's been years. And for some reason, nothing about the park seems as magical as it used to, not even the old merry-go-round. Even though it was before everything started with Jenna.

Good times. Bad times. Boring times. We've spent every kind of time together at Jolliet. But now, we're without Jenna, and even if she does return, I'll never be able to think of this as her magical, safe place again. I always assumed she thought of it that way just like Delaney and I, but now I wonder if I was wrong. How could any place feel magical or safe for her? Maybe that's why she loves running so much. Maybe being in one place makes her feel like she can't escape the pain she feels. Maybe that's why the spinning helped too. Like a dizzying type of therapy. But now I realize the brain numbness that spinning elicits has always been a temporary solution to combat the demons that are probably always active in her mind—maybe that's why she's drinking and doing drugs now. No amount of hypnotic spinning or alcohol or drugs could possibly eliminate those thoughts for good.

chapter forty-eight

SUNDAY, OCTOBER 22, 2017
FIVE DAYS BEFORE JENNA'S DISAPPEARANCE

As Jenna sat in church that Sunday morning, she thought about everything but the sermon, which was being delivered by none other than Thomas because her uncle was feeling under the weather.

She watched as Mr. Kimble held out his hand for Mrs. Kimble when it was time to rise for The Lord's Prayer. When he helped pull her to her feet, Jenna thought about all the old, frail people in Jacob's life who he'd taken care of.

For the past couple weeks, it was like he'd been taking care of her too, being there for her to tell someone how her week was going, being there to listen when she was hurting about the fact that Dustin and Delaney were dating and telling her how beautiful she was when she finally sent him a selfie. Since then, though, things had changed. He'd asked her on Tuesday night what she was wearing and then asked if she'd send a full shot selfie so he could see all of her. Then Friday night, when he'd called her around midnight, he asked if she'd be willing to say certain things to him. She tried to play along, but it made her uncomfortable, so she ended up clamming up and telling him she had to go. He apologized the next day by text, and when she didn't respond, he called her that night even though he said he could never talk on Saturdays. He felt bad for whatever he'd done to upset her, which made Jenna feel bad because it wasn't about him. It was about her. So, after contemplating sharing with him the way he'd shared so much with her, she told him about Thomas. He was outraged and told her how badly he wanted to help her feel safe and comfortable with him. But she was beginning to sense that she didn't feel the way for him that he felt for her, which made her realize she might have to stop talking to him.

When it was time to take communion, Jenna thanked God for the friend he'd given her in Leighton who had served a purpose much like Jacob in Jenna's life. As crazy as it seemed, Leighton also offered a certain level of comfort. Jenna wondered if it was because damaged people are drawn to other damaged people, and the comfort was an empathetic response, sort of like a sixth sense. Maybe two wrongs don't make a right, but two negatives do make a positive. And that's exactly what her friendship with Leighton reminded her of.

As people stood for the final hymn, Jenna watched Audra and Stella. She found herself looking back and forth between them out in the congregation and Thomas standing at an elevated position in front of them. Jenna felt a sudden need to protect them from Thomas.

When the time had finally come to file out of the chapel, Jenna purposely switched sides so she could be in Thomas's line. She saw the shock in his eyes when she shook his hand and held his gaze. Doing so had helped her stand a little taller. But shock wasn't the only thing she sensed behind his dark bottomless pits for eyes. Was it remorse? She wondered. When she released his hand and walked past him, not only did she feel a sense of relief, but she also felt as if the gauntlet had been thrown down. It had been her warning to Thomas that she wasn't going to stay silent any longer.

chapter forty-nine

"I need to talk to Detective Collins. Tell him it's important."

"Mrs. Kemp, he's in—"

"Now," I demand, slamming my hand on the counter.

"Mrs. Kemp," the desk clerk says, unintimidated, "He's . . . in . . . a meeting."

The way she draws out the words infuriates me, but I need this woman's help, so I know I need to reign it in.

"Please listen to me." I lean over the desk. "Someone hurt her. And I think he's the reason she's missing."

An alarmed expression crosses the clerk's face. "I'll see if I can get Collins' attention. Please have a seat."

"Thank you," I say, remaining on my feet.

Moments later, Collins appears, and he doesn't look happy. "Mrs. Kemp, you've been down here every single day. I promise you we're doing—"

"I brought you new evidence," I interrupt, shoving the entire stack of Jenna's diaries into Collins' arms. He staggers a bit as he steadies the pile and gets a better grip on it.

"What are these?"

"Those are Jenna's diaries from the past eight years. They prove that Pastor Thomas Steele abused her."

"Mrs. Kemp," Collins whispers. "Please keep your voice down." He looks over at the desk clerk and asks, "Can you buzz us in?"

When we get to Collin's office, he offers me a seat, but I refuse. Why do these people keep suggesting I sit? How can I sit at a time like this? Instead, I pace his office from wall to wall. Collins sits behind his desk and watches me for a few moments before talking.

"Mrs. Kemp, please sit. You're going to want to sit."

"What?" I pause mid pace and jerk my neck to look at him. It was something about the way he said it.

"Thomas Steele came in a few hours ago."

"What do you mean?" I ask, taking a seat. "Why?"

"He turned himself in."

"For . . . for what exactly?" Suddenly, I'm scared. Is it possible he's the reason Jenna is missing?

"He confessed to sexually abusing Jenna starting when she was very young."

A sob escapes me, and I lower my face into my hands. How can this be happening?

Collins gives me some time. When I finally raise my head, I see that he's pushed a box of tissue to the far edge of his desk so I can reach it. "Thank you," I say, grabbing one. "How old was she when it started?"

"I can't tell you that right now, and I can't tell you what happened after they met yet either. We're looking into his statement right now."

"What do you mean after they met?"

Collins breaks eye contact with me for a second. "Mrs. Kemp, according to Thomas, he saw Jenna last Friday night. She initiated the contact."

"Oh my God. What did he do to her?"

"No, no, no," he raises a hand, "all he admitted to was talking to her. But he says when they were done talking, they parted ways, and she was fine and heading home, to his knowledge."

"He has to be lying. Why would she want to talk to him? Why would she want to even be near him?" Suddenly it all makes sense. *All the stomachaches and not wanting to go to church and the drinking and drugs. How could I have been so naïve to think it was just some kind of teen rebellion or because I read one lousy entry in her diary? Oh, my God . . . her diary entry. It was about Thomas.*

"He says that she told him she was going to tell someone what he did to her if he didn't confess."

"He . . . he has to be lying. Where is he? Let me talk to him. He needs to tell us where she is." I stand and head for the door, but Collins is up and around his desk blocking my way before I get there.

"We've spoken to his wife. She says he got home that night around ten thirty and didn't leave the house again.

"Well, he still could have done something to Jenna when they were together. What time did they meet? If Jenna left Leighton's a little before nine, that's an entire hour and a half that he could have had to hurt her. And how can you even be sure Audra is telling the truth? That woman worships the ground he walks on!"

"Mrs. Kemp, we need a little time to look into this, question some people around the area where he and Jenna met, check some cameras in the area. But for right now, he's here in a holding cell of his own free will. With these diaries and his own confession, he *will* do some time."

"But where is she? Where is my daughter?" I yell.

Collins just stands there, with his hands on his hips and his head slumped, unable to look me in the eyes.

***

"Audra," I say pounding on the door again. "I know you're here. I can hear Stella."

Finally, the door opens a crack and Audra peeks out. Her eyes are bloodshot, and her usually sleek hair and tastefully applied makeup are a mess. She shakes her head at me and says, "I can't, Bonnie. I'm truly sorry, but I just can't."

She moves to close the door, but I give it a shove sending her backward and the door with her. She stumbles, almost tripping over her daughter who's crawling behind her. What have I done? Stella could have been hurt.

"I'm sorry," I say, reaching out for . . . I don't know what.

Audra sweeps Stella into her arms and holds her close, backing away from me. "Please, go, Bonnie."

"Just tell me. Please . . . was he really here with you that night? Did you know what he did to Jenna?"

Audra begins crying at the mention of Jenna, and she won't look at me. "I can't talk to you. I don't know anything," she says to the floor. "Please, just go. Or I'll call the police."

Shocked by her threat, I walk backwards out the door. When I get on the doorstep, she lunges forward and slams the door in my face. I can hear her sobbing on the other side of the door, but I feel no sympathy for her. She's married to a monster. How could she not know?

I turn and rush to my car. Greg and Lenore need to know what's going on.

***

"Bonnie," Greg says, opening the door. "What . . ." he looks behind me, to the left and to the right. "What are you doing here?"

Something is off. Why didn't he greet me like he usually does? *Ooooh, Bonnie, my favorite sister-in-law!* To which I typically respond. *Your only sister-in-law.* Why hasn't he invited me in?

"Greg, I need to talk to you and Lenore."

"Okay," he says, holding my gaze as he slowly opens the door.

I step inside and immediately hear the dishwasher running in the kitchen. Then I glance toward the stairs where I hear music and Lenore's and Hannah's laughter coming from upstairs.

"What is it, Bonnie? Did you hear something about Jenna?" he asks in a hushed voice.

I close my eyes and take several deep breaths. When I open my eyes, I step around him to head to the stairs and say, "I need to tell both of you at the same time." But Greg grabs my arm.

I turn, glancing down at his grip on my wrist. And suddenly I realize I wasn't imagining that something was off before when he answered the door. Something is *very* off. "Greg," I say, shaking my wrist loose. "I need to call Lenore down here."

"Please don't," he pleads. "Not yet. I need to tell her myself."

"What are you talking about, Greg?"

He gives me a pained look and then squeezes his forehead. "I'm so sorry, Bonnie. Thomas . . . he—"

"No . . ." I shake my head and back away from my brother-in-law. "No no no no no . . ."

"Bonnie," he reaches out to me.

"How long have you known, Greg? How long!"

"Bonnie, shhhhh." He glances toward the stairs.

"Greg? Is Bonnie here?" My sister comes into view halfway down the stairs. "Oh, hey . . . What's going on?" She looks from me to her husband, her expression shifting from surprise to confusion.

"Thomas sexually abused Jenna for years when she was younger," I blurt, purging myself of the disgusting words.

Lenore descends the last few stairs, her face contorted into an ugly blend of disbelief and confusion. "*What* are you talking about, Bonnie?"

"And Greg knew about it!" I say, pointing at Greg.

"Have you lost your mind, Bonnie?" Lenore roars. "We're all worried and stressed about Jenna, but how dare you make accusations like this!" She looks to Greg for backup, but he's clutching his forehead again, refusing to make eye contact with Lenore or me.

"Ask him, Lenore. ASK. HIM. Or you can read this," I say, handing her the copies I'd stopped to make of two of Jenna's diary entries from August of 2013. Thomas would have been twenty years old at the time.

"Greg?" Lenore asks weakly as she takes the papers from me. He doesn't respond right away, so she glances down, and a new crease appears in her brow with each second that ticks by.

"Thomas confided in me last night after the youth group meeting," Greg says, his eyes on the papers in Lenore's hand. "Bonnie," he says, stepping toward me, an air of desperation in his voice. "He's so sorry for what he did. Please . . . you need to believe me."

I narrow my eyes at him and am about to tell him I don't care if he's sorry, but Lenore falls to her knees, and Greg turns from me and rushes to her. Eli and Hannah must have been listening from the top of the stairs because they come rushing to my sister's side too.

Oh my, God. Hannah. What if Thomas hurt her too?

Intent on speaking to Hannah, I approach the four of them huddled together. But I stop dead in my tracks when Lenore mumbles, "Thomas . . . he wouldn't do something like that. Right? There must be another explanation. Jenna's an imaginative girl, a creative writer, didn't she win a writing competition once when she was in fifth grade?"

"Then why would he turn himself in?" I roar above her disgusting nonsense. "And how dare you insinuate that Jenna would make something like this up!"

All four sets of eyes, each displaying a different emotion, turn to me: sadness, disbelief, disgust, confusion.

"No," Lenore shakes her head. "He didn't . . . he wouldn't. Greeeegggg," she wails, "Why didn't you tell me?"

As Greg wraps his arms around Lenore, edging out Hannah and Eli. They both stand, Hannah picking up the copies of Jenna's diary entries. When Eli notices, he snatches them from her grasp. "No! Don't read those." His face is grief personified.

My niece and nephew look at me, Eli with tears trailing down his cheeks and Hannah confused about what she'd just heard about her oldest brother. I wish I could comfort them, but I can't help feeling like it would be a betrayal to Jenna. So, I turn on them and walk out without another word.

If Thomas did abuse Hannah, the truth will come out soon enough.

chapter fifty

October 26, 2017

Dear Diary,

Sometimes I wish things could go back to the way they were, before Thomas returned. I was still living the same lie back then, but now everything in my life is a mess, not just me. Lately, I've been thinking maybe it's God's way of making me deal with what Thomas did to me. And maybe it's His way of pushing me to help others by telling someone what he did to me. I need to make sure he doesn't hurt Stella, Audra, or anyone else, and I need to make sure he gets what he deserves.

I'm ready to get my life back together, which means after I take care of Thomas, I have to clean up the messes I've made, specifically with Dustin, Keeley, Delaney, and Eli. None of them deserved the way I treated them. Yeah, even Eli.

Oh, and there is one other mess . . . I don't know what I was thinking by getting in so deep with Jake B. (I know what you're thinking . . . I never should have gotten involved with the chat room site in the first place.) Up until this morning, I still planned to meet him tomorrow night at the Holiday Inn on Brown Deer Road, but I called him after school to cancel and tell him that I can't talk to him anymore. He wasn't mad about it, but I could tell he was upset. But then he started trying to talk me back into it and says he'll still go to the hotel room in case I change my mind. And now he's messaged me like five times to see if there's any chance I'll reconsider. It's really starting to creep me out, and I'm worried about how I told him that I live in the duplex across the street from our house. (He never would have believed a 19-year-old could afford to live alone in a house like my parents'.) I also should never have texted him those selfies. Dumb dumb dumb JENNA! Maybe if he won't just go away now that I've stopped answering his calls and responding to his messages, I can have my number changed. And you can bet if I ever see him in our neighborhood, I'll tell someone about him. For now, I have more important things to worry about.

~Jenna

By the way – I was wrong when I said everything in my life is a mess because there is one good thing that has come out of all my confusion and chaos: Leighton. Some people may think all the horrible things I've done are because of Leighton, but those people are WRONG. None of it had anything to do with her. If anything, she's helped me, and there's so much more to her than people know. If I hadn't had her to talk to, then I probably would never have had the courage to break my silence.

chapter fifty-one

I'm sitting at the kitchen counter sipping a tumbler of whisky and staring at the stacks of missing person posters Joseph and I just made at the local copy center. One of the machines had gotten a jam, so we called over a service attendant. When she removed the jammed paper from inside and paused to look at it, my heart leapt because I imagined her telling me, "Hey, I just saw this girl." How sad is that? My daydreams used to consist of family trips to Hawaii or having a private chef, and now they're made of strangers telling me they recognize my missing daughter. What the attendant really said was, "Would you like me to hang one on the door for you?" I was grateful for her offer, and she followed through right away, but as we walked out the door ten minutes later, it occurred to me most people probably won't even stop to look. And of the people who do, what are the odds one of them will recognize Jenna? It had to be one in a million. Otherwise, why are the police having such a hard time finding her?

"Hey, you," Joseph says in my ear. His freshly grown beard tickles my skin as he kisses my cheek.

"Hey. How are they?"

"Oh, you know ten-year-old girls. Giggly, chatty, and shy around other people's dads." I think back to Jenna at that age and remember those things about her. It wasn't constant—preteens have their ups and downs. How did she manage even one giggle with what he'd done to her, though? "They're getting their sleeping bags set up now."

Shaina's birthday had been a few days ago, and we forgot about it. So now her two best friends were spending the night. After a taco bar and ice cream cake, I told the girls they could buy two movies from On Demand, and Joseph and I left to make the copies.

Joseph takes a seat next to me and places a hand on top of one of the stacks. "So what's the plan for tomorrow?"

"I've told everyone to be here between eight and nine. I figure as people arrive, they can choose which area they'd like to canvass, then I'll give them a corresponding list of all the businesses in that particular area." It had taken me hours to compile spreadsheets of places to post flyers. I don't want them hung willy-nilly. I want to know where they are, and I want to be able to make notes of where people saw a poster if they happen to call us with a tip. "The kids in pairs or groups or without cars can take the nearby places or shopping strips and the mall. Then everyone is invited back here for pizza."

"Still no word from Collins with any updates about Thomas?"

"No. And still no word on if they've found anything of interest in her diaries." I sigh. "No one had anything new to tell me when I went down there again today. But the desk attendant," I look over at Joseph, and he nods, "she's going to help with the posters tomorrow."

"Well, that's something."

"Yeah, but it'll be on her own time. Why does it seem like they aren't doing anything? Why do I feel like we're the only people looking for Jenna?"

Joseph takes a sip of my whisky, which he never drinks. "They are looking, Bonnie. They've combed through her social media profiles and followed up on every single connection she made over the past year. And they spent a lot of time interviewing and looking into Jacob Bickers. And now they're piecing together Thomas's movements from that night. We might not see it, but they're looking."

"And what about this?" I unlock my phone and slide it in front of him.

"Don't read this stuff." He shakes his head and slides it right back.

"This police department resource had the nerve to tell this reporter that they haven't found any evidence of foul play, and they haven't ruled out the possibility that Jenna ran away. How could that person say such a thing publicly? Don't you think that plants a seed in people's minds that there's no urgency here? That maybe she's just some troubled teen, especially now that they know what Thomas did to her?"

"They don't think that, Bonnie, and even if they do, it's not their job to pass judgment. It's their job to find Jenna."

"How did I not know? How could I have been so blind? Why didn't she tell us?"

Joseph downs the rest of the whisky in my glass. "You're not the only one who didn't see it." He retrieves the whisky bottle from the liquor cabinet and refills my glass.

"There was this time . . . when she was five or six. I was pregnant with Shaina and taking night classes, and you were working nights with the construction crew. Jenna asked me if maybe someone else besides Thomas could babysit for her. I was busy making dinner and getting lunches ready for the next day, so I was barely listening. I told her no, there wasn't anyone else. I remember thinking what a convenient setup we had and how inexpensive it was to pay him to sit at our house and do his homework while Jenna watched TV or played with her toys. It wasn't the first time she'd asked either, but that day she persisted with asking why. I lost my temper and yelled that I didn't have time to find a different babysitter for her. I just assumed she was bored with him because he was so much older, and she wanted someone who would play Barbies with her. But she was just trying to protect herself. And I'd yelled at her because I was too busy to stop and look at her and actually ask her why she didn't want Thomas watching her. That was my chance to help her, and I missed it." I slam my glass of whisky and lower my head to my forearms on the counter.

Joseph places his hand on my back, and after a bout of silence, he says, "It's not your fault, Bonnie. We were so busy back then. We barely had time to breathe."

"People are going to blame me, though. They're going to wonder how I didn't notice what was happening to her at the hands of my own nephew."

"I didn't notice either, Bonnie."

I pick my head back up and look over at him. "You don't understand. You didn't know Jenna like I did because she wasn't yours."

He removes his hand from my back, slides his chair a few inches away from mine, and averts his gaze away from me.

"Joseph, I didn't mean . . . what I meant to say is that you weren't there for her first four years. So you wouldn't have noticed any changes in her as easily as I should have."

"I know what you meant."

I'm about to reach for him, but there's a knock on the door, and he rushes away to answer it. I hear a woman's voice at the door, and my first thought is that it's Lenore since I haven't been responding to her calls or texts since last night. But then I hear a baby.

After Joseph passes through the entryway from the back hall into the kitchen, Audra and Stella come into view.

"Audra," I say. It's not a greeting. I'm just surprised to see her.

"H-hi, Bonnie. I just . . . wanted to apologize . . . for yesterday."

"Oh . . . well, thank you. I . . ." I realize Audra must be suffering right now too, just like me. It's just a different kind of grief. Lenore and Greg too. I pull a chair out for her at the kitchen table. "Come in. Sit. I can't imagine what this must be like for you." Joseph and I sit on either side of her. She immediately begins bouncing Stella on her knee. Stella coos and gnaws on her fingers. I remember Jenna doing that when she was a teething baby. "Would you like something to drink?"

"No, thank you." She shakes her head and removes the hat she's wearing. Her hair looks like it hasn't been washed for days. This draws my attention to her disheveled clothing. I've only ever seen Audra in dresses and pleated pants and skirts, never in sweatpants and faded, stained sweatshirts. And Stella has something orange and crusty on her cheeks and around her mouth. Normally, I would get a wet paper towel and clean her up, but I don't have time for that right now, not with Audra sitting in front of me.

"Audra, you told the police Thomas was home with you last Friday night. Was that true? Or did he ask you to say that?"

Her eyes widen a bit, and I see a flicker of contemplation. After a few seconds, Joseph clears his throat and crosses his arms, and I shift in my seat. Finally, she speaks, but she doesn't say what we want to hear.

"Yes, he arrived home around ten thirty. I swear he doesn't know anything about where Jenna is."

Both mine and Joseph's chests deflate. Joseph stands, and I look back to Audra, ready to console her. She must be devastated about Thomas. But she starts talking again before I have a chance.

"Thomas is sorry, you know. That's why he does what he does, bringing people closer to God. It's his way of repenting for his sins every single day . . ."

Joseph and I glance at each other, both of us wondering where this is going.

"Please," she says, hugging Stella tight, "you have to believe me. He's not the same person who did those things to Jenna. Please forgive him. Please tell the police that you don't want to press charges. There has to be a better way to reconcile this."

I squeeze my hands into fists under the table, digging my fingernails into my palms.

"All right," Joseph roars, "that's enough. Audra, you need to leave right now." He stands and holds up his arm indicating she can let herself out.

I'm just as outraged as he is by what I'm hearing, but she can't be this naïve.

"Wait," I say to Audra as she stands to leave. She looks at me, tears in her eyes. "Audra, do you understand that Thomas raped our daughter?" Her only response is a blink, causing more tears to fall. Stella starts to fuss, so Audra turns her around to face me. I can't help but wonder if it's a ploy for sympathy, so I avoid looking at my great-niece. "Do you understand that even if we did say we didn't want to press charges, which would be completely insane, it wouldn't matter. What he did to Jenna is a Class C felony, and he could be sentenced to forty years in prison, whether we press charges or not. Why do you want to protect him? The only person you should be thinking about protecting is that little girl in your arms."

"I'm trying to protect her. She needs her father."

"Joseph is right. You need to leave right now, Audra."

chapter fifty-two

"So, what's going on with Jake B?"

Jenna emitted a sigh that had multiple meanings. When she'd first realized she had to stop talking to Jacob because of the obsession he seemed to be developing for her, she genuinely felt bad—for lying to him about her age, for leading him on with inappropriate talk and selfies, and for accepting the comfort and support he offered. But then when he got upset when she'd canceled their plans to meet in person and wouldn't stop texting and calling her, she felt scared and stupid for getting involved with him in the first place. Yet, she still felt gratitude toward him for listening to her vent about Thomas and other things in her life that had fallen apart as a result. So, her sigh was one big cluster of emotional chaos that Leighton simply took as the sign of a girl who was done with a guy.

"Well, I told him yesterday that I had to stop talking to him, and he was pretty upset."

"That sucks. Why'd you decide to stop talking to him?"

"I don't know. I guess I felt bad for not liking him the way he likes me. I mean, I like him, but not that way. But it's not like we could date anyway . . . he's an adult."

Leighton nodded her agreement. "So, what did he say when you told him?"

"He just kept asking me to reconsider and wouldn't stop messaging me. It got to be really annoying, and it really creeped me out."

"Well, I told you not to get all serious with ChillChat. Just shits and giggles from now on, right?"

Jenna nodded and laughed. Then her expression turned serious again. "Hey, I need to talk to you about something."

"Okay . . . shoot."

"I'm so tired of living with my secrets, Leighton. Do you know what I'm talking about?"

"Yeah," Leighton said with a nod. Then she lit up a cigarette.

"I'm tired of letting it eat me up inside."

"Do you think it would help if you told someone? You know, like a therapist? Someone who can help you."

"*You've* helped me, Leighton. You're the only friend I've ever had who I didn't feel like I had to pretend around. I'm thinking that's why I told you about Thomas that night in Sticks' car."

It had been years since Leighton was close to anyone but Sticks, so the endearing comment made her uncomfortable, and she shifted away from Jenna where they were sitting together on the couch and pretended to check the time on a wall clock in the dining room. Jenna didn't notice because she was so immersed in the thoughts that had been tumbling around in her head for days.

"Putting aside what he did to me, what if he does it to someone else? Especially with his new position as youth pastor? I can't let what happened to me happen to anyone else," Jenna said, shaking her head. "So, I totally agree with you that I need to tell someone else."

Leighton nodded. "But what are you going to do? Go down to the police station and file a report? Because it'll be your word against his. And I hate to say this, but they might not believe you. Because of his respected position at the church. And because you waited so long." Leighton felt like an asshole for bringing these things up, but she didn't want Jenna to confront Thomas without thinking through what the results could be.

"I know." Jenna gave Leighton a grateful smile and patted her knee a few times. "I've thought about all of that, and I don't care anymore. But I'm not going to go to the police. I'm going to talk to Thomas and tell him he needs to tell the police what he did to me. And I'm also going to tell him that I told you. Well . . . I won't say you, but I'll tell him I told *someone*. Then if he refuses, I'm going to the police myself."

"Sounds like you have it all figured out."

"Yeah, and his wife and daughter are out of town visiting her family in Illinois, so tonight is the perfect night."

"Jenna," Leighton says, turning her entire body to face her, "you can't be serious. Tonight?"

Jenna nodded then looked down at her phone. Leighton watched as she navigated to the His Grace Community website where Thomas's cell number was listed.

"Are you sure you're ready to do this?" Leighton asked.

Jenna pressed on Thomas's number populating it into her caller app. Then she pressed to connect. Her heart was beating so fast she thought she might pass out. And just as she was about to chicken out, he answered.

"Hello, this is Pastor Thomas."

"Thomas?"

"Yes?"

"Thomas, this is Jenna. Your cousin." The line went so quiet that Jenna held the phone away from her ear to see if the call was still connected. When she saw it was, she put the phone back to her ear and said, "Hello? Are you still there?"

"Yes. Forgive me for not responding at first. I'm just . . . shocked to hear from you."

"Yeah, well, you should be."

"How are you? We haven't really gotten to talk since I've been back."

Leighton was hanging on Jenna's every word, so Jenna glanced at her, hoping it would give her strength.

"How am I? How do you think I am?" She sounded way more confident than she felt.

"Jenna, I'm so—"

"Look, I didn't call you to catch up. I called because there's something I need to say to you, and I need to say it to you in person."

"Jenna, I don't think that's a—"

"I don't care what you think, Thomas. I know my mom helped with youth group this week because Audra and Stella are out of town, so we should meet tonight."

"Jenna, I—"

"At the Walmart on Capitol . . . in the parking lot. Look for my parents' red Honda Civic. I'll be there at nine o'clock."

Again, he didn't answer, but Jenna didn't bother checking to see if the call was still connected this time because she could hear his heavy breathing. Finally, when she thought she might have to say what she needed to say over the phone, he responded.

"Okay. I'll be there."

Shocked by what she'd just done, Jenna couldn't answer at first when Leighton asked if Thomas had agreed to meet her.

"Hey," Leighton snapped her fingers a few times in front of Jenna's eyes. "Are you sure you're up for this?"

"Yeah," Jenna finally spoke. "He's meeting me at nine. I want to see his face when I tell him how much I hate his guts and that I'm going to tell everyone what he did to me if he doesn't turn himself in."

"You can't go alone. I should go with you."

"No. He might leave if he sees you there with me. It'll be fine. We're going to be sitting in a busy parking lot so he's not going to try anything. Besides, my dad keeps pepper spray in the car for me."

"Okay, well, text me when you're done."

"I will."

Jenna pulled into the Walmart parking lot fifteen minutes before she was supposed to meet Thomas. Even though it had been instilled in Jenna to be early for any appointment, that's not why she'd allowed herself so much extra time before he arrived. She needed the time to text her friends.

Now that Jenna had taken the biggest step of her life in finally confronting Thomas, she felt the need to come clean to her friends about what she'd been hiding. She wanted them to finally understand why she'd spiraled out of control and destroyed her friendships with them in the process.

First up was Dustin. Jenna had the most to say to him and hoped that they might even be able to meet that night.

JENNA: CAN WE PLEASE TALK? NOT BY TEXT, ON THE PHONE OR EVEN IN PERSON.

Jenna waited a few minutes for Dustin to respond before texting Keeley.

JENNA: HEY KEELEY. I NEED TO TALK TO YOU ABOUT SOMETHING. ANY CHANCE WE CAN GET TOGETHER TOMORROW?

Jenna thought for a second before moving on to texting Delaney. There was one more thing she had to say to Keeley.

JENNA: BTW, I MISS OUR RUNS AND I MISS YOU.

Then she texted Delaney.

JENNA: HEY LANEY. I COULD USE A HAIRCUT SO WONDERING IF MAYBE YOU'LL BE AT YOUR MOM'S SALON TOMORROW. I'D ALSO REALLY LIKE TO TALK TO YOU ABOUT SOMETHING. NO, NOT DUSTIN. I'M OVER IT. IT'S SOMETHING WAY MORE IMPORTANT . . .

After she'd texted her friends, Jenna leaned back in the driver's seat of her parents' car and stared up at the light she'd parked under. It reminded her of when she used to wish on stars when she was a kid. It was so silly because the wishes never came true. Even so, as she looked up at the parking lot light, she pretended it was a star. Her phone vibrated right when she'd finished making her wish.

DUSTIN: WHY?

Her heart fluttered, and her palms instantly became sweaty when she saw Dustin had responded. She wanted so badly to see him that night, to get everything off her chest and hopefully start over with him.

JENNA: I NEED TO TELL YOU SOMETHING IMPORTANT.

JENNA: SOMETHING THAT WILL HELP YOU UNDERSTAND.

JENNA: I'M SO SORRY FOR EVERYTHING . . .

DUSTIN: I'M AT A MOVIE SO CAN'T TALK NOW. CAN I GET BACK TO YOU IN ABOUT AN HOUR?

Jenna's chest deflated, squashing her heart flutters. She realized starting over probably wouldn't be easy, but she was willing to work just as hard to rebuild the relationships with her friends as she had worked to tear them down. Confronting Thomas would be the first step.

JENNA: SURE.

Just as she hit send, a car pulled up next to her on the passenger side. She forced herself to look over and locked eyes with Thomas. Instead of giving in to her self-preserving impulse to look away, she forced herself to hold his gaze until he was the one to break eye contact. Then, as he turned off his car, she hid pepper spray between her legs.

Thomas opened the passenger door and slid inside the car Jenna had driven there. Without his church clothes on, he looked a lot less intimidating for some reason. Jenna hated how his profession gave him an invisible shield of sorts. They both sat looking out the front window for a few moments before Jenna turned to Thomas and asked, "Why? Why did you do those things to me?"

"Jenna," he said, turning to face her, "I'm so sorry for what I did to you. You have to believe me."

"Your apology means nothing to me. *Why* did you do those things to me?" Jenna asked the question much louder this time.

"I . . . I don't know." Thomas gripped his forehead. "There was something wrong with me. I was sick. Trust me, I hate what I did to you, and I swear I've confessed my sins to God."

"Trust you?" Jenna laughed. "I did trust. So did my mom and my dad. So do all the people you preach the word of God to. But you're such a liar. You lie to people every day just by being you. No one should ever trust you. Not even your wife or your daughter."

Jenna is taken aback at the groan that escapes Thomas when he begins to cry and covers his face with his hands. But instead of backing off, she keeps right on going.

"I hate you, Thomas. That's the first reason I wanted to see you in person." She suddenly realized she hadn't accomplished one of her goals yet, so she reached out and pulled his hands from his face. As she did this, she screamed, "Look at me!" Then when she was sure he wasn't going to cover his face again or look away, she repeated it. "I hate you. You ruined my childhood, and you being here now just about ruined my entire life. But I'm going to fix it, starting right here and right now."

They stared at each other, Jenna's face fierce and fearless for once, and Thomas's remorseful and petrified. Jenna couldn't stop wondering if his silence and timidity was some sort of trick. Was he going to pounce on her? Was he going to grab her hand and try to make her touch him the way he did when she was a little girl? She shook her head to clear it of the poisonous thoughts. When Jenna finally looked away and out the front window, Thomas did the same. Then after a few more moments of silence, he finally spoke.

"I understand why you're upset, and I truly am sorry. I pray that you can find it in your heart to forgive me someday. I can't think of any other way to fix what I've done, Jenna."

"I can," Jenna said, looking over at Thomas. She waited for him to look at her before she continued. "You can turn yourself in."

"Jenna, I can't . . ." Thomas's mouth opened and closed a few times, but no other words came out.

"If you truly want to repent, then you will."

"Jenna, what about Audra? And Stella? Our lives . . . their lives would be ruined."

Jenna shook her head. "Yours would, but not theirs. Their lives would be better without you in it, just like mine would have been."

Thomas clenched his jaw and stared out the front window again.

"If you don't go to the police station and tell them what you did to me within a week, I'm going to do it for you. I'm done keeping it to myself and letting it poison me. It's your turn to suffer. Now get out."

And that was the last time Thomas ever saw Jenna.

chapter fifty-three

Since my mom forgot that I needed a ride over to the Kemps' house this morning to pick up flyers, I arrive late, and no one is home.

"Thanks a lot, Mom," I say when I get back in the car. "I should have just walked over."

"Leighton, I told you I'm sorry. I know this was important to you. How about if we just drive around and look for people passing out flyers? Or is there anyone you can contact to find out where people are?"

That's actually a good idea, but I won't admit it to her. "Yeah, I know someone." I pull up Keeley's number on my phone.

Even though it's only been open for thirty minutes, Bayshore Mall is already so busy it makes my skin crawl. But I'll stomach the crowd if it means finding Jenna.

"Mom, stop. There they are," I say, pointing to Keeley and Delaney standing on the sidewalk in front of American Eagle. Keeley sees me and waves.

My mom pulls over as close as she can get without blocking traffic. "I'll find a place to park."

"What do you mean? Just go."

"Leighton, I really like your friend Jenna. I'd like to help distribute flyers."

"Well, you might want to hurry up because I don't know how long they'll be standing there or what the game plan is."

"That's fine. I'll find you." She waves and drives off. If I know her, she'll park in one of the parking structures to avoid paying for street parking.

When I get to where they're standing, I get a better view of the square in the middle of the outdoor mall. I hate shopping so the sight makes me want to vomit, but I reign it in for Jenna's sake. There are no less than twenty stores in our line of sight, and this is only about a quarter of the mall. Keeley said Dustin, Eli, and some of their other friends who I couldn't care less about are covering the inside portion of the mall, and we're supposed to meet them all back at the Kemps' house when we're done.

"Where do we even start?" I ask.

"We don't really know, but we have to start somewhere. It's overwhelming isn't it?" Delaney says to me.

"Yeah," I say with a nod. "Just give me some flyers."

Keeley opens the bag she has slung over her body, pulls out a stack of at least fifty and hands it to me. "Do you want to hand these out to people as they walk by, and Delaney and I can go store to store."

Not having to go from store to store is music to my ears. "Sure. Sounds like a plan. Let's just get moving."

The two of them walk into American Eagle, and I start holding flyers out to people who walk by. I try to, anyway. A lot of people shake their heads and keep walking without even looking to see what I'm trying to give them. It makes me so angry. By the time I see Keeley and Delaney go into their fifth store, I stop trying to push flyers on people, and I just sit down on a bench and look at the flyer on top of the stack in my lap. There's a big picture of Jenna in the center with the words "MISSING: Jenna Kemp" above it. There's also a physical description including her height, weight, and the clothes she was last seen in. Also included is her last known location: the Walmart parking lot where she met Thomas. At the bottom of the flyer is Mr. and Mrs. Kemp's names along with their phone numbers. I've seen posters like this before but only in passing. I've never once stopped to really look at the people on them.

"Leighton?" my mom says, approaching. "What are you doing? Why aren't you passing out the flyers?"

"Because it's pointless. No one is going to look at them."

"Then you make them look. Just like you tried to make me look at what a jerk your father was years ago." With that surprising gem of a comment, she begins talking to every person who passes by and making them look at Jenna's face while she says her name. Some people even take the flyers with them after, and some ask for another to hang where they work or where they work out or where they go to school. Eventually, I'm pushing the flyers on people as hard as my mom is. We do this until our stack is gone.

"There. See? That wasn't so hard," my mom says, giving my back a rub.

I resist the urge to pull away from her because I appreciate her help.

When we get to the Kemps' house, we have to park three houses down near the corner because there are so many other cars lining the street. As Keeley, Delaney, my mom, and I file out of the car, movement in the large picture window at the front of the house on the corner makes me pause.

"That's just Mr. Fitzgibbons," Keeley says. "He can be kind of nosey."

I squint my eyes and can see that a small section of one of the curtains is out of place, and when I look a little harder, I see eyes. *Creepy,* I think to myself. Then the curtain falls flat again.

"Yeah, his dog usually barks too," Delaney says. "It must be in the backyard."

When we get inside, there's barely any room to stand. People are holding paper plates with pizza on them or cups containing coffee or cans of beer, soda, or sparkling water. It strikes me as odd at first that all these people are here eating and socializing when Jenna still hasn't come home. But then it occurs to me that no one is talking about anything other than Jenna, newspaper articles and TV news reports about her, or how their search went today. The mood is somber and raw and real. And Jenna would approve.

"Girls! You're back." Mrs. Kemp comes rushing toward us and gives each of us a hug, including my mom. I introduce them, and my mom expresses her sympathy, and Jenna's mom graciously accepts. When we're all done greeting each other, Mrs. Kemp asks for our checklist of places and adds it to the red folder she's carrying around. "We're so thankful to all of you for helping out today. Please, go to the kitchen and help yourselves. There's plenty."

In the kitchen, Keeley and Delaney find all their other friends, and my mom gets pulled into a conversation about our healthcare system. That leaves me standing on the outskirts by myself until Dustin and Eli appear in the empty spot next to me. I can't help but eavesdrop on their conversation.

"I didn't know. I swear. If I had, then . . ." Eli doesn't finish because Dustin pipes in.

"Nobody is saying you knew. Do not beat yourself up, man. I didn't know either. How would we? She never said anything." Dustin glances around the room, and just as he's about to look at me, I avert my eyes down to my phone in my hands.

"He's not my brother anymore. I . . . I could kill him," Eli says. "If I ever see him again I will. I'll kill him." He hangs his head, and Dustin puts a hand on his shoulder.

I never really got to know Dustin, and Jenna didn't talk about him much, but I can tell from the expression on his face that he's feeling just as miserable as Eli sounds.

"Eli, I heard that Jenna met with your . . . brother that night. Do you know if the police think he might know where she is?" Dustin asks.

"No," Eli shakes his head. "I don't know. My parents . . . they won't tell me anything. I don't even know if they know anything other than what he told them. But anything he says could be a lie, so I'm not interested in hearing what he has to say. They just don't get . . . it's like they don't care what he did . . ." Eli says to the floor.

Suddenly, Dustin looks over at me without warning, and I'm so afraid of what he must think of me, that I begin to walk away.

"Leighton, wait," he says, pinching the sleeve of my shirt. I stop and slowly turn to face him and Eli but keep my eyes down. "How are you doing?"

I look up, shocked by the concern in his voice. "I'm . . . okay. Just missing Jenna . . . just like all of you." Suddenly, I'm overcome by emotion because no one else has asked me how I'm doing, probably because no one knows how close Jenna and I have become. No one knows how important her friendship is to me. I've felt like an outsider trying to be part of the search for her, even when I delivered her diaries to Keeley. All these people have known her for so long, so it's reasonable to think that their grief over her disappearance is deeper than mine. But it's not. In some ways, I feel like I know Jenna better than any of them. Time doesn't necessarily make a friendship stronger.

"Hey, it's okay." Dustin puts his hand on my shoulder, just like he did with Eli.

"Thanks," I say.

"Hey, everyone, could we all please gather in here for a moment?" Mrs. Kemp's voice fills the air, and people begin squishing into the living room where she's standing on a chair in the corner. "Joseph and I just want to thank you all for helping today. I can't believe we got every place on the checklists covered. I mean, you all plastered Jenna's posters across the city from downtown to the lakefront, the area all around UW-Milwaukee to the far north shore, and within all the busiest areas of surrounding communities. We've already gotten a few calls, but I don't know how helpful the information is yet. For those of you who don't know, my cousin Mary— over there in the red shirt—" Everyone looks at Mary for a moment and back at Mrs. Kemp. "She's created a Facebook page where we can keep all of you informed of any information we find. Please share it, and there are also extra flyers on the table by the door if you'd like to take some just in case you come across somewhere that doesn't have a poster of Jenna. We don't . . ." Suddenly Mrs. Kemp has lost her train of thought, and Mr. Kemp steps beside her and finishes with a few more words.

"We don't know what we'd do without all of your support. We're hopeful that these posters will be seen by someone who saw her that night or that weekend . . . So," he brings his palms together in an appreciative gesture, "thank you all. You're all welcome to stay or go, and please, feel free to take some food with you. We have more than enough. But before anyone goes anywhere, we'd like to take a moment of silence now, just to pray or think about Jenna."

The room goes silent and eyes all around me drop to the floor, so I follow suit. My family is not religious, and I can't remember the last time I prayed, but I decide to try it because what else have we got at this point?

A few moments into the requested silence, the front doorbell rings, causing heads to start popping up all around the room. All eyes are on Mr. Kemp as he makes his way to the front door and opens it. It's still so quiet in the room that everyone clearly hears the woman at the door say, "Hi, I . . . I'm sorry, I see you have company. I should just—"

"No, come in, please," Mr. Kemp holds the door open for her, and she steps inside.

She recovers surprisingly fast after the shock of seeing so many sets of eyes on her when she steps inside. Mrs. Kemp is already in front of her reaching out to shake the woman's hand. By this time, some people are whispering, wondering who the woman is, and some have wandered off to the bathroom or back to the kitchen, but I'm not going anywhere until I find out who this lady is, and neither are Dustin or Eli. I notice Keeley, Delaney, and a few other girls who are sitting on the stairs looking on as well.

"Hi, I'm Bonnie Kemp, and you already met my husband, Joseph." Bonnie gestures to Mr. Kemp who's closing the door. "How do you know Jenna?"

"I . . . I'm Julie Bickers, Jacob Bickers' wife."

Several gasps travel through the room, Dustin and Eli move closer to where Mrs. Kemp and Mrs. Bickers are standing, and Keeley's jaw drops as she brings her hands up to cover her mouth. Mrs. Kemp reacts with the widest eyes I've ever seen, and Mr. Kemp circles the women to stand behind Mrs. Kemp, blocking my view of Mrs. Bickers' face.

"Why are you here?" Mrs. Kemp asks flatly.

"I . . . I feel terrible that your daughter is still missing, and I just . . . wanted to reach out to you to let you know I care." She glances around the room as if she's just realized whatever she says will be heard by many. So, she lowers her voice, but I'm still close enough to make out what she says, "I also wanted to apologize for my husband's behavior. The way he connected with your daughter on that site is just deplorable. And if I ever find any reason to think he might have had something to do with her disappearance, I want you to know that I will not hesitate to turn him in. I'm sorry to have interrupted."

And within seconds, Julie Bickers is gone.

chapter fifty-four

"Let all that I am praise the Lord; may I never forget the good things he does for me. He forgives all my sins and heals all my diseases . . ."

After talking to Jenna, Thomas recited scripture as he drove to His Grace Community Church, but for the first time in his life, his faith in the power of prayer was faltering. When he arrived at the church, he proceeded straight to the front row of the chapel where he sat every Sunday during Audra's weekly youth message. He bowed his head and continued to beg for forgiveness for the things he'd done to Jenna.

Between prayers, he contemplated his next move. *If I confess, it isn't just me who suffers. It's Audra and Stella too. Why couldn't I have come clean before I had them in my life? Before my demons quieted? Then again, if I'd confessed my sins prior to graduate school, there would be no Audra, because instead of being at that topless club in St. Louis the night we met, I probably would have been in prison and still suffering from my affliction to this day. Audra is what saved me.*

This led Thomas to reflect on his relationship with Audra and how she'd been the Godsend that helped him overcome his demons. He thought back to when he was earning his master's degree in theology and needed a way to unwind, which led him to become a regular at the gentleman's club where Audra worked. She quickly became his favorite dancer. He was shocked when he found out she was twenty-two because she looked so much younger. He'd let his surprise over the fact that she was of legal age slip early on in their relationship—but she didn't seem to care. That's when he began to wonder if she was the one he'd been looking for. Then, after they'd been dating for a couple weeks and Audra moved in with Thomas, she found his picture stash. He knew a normal woman would have dumped him or turned him in, but Audra didn't do either. Instead, she'd asked him to tell her about the pictures. It was appealing to Thomas the way she'd flipped through the photos and put them into piles like she was organizing a deck of trading cards. When she was done sorting the girls—it appeared by age—she asked him to tell her about all of them. When Thomas got to Jenna's picture, he told Audra the only lie he'd ever told her. He said Jenna was a girl he'd met when he was a camp counselor his Junior year in high school. After they'd gone through the entire box of photos, Audra waited until Thomas had to use the bathroom to douse his photo collection with nail polish remover. Then when he returned, she dropped a match on them, and they burnt to a crisp. When Thomas realized what she'd done, he wanted to be angry with her, but he wasn't. How could he be? The pictures had represented his temptations, his filthy desires, his demons. When he asked her why she'd done such a thing, she said, "Because you're mine now." From that point forward, Audra became the only girl for him, his godsend, and since then, he couldn't stop wondering if he'd really changed or if his demons were simply masked. But he always came to the same conclusion; he would never know the answer. All he knew for certain was that the remorse he felt for what he did to Jenna had become a new demon that had begun to slowly eat him up from the inside out.

Praying was not going to help.

As Thomas drove home, he thanked God that his family was still out of town because he wasn't ready to tell Audra what he'd decided to do. But then when he got home, he found Audra's car already in the garage. The only thing that stopped him from going straight to the police station instead of facing Audra was the sight of Stella's beautiful face staring back at him from the screensaver of his cell phone.

Without another moment's hesitation, he turned the car off and went inside, accepting his fate.

"Surprise!" Audra rushed over to Thomas from where she was standing at the counter reading a cooking magazine and threw her arms around him.

When he didn't hug her back as tightly as he normally would, she pulled back and examined his face. "Something wrong?"

How does she know me so well? Thomas wondered as he silently led her into his office, which was the room farthest away from Stella's bedroom. He steered Audra toward the only chair in the room and made her sit. Then he knelt before her.

"Thomas, what is going on?"

"Do you promise not to say a word while I explain?" he'd asked.

"Well, I suppose that depends on what you have to explain."

"Audra, I need you to promise."

"Fine," she said with a sigh. "What is it already?"

"Jenna contacted me tonight."

"Jenna, your cousin Jenna?"

"Yes."

"Okay? Did something happen to that sweet girl?"

"Yes."

"Well, what is it? Is she okay?"

"See . . . the thing that happened to her happened a long time ago . . . before I met you."

Audra tilted her head slightly, a glimmer of understanding appearing in her eyes.

"Do you remember those pictures I used to have—my collection?"

Audra nodded and narrowed her eyes at Thomas.

"One of the girls was Jenna."

Audra exhaled harshly, placed her hand on her chest, and stared over Thomas's head at a memory. "The girl you said you met at summer camp," she whispered.

Thomas nodded and lowered his head to Audra's knees for a moment, just to collect himself.

"Audra, Jenna has suffered horribly because of the things I did to her when she was younger."

"What did you do to her, Thomas? She asked it as though she was clueless, which confused Thomas. How could she be clueless after seeing those pictures?

"It started out as curiosity, but then . . . I went way too far and kept pushing it even further. And now it's time for me to come clean . . . to pay for what I did."

"No . . ." She shook her head, a horrified expression appearing on her face. "You can't."

"Audra," Thomas said, gripping her hands, "if I don't turn myself in, Jenna is going to file a police report. So either way . . ."

"NO." Audra pulled her hands from Thomas's and stood so fast he fell backwards. She was now hovering over him. "You can't, Thomas. Our reputations and our lives will be ruined. Please don't."

"I have to, Audra. For Jenna . . . and for myself."

"What about me? What about Stella?" She folded her arms across her chest and thought for a moment. Then she continued as if she'd come up with a solution. "I'll talk to her, reason with her, and you'll beg for her forgiveness and tell her you've changed. I don't know her that well, but I can tell she's a smart girl. She'll listen to reason. Come on, Thomas." Audra held a hand out to him. "We'll call her right now, ask her to come over. I'll make some cocoa."

Ignoring Audra's hand, Thomas pried himself off the floor. Then he pulled her close and held her tight, but her body remained stiff, and she started up again about how they could fix everything with Jenna. No one had to know. Finally, his mind made up, Thomas had had enough. He pulled back, gripping Audra's upper arms and looking her in the eyes. She tried to look away, but Thomas adjusted his head left and then right, not allowing her to escape his gaze. "I've made up my mind, Audra. God will take care of the rest."

"No, Thomas! No!" She threw her arms up and out with such force that Thomas immediately felt a bruise forming on one of his forearms.

"Think about Stella!" As if on cue, Stella started wailing. "You'll go to Jail! What will happen to her without a father? She'll end up like me, Thomas!"

Audra stormed out of the office, down the hall, and into the living room. Thomas rushed after her, knocking a picture frame off a table in the hall. There was another wail from Stella when the frame crashed to the floor. Thomas paused, unsure whether to go upstairs and comfort his daughter or proceed into the living room in pursuit of Audra. The sound of the garage door opening helped him decide. But by the time he got into the garage, Audra was already gone. Thomas had no other choice than to go to Stella whose frightened wails could still be heard from upstairs.

chapter fifty-five

KEELEY

THURSDAY, NOVEMBER 16, 2017

THREE WEEKS AFTER JENNA'S DISAPPEARANCE

As I pull into a spot in the Starbucks parking lot, I see Eli. He's staring out the window facing the opposite direction from where I'm parked. The fact that he's sitting at a table in a far corner away from any other customers makes me nervous about what he wants to talk to me about. I check the time and realize I'm nearly fifteen minutes early. I wonder how long he's been sitting there.

He spots me right when I enter, so I go over and say hi before ordering something.

"Thanks for coming," he says as I lean down and give him a hug. It feels good and makes my chest flutter.

When we part, we pause to just look at each other, our faces only inches apart. His lips quiver a little, and his eyes are full of sadness, confirming that this meetup has everything to do with Jenna and nothing to do with us.

"I'm going to get a latte," I say, standing and pointing my thumb at the counter. "Do you need a refill?"

"No, thanks," he says, turning his head to look out the window into the darkness again.

"So, how are you?" I ask when I return.

"Not great. You?"

I shake my head. "How are your parents and your sister? Any news about . . ."

"Thomas?" His voice is filled with such hatred. "All I care to know is that

316

he's locked up right now. I know it won't be that way forever since he's been cleared of having anything to do with Jenna's disappearance and since our legal system is total bullshit and my parents are standing by their Golden Boy." He clenches his teeth and looks out into the darkness on the other side of the window.

News spread fast earlier this week that Thomas's whereabouts that night had checked out. The police were able to secure video footage from the Walmart on Capitol Drive to verify the time Thomas and Jenna drove in and out of the parking lot, and a witness came forward to say they'd seen Thomas's car at the church that night after he'd been with Jenna. The final thing that ruled him out was his wife's statement that he was home no later than ten thirty and the fact that Dustin received a text from Jenna later than that.

"Yeah, my parents said the same thing. What about Audra and Stella? How are they?"

"I don't really know, and I don't really care . . . about Audra anyway because she's sticking right by his side just like my parents. I feel bad for Stella."

The thought of people standing by Thomas after what he's done makes me sick. I close my eyes and try to breathe away the anger I'm feeling until Eli speaks again.

"You know, all this time I've wondered why Jenna didn't want me around and was so hostile toward me. Did she just need time to get used to me all grown up? Of course, that theory didn't last long," he adds as an aside. "So, now I wonder if maybe I look too much like Thomas and she couldn't stand to see my face. I'm still not sure about that one, though. Then there's this theory that I think might be the most plausible, but . . . it puts me at fault."

"Eli, stop it. It's no one's fault. As much as I hate to say it, Jenna disappearing isn't even your brother's fault, not if all the evidence is accurate."

Eli shakes his head. "You don't understand."

"Okay, then tell me what this theory is, but I promise you, nothing puts you at fault for Jenna's disappearance or anything that Jenna did before she disappeared."

He stares at me for at least ten seconds before he begins. "So, one time, when Jenna and I were nine, my siblings and I stayed overnight at her house for a weekend while my mom and dad were house hunting in South Dakota. I remember wanting to play Nerf air darts with Thomas and a couple of kids in their neighborhood instead of hanging out with Jenna. At one point I went inside to use the bathroom, and she called me into her room where she had her dolls splayed out along with this anatomy book her mom had brought home from the library. She showed me a picture of a naked man and asked if she could see mine if she showed me hers. So . . ."

Eli takes a few breaths and then looks out the window again. I just sit and wait, wondering what could have happened that would make him think anything that's gone on with Jenna was his fault. When he turns to face me, there are tears in his eyes. I hand him a napkin and give the top of his stationary hand a rub. Then I wait quietly as he composes himself and continues.

"So, after Jenna asked if we could see each other's private parts, we went into her closet, which she used as a fort, and we took off our clothes. Then she asked if we could touch each other, and I said no way, because I knew it was wrong. Hell, I knew even looking was wrong, but she was my favorite cousin, my favorite girl, so I wanted to make her happy. Plus, I felt bad for ditching her for Nerf darts. Anyway, she got all embarrassed, and we both put our clothes back on real fast. Then she ran out of the closet and into the bathroom, and I went back outside to finish the Nerf gun war. Later on, throughout dinner and after, she tried to avoid me until Hannah and I busted into her room and waged a Nerf air dart attack on her. It ended in smiles, and we never talked about the incident again, but I've wondered about it a few times over the years. And I've always felt ashamed for even looking at her privates and showing her mine, and I've wondered where she would even get the idea." Eli looks up at me. "Now, after all these years, I know the answer. That's what she meant that night, at Tommy's party, when she asked why I protect my brother. She thinks I know what he did to her." His lips begin quivering again.

I place my hand back on top of his hand and leave it there this time. "Eli, why do you think what happened between you and Jenna makes her disappearance your fault.?

"Because maybe if I'd said something to someone, like my Aunt Bonnie, maybe Jenna could have been questioned, and all the stuff about Thomas might have come out sooner." He pulls his hand away and looks me in the eyes again. "Keeley, she's lived with what he did to her for all these years.

Can you imagine what that must feel like? To keep a secret like that? To have to repeatedly see the same horrible memories over and over forever? I still can't stop thinking about what happened between Jenna and me in her closet, and that was nothing compared to what Thomas did to her." He picks up a fresh napkin and cleans the tears from his face and blows his nose. Then he looks back out the window. "That's why everything that's wrong with Jenna is partly my fault."

chapter fifty-six

The weather has turned cold, and they say we're in for one heck of a winter, but I'll continue to canvas the area on foot with Lulu as long as it takes. A little cold and snow isn't going to hold me back. I know from the way Joseph looks at me whenever I return from my walk, that he's beginning to pity me. But I don't care.

When you're the mother of a girl who's disappeared into thin air, you don't care about much of anything anymore because all you can think about is what happened to your daughter.

The most recent word from Detective Collins is that Jenna's case is open but resources are too slim to keep an active team on it. In other words, they've stopped looking. They just can't say it like that.

At least once a week there's a new article that pops up about Jenna. The only problem is these articles keep repeating the same information mixed in with all new completely useless information and speculation. Dried up leads including the rehashing of Jacob Bickers and Thomas as persons of interest, speculation into whether the police might have missed something about either of the men even though they both had alibis. Interviews with long lost friends of the men dating back to grade school, old college roommates, and past girlfriends and employers. Everyone has an opinion to share, and no one seems to agree on anything. So, all we can do is rely on the evidence available, which doesn't provide any real closure at all. Even though I know it's all for clicks, I'm grateful that reporters and news outlets are still circulating her name.

A few days ago, there was an article on the *Milwaukee Journal Sentinel's* website about the land that used to be owned by Jacob Bickers' in-laws which now belongs to him and his wife since the recent passing of his mother-in-law. The reporter suggested that the land could be a crucial area that was ignored when the police dismissed Bickers as a person of interest. Julie had called me, outraged that anyone could suggest such a thing, and wondered if I thought she could sue the newspaper. It seems no one can sue the media for printing speculations, even when it results in vandalism. Poor Julie. First, she loses her mom, then the cabin that's been in her family for decades is nearly destroyed all because of speculation from a reporter. So, there are also negatives to having the media continue using Jenna's case as clickbait.

The calls from concerned family and friends have slowed. Of course, I still hear from Keeley, Delaney, and their mothers every few days, whether it's a text or a quick phone call just to see how I'm doing. Dustin hasn't called at all, but he has stopped over to see how we're doing. He even played checkers with Shaina a few times—that was hers and Jenna's favorite game to play together. Leighton has been by too, but she doesn't say much, and she never stays long. I thought it was peculiar the way Jenna had befriended her at the beginning of the school year, given how different I'd assumed they were, but they must have developed quite a special friendship based on the way Leighton tears up every time she leaves our house.

But with Christmas right around the corner, I expect that even communication from Jenna's closest friends will decrease as well. I honestly don't know how we're going to make it through the rest of the holiday season, especially since Christmas has always been Jenna's favorite. Never mind that we don't even have a church anymore. Even though Greg has resigned at the urging of angry parishioners and protestors, and reporters have stopped standing out front of the place where a pedophile rapist once served as a youth pastor just to get their perfect shots to accompany their articles, it'll still never feel like a safe place to me, not when I think about all the times we forced Jenna to go there and have to agonize over seeing Thomas. The guilt I feel about that is overwhelming, and I will never forgive myself.

chapter fifty-seven

As Jenna drove home after talking to Thomas, she thought about whether she felt his apology was sincere. Not once did she feel bad for him as he cried because his tears were nothing compared to all the tears she'd cried over the years. She quickly decided she didn't care whether the remorse he'd expressed was real. He could rot in Hell for all she cared.

She moved on to thinking about how proud she was of herself for staying strong and not showing how scared she was. Even though she still felt disgusted just being near him, she didn't allow herself to feel threatened by him. And now that she'd confronted him, she could feel relief oozing throughout her body.

When Jenna pulled onto the parking slab next to the garage, she checked her phone for the time and to see if Keeley or Delaney had responded to her texts. She emitted a sigh upon seeing that neither had. As for the time, it was only nine forty-five. If Dustin was at a movie, he wouldn't be calling her for at least thirty more minutes.

She stared at the back of her house and thought about how it wasn't just her friends who needed to know the truth. Her parents needed to know too, but she was still a bit upset with her mom for invading her privacy. She couldn't help it. She would let it go eventually, but for now, she'd focus on straightening things out with her friends. She would definitely tell her parents within the next couple of days, though.

Not wanting to go inside to wait for Dustin's text, Jenna decided to go for a run through Jolliet. She'd always done her best thinking while running.

Before getting out of the car, she threw on the windbreaker and sneakers she kept in the backseat. She was already wearing leggings and a hoodie with short and long-sleeved shirts layered underneath, so despite the dropping temperature, she knew she'd be fine after she ran for a few blocks.

When she got out of the car, she hid her bag under the front seat, threw her hair up in a ponytail, and started jogging up the alley behind her house. Once she had a good stride going, she allowed her mind to begin processing everything that could occur as a result of people finding out about Thomas. She thought first about Audra and Stella and how hard it would be for Audra when she found out. Then she thought about her aunt and uncle and Eli and Hannah. The thought of Aunt Lenore made her wonder if she was doing the right thing. She couldn't imagine a mother finding out the child she'd carried inside of her was a monster. How could someone not feel partly to blame? She also circled back to what it would mean if Thomas really was better like he said he was, then was it worth breaking so many hearts and ruining so many lives? She picked up her speed and ran as hard as she could to dispel this thought. It was time for Jenna to think only of herself, and she couldn't go on living with the secret anymore. She also couldn't live with the *what ifs* that were swirling around in her brain colliding with the second thoughts that were also present. What if Thomas isn't better? What if he abuses Stella? No, if Thomas didn't turn himself in, Jenna had to follow through with what she'd said she'd do. And that meant she had to tell everyone close to her, starting with Dustin. Almost more than anyone, he deserved to know the truth and to hear her say she was sorry in person for everything she'd put him through.

When Jenna arrived at the park, she noticed headlights behind her for about two blocks. Paranoia made her glance back, just to make sure it wasn't Thomas's car. It wasn't, but just to be safe, she sprinted onto a path to take a shortcut to the old playground. Once she was under the cover of the woods, she stopped under one of the lights illuminating the path and texted Dustin to see if he would still meet her.

JENNA: HEY, CAN YOU STILL MEET ME? I'M AT THE MERRY-GO-ROUND.

chapter fifty-eight

"Mr. Bickers, I'm going to level with you here, things aren't looking good for you. Are you sure you don't want to call your attorney?"

"I don't have an attorney, and I don't need one because I've done nothing wrong."

"Okay, then. Here we go, I suppose," Collins said.

What the hell was that supposed to mean? Here we go, I suppose. I'd been up at the land Julie's parents left to us just to survey things now that all the snow has had time to thaw. I'd spent hours repairing as much damage to the cabin as I could so Julie wouldn't have to see it all again. It was hard enough for her the first time she saw it after vandals trespassed on the property. That was when my name was released to the public when Jenna first disappeared. But that was months ago, so I have no idea why I'm sitting here in front of Collins again. Julie and the kids weren't even there this morning when I got home, so they have no idea I've even been there and no idea where I am now. In fact, I thought it was Julie or Brady knocking on the door shortly after I'd gotten home. I thought maybe she had her hands full of groceries and couldn't unlock the side door herself.

"Let's just get this over with. My wife is expecting me home," I say, irritated.

Collins raises his eyebrows. *Again, what the hell was that supposed to mean?*

"Mr. Bickers, we've received some new information that leads us to believe you weren't completely honest with us the first time we interviewed you regarding the whereabouts of Jenna Kemp back in October."

"Well, that's news to me," I say, crossing my arms and leaning back in my chair.

Collins nods. "You had initially stated that your relationship with Jenna was strictly through calls and texts . . ."

I nod emphatically.

". . . and that you and Jenna never made plans to meet each other in person."

"That's right, we never made plans to meet in person. And I told you, I'd cut off communication with her."

"Right, we're aware of what you said. Here's the thing, we now come to possess Jenna's most recent diary, which details the progression of your relationship with her."

"Oh, well, whatever it says, you can't—"

"And, Mr. Bickers, based on Jenna's final entry in her diary, we believe you did, in fact, have plans to meet her at . . ." He opens his manila folder and glances inside. "Holiday Inn in Brown Deer. And before you say anything, just know that we have taken a peek at the hotel's video footage from that night, and you were in fact captured by one of the backdoor cameras several times that night. Do you have anything to say about that?"

"Well, clearly it's not me in the video. I was home. My wife . . . Julie told you that—"

"Mr. Bickers, Julie spent some time talking with us yesterday."

My jaw drops. I think about the messages I left her and the texts I sent, all unanswered. When I don't say anything, Collins continues.

"And you should probably know that Julie wasn't too pleased to learn about your relationships with Cynthia Morris and Faith Perkins, and she has recanted her statement that you were home with her the evening of Friday, October twenty-seventh."

I shoot to my feet, unintentionally throwing my chair back a few inches.

Collins stands just as quickly. "Mr. Bickers," he warns, "do I need to ask for another officer to sit in with us?"

"No," I say, breathing heavily. I adjust my chair and plop back down in it. "I'm sorry, but this is bullshit. The only reason Julie would do that is because we've been working on our marriage, so of course she's upset to learn that I was unfaithful."

Collins narrows his eyes and nods and opens the damn manila folder again. When he closes it and looks back up at me, I sense things are about to get worse.

"On the evening Jenna disappeared, the Briarwood Police Department received two phone calls from a concerned neighbor who lives a few houses down from the Kemps. His calls were received between the hours of nine and ten that night and were to report a suspicious vehicle driving back and forth down Berkeley Street. There had been a few car break-ins in the area recently, so he was keeping watch that night. Funny thing is, he reported the make, model, and color of the vehicle that appeared to be, in his words, "casing the neighborhood." Mr. Bickers, did you happen to drive down Berkeley Street that night?" For good measure, Collins adds, "I don't suppose I have to tell you that the car matches the description of the car you currently drive, Mr. Bickers."

Shit. I don't even have to say it out loud for Collins to know that he's got me on this one. Why did I have to drive down her street that night? Ever since I found out she was sixteen, I thought she'd made up living on that street.

"No, you don't have to tell me that."

"So, is there anything you'd like to tell me that you may have accidentally left out the last time we spoke?" Collins asks. "The only thing you can do to help yourself now, Mr. Bickers, is tell the truth."

"Fine, I admit it. Jenna and I were supposed to meet that night, but she canceled on me the day before. I'd told Julie that I had to attend a conference in Madison early on Saturday morning, so it would be easier for me to just spend the night. What I really did was get a room at the Holiday Inn. After Jenna canceled, I figured I could use some alone time anyway, so I stayed in the room by myself. I really did go to Chasers Pub, though, like I told you the last time we talked. But another thing I left out was that I took a ride to Briarwood and drove down Berkeley Street because that's where Jenna said she lived . . . in a duplex . . . alone. But I swear I never saw her in person that night or ever. I had nothing to do with her disappearance, and I have not spoken with her since that Thursday when she called to cancel on me."

"Mr. Bickers, will you grant us permission to search your property up in Kewaskum then?"

"Why?" I ask, my patience running thin. "Why would you have to do that?"

"Because we believe there may be evidence on that land that could lead us to Jenna."

I stare at him, dumbfounded. "No, absolutely not. You'll have to get a warrant if you want to step foot on our property."

"Mr. Bickers, I was just asking as a courtesy. The warrant has already been secured, and officers are already on their way to the property as we speak."

chapter fifty-nine

Why? Whyyyyyy did he have to do this? Audra thought, slamming her hands against the steering wheel. Then she put the car in reverse and checked her rearview mirror as she backed out of the garage. As soon as she cleared the threshold, she hit the button on the garage door remote. When the door was about halfway closed, she caught a glimpse of the inner door opening and Thomas's feet scurrying down the steps into the garage.

For a while, Audra drove aimlessly, unsure where she was going or what she was doing. But then it hit her. She could talk to Jenna. She could make Jenna realize how detrimental it would be for so many people if Thomas turned himself in. She could convince Jenna that Thomas was sorry and that he was ill when he did whatever he did to her, but he was better now.

She's just a girl. Audra thought. *I know I can convince her. And if she doesn't listen to reason, then I'll tell her no one will believe her. Why would they when she's been drinking and doing drugs and God knows what else. I've heard the rumors, but I'm too polite to partake in spreading them.*

Still unfamiliar with Briarwood, Audra found the Kemps' address in her Google Maps history and started the navigation. As she followed the monotone directions, she thought of an alternative way to make Jenna listen. Maybe if she shared the way she'd once walked a broken path littered with abuse at the hands of her own father, Jenna would be more sympathetic about how losing Thomas would affect Stella. Surely Jenna would reconsider if she knew Thomas had rescued Audra from the drugs and abuse and had helped her realize that she was worthy of God's love and forgiveness. Maybe if Audra told Jenna all about her own past, Jenna would confide in her instead of thinking she had to involve the authorities.

No man should pass judgment on another man. That is God's business. It's my business to protect the ones I love.

Audra turned down Berkeley Street and was disappointed to see how dark the Kemps' house was. She needed to figure out a way to talk to Jenna without waking Bonnie and Joseph, so she looped around the block for a little extra think time.

Should I go to the door? What would I say if Joseph or Bonnie answer?

As Audra looped around the block a second time, it was as if God had answered her prayers when she saw Jenna exiting the alley that runs behind the Kemps' house.

This girl has just threatened my husband's integrity and the well-being of our family, and she's out for a leisurely run?

Audra did her best to follow Jenna at a distance without losing sight of her. She certainly didn't want to risk Jenna spotting her yet because she hadn't decided exactly what she planned to say. When Jenna turned down a street that cut off in a T at Jolliet Park, Audra had two options—go right and stick out like a sore thumb behind Jenna or go left and potentially lose Jenna. She chose right, but to her dismay, Jenna increased her speed and entered a path into the woods surrounding the park.

Damn it.

Audra didn't know whether to park her car and follow Jenna or drive into the park and see if she could find her. Within seconds, she decided to drive because she had no idea how far the trail Jenna was on went into the park and no idea where it exited. If she couldn't find her, she'd just have to go back to the Kemps' house and wait outside for Jenna to return home.

Jenna sat on the merry-go-round, remembering the last time she was there. It had been right before Thomas moved back into town and things went to hell. She couldn't stop wondering when Dustin was going to text her back, so she decided to spin to keep her mind off of it, which worked because then she started thinking about how out of control she'd spun over the past couple months. She'd let things spin out of control way too fast and couldn't figure out how to slow it all down. It was like she was stuck on the merry-go-round and no one was there to help her slow it down. As a result, she was dizzier than she'd ever been before—dizzy with fear, dizzy with remorse, and dizzy with shame.

As she lay there, spinning at a nice calming speed and looking up at the stars, her phone vibrated. When she moved to jump off the merry-go-round, headlights appeared from a car that must have just pulled into the old parking lot just up the trail from the old playground. She wondered with anticipation if maybe it was Dustin, but his text said otherwise.

DUSTIN: I'M ON MY WAY. ABOUT 15 MINUTES.

The news that Dustin would be another fifteen minutes was unsettling to her. She thought about the car that she could have sworn was following her before she'd run onto the trail, and now she was looking at this other car that appeared to only have one occupant. When the car's lights went out and a person got out of the driver's side, Jenna thought maybe she should run. But then she recognized who it was.

chapter sixty

"Good morning," I say, immediately wondering why I've said it. It isn't a good morning at all. Not with the new information that Mrs. Kemp discovered in Jenna's hidden diary coming to light. I could barely sleep because I needed to know if any of it will help find Jenna.

My mom and dad are sitting together at the kitchen table, which is unusual. Normally by now, she's standing at the counter eating breakfast, and my dad is rushing to fill a travel mug with coffee because he's running late.

My dad looks up from the morning paper. "Good morning, sweetheart." His eyes migrate over to my mom. I didn't notice at first that her chair is scooted over right next to his.

"Good morning, Keeley. As soon as you get that milk poured, why don't you bring your cereal over here so we can have a chat?"

"Okay . . ." Again, unusual. We never sit together during breakfast on weekdays. I put the milk back in the fridge, grab a spoon and make my way over to the table. "What's up? Did you tell Dad all about Mrs. Kemp's call yesterday and Jenna's hidden diary?"

"Yeah, and that's actually related to something we need to talk to you about." She slides the newspaper across the table so that it's right under my nose. I stop mid-chew when I see the headline. I glance up at my dad. He sighs deeply and folds his hands under his chin, prompting me to start reading.

Man in Custody in Connection with Disappearance of Local Teen

Jacob Bickers (43) of Thiensville was taken into custody late last night in connection with the disappearance of local teen, Jenna Kemp, who was reported missing by her parents on the early eve of Saturday, October 27. A police department representative revealed that the arrest was made, based on new evidence, including verified reports from an unidentified witness who saw Bickers' car near the Kemp residence on the night of Kemp's disappearance.

When questioned by authorities, Bickers admitted to having plans to meet with Kemp at the Holiday Inn located in Brown Deer on Friday, October 26, the last day she was seen by anyone. He then claimed that Kemp had canceled plans with him the day before. He denies having any contact with Kemp since. According to police reports, Bickers did not disclose information about his plans to meet with Jenna back when he was first interviewed in November 2017.

According to his wife, Bickers claimed to be out of town for a work-related event on the evening of Kemp's disappearance. Bickers' employer, Pax Pharmaceuticals, was also contacted by authorities. A human resources representative said they have no knowledge of any work-related business that would have kept Bickers overnight on that evening.

Bickers is associated with Kemp via a popular chat room site. Authorities are still looking into the screening protocol used by this site to ensure that users adhere to legal age requirements and are who they say they are.

Anyone who may have information about the whereabouts of Kemp is encouraged to call the Briarwood Police Department.

I turn the page to see if there's more, but there isn't. "Since he's in custody, does that mean they think he did something to Jenna? Like he hurt her or he . . ." I can't even bring myself to say it.

"We don't know, Keeley, but what I can tell you is that it isn't a good sign that this guy lied to his wife about where he was going. On top of that, they both lied the first time around when he was interviewed back in October." My dad places a hand on top of mine. "Keeley, we thought you should know that it was on the news this morning too. Everyone knows, and this whole case is likely to blow up now. I imagine reporters might start showing up at your school."

Shaking my head, I mumble, "She's not coming back, is she?"

"Oh, honey, don't say that." My mom gets up and wraps her arms around me from behind. "We don't know that. I'm sure there's more to it than what's in that article. The police don't reveal everything they know to the press. And things aren't always as they seem. Thomas Steele certainly taught everyone a lesson in that department, didn't he?"

chapter sixty-one

Audra looped around the park a few times with no luck. Then on her fourth pass, she noticed a turn she hadn't seen before. There was a sign that said OVERFLOW LOT as she veered to the right. The lot was completely empty, so Audra pulled into a spot with the intention of turning around and heading back the way she'd come from. That's when she saw Jenna standing next to the merry-go-round.

Jenna didn't appear to notice Audra at first because she was looking at her phone, but then she glanced in the direction of the lot, and it looked like she might take off running again. This made Audra nervous because she didn't want to miss what could be her only chance to talk some sense into Jenna. So she turned off her car and hopped out, ready to call out to Jenna. But to Audra's surprise, Jenna was already walking toward the car.

Thank God I can finally talk to her and help her understand that turning Thomas in would be the wrong thing to do.

Audra rushed to meet Jenna on a trail halfway between the lot and the playground.

"Audra? What are you doing here?" Jenna asked.

"Oh, Jenna," Audra paused and looked up because a light trickle of rain had started. "I was hoping we could talk, sweetheart."

"Did Thomas send you?"

"Oh, no. He told me not to come. I swear." Suddenly, Audra realized she needed to make Jenna think she was sympathetic to her if she hoped to attain positive results. "I'm so sorry for what he did to you."

Jenna folded her arms across her chest and looked up at the increasing rain.

"This rain is coming down pretty hard. How about if we talk in my car?" Audra suggested.

Jenna nodded, and they scurried up the path and into Audra's car. They both took a moment to wipe their faces, and Audra smoothed her hair.

"Jenna," Audra said, turning to her, "you know, Thomas is truly sorry for what he's done."

"No," Jenna rapidly shook her head. "I don't care."

Audra was shocked that such a tiny, timid girl could speak with such firmness.

"Thomas was sick, Jenna, but he's better now."

"Audra, do you know what he did to me?"

"Jenna, as soon as he got done talking to you, he came home and confessed to me. He's repentant, and he won't ever hurt you again."

"How can you say that? How are you not worried to death that he'll do the same thing he did to me to Stella. There's no doubt in my mind Thomas has a sickness, but it isn't the kind that can be healed."

"Jenna . . ." Audra reached for Jenna's hand, but she slapped Audra's hand away.

"Do you know how old I was in the first memory I have of him assaulting me? Three. I was three years old, Audra. It's one of my earliest memories . . . You need to be concerned about your daughter, Audra."

Jenna placed her hand on the door handle, but Audra couldn't let her go just yet, so she locked it and kept her finger poised over the master auto lock just in case Jenna tried to leave again.

"Let me out, Audra."

Audra decided it was time for her to cry. As she'd hoped, the forced waterworks led to Jenna taking her hand off the handle and turning in her seat to face Audra.

"Please understand how hard it is for me to accept this, Jenna. I thought I knew Thomas. My daddy was a sick son of a bitch, and here comes Thomas, riding into my life like a white knight coming to rescue me. I thought I could trust him, Jenna."

"I did too."

Good, she's confiding in me.

"But he's dangerous, Audra. He's a liar. And Stella will be safer if he's not around."

Damn it. Damn it damn it damn it!

"Will you go with me to the police station right now, Jenna? Please?"

"I . . ." Jenna pulled her phone out of her pocket, causing Audra to panic until she saw the red bar at the top of the screen and the phone shut off. "Shit," Jenna cursed under her breath. "I'm supposed to meet Dustin here pretty soon."

Audra continued to sob. "Please, Jenna," she pled. "You're right. I need to protect Stella." Audra didn't know where the situation was headed, but she knew she needed more time with Jenna. She couldn't let her leave until they'd come to an understanding, one that worked for everyone. "We can go to the police station, and you can file a report tonight. I promise I'll stay with you, and I'll tell them everything Thomas told me."

Jenna nodded. "Okay, but I need to use your phone.

"Okay . . . okay," Audra sniffled and started up the car. "Just . . . let's get going. And then I'll tell you where my phone is."

Audra pulled out of the parking lot and drove, the whole time wracking her brain to think of what else she could say to sway Jenna to not ruin their lives.

"Audra, your phone, can I please use it?"

"Oh shoot, Jenna, I just realized I don't have it. I was such a wreck after talking to Thomas. He was a wreck too, of course."

"Audra, you were supposed to turn there. That's okay, though, you can take the next right."

"He's just sick to death over the pain he's caused you, Jenna."

When Jenna didn't respond, Audra looked over at her, and her face was filled with fear. Audra recognized the look. She used to see it all the time on her mom's face when her dad would come home in one of his moods.

"Audra, you have to take me home . . . right . . . now." Jenna began to plead, reaching for the door handle.

What is she going to do jump out of the car? Audra wondered.

Jenna realized how silly it was to consider jumping out while the car was moving, so she pulled her hand back into her lap and tried to turn her phone back on, but it was completely out of juice. Desperate to contact Dustin, Jenna threw open the glove box and rummaged around for a charging cord. Audra observed silently, looking back and forth from the road to Jenna until Jenna gave up and slammed the glove box closed.

"Audra, I don't understand what you're doing here, but we need to turn around. Please." Jenna's voice was laced with desperation.

"I don't understand what I'm doing either," Audra said, her eyes struggling to see through the downpour. *And it's true*, she thought, *I know what I need the outcome to be, but I don't know how to get there just yet.* "Can we just drive, Jenna? So we can both think things through." Jenna stared at Audra, her eyes wide with disbelief. "I just . . . need to think things through a little more, prepare myself for what's going to happen next. I can't imagine what living with this has been like for you, but please try to understand what it's like for me right now too."

Finally, Jenna appeared to relent and leaned back in her seat. They continued to drive for a few more miles as Audra debated how to proceed. The only sound was the heavy rain pouring down as if God was crying for both of them.

Jenna was scared to death of Audra because she was certain Audra had lost her mind when Thomas told her about what happened. She didn't know what else to do other than sit back and give Audra time to calm down and come to her senses. But with each mile that passed, Jenna became more and more nervous. After about twenty-five minutes of driving, she was beginning to think Audra was never going to turn around, so she decided to tell her what she wanted to hear.

"Maybe you're right, Audra. I'm so confused."

Audra glanced over at Jenna, hopeful that maybe they could work things out. "Oh, Jenna," she said with a sigh, "I've been over here praying that you would say that."

Jenna rubbed her face with her hands, then looked over at Audra. "Do you really think Thomas is better? Do you think he's truly sorry?"

"I do, Jenna. One-hundred percent cross my heart and hope to die. He feels so much remorse."

"Do you promise that if I agree not to say anything *for now*, that he will go and see someone, like a therapist?"

Audra kept her eyes on the road as she nodded whole-heartedly. "I do. And I believe he would be more than willing to do that too. The three of us can figure this out, and I'll be there for you every step of the way."

"Okay, we'll figure it out," Jenna said. "Can we please turn around now? It's close to eleven, and if we drive any farther, I'll never make my curfew."

Audra threw on her blinker even though there weren't any other cars around them. As she exited the freeway, Jenna looked around to see if she recognized where they were, but she didn't. She was hoping there would be a gas station or a house or anything because she didn't want to be near Audra for one more second if she didn't have to. She didn't even care about the rain because her jacket was waterproof so it would at least keep the top of her body dry if she saw a place she could make a run for. But as far as she could see, there was nothing near that exit.

Audra looped around to get to the freeway entrance on the other side, but to Jenna's dismay, the entrance was closed and there was a detour sign pointing them farther down the country road.

"Oh, boy, I guess I picked the wrong exit," Audra said as she sped through a stop sign she didn't see.

A little farther down the road, Jenna saw a light through a thick patch of trees to the right of them. It appeared to be a house off in the distance, probably the owners of the rundown farm they were about to pass. At that moment, Jenna made up her mind. She wanted out of Audra's car. Even if there wasn't anyone home at the house in the distance, she wouldn't have more than a mile run to get to the nearest gas station. It's not like they were *that* far away from civilization.

When Audra slowed the car down at the next stop sign, Jenna threw open her door and made a run for it. She moved along the side of the road looking for the best path to run to make her way to the trees, but it was hard to see in the dark and through the pouring rain. When she heard Audra's car speed up, she cut right and nearly lost her footing when her ankle started to roll down a slope toward a culvert on the side of the road. She righted herself quickly and then tried to leap over the water rushing out of the tunnel, but she misjudged, and her right foot came down hard on a slippery rock causing her to lose her balance and crash headfirst into the exposed concrete section of the culvert.

"Jenna! Oh my God! Jennaaaaa! Oh, dear Lord, what have I done?"

Jenna heard the faint sound of Audra's voice calling her name as she fell face down into the water that was pouring out of the culvert. She knew she had to get up, but she couldn't move. Her head was throbbing, her lungs were filling with water . . . every part of her body felt cold . . . everything went black.

chapter sixty-two

THE MILWAUKEE JOURNAL SENTINEL
TUESDAY, MAY 15, 2018
SIX AND A HALF MONTHS AFTER JENNA'S DISAPPEARANCE

Suspect charged in murder of 16-year-old Jenna Kemp

A 43-year-old man has been arrested and charged with the killing of 16-year-old Jenna Kemp. Kemp was reported missing by her parents in October of last year.

The suspect, Jacob Allen Bickers of Thiensville, Wisconsin, an employee of Pax Pharmaceuticals, was previously questioned in the disappearance of Kemp back in November. At the time, police found no evidence that Bickers had been in contact with Kemp on the evening she was last seen. In addition, Bicker's wife told police that he'd been home with her and their two young children that evening.

New evidence suggests that Bickers provided false information in his first statement to police, and Julie Bickers has since recanted her statement. Eyewitness testimony also places Bickers near the Kemps' home on the night of her disappearance. Another key piece of evidence was found during a search of land in Kewaskum which belonged to Bickers' in-laws at the time of Kemp's disappearance. The land has since been re-deeded to Bickers and his wife after the passing of her mother in late November.

According to the Briarwood Police Department, Bickers met Kemp on the popular chat room website ChillChat.com.

Bickers has been charged with second-degree intentional homicide and is being held without bond at the Milwaukee County Jail until he appears in court early next week.

chapter sixty-three

Thomas handed the photo of Stella in the backyard chasing her new puppy back to Audra. He missed his little girl more than anything. A tear threatened its way out of his eye, but he wiped it away quickly, not wanting Audra to see him cry. He would have plenty of time for crying later. There wasn't much else for someone like him to do in prison.

"She's growing so fast. Thanks for letting her keep the dog."

Audra nodded. "It would have been nice if your parents had asked if it was okay, but under the circumstances, what was I supposed to do?"

She gave Thomas the look he'd grown to dread, so he checked the time. Ten minutes remained of their visit. He knew he had to choose his next words wisely if he wanted to avoid another one of Audra's breakdowns.

Thomas reached across the table for Audra's hand, and she eagerly gave it to him. The way she still loved him after everything he'd confessed to doing to Jenna continued to amaze him.

Sometimes he wondered if he should confess about the other things he'd done, but he kept coming to the same conclusion. If the police found out about *all* the girls over the years, he'd end up watching Stella's entire childhood through pictures from behind bars. He decided his remorse for everything he'd done and the time he would serve for what he did to Jenna was enough of a price to pay for his sins. "Will you bring Stella next time?"

Audra nodded, her pained expression growing more prominent by the second. She wasn't going to be able to contain herself.

"Audra, I think we should say goodbye now." Thomas gripped one of her hands with both of his. "You look like you could use some rest. Maybe take a nap or get yourself one of those facials you like before you pick up Stella from my parents' house."

"I don't need rest, Thomas. I need you home with Stella and me." Audra started to cry.

"Audra, please. We've been over this a million times. What's done is done. I need to pay for my sins. I need to make up for what I did to Jenna."

Audra responded by crying even harder, just like the last time she'd visited. Thomas released her hand, pulled a tissue from the box on the table, and handed it to her.

"What about Stella? What about me? Why did you have to do this to us, Thomas? Why couldn't you have just let God judge you? You're a good man now. You've changed. I know that counts for something in His eyes."

"What's done is done, Audra."

"Poor Stella. Everyone knows. We'd have to move across the country to escape all of their judgmental eyes and whispers." Her body shuddered as she started rocking in her seat. This was something Thomas hadn't seen before, and he wondered if maybe his mom was right. Maybe Audra needed to see a therapist.

"Audra, I've told you, you don't have to stay so close to visit me. You can move, start over someplace else. I won't be in here forever. We can talk on the phone and write letters until I can join you and Stella when I get out. Things will work out. You'll see."

"How? You're going to be a registered sex offender for the rest of your life. What will you do for work? Why couldn't you have just kept your mouth shut? Those diary entries of hers wouldn't have held up in court. It would have been her word against yours. A respected pastor versus an out of control teenager."

"Stop, Audra. Just stop. It was what I did to Jenna that caused her to act the way she did. I don't doubt that for a second." Thomas grabbed a tissue for himself and dabbed his downturned eyes. The remorse he felt was unbearable. "It's my fault she's gone . . ."

"No, that's not true," Audrea whispered as a vision of Jenna running and falling on that rainy night flashed before her eyes.

". . . because had she not been in such emotional turmoil over what I did to her when she was younger . . ."

"No, you're wrong." Audra wished she'd never shone her phone's flashlight on Jenna's face that night because for the rest of her life, every time she closed her eyes, she'd see Jenna's dead eyes and all the blood that had been seeping from her forehead.

". . . she never would have met Jacob Bickers . . . And she wouldn't be gone now. So, I deserve to be here for that too."

Bile made its way up Audra's throat as she recalled dragging Jenna's limp body to the abandoned barn near the ditch where she'd fallen and hit her head on the culvert. She'd panicked that night and figured it was only a matter of time before Jenna's body was found, but days turned into weeks, and then weeks turned into months. Audra never felt any sense of relief, not for a second.

"Thomas, I have to tell you something."

Thomas wiped a stray tear from his chin and looked up from the table to meet Audra's tortured gaze. Her chest heaved, and she gripped the edge of the table as if she would tip it at any moment. Tears were cascading from her chin. Thomas didn't even recognize the woman before him, the way her eyes darted from one corner of the room to the other like a caged animal.

"What is it?" he asked.

"You're not responsible for Jenna's disappearance. And neither is Jacob Bickers." Audra thought about how she'd driven to the Bickers' property in Kewaskum after reading an article about the land they'd inherited from Julie Bickers' parents. She closed her eyes and pictured herself tossing Jenna's phone out the window into a patch of evergreen trees as she drove by.

"Audra, what are you talking about? How do you know that?"

"Because I was the last person to see her that night."

chapter sixty-four

We had a beautiful memorial service for Jenna today. The entire ceremony took place outdoors, and everyone was asked to wear a pair of sneakers. Pastor Jensen, who retired from the position Greg took over back in September insisted on leading the service even though he can barely walk. Jenna always liked him and always had a smile for him.

Everyone who loved Jenna was there—Keeley's family (including her brother who came home from Madison), Delaney's mom and dad, Dustin's family, and Leighton and her mom. Besides Jenna's closest friends, there were dozens of other classmates, teachers, administrators, colleagues of Joseph's and mine, and most of our extended family.

Even Julie Bickers showed up for the gathering at our home after the burial. I'd invited her to the entire day's events, but she had an appointment to close on the sale of hers and Jacob's house this morning. During the time Jacob was in prison, she'd filed for divorce and put their house on the market. It made no difference to her when Jacob was cleared of the charges against him after Audra confessed to witnessing Jenna's fall and concealing her body. She's still intent on putting all of Jacob's lies and infidelity behind her, and I don't blame her one bit.

I was surprised when Lenore and Greg didn't show up. Eli had told me he planned to bring Hannah, but his parents, still angry over the fact that we'll never forgive Thomas for what he did, refused to attend. Lenore had called last week and said if we couldn't accept Thomas back into our good graces, then we couldn't accept them either. I didn't disagree and told her they could consider themselves uninvited. I never thought in a million years that they'd skip Jenna's funeral, though. It just goes to show that it's possible to not even really know your own flesh and blood.

But Eli was there with Hannah like he said he'd be, and they even brought Stella. I'm sure that was one heck of an argument with his parents, but I'm also positive Eli wasn't going to have it any other way due to the promise he's made to himself to make sure Stella grows up knowing that Jenna is not the reason her mother and father will both end up spending decades in prison, the way her grandparents would lead her to believe. For now, Greg and Lenore have temporary custody, while Audra is in jail awaiting sentencing for not reporting Jenna's death and hiding her body. Audra's recovering drug-addict mother has also filed for custody of Stella. She's even fighting Thomas's right to see Stella at all, given what he did to Jenna. Lenore was outraged by this because "Audra is a murderer, for crying out loud." I can only laugh at my sister's ridiculousness. Honestly, is one of Stella's parents really any better than the other? In all the confusion, I pray that Eli will remain steadfast in his promise to watch over Stella.

epilogue

My quadriceps are beginning to ache, and my hands are numb, but I just passed the mile twelve marker. At least I don't have much farther to go. I only signed up for this race four weeks ago, so I'm not as prepared as I should be, but any pain I'm feeling is nothing compared to the pain Jenna must have felt all those years.

Jenna and I had a bucket list of ten marathons we wanted to complete someday. The one I'm running now—the Hawaii Ultra Run—is number one on that list. I plan to check off every event in as short of time as possible, mostly for Jenna but also because you never know what life has in store for you.

In the last stretch, I reach up and grip the silver locket I've been holding off and on throughout the race, whenever I've felt like I can't go another step. Mrs. Kemp gave me the necklace on our flight to Honolulu. Inside the small oval is a picture of Jenna and me from the first 5K fun run either of us ever participated in. With the locket around my neck, Jenna will be with me for each event, cheering me on every step of the way.

Just when my muscles are beginning to lock up and I don't think I can continue, I see signs up ahead with mine and Jenna's names on them. They say things like *Go Keeley and Jenna!*, *You've got this Keels and Jenaboo!*, and our names inside a big heart. Holding the signs are Mrs. Kemp and my mom, Delaney, Leighton, and Dustin. The closer I get, the louder their cheers become, but for some reason, the only thing on my mind is a memory from when Jenna, Delaney, and I were kids and at the merry-go-round. Jenna had just gotten done telling Delaney and I a story she'd written about a little girl who was lost and couldn't find her way home. She'd met many new friends along her journey back to where she came from, but she never ended up finding her way.

"That's it?" Delaney had asked.

"Well, it doesn't have an end yet," Jenna replied.

"What do you mean, it doesn't have an end?" I said. "I like how you ended it. I like unsolved mysteries."

"Yeah, me too, I guess," said Delaney.

"Not me." Jenna shakes her head. "Every story should have an ending. A happy ending. So it's not done yet."

"Fine, can we help you figure out how it ends then?" I asked.

She nodded, and we spent the rest of the afternoon spinning and staring up at the sky as we brainstormed ways for the little girl in Jenna's story to get her happy ending.

When I stagger across the finish line, everyone rushes to me and gives me hugs. Jenna's mom whispers in my ear. "Thank you, Keeley. Jenna would be so happy if she was here right now."

a note from the author

Thank you for reading SPIN. Please let others know about your experience by leaving a review on the retail site(s) of your choice, Goodreads, and/or any other book-related platform. Your support is greatly appreciated.

I love hearing from readers! Please connect with me on Facebook, Instagram, or Twitter. ~ K. J. Farnham

about the author

K. J. Farnham was born and raised in a suburb of Milwaukee. She graduated from UW-Milwaukee in 1999 with a bachelor's degree in elementary education and went on to earn a master's degree in curriculum and instruction from Carroll University in Waukesha. She then had the privilege of helping hundreds of children learn to read and write over the course of twelve years. Farnham now lives in western Wisconsin with her husband and three children.

afterword

I'm not a trauma expert, but I know what it's like to live with memories of sexual abuse. If you or someone you know has been sexually abused or assaulted, please reach out for support or counseling if you haven't already done so. The following resources can help.

Australia
1800RESPECT – https://www.1800respect.org.au/

Canada & United States
RAINN (Rape, Abuse & Incest National Network) – https://www.rainn.org/

United States
National Sexual Assault Hotline at 800.656.HOPE (4673)
The National Child Traumatic Stress Network – https://www.nctsn.org/what-is-child-trauma/trauma-types/sexual-abuse
Jade Eby, Childhood Sexual Abuse Survivor and Coach – http://jadeebycoaching.com

UK & Ireland
The Survivors Trust – http://thesurvivorstrust.org/

Chat Rooms and Message Boards for Sexual Abuse, Incest, Ritual Abuse and Rape Survivors
Fort Refuge – http://www.fortrefuge.com/

Recommended Literature
Maltz, W. (2012) The Sexual Healing Journey: A Guide for Survivors of Sexual Abuse. New York, NY: William Morrow Paperbacks

acknowledgments

First and foremost, thank YOU, the reader, for the time you devoted to Jenna's story. Your readership and support mean the world to me.

I'm so grateful for all my wonderful beta readers. Kayla, Abby, Ella, Sonia, Brooklyn, and Phoebe – Your feedback helped make this book so much better! Polly Barreto, Marnie Ide, Alica Flechner, Jenny Hanson – Thank you for taking time out of your busy schedules to read and critique this book. I sincerely appreciate your continuous support and encouragement!

Jade Eby – Thank you not only for being a beta reader, but also for offering to be a source of support for survivors of sexual abuse. I'm in awe of your bravery.

To Jessica Wink with the West Allis Police Department – Thank you for sharing your expertise on missing persons investigations!

Thank you to all the individuals who helped piece together and promote this book: Amy Queau of Qdesign (cover), Carol Ann Eastman (blurb), Leah Campbell (editing), Karan Eleni of The Letterers Collective (editing and formatting), Giselle Cormier of Xpresso Book Tours, and Kylie Frankel of Kylie's Fiction Addiction.

Shout out to Farnham's Faithfuls! Together we have built an amazing online community, and I'm so grateful for your support. I hope you all stick around for many books to come. (Extra special thanks to Marnie, Polly, and Jenny for being the best group administrators around!)

To my husband and children, who collectively asked if I was done writing this book no less than one million times, thank you for your patience and support. I love you guys so much! Also, to my son Cole, you're the best brainstorming buddy ever. Thank you for listening to me talk about this book nonstop, for your enthusiastic questions, and for encouraging me to *just keep writing* whenever I hit a rough patch.

www.ingramcontent.com/pod-product-compliance
Lightning Source LLC
Chambersburg PA
CBHW031610100726
47898CB00006B/1726